To Joanne & John.
May no such war trouble
us, in the future.
K 1/8/22

WAR BETWEEN
US AND CHINA

WAR BETWEEN US AND CHINA

WINSTON LANGLEY

To order additional copies of this book, contact:
Xlibris
844-714-8691
www.Xlibris.com
Orders@Xlibris.com
828182

DEDICATION

To the young people of the world, who should not
be forced to experience World War III.

CONTENTS

PART I
The Trap and Its Application

PART II
Case Studies, Gathering Storm, and Another Past

PART III
Counter-Narratives on Case Studies

PART IV
Dynamics of US–China Relations

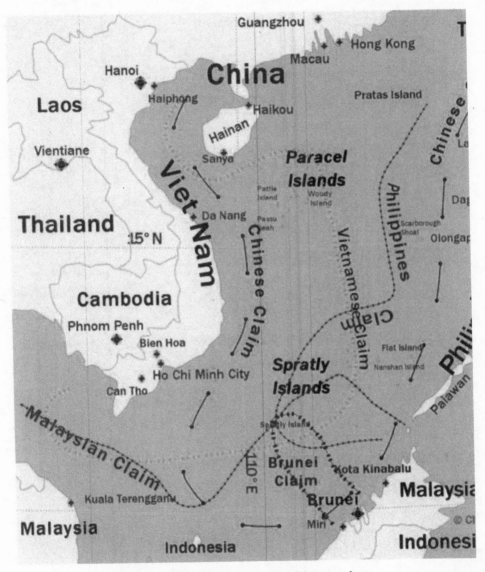

https://chinasage.info/south-china-sea.htm

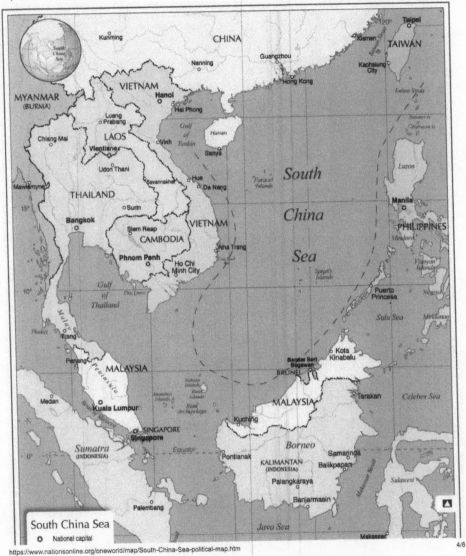

https://www.researchgate.net/figure/South-China-
Sea-Map-The-red-dotted-line-shows-the-furthest-
extent-of-Chinas-island_fig1_323214499

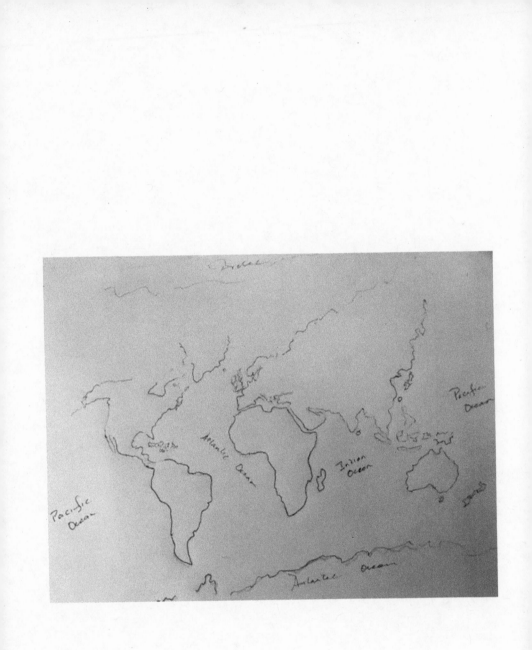

ACKNOWLEDGEMENTS

This volume is the result of four interrelated concerns having to do with the future of US–China relations, perhaps the current most important bilateral international relations for each country and the peoples of the world. Each of these concerns is centered on a book, *Destined for War*, which was published in 2017 and became a best seller among scholarly works.

I read the book in 2018 and became very disturbed by its tone and much of its content. Many facts and issues are presented in a distorted manner; some partake of prejudices, including subtle racial ones, that have been part of the West since the latter term emerged as a geopolitical and cultural category, and it subtly embodies scenarios that, on their face, offer the appearance of insightful possibilities when, in fact, they are part and parcel of an overall strategic position of the US. Second, I began to hear people, many outside international relation or politics, speak of the "Thucydides Trap," the central concept in the book, and to realize that the work was having an even greater impact than I had assumed. When a physician colleague of mine asked what I thought about the concept, I began to think that the work ought to be rebutted. That which proved to be a turning point in my decision, however, was my meditating on the fact that the author is a professor at perhaps the nation's most prestigious university, teaching students, doctoral students—tomorrow's leaders—who often have little historical appreciation (because of the limited historical content found in the approach to teaching international relations in the US) to question, seriously, the claims of the book and what such teaching can come to mean for a broader socialization, including that for potential future decision makers and policy influencers.

The fourth concern stems from the Cold War, under which I grew up, and its damaging impact on the world, including possibilities envisioned by individuals and subnational groups. The tensions occasioned by that war, although not ever having resulted in an actual physical exchange between its two principals—the US and the former Soviet Union—never ceased to threaten one, and other countries and areas of the world, especially the Global South and the least socially favored everywhere, who experienced conflict, destruction, and socio-political reversals in their processes of development. For many young people in the US, disillusionment and distrust of the government increased, and a progressive militarization of international and national life came to be. Almost every social institution was adversely affected.

Another war, a second Cold War, this time between the US and China, would return the world to a regrettable and, in some cases, shameful past, with even greater socioeconomic damage resulting, because of the increased interdependence among peoples and countries and our being faced with threatening global problems that the world of 1945–1989 (duration of the Cold War) never faced. The lethality of weapons of mass destruction has also grown, and more countries have those weapons.

In writing this book, I tried to show (where the evidence suggests it) that in many areas in which the US has been depicted in ideal terms and China as the opposite of those ideals (the US), Washington may not be as cast and, often, China as well. In so doing, the appearance of my being less than objective could be mistakenly inferred. All such efforts, on my part, in fact, are either to expose certain hypocritical behaviors or claims or to suggest that an item of conduct is incident to all states or individuals (not peculiar to China or the Chinese) or that a weakness ought not to be used to define a country or people when all countries have weaknesses.

I offer thanks to the Boston Athenaeum, Boston University Law School, Harvard University Law School, the Avalon Project Collection at Yale Law School, the Healey Library at the University of Massachusetts Boston, and the Lamont Library at Harvard. A special "thank you" goes to all those who helped me to procure important research materials. I, of course, am solely responsible for the contents of the work.

INTRODUCTION

Destined for War, by Graham Allison, argues that war between the US and China is very likely because both countries are caught in a trap from which neither can easily escape. That trap, called the "Thucydides Trap," argues that when an up-and-coming power acts to challenge a ruling one, this challenge lets loose or unbinds so many destabilizing and disruptive forces that the latter overwhelms decision makers and war results. In making this claim about the trap, Allison did not simply operate on the basis of an abstract assertion. He located this claim within the office of history and, to substantiate it, brought to bear persuasive eye-witnessing historical events. He also invited, to support his argument, respected contemporary experts in international relations and politics, country-specific specialists, and even a respected former statesman ostensible clothed with what is often called "inside information."

Among the eye-witnessing accounts are many case studies of historical conflicts and wars, which are advanced as precedents—precedents evidencing parallel or similar circumstances and like results. With an urged proper respect for the past, Allison then invites readers and policy influencers to pursue the path that prudence counsels and see whether it might be possible to avert that for which we are seemingly destined. He, however, presents no course of action that does relieve the US of its current position as *ruling* power, one of the two cornerstone conditions that supposedly bring the trap into being in the first place. This would appear to mean that "ruling" powers, perhaps by divine right, should not be challenged, or there will be a war, in which case the blame should be on the audacity of would-be challengers. This has been the case throughout history—blame the challenger, unless the latter wins in such wars and can write its own history.

In this book, I argue that war may very well come about between the US and China, stemming from the increasingly escalating differences between them, but the core cause will not be because of the trap suggested by Allison. Further, it contends that there is no "Thucydides Trap," namely, when a ruling power's standing is challenged by an emerging one, the fear of that rise and the likely replacement that the rise entails for the ruling power result in war. Rather, the historical evidence advises that wars, in the circumstances described, result from the ruling power's inability or unwillingness to accept equality and live by the norms that principle embodies.

Suffusing Allison's work are three other associated factors in the elaboration and application of the trap. First is the expressed or implied position that human moral agency is weak and can be easily overridden by historical "forces." I again dispute this position (and one wonders why, in face of such weakness, we would insist on gaining and retaining nuclear weapons or weapons of mass destruction in general) by showing how leaders associated with the very case studies that he selected to persuade readers deliberately manipulated events to invite war or to justify entry into war. Second, the structure of thinking that governs the entire presentation of *Destined for War* is one that is the offspring of a theoretical outlook in political science called realism, which sees human nature in the most negative light. This outlook (and belief) is pervasive in the book because Allison argues that it is present in all human group relationships—the son seeking to topple his father from the standing the latter has in the family, the sports team or business that seeks to replace the champion, forgetting the role of government, including umpires, and the "rules of the game" that forbid the father, champion team, or business from being rule maker, prosecutor, and judge in defense of their respective dominant positions. Given the view that human nature is evil and the weak position of human moral agency, the exercise of power and dominance is the only reliable means by which social and political order as well as human thriving can be established and securely protected.

The third is more protean than the first two and so, especially for the general consumer of foreign policy, difficult to master. It has to do with a widely shared view, often supported by popular news presentations, their associated commentators, and, as well, "experienced specialists." It is that the US's worldwide preeminence is more the result of makeshift or improvised decisions made to satisfy domestic constituencies and unpredictable international developments rather than a product of a coherent, strategic design.[1] When this view is presented by scholars such as Allison (his scenarios encourage it), that presentation makes it easier to attribute results to wrong causes and manipulate facts to lend the appearance that the US but reacts to events. It is true that the US's foreign policy has been significantly influenced by domestic constituencies and international events, as is the case with all countries. The evidence suggests, however, that responses to domestic and international constituencies are, on most occasions, the periphery that operates around a strategic core, referred to as the Grand Area (to be elaborated later), as well as an ideological conception of the self and that self's purpose that is global in reach and has been either unchanging or resistant to all but minor changes.

The War Between US and China seeks to prove its attempted refuting arguments by way of making its readers acquainted with an alternative history, including the history of a selected number of historical case studies that Allison, in *Destined for War*, proffers as proof for the claims it makes. This refuting covers fifteen chapters plus a conclusion, and the chapters, in turn, are arranged in four parts.

Part I, entitled "The Trap and Its Application," consists of the first three chapters and deals with the trap as understood by Allison, its application to China, and its dramatic historical expression in the Peloponnesian War, between Athens and Sparta—a likely mirror of the US–China relations. Part II, entitled "Case Studies, Gathering Storm, and Another Past," covers Chapters 4, 5, and 6 and brings to bear on our discussion the case studies of Japan versus the US and Germany versus Britain, along with some underlying ideas and the international political structure that governed the thinking of the periods under discussion.

---

[1]   See p. 10 of a later cited work by Henry Kissinger, "America at the Apex."

Part III, entitled "Counter-Narrative on Cases," encompasses Chapters 7, 8, and 9 and has, as its burden, the elaboration of a past that differs substantially from the one portrayed by Allison and is supportive of the idea that *equality*, not *replacement*, has been the historical problem (if one wishes, the trap) that has troubled the instances of leading powers and their paired historical challengers, as evidenced in the cases of Germany versus Britain and Japan versus the US. Part IV, entitled "Dynamics of US–China Relations," roofs Chapters 10 to 15. It continues the alternative history and includes issues of race, cultural outlooks, trade, technology, economic development models, and how the changes of fluctuations in the sweep of Washington–Beijing relations have encompassed the globe as a whole, including the Global South, in part because of the US's ideological and geopolitical identity, in part because of changing international norms and problems, and in part because of Beijing's efforts to deal with Washington's policy of containment.

As revealed by the evidence in the previous case studies, including that of Athens versus Sparta, a fairly extensive examination of US–China relations discloses very clearly that the principal issue between them is not and has not been the publicly asserted or textually offered threat of replacement but the feared prospect, on the US's part, of equality with China. This equality would mean, mainly, that the US would no longer have its relatively unrestricted way in the world. This is what is and has been at stake and the unswerving strategic focus, on China, sponsored under various modes of containment, regionally and globally. Until today, there has been no official, public reference to China other than as a regional power, as we now refer to Russia, and when China has refused to conform to this ascribed status—as in the case of women, minorities, and small or "weak" states—that refusal is characterized as angry, hostile, ambitious, or informed by indignation.

The conclusion attempts to summarize much of what the first fifteen chapters house, looks at the direction in which globalization is seen as going as well as the extent to which the values espoused by the US and China better prepare them for adjustments consistent with that direction, and suggests some area within which, for the sake of the well-being of each and the rest of the world, the US–China relations might be selectively restructured. The latter implies moral agency capable of controlling historical forces.

The principle of equality, so manifestly implicated in this study, is not being emphasized only as the accurate historical foundation on which to judge the case studies of wars covered in this volume. It is not, in other words, in its evidentiary use in this work, simply an exercise in the refutation of a thesis, as important as doing so is and should be. It is also a wrestling with what undergirds the US Declaration of Independence—a self-evident truth, the drafters of that declaration claimed—and the basis of what we regard as human dignity. It is also the conceptual substructure of liberty and freedom and of self-determination writ large. It is the obverse of domination, and almost every ethno-racial, indigenous, linguistic, religious, sexual orientation, woman, worker, or immigrant minority, among others, will attest to it.

To have any country claiming to be a democracy, in antiquity or today, frown at the principle in favor of domination is to lay bare a hypocrisy that is subversive to all the other associated values just mentioned. (Of course, since democracy is a moral entitlement of everyone under the Universal Declaration of Human Rights (UDHR), it is also hypocrisy on the part of any state engaged in a like frowning.) It is also to remove from the historical and future challengers to domination the heavy burden of responsibility that they have unfairly borne for wars and to unveil the often equal or greater responsibilities of ruling powers in causing such wars. An emphasis on the truth of equality in the complex relationship among countries can also help in the mapping of our individual and collective path toward our common future, in which equality is playing and will play a very important role. From all the evidence I have garnered in US–China relations, I have found nothing to indicate that China has been other than defensive in its military behavior, including in the Korean War, and pre-modern China exhibited a like defensive orientation.

The fact that the "never again" mantra against war and the United Nations' (UN) legal and moral structure, as well as that structure's review and amendment, were not points of any significant focus in *Destined for War* speaks eloquently. We are left with political realism alone, condemned to an indefinite replication of the "Thucydides Trap."

My view is that we have many alternative futures and should leave behind the realist thinking that has kept us trapped.

The approach that the book has followed is a largely historical one, with concepts linked to time and circumstances, although some have become trans-historical (and are treated as such). Use was made of a variety of sources, including original documents, policy statements of presidents, secretaries of state, or foreign ministers, intergovernmental resolutions or treaties, judicial decisions, historical studies by reputable historians, economic treatise, scholarly and semi-scholarly journals, popular magazines and newspapers (the latter from both China and the US), statements from lectures, and even television appearances by officials. In all these areas of sought help, I have tried to be fair, although not always neutral.

WAR BETWEEN US AND CHINA

There Is No Thucydides Trap

PART I

The Trap and Its Application

CHAPTER 1

The Trap as Understood by Allison

Who Was Thucydides?

Thucydides was an Athenian general and historian who wrote about the fifth-century war between Athens and Sparta, which lasted from 431 to 404 BC. Because of his approach to the writing of history—which, unlike that of earlier historians, excluded speculation, spectacles, or the invocation of divine intervention—his work came to attract favorable attention. This work, under discussion in this book, has been known for more than what it was not, however; indeed, it is best known for what it was and has been regarded as representing. It has come to be viewed as limiting its focus to evidence-based analysis, recounting what has been observed according to the highest standards of impartiality. As such, Thucydides has come to be called the father of "modern" or what is sometimes labeled "scientific" history.

He is also regarded as the father of a school of political thinking (one may say political theory) that has been known as political realism. This school views political behavior—at the individual or group level, including states—as grounded on and fundamentally influenced by self-interest. His historical masterpiece, *History of the Peloponnesian War* (a war between Athens and Sparta), is shaped by this thinking, which has informed the deliberations and actions of political leaders, policy makers, and policy scholars (especially in the West but elsewhere also) for centuries.[2] Associated with realist thinking is what has come to be called moral skepticism, a view that is defined by a deep doubt about the effectiveness of morality in international relations, where, it is believed, power and only power is determinative of outcomes.[3]

Born in a leading Athenian family, this Athenian general was stationed in Thrace (part of Bulgaria, Greece, and Turkey today), where he was exiled and spent most of the war years as punishment for his failure to prevent the capture of Amphipolis (a small Greek city) by Sparta. It is possible that the time and other opportunities allowed by this exile facilitated his writing of the book. The seeming independence and scholarly integrity that have characterized his recounting of the war, along with the lessons he claims to have deduced from the events narrated, have made his *History* a manual of sorts to future would-be political leaders and actual statespersons, serving as a "lighting of the way" on the decisions, motives, circumstances, and nature of leadership that produce war, inform its continuation, and define its contours and consequences. Aptly, Thucydides himself tells us why he wrote the book and, in the process of so writing, distinguished it from other histories. He indicated that he did not write his book to elicit excitement and sensation (romance):

---

[2]   One finds this thinking dominating the foreign policy of the US, from the beginning of the republic, but especially so after World War II, when Washington assumed leadership of the West. George Kennan, Henry Kissinger, Reinhold Niebuhr, Hans Morgenthau, and Brent Scowcroft were or have been among the names of the more influential thinkers, practitioners, or mentors in the field. Niebuhr's *Moral Man and Immoral Society* (New York: Charles Scribners, 1932) and Hans Morgenthau's *Politics Among Nations* (New York: Alfred A. Knopf Inc., 1954) have served as teaching tools for generations. Kissinger, whose dissertation at Harvard dealt with the balance of power concept and practice in post-Napoleonic Europe, has never been able to move outside this concept, so dear to political realists.

[3]   See Niebuhr's work cited above as well as Terry Nardin's *Law, Morality, and the Relations of States* (Princeton: Princeton University Press, 1983). The latter work provides a broader context within which to reflect.

The absence of romance in my history will, I fear, detract somewhat from its interest, but if it be judged useful by those inquirers who desire an exact knowledge of the past as an aid to the interpretation of the future, which, in the course of human things, must resemble if it does not reflect it, I shall be content . . . I have written my work not as an essay which is to win the applause of the moment but as a possession for all time.[4]

Thucydides embraced a cyclic outlook on history, meaning he saw past occurrences as recurring, in analogous if not identical forms, as indicted in the just-cited quote. Humans, therefore, could profitably learn from certain causes and effects and deduce patterns or trends despite apparent ambiguities. As such, particular occurrences, properly understood, hold within them distillable lessons from which generalizations can be made.[5] Graham Allison shares this view—that Thucydides' work has direct relevance to this century and beyond and is a reliable guide to the future. The position of this book is that the work of Thucydides is *not* a reliable guide for the future because—at least in the claim concerning the cause of the war—he erred. Allison, in relying on him, has likewise erred.

Statement of the Trap

The term "trap" refers to something (including circumstances) by which an entity is caught or otherwise confined without having foreseen the developments leading to the confinement or entrapment and its consequences. Allison begins his book, *Destined for War*, by noting that none of the leaders of the major powers of Europe wanted World War I—at least, the war they faced—and that none of them would repeat the choices made (they were all men) if given opportunities to make them

---

4   See Thucydides, *The Complete Writings of Thucydides: The Peloponnesian War*, unabridged Crawley translation with an introduction by John H. Finley Jr., Eliot professor of Greek literature, Harvard University (New York: The Modern Library, 1954), pp. 14–15.

5   Ibid., p. xii in Finley's introduction.

again. In short, each of them was trapped. More important than specific sparks that may be seen as causes of a war, as Thucydides (according to Allison) teaches us, "are the structural factors that lay at its foundations: conditions in which otherwise manageable events can escalate with unforeseeable severity and produce unimaginable consequences."[6]

Focusing on what he saw as the central structural factor that sponsored the war, Thucydides wrote that the "real cause, I consider to be one which was formally most kept out of sight. The growth of the power of Athens and the alarm which this inspired in Lacedaemon [Sparta] made war inevitable."[7] In other words, while others may have focused, in his view, on an array of contributing causes, they overlooked what he considered the "real cause." Allison, in turn, sees this "real cause" as a "primary driver at the root of some of history's most catastrophic and puzzling wars."[8] He then elaborates,

> Intentions aside, when a rising power threatens to displace a ruling power, the resulting structural stress makes a violent clash the rule, not the exception. It happened between Athens and Sparta in the fifth century BCE, between Germany and Britain a century ago, and almost led to a war between the Soviet Union and the United States . . .[9]

Sparta and Athens: An Elaboration of the Trap

Athens and Sparta were two city-states in ancient Greece, between which developed a rivalry that resulted in a catastrophic thirty-year war. Sparta, defined by an agriculture economy, was a land-based society that built its identity around a culture grounded on military discipline.

---

[6]   Graham Allison, *Destined for War: Can America and China Escape Thucydides' Trap?* (Boston: Houghton Mifflin Harcourt, 2017), p. xiv.

[7]   Thucydides, op. cit., p. 15.

[8]   Allison, *Destined for War,* op. cit., p. xv.

[9]   Ibid.

4

At age seven, for example, boys were inducted into military schools for disciplined training, and they, together, with a kind of collective identity, would succeed their elders as part of a warrior class in the pursuit of rendering service to the ideal of creating the perfect state.

Spartan citizens themselves did not indulge in farming; that activity was engaged in by a semi-enslaved group or class called helots, who lived on Spartan-owned estates and, along with members of other groups such as those which had been liberated from slavery, were allowed to keep a portion of that which they cultivated.

The values of discipline, frugality, sacrifice, and collective identity, within the warrior class, were nurtured. Spartan women citizens (unlike their Athenian counterparts, who were largely homebound and had little education) were expected to deal with the household economy and the early training of children, engage in civic life, and be disciplined, frugal, and prepared for sacrifice just as their male citizen counterparts. They partook in athletic activities with men and were known for their independence, proficiency in dancing and music, and beauty. (The famed Helen of Troy was a Spartan woman.[10]) They could and did own property also.

Athens, on the other hand, was a commercial city and the commercial center of Greece, with ever-expanding economic interactions with the rest of the Mediterranean and beyond. Unlike Sparta, which was governed by a monarchy, Athens had elected leaders called archons, a major one of whom was Pericles, to whom we will later refer. Because of this election of public leaders, Athens is often viewed as a democracy. It should be understood, however, that only the male citizens of the city could vote, and they constituted less than 15 percent of a population, at least a third of which were slaves. Like Sparta, it also had helots or semi-slaves.[11]

Both Athens and Sparta fought together defending Greece against the Persian Empire, especially during a series of famous battles:

---

[10] See Peter J. Brand in "Athens & Sparta: Democracy vs Dictatorship" for a well-written summary of Spartan and Athenian societies, with maps and other visual features that contribute to one's understanding. It, of course, reinforces certain common assumptions in Western culture (www.uopeople.edu).

[11] Ibid.

Thermopylae (August of 480 BCE), Salamis (August–September of 480 BCE), and Plataea (479 BCE). Athens was the star at Salamis, which, like that at Plataea, was a naval battle. There might not have been a Salamis, however, had it not been for the bravery of Sparta in the losing effort at Thermopylae—a bravery that delayed Persian advance and gave Greece more time to organize. After the decisive battle of Plataea, when the Greeks overcame the Persians, two important developments became apparent. First, Athens (unlike Sparta, which had rich agricultural lands to which it could and did return) focused on expanding its commerce, on which it depended, having so little land of its own for agriculture. Second, it progressively began to see its achievements at both Salamis and Plataea (but also during the 490 BCE Battle of Marathon, the first attempt by the Persian Empire to subdue Greece) as entitling it to the leadership of Greece. So consistent with the growing breadth and self-assessed weight of its interest, it used its expanded superior navy to extend its influence, sometimes pressing its allies to pay for the security its navy had before freely offered as a public good. The material returns from this pressure, as well as from commerce, considerably increased Athenian wealth.[12]

It is this expansion of Athenian influence and power, this felt entitlement to have its claims assume greater sway, that Allison contends induced insecurity and fear in Sparta, a country that had hitherto enjoyed a determinative say in the political and military order of Greece. Sparta wanted to preserve the status quo in which it was, according to Allison, dominant; Athens challenged it.

The claimed trap was then in place, associated as it was, in the "natural, inevitable discombobulation that occurs when a rising power threatens to displace a ruling power," contends Allison.[13] The threat of displacement "can happen in any sphere," he argues, and he points to examples of the younger sibling surging to overshadow his elder, or even his father, in family life, an upstart company with disruptive

---

[12]   In the Battle of Marathon, where Athens played the leading role in defeating Persia, Sparta did not participate. See Jennifer T. Roberts, *The Plague of War: Athens and Sparta and the Struggle for Ancient Greece* (Oxford: Oxford University Press, 2017).

[13]   Allison, op. cit., p. xvi.

technologies, such a Google or Uber, threatening older companies, such as Hewlett-Packard, or a young gorilla seeking to replace an older alpha male. In international relations, however, he contends, the "implications are most dangerous." Why? Just as "the original instance of Thucydides' trap resulted in a war that brought ancient Greece to its knees, this phenomenon has haunted diplomacy in the millennia since. Today it has set the world's two biggest powers on a path to cataclysm nobody wants but which they may prove unable to avoid."[14]

The reader will perceive, from the last-quoted statement, that the trap is defying of subjective human actions.

---

[14]   Ibid.

CHAPTER 2

The Trap's Application to China

During the middle of World War I, the US became the world's creditor country. Since that time, it has exercised economic and, by the end of World War II, worldwide military domination. This dominance, contested by the former Soviet Union after 1945, became all the more so in the wake of the disintegration of the latter county in 1991. This crumbling of its principal international challenger allowed the US the opportunity to extend its power beyond existing territorial spheres— Latin America and the Caribbean, Western Europe, the Middle East, East Asia (with the exception of China and North Korea), Australia and New Zealand, and the continent of Africa—to the areas of Eastern Europe that were parts of the former USSR. Officials in Washington began to speak of Washington's style of liberal democracy extending itself from Vancouver to Vladivostok if American "principles and values" were adopted.[15]

It is this domination to which Allison refers when he speaks of China's challenge—a challenge that he, in his introduction, puts in dramatic terms, asking his readers to suppose that the US were a corporation. In that case, it would have accounted for 50 percent of the global economic market in the years immediately after World War II. That commanding economic position had, by 1980, declined to 22

---

[15] See, for example, James Baker's December 12, 1991, speech at Princeton University.

percent, and following three decades of double-digit Chinese growth, he offered, the US's share was further reduced by 16 percent. Far more important, from the standpoint of his contention, if "current trends continue," the US's share of global economic output will decline further over the next thirty years to approximately 11 percent, while China's will have grown from 2 percent in 1980 to 18 percent in 2016, on its seemingly irreversible way to 30 percent by 2040.[16]

The use of these quantitative data is misleading (as we will see), but let us accept them for purposes of discussion. It gives the impression that the indicated, seeming economic decline of the US is primarily attributable to Beijing. In 1980, when China's share of world economic output was but 2 percent, the relative decline of the US from 50 to 22 percent was due to what had happened in Western Europe, especially within the European Union (EU), in Japan, as well as what had taken place in Canada, among other countries or regions of the world. By 2016, other areas of the world such as Brazil, India, Mexico, South Africa, Turkey, South Korea, Australia, and the nations of the Association of Southeast Asian Nations (ASEAN), among others, had been increasing their relative share of global economic output also. Let it be sufficient to say, at this juncture, that one can agree with Allison that the rise in China's share of world economic output has posed the only challenge to US dominance.

Scope of Threat and Trends

Even more important than Allison's focus on certain statistical claims is his use of the conditional "if current trends continue." He elaborates on current trends, as he understands them, in a number of areas: the reality of the US becoming "number two"; the psychological difficulty of facing such a status; the rapidity of change that China has been leading; the latter country's success in education, including its "STEM revolution"; Beijing's emerging military power; and a *new* balance of power orientation. We will touch on each in the order indicated.

With respect to the first, he noted that China's gross domestic product (GDP), which was but $300 billion in 1980, had grown to $11 trillion by 2015 (over $14 billion by 2019); its increment of growth

---

[16]   Allison, op. cit., pp. xvi–xvii.

every two years since 2008 was larger than the entire economy of India and was adding the equivalent of the whole economy of Greece every sixteen weeks. Further, although workers in China were but a quarter as productive as their counterparts in the US, were they to become even half as productive as the US's workers, Beijing would be leading a national economy twice the size of Washington's. Coupled with the issue of productivity are the rate of China's economic growth and the reach of its manufacturing. In the former, Allison observed, China has been increasing three times (it is now two plus) the US's rate; in manufacturing, it has surpassed the US as a producer of ships, steel, aluminum, cell phones, clothing, and computers, among other items, to become the "manufacturing powerhouse of the world."[17] Most "devastatingly for America's self-conception, in 2016" (largely because of the 2008 worldwide financial crisis), China became and has continued to be the primary engine for economic growth.[18]

The national self-conception among US citizens is that the US enjoys first standing, in terms of economic power, throughout the world. Allison, to reinforce his claim concerning China's threat, is contending that the US actually occupies second place to China—something that, he admits, "any American citizen" since roughly 1870 (the date that the US surpassed Britain as an industrial power) would find "unthinkable."[19] Using the yardstick of what is called purchasing power parity (PPP) instead of the conventional GDP, he contends that the size of the US's economy in 2014 was $17.4 billion, compared with China's $17.6 billion, and marshals supporting stances in the form of included quotes from the CIA, former MIT professor Stanley Fisher, and the International Institute for Strategic Studies to boost his contention that PPP is the standard to be used when national economies are being measured. By this measurement (and what this yardstick does is measure the rate at which the currency of one country must be converted into that of another country to make it possible to purchase the same goods), China

---

[17]　Ibid., p. 9. Most of the data under the "reality" of the US becoming number two can be found on pp. 6–9.

[18]　Ibid.

[19]　Ibid., p. 10.

could rightly be said to be number one and the US number two. This is the point that Allison, understanding how interlaced being number one in economic size has been to US national identity, is bent on making.[20]

Allison continues in reinforcing the idea of the threat that China is claimed to pose to the US by next looking into the rapidity with which China has been changing (and, by extension, changing the world), its transformation in the area of education, especially STEM (science, technology, engineering, and mathematics) education, and its evolving military power. At the physical infrastructure level of change, he notes that China built 2.6 million miles of roads, including 70,000 miles of highways, between 1996 and 2016, thereby connecting 95 percent of that country's villages and, in so doing, surpassing the US as the country possessing the most extensive system of highways. He then proceeds to touch on bridges, high-speed trains, and high-speed rail tracks (more than the rest of the world combined) during the period and then exposes the reader to the rapid transformation taking place, in China, in the areas of social change and human development. Here, he notes that Beijing increased the average per capita income of its citizens from $193 in 1980 to over $8,000 in 2016 and that between 1981, it succeeded in lifting over five hundred million people out of poverty, an achievement that has no precedent in history. China, he further observed, also rivals the US in the number of billionaires it has and is leading Asia toward surpassing North America (it has already done so in respect of Europe) by 2020.

Linked to the above achievements, the People's Republic of China (PRC) has been equally effective in the rapidity with which it has effected improvements in education, health care, and other areas of human social well-being. For instance, while 80 percent of China's population was illiterate in 1949 (when the PRC assumed control of China), with a life expectancy of thirty-six, by 2014, life expectancy rose to seventy-six years, and the rate of its literacy was 95 percent. Perhaps the category of education in which China's achievements have been most admired and feared is that of STEM, where Beijing "rivals and, by some measures outperforms, the United States."[21]

---

[20]   Ibid.

[21]   Ibid., p. 16.

The conclusion of the preceding sentence finds offered support in a number of areas, including four mentioned below and their ties to planning and the military capability of China. The first is the performance of high school students, as evidenced through "the internationally recognized gold standard" for comparing educational achievements among high school students, the Program for International Student Assessment (PISA), and Stanford University's comparison of students entering college in the fields of computer science and engineering. In the case of the 2015 PISA, China was ranked sixth in math, while the US ranked thirty-ninth (China and the US ranked first and twenty-fifth, respectively, in 2018), and the just-mentioned Stanford assessment found that Chinese high school graduates "arrive with a three-year advantage over their American" peers in "critical thinking skills."[22] Second, he looks to schools of engineering and engineering graduates, including PhDs in STEM fields, and finds that according to the US News & World Report rankings of 2015, Tsinghua University (frequently referred to as China's MIT) had become the number-one university in the world for engineering. Further, he claims, of the top ten schools of engineering in the world, China and the US had four each, and in terms of the core competencies of STEM that drive "advances in science, technology," and the most rapidly growing sectors of "modern economies," China was annually graduating about four times as many students as the US.[23]

Third, he focused on the diffusion of STEM education across China's economy, attributing to that diffusion China's high-tech manufacturing increase from 7 percent of the global market in 2003 to 27 percent in 2014 as well as US decline during the same period from 36 percent to 29 percent. Associated with said diffusion also is Beijing's achievements in the "fast-moving field of robotics," where China doubled the US registered number of applications for new patents and added "two and a half times as many industrial robots to its workforce."[24] As compelling, Beijing filed "almost twice as many total patent applications" as *second-place* Washington (emphasis the author's) and became the first country

[22] Ibid.

[23] Ibid.

[24] Ibid., p. 17.

from which originated "more than one million applications in a single year."[25] He moves on to quote a 2014 warning from the American Academy of Arts and Sciences that if the US does not quickly expand and strengthen its own scientific commitments and daring, it will "squander" the advantage it has long held as the leading engine of innovation, economic growth, and job creation.[26]

Allison rejects the frequently asserted claim or implication that China's industrial and technological success has been based on imitation and mass production, contrary to what he will contend in the areas of Beijing's culture and identity. He does, however, strongly associate himself with those who focus on China's alleged "theft of intellectual property," as an important part of its research and development program— the fourth area of evidence he brought to bear on his conclusion that China—in the STEM field—rivals and in some cases outdistances the U.S. He sees China as indulging in this theft through the old-fashioned way, with spies, as well as through the more modern cyber methods. He notes, however, that China has become "an innovator in its own right" and presents as examples its leadership in supercomputing since 2013 (the US regained this status in 2019). As well, in 2016, Beijing launched the world's first quantum communication satellite, designed to provide hack-proof communication. In the same year, China also completed the world's largest radio (as distinguished from optical) telescope, a device that augments China's capacity to explore deep space.[27] The success of China in these technological achievements, for Allison, is a demonstration of Beijing's capacity to undertake, successfully, "costly, long-term, path-breaking projects and see them through"; this is a capability that, in the case of the US, he sees as having atrophied.[28]

The scientific and technological accomplishments enabled by STEM education in and the overall economic performance and social development realized by China made it possible for that country to

---

[25]   Ibid. One can read pp. 16–17 for Allison's focus on STEM in China.

[26]   Ibid., p. 17.

[27]   Ibid., p. 18. In 2019, China's rover, *Jade Rabbit 2*, set off to explore the far side of the moon.

[28]   Ibid.

boost its military power. Allison cites the increased military spending of China (and again, he uses PPP as his measurement) in the amount of $314 billion to demonstrate that increase. As well, he cites a report from RAND Corporation that speaks of China as having, by 2017, an "advantage" or "approximate parity" in six of the nine areas of conventional military capability and concludes that between 2020 and 2030, Asia will become a receding frontier of US dominance. As in the case of its economic progress, China's military advances, Allison is arguing, are rapidly cutting into America's status as a global hegemon and thereby are forcing Washington "to confront ugly truths about the limits of American power."[29]

The final area trend that, if continued, portends war between the US and China is what Allison calls the "new balance of power," with "new" understood to mean a movement away from the old concept of balance that largely or exclusively emphasized military power to one that focuses on a combination of the economic and the military. This new focus, sometimes called geo-economics (really the old economic geography), uses economic instruments (from trade, investment, and technology transfer to cyberattacks, foreign aid, and currency manipulation) to achieve what are considered important geopolitical goals.[30] To Allison, "China primarily conducts foreign policy through economics," and this assertion is favorably backed up by two scholars, cited in the last footnote, who contend that China "is the world's leading practitioner of geo-economics" as well as the major inspiration in returning regional or global power projections to economic, as distinct from merely a political–military, exercise.[31]

To lend further support to the claim that China is the leading practitioner of geo-economics (and one has but to review the US's policy toward Japan before and after World War II or its open door policy toward China to dissent from this claim) and is using this practice to threaten the US, Allison

---

[29]   Ibid., p. 20.

[30]   Ibid. See also Robert D. Blackwill and Jennifer M. Harris, *War by Other Means: Geoeconomics and Statecraft* (Cambridge: Harvard University Press, 2016), which Allison quotes.

[31]   See quote in Allison, op. cit., pp. 19–20. See Blackwill's and Harris's introduction, especially (p. 11), to understand this important but inaccurate claim.

points to China's trade with 130 countries, including those of ASEAN (Brunei, Cambodia, Indonesia, Laos, Malaysia, Myanmar, the Philippines, Singapore, Thailand, and Vietnam). Trade with this group of countries (15 percent in 2015) exceeded the percentage of trade with the US (9 percent), Allison observes, and he contends that the economic leverage that China holds in its relations with these countries (as it does with other countries, such as Japan, from which it banned the export of rare metals in 2010) offers evidence of Beijing's readiness to use its economic power—buying, selling, sanctioning, investing, and bribing—to force countries to "fall in line." Also, when it (China) could not get its way in the US-dominated Bretton Woods institutions (the World Bank and the International Monetary Fund or the IMF), it stunned Washington in 2013 by establishing its own competitive institution, the Asian Infrastructure Investment Bank (AIIB).[32] What, to Allison, is even more troubling is that despite "an intense campaign by Washington" to pressure nations not to join this China-led bank, fifty-seven signed up even before it was launched in 2015, and those signatories included some of the US's key allies, "with the UK in the lead."[33]

Other Trends

Three other international "realities" suggest that the trends dealt with above remain unpromising, from the standpoint of Allison. In 2008, China also decided to establish its own club "rather than play by the West's rules." It organized BRICS—Brazil, Russia, India, China, and South Africa—a "group of rapidly expanding economies capable of making decisions and taking actions without supervision from the United States or the G7."[34] In 2013, China struck again; this time, it launched what has come to be known as the One Belt One Road (OBOR) initiative, "a network of highways, fast railroads, airports, ports, pipelines, power transmission lines, and fiber-optic cables across Eurasia," also the physical foundation

---

[32] Allison, op. cit., p. 22.

[33] Ibid.

[34] Ibid., p. 23. The Group of Seven (G7) is a forum of seven countries that boast the world's largest developed economies—Canada, France, Germany, Italy, Japan, the UK, and the US.

for social and economic development of a tri-continental region.[35] Indeed, this initiative is designed to link some sixty-five countries, encompassing portions of Asia. Africa, and Europe and creating a new "Silk Road," representing populations of over four billion people with an investment of about $1.4 trillion.

To Allison, this economic (geo-economic) plan or initiative is nothing less than what the great military strategist of China, Sun Tzu, had taught that "ultimate excellence lies not in winning every battle but defeating the enemy without fighting." China, in Allison's view, is preparing for victory without a conventional military battle, and he quotes Henry Kissinger to reinforce this view: "Far better than challenging the enemy on the field of battle" is the act of maneuvering that enemy into unfavorable positions "from which escape is impossible."[36]

He (Allison) concludes, in part, by saying that whether one sees China's policies as defined by largesse or economic imperialism, its economic networks are spreading across the globe in a manner that is changing the international balance of power in favor of Beijing and unfavorably to Washington. Even longtime allies in Asia often tilt toward China.[37] Before 1998, the first question that Asian leaders would ask in relationship to international issues was "What does Washington think?" Today they are apt to ask, "What does Beijing think?"[38]

---

[35] Allison, op. cit., p. 23.

[36] The quotes are from Sun Tzu and Kissinger, respectively, and they are contained in Henry Kissinger's *On China* (New York: Penguin 2011), pp. 28–29. The last quote is Kissinger's rather artful summary of Sun Tzu's main point. See Sun Tzu, *The Art of War*, with a new foreword by John Minford and translated by Lionel Giles (Tokyo: Tuttle Publishing, 2008), p. 10.

[37] Allison, op. cit., pp. 23–24.

[38] Ibid., p. 24.

CHAPTER 3

Athens and Sparta: Mirror of China and the US

The recounted accomplishments of China in the last chapter, taken separately or together, constitute "a relentless rise" that is a threat to the US, according to Allison. He emphatically contends also that, as pointed out in Chapter 1, the Thucydides Trap causes wars that "nobody wants," including the two principals in the Peloponnesian War, as is the case in the current instance with the US and China. The dynamics of the trap, however, are such that the fear caused by the "relentless rise" of Athens and China—challenging the status quo countries of Sparta and the US, respectively, generated in ancient Greece and today—stresses that "not just extraordinary events" but even seemingly passing or ordinary "flashpoints" in interstate relations can invite or "trigger large-scale conflict."[39]

After briefly going through the perceived differences between Spartan and Athenian culture, political systems, and interest, as well as a treaty, the Thirty Years' Peace, Allison takes his reader to the flashpoints that triggered the war. We will reverse the order of these pointed-to differences, beginning with the peace treaty.

The Thirty Years' Peace was a treaty signed by Athens and Sparta in 446/445 BCE. It brought to an end the conflict commonly known as the

---

[39]   Ibid., p. 29.

17

First Peloponnesian War, which began in 460 BCE, and, as well, provided conditions under which the Greek city-states could coexist peacefully in the future. Included in its terms (and those terms seem not to be fully known) were indicated commitments to ensure a certain minimum order and security. First, allies of the dominant two rivals (Athens and Sparta) could not realign—meaning they could not change their existing membership in the respective alliances—the Delian League, led by Athens, and the Peloponnesian League, led by Sparta. Allowing for such realignment would, it was thought, be too potentially destabilizing and, as such, could lead to war. Second, neutrality would be honored, but a former neutral city-state could, if it were to independently choose to, join one or the other of the two alliances. This provision, in a rather sophisticated manner, gave recognition to the fact that there were city-states that saw their interests as actually or potentially less well served by joining either of the alliances than remaining outside of them—remaining neutral. Were they to find reasons to change their thinking, they could voluntarily join one of the alliances. Third, disputes arising between Athens and Sparta or between members of their respective alliances should be addressed through arbitration—a third-party mode of dispute settlement, with such third parties deemed to be impartial.

In other words, the thinking of Athens and Sparta (and ostensibly other Greek city-states) reflects the understanding that despite what appears as a nonaggression pact between them, there were likely to be incidents (in Allison's words, "sparks") that would arise from time to time. Such incidents could result in a war, which they would rather avoid, between them. To avoid such a development (in cases where negotiations between them or between members of their respective alliances were unsuccessful), they would have or put in place some institutional machinery to help reduce the likelihood of war. During the interlude between 445 BCE and the beginning of the Second Peloponnesian War, 431 BCE, there were a number of breakdowns that took place in the relations between Athens and Sparta, including two linked to "local" disputes. The first in 435 BCE involved Corcyra, a neutral country and possessor of the second largest navy after Athens, and Corinth, an ally of Sparta that boasted the third largest navy but at considerable distance behind Athens. The second, in 432 BCE, involved Megara, an ally of

Sparta, in what has come to be known as the Megarian Decree issued by Athens.[40]

In the case of the first, Corcyra, a colony of Corinth, had, in accordance with the terms of the treaty just dealt with, elected to remain a neutral power and, for many years, had failed to give the type of recognition to Corinth, which colonies were expected to accord to mother countries. On the latter account, among others, relations between the two were not good. When Epidamnus, a colony of Corcyra, in seeking to deal with internal factions, approached Corcyra and the latter refused to offer help, it turned to Corinth, which offered to help. Corcyra saw this offer of help by Corinth (without even the proper customary consultation) as an unacceptable course of action and intervened in Epidamnus, defeating the ruling faction and taking action against both the interests of the latter city-state and Corinth. The Corinthians, responding with their navy, were routed by the Corcyraeans. Humiliated, Corinth spent a year upgrading and expanding its navy and preparations for another battle with Corcyra. On coming to know this, Corcyra appealed to Athens, and Corinth, aware of what Corcyra's action meant, appealed to Sparta.

Both Athens and Sparta now faced a dilemma. From the standpoint of Athens, it was desirable that Corcyra, which once saw neutrality as a "wise precaution," should now be offering itself as an ally, but accepting such an alliance (with a state that had the second most powerful navy) could incite anger in Sparta. To refuse the offered alliance, however, brought with it the possibility that a defeat of Corcyra by a rearmed Corinth would allow the latter to have not only its own navy but that of Corcyra as well. Further, since Corinth was an ally of Sparta, a strengthened Corinth would mean an equivalently strengthened Sparta. There was also the issue of whether offering aid to Corcyra constituted a violation of the Thirty Years' Peace (we will use the acronym TYP in all subsequent references to this agreement). Athens, through the leadership

---

[40]   Although we will be focusing on works of Allison and Thucydides in these early chapters, one may profitably read certain works on Greece, such as Malcolm F. McGregor's *The Athenians and Their Empire* (Vancouver: University of British Columbia Press, 1995) and Nigel Bagnall's *The Peloponnesian War: Athens, Sparta, and the Struggle for Greece* (New York: St. Martin's Press, 2006).

of Pericles, its "first citizen" (or equivalent of prime minister), sought to deal with the dilemma by agreeing to a "defensive alliance": it would not join Corcyra in *attacking* another country, but it would offer assistance if Corcyra were the victim of an attack. Corcyra was likewise bound. In part, to give effect to this understanding, Athens sent a small symbolic fleet to Corcyra with instructions to avoid attacking unless attacked.

Corinth saw this development and subsequent conduct on the part of Athens differently. So it had to be, for "it begun now to be felt," according to Thucydides, that the coming of the Second Peloponnesian War was but a matter of time, and no one on the Athenian side was willing "to see a naval power of such magnitude as Corcyra sacrificed to Corinth."[41] So as the latter state moved to prosecute its planned war against Corcyra and had begun to gain the upper hand and noticing that the Corcyraeans were "hard pressed, the Athenians began at length to assist them [the Corcyraeans] unequivocally."[42]

The Corinthians saw this as a breach of the TYP and were enraged. This rage would, in part, be taken out on Sparta too because Corinth felt that its ally Sparta was not acting as firmly as it should to deter Athens. Like Athens, however, as rightly characterized by Allison, Sparta faced a "strategic bind."[43] Were it to support Corinth (as sympathetic as it was toward it and its effort to discipline its colony, Corcyra, and prevent the latter from joining Athens), gaining control of Corcyra and its naval capabilities would be interpreted by Athens as an attempt by Sparta to match its naval capacity (the reader should remember that, as before indicated, Sparta has an advantage in the military area of the army, while Athens enjoyed that advantage in naval capabilities) and irreversibly change the existing balance of military power between them, in favor of Sparta and the Peloponnesian League.

On the other hand, Sparta could not remain neutral or indifferent. To do so would suggest to its allies that it was unwilling to come to their aid, even when such aid was demonstrably needed. It would likewise invite the unwelcome inference that Sparta was fearful of Athens—a

---

[41] Thucydides, op. cit., p. 28.

[42] Ibid., p. 30.

[43] Allison, op. cit., p. 35.

psychological state that no leader of an alliance can long survive. Above all, it would allow Corcyra (with the second largest navy among the city-states) to add its military capabilities to those of Athens, Sparta's principal rival. What ally or Spartan citizen would now believe in the power of Sparta to ensure his, her, or its security?

Immediately after the confrontation between Corinth and Corcyra (and almost concurrent with its later phases) were some "fresh differences ... between the Athenians and the Peloponnesians [Spartans] and contributed their share to the war."[44] Among these fresh differences was an encouraged revolt among the Potidaeans, who were a tributary ally of Athens (meaning they were members of the Delian League who paid monies to Athens); they were also a colony of Corinth, which had encouraged the rebellion. Athens laid siege to Potidaea (432–430 BCE), demanding that it exclude Corinthian advisors and officials and decline to accept them in future years and remove certain city walls so that its defense would be more accessible and vulnerable to Athens. There was also the Megarian Decree, which was a body of economic sanctions imposed by Athens on Megara, an ally of Sparta, in 432 BCE. The decrees—a claimed response to alleged Megarian commission of incursions on lands that belonged to Athens and had, as well, harbored slaves who had escaped from Athens—banned Megarians from the harbors and market sites throughout the Athenian Empire (and this most likely applied to allies or trade partners of Megara, thus undermining the security of its economic activities). This course of action by Athens helped convince Sparta that it had to act, and act it did. It demanded that Athens revoke the Megarian Decree, raise the siege of Potidaea, and respect the independence of city-states.

The Athenians, led by Pericles, rejected the ultimatum, indicating that it would allow states their independence only if they enjoyed that status before the TYP; it would not raise the siege of Potidaea and would allow Megara to resume trade in Athenian markets and harbors only if Sparta were to engage in certain courses of action in favor of Athens.

To Allison, the message is clear: "the rise of Athens could destroy a key alliance that, for centuries, had helped to keep the Spartan homeland

---

44   Thucydides, op. cit., p. 33

secure."[45] His claim here is reinforced by Thucydides, whom he quotes. The Spartans voted that "war must be declared, not so much because they were persuaded by the arguments of allies [many of which were critical of Athens but also critical of Sparta for its relative inaction in the face of Athenian aggression] as because they feared the growth in the power of the Athenians, seeing most of Hellas already subject to them."[46] In short, Sparta looked to the future and concluded that its position, given the then perceived trajectory of Athenian power and expansion, could only be worse. The ensuing war, lasting for nearly thirty years, resulted in the complete destruction of Athens and the Athenian Empire, and Sparta, although emerging as "victor," was depleted and would be defeated many years later (372 BCE) by Thebes. So in Allison's words, "was the war inevitable?"

He concedes that Thucydides' use of the term "inevitable" should not be taken literally but that it captures a dynamic in human affairs that is difficult to manage when a state that exercises supreme power finds itself challenged by a rising power, especially when fueled by the psychological drivers of fear, interest, and honor. In the case of the latter, for example, the Athenian sense of "entitlement" created problems, but so did the fear and anxiety of Sparta as Athens expanded its influence. The leaders of the "two states could not stop a relentless realignment from tipping into bloodshed . . . In spite of great statesmen and wise voices in both Athens and Sparta warning that war would mean disaster," the changing balance of power induced both sides to conclude that "violence was the least bad option available."[47] This, to him, is a likely fate for China and the US.

My aim is to rebut Allison later in this work, but I must, at this stage, indicate that in his thirst to focus so much on the operations of non-human forces (the balance of power, for example), he deliberately deemphasized and, to an extent, overlooked the critical role of Pericles, who, on at least two crucial occasions, was able—through his unbending preference for war, accompanied by his unequalled capacity to persuade—to swing

---

[45]   Allison, op. cit., pp. 36–37.

[46]   Thucydides, op. cit., p 50.

[47]   Allison, op. cit., p. 40.

sentiments in favor of either going to war or continuing it. One has but to study his speech in the context of the balance of expressed sentiments or the indicated psychological state at the second congress at Lacedaemon (432 BCE) and his funeral oration in 431 BCE. In each, he was able to either remove doubts about going to war or continuing it or silence those who had expressed doubts about going to war or, in some instances, saw such a war as a price that Athens should be unwilling to pay for the peace to be lost.[48] We will be returning to this theme.

---

[48]   See Thucydides, op. cit., pp. 79–83, 102–109.

PART II

Case Studies, Gathering Storm, and Another Past

CHAPTER 4

Case Studies

The first chapter of this work deals with, among other things, a definition of the Thucydides Trap. Chapter 2 seeks to show that both the US and China are caught in this trap, while the Chapter 3 occupies itself with efforts to demonstrate that there was an analogue, in ancient Greece, in the political form of Athens and Sparta, to our current confrontation between China and the US. This chapter seeks to say that the problem of the trap has always been with human beings; it is not just a phenomenon of ancient and contemporary times. One, therefore, as was the hope of Thucydides, can come to understand better the true nature of the danger that the trap represents by studying, as Allison has done, other manifestations of its type. Among those manifestations are two case studies that I have chosen from six presented in Allison's book: Japan versus the US and Britain versus Germany.

Japan versus US

The focus here is the 1941 attack by Japan on the US naval headquarters at Pearl Harbor, Hawaii, resulting in the destruction of most of the US fleet that was stationed in that harbor. To Allison, that which sponsored the attack was the rivalry between Washington and Tokyo, a rivalry that began in the late nineteenth century as a byproduct

27

of the Spanish–American War of 1898 and the so-called open door policy, which Washington adopted in 1899.

In the case of the 1898 war, the US gained a number of possessions—including what is often regarded as its first colony, the Philippines, along with Guam—to enable it to expand its military and commercial interest. With respect to the open door initiative, it represented a foreign policy stance by the US that it would not recognize the actions of foreign powers in China that lent themselves to monopolizing or creating exclusive or preferential commercial positions in that country. Rather, that country should be open to all commercial interests "on an equal basis," as is understood by Allison.[49]

Japan, in Allison's view, saw the US's stance as unfair. First, Washington was extending, long distance, its own exclusive commercial interests in areas such as Guam and the Philippines but was seeking an "open" door in China. Second, other countries—the UK, in India, Holland, in Indonesia, and Russia, in Siberia and the Sakhalin Islands—were extending their respective interests closer and closer to Japan, and the latter was being pressured to withdraw from territories it had gained (in its 1894–1895 war with China, in which the latter country was defeated). So after carefully preparing itself militarily, it moved in three directions to advance its interests.

It went to war (1904–1905) with Russia, with which it had had differences over Korea and Manchuria, and administered a stunning defeat of Moscow, taking control of Port Arthur (now called Lushunkou District in the city of Dalian, China), the South Manchurian Railroad (SMR), and the southern half of the Sakhalin Islands. (It had, by then, also wrested control of Taiwan from China and occupied Korea.) The second direction that Tokyo pursued involved the 1931 invasion of China, moving some five hundred miles into the latter country's interior, from where it could control commercial and other interactions with many cities and ports (many of the latter controlled by Western countries, including the US) and dominate over half the country. The third direction was largely ideological, including Japan's version of the Monroe Doctrine, which stated that as of 1933, Japan would be

---

[49]   Allison, op. cit., p. 45.

"responsible for the maintenance of peace and order in the Far East."[50] This doctrine, associated with the idea of "Asia for Asians," bespoke Japan's view that Asia was being dominated by non-Asians, who allowed no reciprocal opportunity to Asians to thrive within their respective areas, and it was also part and parcel of Japan's focus on shaping the to-be-advanced-later Greater East Asia Co-Prosperity Sphere (GEACPS), dominated from Tokyo. To Allison, Japan's strategy constituted a kind of "uncompromising win-or-lose conviction" that if it did not ascend, it was in decline.[51]

In the case of the US, its "self-proclaimed guardian of the Open Door," according to Allison, found Japan's ambitions and actions "unacceptable,"[52] essentially arguing that Washington was bound to adhere to its own doctrinal position and favorably quoting Prof. Paul Kennedy's position that Tokyo's aggression was actually more than a contravening of US open door policy; it was also a "threat to" a principle, at least in theory, on which the American way of life is quite dependent.[53] In other words, it was an identity matter, and so the US could not simply turn its head; it had no choice but to respond.[54]

The US, therefore, according to Allison, proceeded to impose a number of sanctions on Japan, including "essential raw materials such as iron, brass, and copper—and, finally, oil."[55] These sanctions, he argues, proved to be the "the proverbial straw," with oil proving to be of utmost importance. War became inevitable as Japan decided to effect a "knockout" blow to the US. He concludes that the "contest between a rising and ruling power often intensifies competition over scarce resources . . . The attempt to deny a state imports it judges crucial for

---

[50] Ibid.

[51] Ibid., p. 46.

[52] Ibid.

[53] Quoted in Allison, ibid., p. 46.

[54] See Paul Kennedy, *The Rise and Fall of Great Powers* (New York: Vintage Books, 1989), p. 334. His views of Japan and its actions are, as the reader will later see, somewhat narrow.

[55] Allison, op. cit., p. 47.

survival can provoke war."[56] There was no ruling and rising power here, regionally or globally. The US and Japan were competitors, as we will see later. Allison's to-a-degree sketchy presentation of the case obscures the true character of the competition.

Britain versus Germany

The other case study that I chose is that of Britain versus Germany. To Allison, the challenge of Germany to Britain's worldwide hegemony was the cause of World War I.

He begins by noting that if one were to use 1900 as a temporal benchmark, Britain or the British Empire encompassed modern India, Pakistan, Bangladesh, Malaysia, Myanmar, Singapore, Australia, New Zealand, and Canada, along with much of the continent of Africa. As well, it exercised strong influence in Latin America and the Caribbean (areas within which it had colonies) and held strategic positions and/or protectorate relationships from the Falkland Islands to Cadiz, Cyprus, Suez (Egypt), the Persian Gulf, Sri Lanka, and Hong Kong, among others.[57] It also boasted the world's most impressive navy, owned the world's key currency, the pound (which operated as the functional equivalent of the US dollar today), functioned as the world's banker, with London serving as the commercial center of the world, and ascribed to itself the role of world's policeperson. "Britain thus saw itself and expected others to see it as number one."[58]

He then underlined the view that the UK had of itself and how that view was legitimized in the imperial setting through the voice of young Winston Churchill (without doubt reflecting the sentiments of most other Englishpersons, as will be seen) that Britain would continue the path that had brought it to the status of "top dog." That path was to "pursue that course marked out for us by an all-wise hand" to "carry

---

[56] Ibid.

[57] Countries or ties that were left out were included by the author.

[58] Allison, op. cit., p. 60.

our own mission of bearing peace, civilization, and good government to the utmost ends of the earth."[59]

He then sought to contrast this vision by Britain, concerning its self-assessed status and its mission for the future, with Germany's search for its "place in the sun." In his mind, Germany's pursuit of its "place in the sun" was in conflict with Britain's "top dog" status and was analogous to (and a repetition of) the power dynamics between Sparta and Athens, in which one comes face-to-face with the fear felt by the ruling power when a rising rival appears to endanger the security of its status. How was the fear, in Allison's view, generated? What did Germany do to generate that fear?

Three categories of conduct, in his view, fueled that fear—a fear that led to war. They were in the areas of economic and technological growth, responses to the formation of alliances, and the increases in armed forces, principally the navy. In the area of economic and technological growth, Berlin had, by 1914, moved past London in global manufacturing output (not as much as the US had) and had overtaken it in heavy industry and factory products as well as in the emerging, all-important sector of organic-chemical industry. Also, although Britain's exports to Germany doubled between 1890 and 2014, those exports represented but half the value of what it was importing from Germany. The latter country's rising economic power was cutting into Britain's prosperity, and its control of 90 percent of the world market in the then emerging organic-chemical industry occasioned anxieties in London. Between 1901 and 1914, Allison observes, German science and technology had also surpassed that of Britain to become "the best in the world," reflecting strong advancement in university research and a supportive state. He offers as evidence of this development the fact that between 1901 and 1914, Germany, boasting scientific breakthroughs, won eighteen Nobel Prizes, twice as many as the UK and four times as many as the US.[60] Let us turn to the military capacity and to political alliances.

---

[59] Quoted in Allison, ibid., p. 61.

[60] See Allison, ibid., pp. 62–65. These pages cover the data mentioned in the area of economic and technological achievements.

In the matter of military capability, emphasis is placed on the navy because this is where the UK was supreme and where Germany, in his view, had to challenge. This is indeed where Germany was perceived to and did, in fact, challenge, with its First Naval Law in 1898 and its Second Naval Law in 1900, on a planned path to make Germany's navy one that could challenge Britain's. The first law called for nineteen battleships, and the second required a doubling of the size of the first. Britain, which had what was called a "two-power standard" (meaning that London would maintain a number of battleships that was at least the equal of the combined naval strength of the next largest two navies in the world), sought to maintain that standard.[61] The latter had become, in the thinking of Britain, a reliable way by which it could (quoting from a famous 1907 memorandum from the foreign office with which we will be dealing) ensure that the "virtual 'law of nature' inherent" in London's foreign policy—to prevent any single state from dominating continental Europe—would continue to be faithfully executed. That prevention, in turn, was concomitantly viewed, by Britain, as instrumental in maintaining its global ascendency. For Germany, this instrumental policy represented an unacceptable containment.

The UK also had fears about the physical proximity of the German navy (headquartered at Kiel on the Baltic, fewer than five hundred miles from London), but this fear was matched by Germany's anxiety that Britain might use its superior navy to attack that headquarter, not unlike it had done to Copenhagen in 1807 as Britain faced Napoleon.

With respect to alliances, the first significant one, from the standpoint of our subject, was the 1902 UK–Japanese defensive alliance. It was primarily directed against Russia, in the so-called Far East, where Moscow constituted a challenge to both Britain and Japan; it also reduced the need for London to maintain many forces in that region and to concentrate more elsewhere, including Europe. Certainly, this was part of how Germany, which was conscious of Britain's weakness in potentially having the latter's navy overstretched

---

[61] While Britain found it difficult to maintain this standard, in the face of many more countries developing large navies—France, the US, Japan, and Italy and, to an extent, Russia—it was able to maintain roughly a 2:1 tonnage ratio with Germany between 1880 and 1914.

throughout the world, saw things.[62] The second alliance began with the 1904 creation of what was initially called the Entente Cordiale (a cordial agreement or understanding) between Britain and France, with a view to accommodate, mutually, their long-standing disputes, especially those involving rival colonial claims. By 1905, however, both countries began secret military talks, which led to a 1907 trilateral alignment (France already had some ties with Russia) among France, Russia, and Britain, which later became known as the Triple Entente—really a defensive alliance among the countries.

Germany, of course, which had been feeling "encircled," felt all the more so and sought to find opportunities—in Morocco, in Libya, and, to an extent, in the Balkans and Tunisia—to create estrangement among the members of the Triple Entente, thus increasing tensions among European powers. Berlin also pursued steps to link itself more closely to the much earlier created 1882 Triple Alliance, among Germany, Austro-Hungary, and Italy. For Allison, Britain embodied the view that "the growth of the German navy and its geographical proximity" to its borders "posed a unique existential threat" and thus, from the standpoint of London, made Berlin "its [Britain's] primary enemy."[63] This threat, he claims, made war "preferable to the prospect of Germany achieving dominance on the continent and then threatening Britain's survival."[64]

As such, the UK, viewing Germany's 1914 planned move through Belgium as a path to France and fearing the defeat of France—and, with that defeat, the control of the continent by Germany—used the issue of Belgian's neutrality (of which Britain was a guarantor) to help mobilize public opinion to go to war. Here, he quotes British historian Paul M. Kennedy to reinforce his position[65] that London sought to preserve, as

---

[62]   Allison, op. cit., p. 70.

[63]   Ibid., p. 81. As we will see later, Germany was not even seeking naval equality with Britain.

[64]   Ibid.

[65]   Paul M. Kennedy, *The Rise of Anglo-German Antagonism, 1860–1914* (London: Allen & Unwin, 1980).

did Sparta, the existing state of affairs, while Germany, for a mixture of offensive and defensive reasons, sought to change it.[66]

As in the case of Germany, according to Allison, China feels that it has been cheated out of its "rightful place" by countries that enjoyed powerful international standing while it was weak. Like Germany also, China possesses the will and the means to change the existing international arrangements. In the meantime, like Britain, the US jealously guards its primacy on the world stage (the status quo) and is determined to resist China's attempts to "revise the global political order."[67]

---

[66]   Ibid., p. 470. See also Allison, op. cit., p. 83.

[67]   Allison, ibid., p. 85.

CHAPTER 5

A Gathering Storm

Having constructed an apparently persuasive case for many readers that Germany versus Britain and Japan versus the US, among others, furnish appropriate, underlying historical support for his thesis, Allison moves to what he sees as the "gathering storm," a term used by Winston Churchill for the title of the first of his six-volume work on World War II—a volume in which he captured the movement toward war. In other words, in Allison's view, we are moving toward war with China.[68]

In Part III of his book, "A Gathering Storm" (divided into Chapters 5, "Imagine China Were Just Like US," 6, "What Xi's China Wants," 7, "Clash of Civilizations," and 8, "From Here to War"), Allison seeks to clinch his point concerning the trap. The first of these four chapters covers a history of the US's conduct in its march to becoming a global power and then to *the* global power. The latter status was acquired through aggressive actions varying from the declaration of the Monroe Doctrine, its corollary, and their enforcement; the 1846–1848 war with Mexico, therefrom acquiring from that country the area now constituting Arizona, California, Colorado, Nevada, New Mexico, Utah,

---

[68] Winston Churchill, *Gathering Storm* (Boston: Harcourt Mifflin Company, 1948). For the reader who wants to have a less side-leaning and more theoretically grounded view of the more immediate political and psychological crosscurrents leading to the war, see John G. Stoessinger's *Why Nations Go to War* (New York: St. Martin's Press, 1988), pp. 1–23. Earlier editions are, in some respects, better.

and Wyoming; the annexation of Hawaii; the attack on Spain in 1898 (the Spanish–American War), which resulted in the acquiring of Cuba, Puerto Rico, the Philippines, and Guam; the separation of Panama from Colombia to facilitate the building of the Panama Canal as a strategic link between the Atlantic and the Pacific, to serve commercial and naval purposes; the "Manifest Destiny" doctrine, which was used to justify the "Western march," eliminating, through wars, any and all opposition that Native Americans posed to the increased taking of their land and other resources; and the controversy with Britain (and threat to Canada) over the Alaska boundary.[69]

It is not only that the US's conduct was aggressive in all the instances cited, as examples, to extend its territory and political influence as well as security but that they were largely used to exclude or limit other nations' political and economic intercourse with the areas acquired. The Monroe Doctrine, for instance, was designed to limit European countries' engagement with Latin America. As well, the claim (under Manifest Destiny) that the US was chosen to lead and improve the lives of others is an exclusivist stance, associated with Washington's self-righteousness. Allison rightly thinks that we would not want China to emulate the US's behavior and that a China "Monroe Doctrine," in respect to its "neighbors and the South and East China seas along its borders," would be unwelcomed by the US.[70] Although China has not emulated the US in the latter's historical (or contemporary) aggressiveness, Allison claims that "we ain't seen anything yet."[71] The storm is gathering.

With respect to what Xi's China wants (Chapter 6), Allison does not so much seek to analyze China's behavior as he deduces that supposed or likely behavior or ascribed ambitions from the view of others, especially the views of the late prime minister of Singapore, Lee Kuan Yew, whose reported, relevant views of Beijing (and Washington) have been fairly

[69] Allison, op. cit., pp. 91–106.

[70] Ibid., p. 106.

[71] Ibid.

broadly circulated.[72] Neither does Allison focus on China as he does one Chinese leader, Xi Jinping, and then generalizes what he claims to see as China's ambitions and intentions. What are these ambitions? In aggregate, to make China "great again" and to "become number one in Asia and, in time, the world."[73] To be number one in Asia begins with returning China to the prominence it enjoyed before the West intruded in its affairs; reestablishing control over "Greater China," including Tibet, Taiwan, Hong Kong, and other areas; recovering historic spheres of influence along its borders and adjacent seas; and commanding the "respect of other great powers in the councils of the world."[74]

Allison then goes on to discuss a number of other areas in Chapter 6, including the "world according to China." For instance, the country is depicted as "profoundly ethnocentric and culturally supremacist," hierarchical (one should know one's place), inclined to expand by cultural osmosis, in contrast to the missionary zeal that characterizes the US, and burdened by a past that is defined by millennia of Chinese dominance that abruptly came to an end in the nineteenth century by an industrializing West (the US and Europe), economic colonization, and occupation by outside powers—"first by the European imperialists and later by Japan."[75]

"Who Is Xi Jinping?" followed by "Realizing China's Dream," "Xi's Nightmare," "Making China Proud Again," "Sustaining the Unsustainable," "A Message to America: Butt Out," and "Fight and Win" are the other subthemes of the chapter. The first focuses on President Xi, who—from the social humiliations, deprivations, and general disappointments of the Cultural Revolution (1966–1976), including its impact on his father, who was imprisoned, and on his elder half-sister, who committed suicide—"chose to survive by becoming redder than

---

[72]   See, for example, Belfer Center for Science and International Affairs, *Lee Kuan Yew: The Grand Master's Insights on China, the United States, and the World,* interviews and selections by Graham Allison and Robert Blackwell, with Ali Wyne and foreword by Henry Kissinger (Cambridge: MIT Press, 2013). We will hereafter cite this work as *Lee Kuan Yew.*

[73]   Ibid., p. 2; see also Allison, op. cit., pp. 108–109.

[74]   Allison, ibid.

[75]   Ibid., p. 111.

red"[76] and gained supreme power largely by purging powerful rivals using a "highly visible" anticorruption campaign. In the case of realizing "China's dream," Xi has set out to revolutionize the Communist Party of China (CPC), to revive China's nationalism and patriotism (by way of instilling pride in being Chinese), to shape a third economic revolution (restructuring the country's economy to ensure greater emphasis on internal consumption), and to rebuild China's military.[77]

The rest of the chapter, in all the cited subcategories, revolves around Xi. In Allison's view, he faces a continuing "nightmare"—the possible loss of control by the Communist Party, as had taken place in 1989/1990 under the Gorbachev-led, former USSR and generally seen as having led to the disintegration of the latter country. He is also burdened by "making China proud again" through nationalist sentiments, not the idea of a "new socialist person," as espoused by the revolution, and "sustaining the unsustainable"—maintaining the rapid rate of economic development China has had while undergoing the previously mentioned internal restructuring as well as the external initiatives such as the OBOR (or the Belt Road Initiative or BRI) project. Allison sees the latter as China's seeking to control the "world Island" (a geopolitical term for the Euro-Asian geographic core), a step toward gaining control of the world.[78]

In the case of "A Message for America: Butt Out," its central focus is on the sentiment, voiced by Xi, that Asians should control their own affairs; Allison combines this sentiment with his efforts to show how Xi's China has been expanding its influence in Southeast Asia and its efforts to reclaim the areas in the South China Sea. In his view, China's "longer-term objective is clear"—it seeks to use its ability to project

[76]   Ibid., pp. 113–116.

[77]   Ibid., pp. 116–117.

[78]   Ibid., pp. 125–126. The term "world Island"—also referred to, at times, as the "pivot area" or "the heartland"—denotes the largely landlocked area of Central Euro-Asia that has been seen by geopoliticians as the key to the control of the world. See, for a path-breaking work, Halford J. Mackinder, "The Geographical Pivot of History," in *The Geographical Journal*, Vol. XXII (April 1904), pp. 298–321. https://www.iwp.edu-content/uploads/2019/05/20131016MackinderTheGeographicalJournal.pdf

power in the area of that sea to exert greater influence over the estimated $5.3 trillion trade that passes through it every year, to muscle the US out of those waters, and to absorb, within its economic orbit, the nations of Southeast Asia—perhaps even including Japan and Australia. "It has so far succeeded," Allison contends, "without a fight. But if fight it must, Xi intends to win."[79]

The last referred-to subject, war and fighting to win, encompasses the scope of military reforms that have been initiated by Xi, including his fight against corruption (including corruption in the armed forces) and his emphasis on his building of China's navy, not unlike Germany, after the latter had become aware of the thinking of US's Alfred T. Mahan (conceptual father of Washington's thinking on the navy and sea power) and more conscious of the ways by which London, as China does Washington today, could use its navy to limit the self-determining interests of other states.[80] Allison also duly notes that the powers that, separately or together, dominated China during the nineteenth century did so by way of naval power. China, in my view, intends to avoid the humiliation that came from the absence of a navy that can protect its political independence and territorial integrity.

Chapters 7 and 8 respectively focus on differences between the US and China in values and culture and on some likely paths to war. In the first of the two chapters, entitled "Clash of Civilizations," Allison is emulating the thinking of his late faculty colleague Prof. Samuel Huntington in arguing that not only does and will culture play a more central role in the relations among states, but also, as in the case of Athens and Sparta, conflicting values will play a major role in US–China relations.

In his "Clash of Civilizations" portion of his book, Allison summarizes the "clash of cultures" between the US and China. In self-perception, the US views itself as "number one," while China views itself as the "center of the universe." On core values, the US is defined by "freedom," while China is defined by "order." In their view of government, the US sees it as a "necessary evil," while China regards

---

[79]   Ibid., p. 128.

[80]   See Alfred T. Mahan, *The Influence of Seapower Upon History, 1660–1783* (Boston: Little, Brown and Company, 1898).

it as a "necessary good," and while the US's form of government is a "democratic republic," China's is "responsive authoritarianism." As well, he posits, the US's attitude toward foreigners is "inclusive," and China's is "exclusive." The US's time horizon is "now," while China's is "eternal." The US sees change in terms of "invention," while China views it in terms of "restoration" and "evolution." Finally, the US, in foreign policy, values "international order," while China emphasizes "harmonious hierarchy." He also contrasts the US's and China's approaches to war. With the above claimed differences in cultural values—combined with all the other earlier narrated areas of constituting, from the perspective of Allison, threats and conflicts of interest—it is understandable why he is disposed to see a disastrous future war between the US and China. He thus, in Chapter 8, focuses on "From Here to War."

The burden of "from here to war," consistent with Thucydides' counsel about and Allison's emphasis on it, is the part played by fate or the "influence of accidents" (unplanned developments) and mistakes (including misperceptions) in causing long-term military catastrophes. Allison takes the reader through two paths—one offering examples of past accidents or near accidents between the US and China, and the other projecting likely or possible areas of future accidents.

Reviewing the past, he looks at the Korean War of 1950–1953, during which the US's General MacArthur dismissively overlooked the "peasant army" of China, which later inflicted stunning reverses on the US-led UN forces—the Sino-Soviet border conflict of 1969, when China is said to have ambushed Soviet border troops to teach Moscow a lesson, a conflict in which the US became involved to prevent Moscow from using nuclear weapons in a preemptive strike. He then touched on the Taiwan Strait Crisis of 1996, during which Beijing—to bring pressure to bear on the possible election of a candidate who was then espousing independence for Taiwan, contrary to the "One China" policy—launched missiles that "bracketed the island and threatened commercial shipping on which it depended."[81] The US responded by

---

[81]   Allison, op. cit., p. 159.

sending the USS *Nimitz* and USS *Independence* aircraft carrier battle groups to help Taiwan, and China backpedaled.[82]

As respects the future, Allison notes the psychological effects of the US's and China's "memory" that the US has either lost or failed to win four of the five wars it has entered since World War II (Korean, he sees as, at best, a draw, Vietnam a defeat, Iraq and Afghanistan unlikely to be a victory, and only the 1991 war to remove Iraq from Kuwait a win). He then touches on new "disruptive weapons" that enable a country to paralyze another's command-and-control systems, cutting off links between headquarters and commanders and troops in the field. Cyberspace, he opines, provides even more opportunities for disruptive actions, and with antisatellite capabilities, a conflict can escalate to untold proportions.

For Allison, this includes an accidental collision at sea; a move by Taiwan toward independence and, by this act, inviting China's military intervention to prevent it (in this case, the US might be tempted to act to help Taiwan); a war triggered by actions of a third party (Japan, for example, over the Diaoyu/Senkaku Islands); and North Korea's hostile actions toward South Korea, the collapse of North Korea, or a move by South Korea to conquer North Korea. He then touches on the possibility to an economic conflict leading to military action. All these could occasion a war that no one seeks.

The Trump administration, he observed, had identified "a clear culprit: China's cheating on trade agreements, currency, intellectual property, industrial subsidies, and artificially cheap exports."[83] He notes that the US is demanding "equal trade without deficits"[84] and moves quickly to observe how malware, which China could use, might disrupt "the integrity of the entire American financial system and cause panic."[85]

Part IV of his book deals with "why war is not inevitable," with a number of suggestions intended to avert war, beginning with the use

---

[82] Ibid.

[83] Ibid., p. 181.

[84] Ibid., p. 182.

[85] Ibid., p. 183.

of the UN, which he quickly dismisses because it does not work. He
does not examine why it does not and spends the rest of his presentation
offering some of the most (from the standpoint to the West and the US)
status quo–supporting prescriptions, seemingly believing that there
is no alternative to the existing liberal international order. In the end,
however, his prescriptions cannot not work because he misidentified
the problem between Athens and Sparta and, as well, each of the case
studies we covered. As such, he also misdiagnosed the problem between
the US and China.

CHAPTER 6
There Is Another Pattern

There is a narrative other than that provided by Allison, even if one were to accept his general interpretation of Thucydides. This other narrative is reinforced when one examines more carefully the thinking that the Athenians represented at the time under review and the limited emphasis given to the role of Pericles, an example of human moral agency, and his thinking (Allison, unlike Thucydides, gave little attention to these factors).

The general narrative presented by Allison—built, as the reader will recall, on Thucydides' position that the "growth of the power of Athens" and the "alarm" that growth had inspired in Sparta made the thirty-year war between them inevitable—is generalized by Allison as follows: when, in the history of human beings, a rising power threatens to displace a ruling power, the resulting structural stress makes a violent clash the rule, not the exception. The case studies we covered were offered to support this generalization. The other narrative contends that the challenge that Athens posed to Sparta was not a displacement challenge but a much more fundamental and socially compelling threat. This threat was troubling in meaning and impact not just to Sparta but even to the allies of Athens, and the means chosen by Athens to mount or manifest the threat, equally frightening, varied from claims to entitlements to a sum of behavior that, in effect, subverted people's sense of honor and dignity.

Displacement

The term "displacement" has several meanings, including changing place with, supplanting, removing from, or taking the place of another. Any of these meanings suggests that Sparta's fear of being replaced by Athens made war inevitable. The other narrative takes the position that Athens had already replaced Sparta as the dominant power in Greece by the time of the outbreak of the Second Peloponnesian War and that its superiority to Sparta was manifested in many areas—including the size of its population, revenues, strategic capabilities (the largest navy and one that could be maneuvered to initiate and maintain an embargo against Sparta), and a commercially based economy, in contrast to Sparta's, which was agriculturally constituted. This superiority was not something implicit but a fact of which both Sparta and Athens were duly conscious.[86] (Pericles, leader of Athens, whom I will later quote, and Archidamus, the Lacedaemonian king, whose words or substance of those words I will present here, were particularly aware of this.)

He, the Spartan king, was a voice of restraint as the 432 BCE debate about going to war with Athens, at the Congress of the Peloponnesian Confederacy, was concluding. He noted that Sparta could act swiftly, if the need arose, and could act from different sites that could offer advantages, but he warned about having to fight with people "in a distant land" who have an "extraordinary familiarity with the sea," who enjoy "the highest state of preparation in *every department*" [emphasis is this author's], who have "wealth, private and public, with ships and horses and heavy infantry" as well as "a population such as no other Hellenic place can equal."[87] He therefore queried, what was the source of apparent confidence (among Spartans and its allies who were trying to induce Sparta to declare war on Athens, which many of those allies saw as oppressive and bullying)?

---

[86]   For a general sense of the time, see Josiah Ober's *The Rise and Fall of Classical Greece* (Princeton: Princeton University Press, 2015). Athens, of course, was vulnerable to Sparta's well-trained land forces that could invade Athens, but the superiority of the latter's navy posed a problem, especially so because it could operate from different locations.

[87]   Thucydides, op. cit., p. 46.

Was it "in ships?" he asked. "There we are inferior; while if we are to practice and become a match for them, time must intervene. Is it in our money? There we have a greater deficiency," he indicated. Then he looked to the area where Sparta had an acknowledged advantage and thus confidence but even here presented a strategic weakness: "confidence might possibly be felt in our superiority in heavy infantry . . . which will enable us to invade and devastate their lands, but the Athenians have plenty of other land in their Empire, and [they] can import what they want by sea."[88] He then went on to note that Sparta could, as is often done today, try to induce insurrection among the allies of Athens, but doing so would require a fleet since most of the allies are islands.

So if the fear of Sparta were not displacement, what was it? The broader goal of Athens—world domination and, as important, the means by which it sought to bring about that goal. Let us look at each, in turn.[89]

Broader End

In the first chapter of this volume, we touched on a number of Greco-Persian Wars (GPW), a series of conflicts between 490 BCE and 479 BCE, led by Athens and Sparta, defeating an invading Persian Empire. It was after these wars that Athens formed the Delian League (478 BCE) as a "permanent alliance" to defend Greece against potential invaders, especially Persia, whose near-defeat of the Greeks generated a long-lasting fear of its possible return. Sparta—which had, in the previous century, organized a coalition of Greek city-states (the Peloponnesian League)—kept that league, which, as we have seen, became a rival of the Athenian alliance.

While the coalition remained a loose confederacy, Athens gradually converted the Delian League into an increasingly centralized institution as that city-state moved from the status of first among equals to supremacy within the coalition to the dominator of what became an empire with an ever-expanding reach. For example, the increased centralization and expanded reach expressed themselves in 454 BCE, when Pericles moved the treasury of the Delian League from the sacred island of

---

[88] Ibid.

[89] Ibid., p. 90.

Delos to Athens—a course of conduct induced by the claimed need to protect the league's funds from Persia but which, in fact, gave Athens greater control of those funds. As well, between 450 BCE and 447 BCE, Athens, by decree, engineered a common currency (a silver coin, the tetradrachm), the use of which was made obligatory for members of the alliance, and it organized an exchange rate in favor of itself.[90] Contributions to the large fleet that had defeated Persia at Salamis (a fleet that became larger and larger) increasingly had to be in the form of money instead of in kind—ships, timber, or grain, for example. It was this reliable body of funds—from the Delian League's treasury, favorable exchange rate, ownership of key currency, and obligation to pay in money rather than in kind—to which King Archidamus referred; it was this same body of funds and the wealth it sponsored that paid for the further expansion of the fleet, the broadening of commerce, the maintenance of the increasing number of colonies, and the payment for impressive expressions of public art. The wealth also seeded the seemingly unrestrained expansion of the Athenian Empire and informed King Archidamus's observation that Athens, in fact, did "aspire to rule the world."[91] This aspiration, along with a frown at the idea of equality, formed the larger aim of Athens.

As the fear of a return of the Persians gradually faded, some of the former grateful allies of Athens began to seek greater autonomy. Others openly questioned the tribute or taxes they were paying to Athens,[92] and still others saw the security they had initially sought under the Athenian-led Delian League as having brought another source of insecurity—the Athenian Empire itself. This questioning of its status and policies by its allies became threatening to Athens. As this threat became clearer, in the form of less and less willing acceptance of its imperial policies, Athens began to employ means designed to further control and expand its empire, means that included norm departures, a claim to privilege and entitlement, the introduction of self-interest as an immemorial and

---

[90]   See N. G. L. Hammond, *The History of Greece to 332 B.C.* (Oxford: Oxford University Press, 1959), p. 306.

[91]   Thucydides, op. cit., p. 90.

[92]   Peter Fawcett, "When I Squeeze You with Eisphoral: Taxes and Tax Policy in Classical Athens," in *Hesperia*, Vol. 85, #1 (January–March 2016), pp. 153–190.

future principle as well as source of legitimacy, and the refusal to accept mutual respect, which is the most important attribute of equality.

A Claim of Privilege

Not only did Athens move from leading a confederation to imposing an empire on Greece, but also, it sought to purchase a form of legitimacy—rightfulness, reasonableness, logicality, and even constitutionality—for its imperial standing. This purchase, it sought to make permanent and secure in a variety of ways, but the principal three modes were defined by a recited doctrine or maxim about the "natural" relationship between the strong and the weak, the historical role of Athens in preserving the freedom of Greek city-states, and an alleged unrequested gift offered to and accepted by it.

In the case of the strong–weak relationship, Athens contended that the weak should observe status subordinacy and submissiveness, accepting of the claims of the strong; be takers of what is offered, not engaged in action to be makers; and be dependent on the lead and discretion of the strong. This status was not something Athens was newly seeking to create; it had "always been the law that the weaker should be subject to the stronger."[93] With respect to the just-mentioned "historical role" of Athens, it refers to that city-state's contention that but for its leadership and its unexampled exertions (in ships, patriotism, risk taking, and successes in the defeat of the Persians in the battles earlier covered), Greece would have been defeated and enslaved by Persia.[94] These successes and their associated benefits that have been bestowed on the people of the various city-states of Greece concurrently conferred on Athens a special status and an entitlement to it.

In other words, Athens merited its imperial position; it enjoyed a kind of self-defined worthiness that, allegedly, others, including Sparta, understood, acknowledged, and accepted until "calculations of self-interest" expressed in the clamors for "justice" intervened. That

---

[93] Thucydides, op. cit., p. 44.

[94] Ibid., p. 43. Here, for example, one finds Athens noting that it had furnished two-thirds of the four hundred vessels at Salamis. It also provided the incomparable commander of the fleet, Themistocles.

intervention was grounded on "calculations of self-interest" no one had previously "ever brought forward to hinder his ambition when he has a chance of anything by might."[95] In short, Athens was asking, when did a city-state or any group of humans ever invoke justice as grounds to bypass opportunities for gain through the use of power?

The view that Athens merited its imperial position above and beyond what has been said above concerning privilege and entitlement was seen by Athenians as strengthened by the contention on the part of Athens that, relieved by the victory it led over Persia, many city-states "spontaneously" offered and attached themselves to it to enjoy its protection. In short, the empire was a gift, and it would not be "contrary to the common practice of mankind" if "we" [the Athenians] accepted an "empire that was offered to us and refused to give it up under the pressure of the strongest motives—fear, honor, and interest."[96]

Common to each of the three indicated areas that make up Athens's reach to legitimize its empire and imperial behavior—the relationship between the strong and the weak, the unequaled contributions to the freedom and prosperity of Greek city-states (through the GPW), and the "gift"—are two attributes: one, that the behavior of Athens was either natural or consistent with the customary conduct of peoples and nations and, therefore, universal; and two, that Athens, in allegedly treating its subjects with greater moderation than other imperial powers, was not only more just but *qualitatively* different. What was the basis for this claimed difference?

It supported a law-governed imperial system, allowing for one of the more unvarnished expressions of noblesse oblige, in which even the inferior, by virtue of the legal order, was able to associate with it as equals. Continuing, Athenians see themselves as having more "respect for justice than their position compels them to do."[97] This asserted legal equality (where the nobility obligates Athens to be generous to its inferiors) really referred to the use of "the impartial laws of Athens"[98]

---

95   Ibid., p. 44.

96   Ibid.

97   Ibid.

98   Ibid

to settle dispute—laws that generally favored Athens and, therefore, made it litigious but giving the appearance of being committed to a law-governed order. Non-Athenians who did not see things this way complained about what they saw as unfair judgments favoring Athens. The latter, offended by what it considered an undeserved reputation for litigiousness and unfairness in the complaints of allies, argued that such complaints came about because these allies were "ungrateful for being allowed to return most of their possessions . . . [and their] indignation, it seems, is more excited by legal wrong than by violent wrong; the first looks like being cheated by an equal, the second like being compelled by a superior."[99] Athens came to prefer the second because it was unbothered by the many complaints and wrangling in court.

For the countries that were materially, militarily, and politically less powerful than Athens, the idea of equality that the law offered was of utmost importance.[100] It was part of custom (as exhibited by the principle that a country could elect to be neutral but could also decide to join an alliance, providing it was done voluntarily—without coercion). Athens, however, came to adopt the idea that self-interest and power were more important than law and equality, a fact that became quite telling in the Melian Dialogue (between Athens and Melos),[101] during which the Athenians told the Melians that they (the Athenians) would bypass reciting how they had a right to their empire by virtue of having defeated the Persians or confessing to some false claims about some alleged wrong that the Melians had done as a justification for their demands that the Melians give up their stance of wanting to remain neutral in the war between Athens and Sparta. A "right as the world goes," said the Athenians, "is only a question between equals in

---

[99]   Ibid., pp. 44–45.

[100]   Ibid., p. 22. Even colonies were considered equals, in my respects.

[101]   This is a rather famous exchange between the Athenians and the Melians, with the latter resisting Athens's insistence that it join the Athenian empire, while the Melians, a colony of Sparta, preferred to remain uninvolved in the conflict with Sparta.

power, while the strong do what they can and the weak suffer what they must."[102] Athens would speak of interest only.

Privilege and Interest

It was the making of naked, self-defined interest as the core of Athenian foreign policy, thereby subverting the legal and moral order with the equality the latter conferred, that compelled or induced Sparta to go to war. Without that order, not only the colonies but also every state that was not superior to Athens would lose its independence. When Thucydides, therefore, said that it was the growing power of Athens and the fear that growth elicited from Sparta that had caused the war, his summary of cause was incomplete, as the quoted portions above from his own writing attest.

As its empire became more and more powerful, Athens wanted nothing to do with the equality that the existing order allowed; it even warned Sparta that if it were to "succeed in overthrowing us [Athens and its empire] and taking our place," substituting Sparta's practices, so leagued to law, it would quickly discover the many condemnations instead of approvals that legal equality would occasion.[103] What Athens wanted instead was the freedom of action that imperial powers at a stage in their respective evolution (perhaps one should say devolution) seek, accompanied by fealty from inferiors—usually flattering offerings to the superior's self-ascribed greatness. The latter attribute, in turn, is used to effect further domination and to exact more favorable returns based on self-interest, without any concern for fairness or the common good.

Sum of Parts

What Sparta saw and experienced, some of which has been included in the immediately three preceding subsections, is not so much a matter of displacement (this, as said earlier, had taken place long before, although its application to specific colonies or allies had continued)

---

102   Thucydides, op. cit., p. 331.

103   Ibid., p. 45.

but claims of privilege and to entitlement, the wholesale substitution of self-interest for the rule of law and custom, and the search for worldwide domination by Athens. So it was not primarily the issue of Athenian gains in power, especially as measured in military and economic terms, that was the critical ingredient; it was rather the mixture of moral and psychological spices that gave taste to Sparta's experiences. They were the collapse of rank, sense of worth, esteem, respect, and consideration of integrity, of moral strength (what the Corinthians saw Sparta seeking to uphold in the principle of "fair dealing" but which was useless when dealing with Athens) and of character.[104] At the heart of this collapse was the spirit of equality, which Athens could no longer indulge (and the reader should bear in mind that equality confers rank and recognized status).

This spirit of equality sprung, as indicated, from "equality under the law," a principle (and its associated sentiments) that generally preexists the disputes it is called upon to judge and, in most cases, resolve. A preexisting army of other principles exercises an internal morality that is inclusive, if they are neutrally applied. Among them are the unchanging precept that one is not the best judge of one's cause; that rules of law apply equally to the rich, the poor, the powerful, and the powerless; and that impartiality is an inalienable attribute of equality. The less powerful, therefore, can face the most powerful on even terms. The latter is what Athens feared because it allowed inferiors a sense of grievance and anger in cases where a superior is seen as having an unfair advantage leading to an undeserved outcome. Compelling impositions from a superior power remove this problem.

Meeting the powerful (in this case Athens) on even terms is what the Melians referred to when they discovered that the self-interest that Athens urged them to pursue, that of taking "the advantage of submitting before suffering the worst," by refusing to do so (the Melians wanted, in the war between Athens and Sparta, to remain friends with Athens without being an enemy of Sparta rather than, as demanded by Athens, becoming an ally of Athens and an enemy of Sparta), was one-sided. In

---

[104] Ibid., pp. 40–41. Here, one finds Corinth doing its utmost to get Sparta to declare war on Athens by noting, among other things, that the Athenians were "addicted" to innovation in commerce and military.

short, self-interest did not mean what the Melians defined it to be but what Athens decided it was or was not, leaving Athens *alone* to define its own interest as well as that of others.

This course of conduct, on the part of Athens, was seen by the Melians as violating not just the law governing neutrality but also the internal morality of the law—the norm of equality. It was, they said, the equivalent of destroying "what is our common protection," of not "being allowed," when "in danger, to invoke what is fair and right."[105] This protection, this common protection, Sparta saw as degraded and, therefore, unavailable—an alarming development for a conservative state seeking to find its way, including its sense of security, in a status quo that had ceased to exist, as Corinth was arguing.

All the above-narrated, anxiety-producing behavior, on the part of Athens, was intermingled with a public belittling of Sparta, in part to augment its own sense of its self-anointed greatness but also to offer instruction to other powerful city-states that they may be subject to the same treatment. In other words, the mutual regard and respect normally extended even to one's enemies was under assault or already corrupted. For instance, the role of Sparta in the GPW was marginalized. It used that state's cautiousness to misrepresent it as being averse to danger and daring. It also disparaged its institutions and culture and openly supported, as earlier pointed out, enemies of its allies.[106]

Indeed, if one were to carefully read the oration of Pericles, at the end of the first year of the Peloponnesian War, he was then trying to defend himself against the charge that he was to be blamed for the war as well as offering recognition to and assigning praise for the fallen in battle, their presented, illustrious ancestry, and the level of standard they provided to future generations. As important, one finds his extraordinary claims about Athens's greatness and its unique and exceptional standing in the world, not just Greece. For instance, he claimed that "we [the Athenians] have forced every sea and land to be the highway of our daring, everywhere, whether for evil or for good,

---

[105] Ibid., p. 331.

[106] Ibid., pp. 18–33, 45, 334.

have left imperishable monuments behind us."[107] Athens, he claimed, was the "school of Hellas"—the model for Greece, the city-state from which others could and should learn.

Therefore, words such as "only," "alone," "singular," "unlike," and "superior" are used through the speech again and again to characterize Athens and its self-adjudged exceptionality. Why would such a state long entertain the idea of equality? It was too restraining, in morals and in law, and even the recognized invocation of the gods. It was under these conditions that Sparta, to keep its remaining allies and enjoy a final chance to preserve its independence, decided to go to war. It was Athens's monumental commitment against equality, so regrettably overlooked, that occasioned the war.

---

[107]   Ibid., p. 106.

PART III

Counter-Narratives on Case Studies

CHAPTER 7
Japan and the US

Having shown that there is another reading to be had from the thesis concerning the cause of the war between Athens and Sparta, we should now move to see how, if at all, this new reading bears on the other case studies that Allison used to support his position. We will use the two additional cases previously discussed—two of those, as the reader should recall—chosen and studied by Allison as part of the proof that he offered for the validity of his thesis. They are Japan versus the US and Germany versus Britain. It is the contention of this work that the cause of war, in both cases, was the search for—and the fear as well as rejection of—equality.

To Allison, Japan (as presented in Chapter 4) was a rising power that was contending with a ruling power, and after focusing on a number of economic sanctions imposed by the leading power, the US, on the rising power, Japan, the latter attacked the former. As with Athens and Sparta, there is a counter-narrative—one revolving around the history of US–Japanese relations from the 1850s (not 1898, as Allison selected as his starting point) to 1941, the structure of the international system between those two dates, and the thinking and values that actuated the behavior of the states during the period under review.

History, 1853–1920

Both the US and Japan emerged from traumatic experiences during the 1850s and 1860s. For the US, it entailed controversies concerning slavery and its place in society, which, in turn, led to the Civil War (1861–1865), followed by amendments to its constitution, providing for civil and political rights (CPR) for non-whites, particularly African Americans. For Japan, it was its new encounter with the West, led by the US, in 1853, the overthrow of the Tokugawa shogunate (a semi-feudal military governance structure that had led Japan between 1600 and 1868), and the modernization policies of the country under a restored imperial rule (called the Meiji Restoration).

The US, which had begun its modernization earlier (and modernization is being used here interchangeably with industrialization), saw it gain new momentum after the Civil War in many ways, including the coming into being of the corporate era, the mechanization of labor, production pursuing economies of scale, wholesale commercialization, the conferring of legal personality on the corporation, the focus on research and education in non–liberal arts areas by public universities, and an impressive emphasis on technology. Central to this modernization was a focus on overseas markets, the latter including commercial, investment, and raw material markets. With respect to Japan, its modernization was more rapid and centrally directed, and it involved governmental reforms that were significantly emulative of the West— indeed imported from the West. It was also defined by a meteoric shift from an overwhelmingly agricultural to an industrial economy. The latter pursuit, the Meiji government decided, was necessary for its very survival. Why so? Japan thought it would have to become as powerful as those states that threatened it, and industrialization was a step in the direction of that development.

First, the country, which had sought limited or no commercial and other forms of intercourse with the international community, was forced, in 1854, under the threat of an armed attack by the American commodore Matthew C. Perry, to open its "doors" to the US's trade (and later to the trade of other countries, including the UK and Holland). Additionally, it had to agree that Americans, while in Japan (called

58

extraterritoriality), would not be subject to Japanese law. They would live under US law and would be tried in the latter's court; Washington would only accept specified rates of tariffs in designated Japanese ports; and coins "would be traded without any duty"—an imposed decision that would lead Japan to hemorrhage gold currency.[108]

It is not surprising, therefore, that Japan sought to know more about how it could become powerful enough to defend itself and about the authority by which war and the threat of war not only was morally permissible but also could be used to exact concessions from others so that it too could avail itself to the terms of that authority. As well, Japan, about the physical size of the US state of Montana (with mountains dominating its topography) has always faced a scarcity of natural resources, including what we today regard as important minerals, many of which are of seminal importance in the process of modernization and the acquisition of international power.[109] Its modernization, therefore, at least in part, would engender a vigorous search for foreign markets, especially to satisfy resource needs in areas where it had weaknesses within its own borders.[110]

With both countries focusing on overseas markets, in some cases particular regions and countries (Asia Pacific, for example), and coveting some of the same opportunities and sharing elements of the then reigning ideological outlook (to be reviewed later), they became bitter rivals. In 1894, incited by differences between Beijing and Tokyo over Korea, Japan attacked China and, within four months, defeated it in the First Sino-Japanese War (1894–1895), The result? China was forced to recognize the "independence" of Korea, ending a long period

---

[108] Donna A. Hathaway and Scott J. Shapiro, *The Internationalists* (New York: Simon & Schuster, 2017), pp. 138–139.

[109] John Hunter Boyle, *Modern Japan: The American Nexus* (New York: Harcourt Brace Jovanovich, 1993). p. 2.

[110] Admiral Perry told the Japanese that God had made the world in such a way that no country was self-sufficient and that trade is one way that the lack of self-sufficiency could be overcome. Any state that refused to trade, therefore, was doing something contrary to the principles supportive of mutuality among nations and the comity or friendship that spring from the expected mutual support from one another. See Hathaway and Shapiro, op. cit., p. 136.

of tributary relationship between the two countries and leaving the latter country as a site for expanded Japanese influence. Taiwan and the Pescadores Islands were transferred from China to Japan, as was the Liaodong Peninsula, the southern gateway into Manchuria. In 1898, the US annexed Hawaii, where, for some years, it competed with Japan (even Britain and, to a degree, Germany, as well) for influence.[111] That year also, the US, as a part of the returns from its war with Spain, acquired, among other areas, Guam and the Philippines, the latter much desired by Japan.

The US, observing that China was being carved up by other powers, especially those from Europe, noting further that it was being left out of this rather important market, developed a diplomatic stance known as the "open door policy."[112] That policy, enunciated in 1899 by the then secretary of state, John Hay, contrary to the then existing practices of imperial powers in China that pursued exclusive trading and other privileges in China, sought to have established a system of trade that would be open to all countries on equal terms. It also sought protection of China's territorial integrity; after all, if the territory of that state were not protected, there would be little or no venue within which to pursue trade and investment. The other imperial powers—such as Russia, France, and Germany but especially Japan and Britain—were not pleased. While the policy, if implemented, offered a relative latecomer to China, the US, opportunities for commercial and other types of expansion, it was viewed by other countries that had earlier claims in and on China as diluting or limiting their commercial and investment possibilities. With certain modifications over time to accommodate "facts on the ground," the US stood by the policy and sought to extend it.

In 1903, the US sponsored the independence of Panama from Colombia. This was done to ensure the building of a canal that would connect the Atlantic and Pacific Oceans and perhaps, even more

---

[111] Merze Tate, *Hawaii: Reciprocity or Annexation* (East Lansing: Michigan State University Press, 1968).

[112] William Appleman Williams, ed., *The Shaping of American Diplomacy*, Vol. 2 (Chicago: Rand McNally & Company, 1967), pp. 440–477. This book contains the texts of important documents and readings covering many areas of US foreign policy and is used extensively in our discussions.

important, to underwrite (infrastructurally) Washington's claims to being a Pacific country, a great power, and its claims to the China market. One year later (1904), Japan, dissatisfied with its sought assurances from Moscow (which was its other principal rival in China) that Russia would not interfere in Korea, launched a military attack on the termination point of what came to be called the SMR, Port Arthur, then the site of Moscow's deep-water port and strategic naval base in East Asia (under long-term lease from China). The Japanese not only won stunning victories in land battles but also, in early 1905, destroyed the Russian Baltic fleet, which was sent to the East to help in the war. The results were many, including the destruction of Russia's ambition to become a great naval power, the elimination of Russia as a rival to Japan in Manchuria and Korea, Tokyo's confounding (no Asian country had, in modern times, defeated a European great power) military ascendency, China's coming to know that it now faced a far more formidable Japan than it had encountered in 1894, and Britain's weighty satisfaction in having forged the 1902 alliance with Japan to contain Russia's rising influence in Asia. The victory, for the US, also brought uncertainty about the idea of an "open door" as well as its companion principle, the territorial integrity of China.

The US [whose leader, Theodore Roosevelt (hereinafter TR), presided over, as mediator, the ensuing Treaty of Portsmouth between Russia and Japan] took very keen notice of the developments and understood that it had a more redoubtable rival in Japan than first thought. In the very year of Tokyo's victory (1905), the US formally sought to contain that rivalry diplomatically by entering into the Taft–Katsura Agreement, accepting Japan's free hand in Korea, in return for Tokyo's disavowal "of any aggressive design whatsoever on the Philippines,"[113] against which the US had, only in 1902, concluded a war. The US, however, did not want to concede too much to Japan, although it knew that Russia's transfer to Tokyo of Port Arthur and the entire peninsula on which the port was located, its withdrawal from Southern Manchuria (which,

---

[113] Quoted in Samuel F. Bemis, *A Diplomatic History of the United States* (New York: Holt, Rinehart and Winston Inc., 1965), p. 493. This agreement was negotiated between the then US secretary of war, William Howard Taft, and the then prime minister of Japan, Taro Katsura.

while returned to China, was subject to important exemptions, ensuring Japan's paramount influence there), and the commitment of Moscow to cease interfering in Korea left Japan in a difficult-to-contest standing in Northeast China and in Korea.

So Washington sought to use less visible means, financial investments, to influence developments in China, but when the Sun Yat-sen–led revolution of 1911 ensued and he, along with the nationalist party, established the Kuomintang (KMT), which gave the promise of uniting a seemingly reawakened China, all those powers that had fed on a divided, almost chaotic China had to begin recalculating their relationship with that country. Japan saw the promise of a unified China as a threat to its emerging dominant position there, and in January 1915, Tokyo presented what has come to be called the "Twenty-One Demands" on China—demands that, if wholly accepted, would have made China a protectorate, "Japan's India," as one author characterized the likely resulting relationship between Tokyo and Beijing.[114]

The demands (and they included encroachments on China's sovereignty in Shandong, South Manchuria, and Eastern Inner Mongolia), intended to be secret, were exposed and immediately elicited a strong reaction from the US, which feared that its open door policy would be permanently closed. (Here, a reminder is prudent: although on the surface, this policy appears to have been altruistic, seeking to protect the territorial integrity and political independence of China, it was but a means by which the US sought to ensure the opportunity to extend its economic interest in China.) Washington, however, especially in the face of the war in Europe, had to be particularly careful about its opposition to Japan—mindful as it was of Japan's alliance with Britain and the fact that, through that alliance, Tokyo was also at war with Germany and its allies. That common war effort could not be weakened, and Japan understood this.

Despite the threat of increased tensions with Japan, the US felt that it should find some balanced way to stake out its position or face exclusion from the Chinese market. That balance was, from the standpoint of Washington, struck through a note from Secretary of State William Jennings Bryan, which informed Japan that while the US could not be

114   Ibid., p. 687.

indifferent to the assumption of the economic or military domination of China, it accepted that "territorial contiguity creates special relations between Japan and those districts" (mentioned at the beginning of the paragraph). The note went on to say, in a most tactful manner, in closing (and in explicitly linking US economic interest with China's independence), that Japan would find it compatible with its interest "to refrain from pressing upon China an acceptance of proposals which would, if accepted, exclude Americans from equal participation in the economic and industrial development of China and would limit the political independence of that country," thereby creating a circumstance it (Washington) was confident Japan did not desire or seek.[115]

The immediately preceding position of Washington may well have contributed to modifications of the demands on China, but by May 7, 1915, Tokyo gave Beijing an ultimatum to accept the modified version of the demands within forty-eight hours, and China accepted. The US, on learning of this new development, reacted forcefully, indicating "that it cannot recognize any agreement or understanding which has been entered into or which may be entered into between the Governments of Japan and China, impairing the treaty rights" of US citizens in China, "or the international policy relative to China commonly known as [the] open door policy."[116]

Japan did not flinch from its policy and activities in China despite the US's refusal to recognize them, although it slowed its pace. In the meantime, it had busily engaged in an extended diplomatic offensive to exploit the problems faced by Britain and its allies in Europe to gain recognition (meaning acceptance) of those activities and policies. For example, in exchange for Japanese convoys in the Mediterranean (thus allowing allies against Germany to redeploy naval forces elsewhere), Britain agreed in February 1917 to support at the anticipated postwar peace conference Japan's claim to Shandong and the retention of German Pacific islands north of the equator. France, in March of the same year, agreed to support the same claim if Japan would get China to cut diplomatic relations with Germany. Later, both Russia and Italy

---

[115]   Ibid., p. 688.

[116]   Ibid., p. 689.

pledged to support Japanese claims in China after the war.[117] Only the US, which joined the war efforts against Germany late, held out.

Japan launched a diplomatic effort toward the US, one of two other developments we should touch on, the other involving President Wilson's return to an earlier initiative pursued by Washington. Together, they show Japan's search for broad acceptance of its policies—a search that the US-led policies frustrated. They also show that while Japan felt that it had to control China militarily, the US thought that its sought control could be effected less intrusively, through economic means.

Seeking to gain US support for its policies in China, Tokyo redoubled it efforts by sending former foreign minister and then distinguished diplomat Viscount Ishii Kikujiro to Washington to accomplish that end. His negotiations with then secretary of state Robert Lansing resulted in a partial reiteration of the US's position in respect of the latter's interest but this time offered some incremental improvements in concessions to Tokyo. An agreement on November 2, 1917 (called the Lansing–Ishii Agreement), states that both the US and Japan recognize that "territorial propinquity creates special relations between countries," and as a consequence, the US "recognizes that Japan has special interest in China, particularly in the part to which her possessions are contiguous."[118] (This meant, among other things, that the US recognizes that Japan had special interest in Manchuria and the surrounding areas.) On the other hand, while the geographical position gave Tokyo "special interests" that it could militarily defend, it (Tokyo) had "no desire to discriminate against the trade of other nations or disregard the commercial rights heretofore granted by China in treaties with other powers."[119]

The term "no desire" is particularly troubling since it suggested something wholly in the control of Japan, but when it is joined with the fact that Japan "declared" that it would "always adhere" to the open door principle or "equal opportunity for commerce and industry in China," Washington appeared to have been satisfied. That satisfaction

[117]   Ibid., p. 690.

[118]   Ibid., p. 692.

[119]   Ibid. It is enlightening to read an article written in the 1930s dealing with the term "special interest." See Franz Michael, "Japan's 'Special Interest' in China," in *Pacific Affairs*, Vol. 10, #4 (December 1937), pp. 407–411.

was partly dashed by strong opposition from China as well as a secret understanding that partly compromised the integrity of the agreement. Pres. Woodrow Wilson, noting the extent of Japan's expansion in China, returned to a 1907 US plan to use financing, though a consortium of bankers (from Britain, France, Japan, and the US), to advance investments in China. Japan was not pleased, especially so because it could not possibly compete then with the US and the rest of the West in the area of financial penetration in China and saw the initiative as a not-so-subtle US attempt to disappoint Tokyo's ambitions in China. It therefore waited until it was satisfied with the terms of the Lansing–Ishii negotiations before it consented to join.[120]

Structure and Ideology

Developments between both countries during and after the peace conference that ended World War I (the Paris Peace Conference of 1919–1920) to the attack on Pearl Harbor in 1941 should allow the reader to gain a sharper appreciation for the true nature of the rivalry between the two countries. Before we touch on those developments, however, we should go back to include here two other major factors, mentioned earlier, shaping the narrative under this case study. They are the structure of the international system within which the US and Japan were competing and the dominant, governing ideologies and their relevant values.

With respect to the structure, the international order was organized around what experts in the field of international relations would call a multipolar system. This system exists when, on a regional or global level, there are many centers (states) of independent decision making, among each of which power is distributed in such a way that no single state, by itself, can dominate another within the system. In other words, an international multipolar system or order exists when and if the major powers (regionally or globally) that constitute it, while not mathematically equal in power distribution, include no single country

---

[120] Thomas A. Bailey, *A Diplomatic History of the American People* (New York: Appleton-Century-Crofts, 1958), p. 637. This four-power agreement was signed in 1920, but it had little influence on Japan.

that, by itself, can dominate another major power of the system itself. This multipolar order contrasts with what is called the bipolar one, which largely existed from 1949 to 1989, during which there were two dominant centers of power (the US and the former USSR), around each of which were grouped all or most of the other major international actors, and the leader of each center enjoyed such overwhelming power that it at times exceeded the power of all the states grouped around it.

A multipolar international order existed during the nineteenth century, especially the latter half and, largely, the first two-fifths of the twentieth century. As a system, it has always been dynamic, with member states often collaborating or forming alliances to augment their respective power and, if possible, limit or diminish that of an actual or perceived potential enemy. In 1902, for example, as we saw earlier in this chapter, Britain allied itself with Japan (later dissolved) to limit the expansion (at London's expense) of Russia and Germany in China, and in 1916, a Russian–Japanese treaty or alliance was negotiated against "any third power whatever, having hostile [designs] against Russia or Japan."[121] This treaty was a secret one—a practice and values embraced by states during the period under discussion—and its vague reference to "any third power," while seemingly applicable to any country, was in fact pointing to the US.[122] Of course, members of the multipolar system, instead of pursuing rivalry among themselves, can, on occasions, unite again one of its members—as was done with China.

The preceding three paragraphs, in part, capture the outer structure, along with a rudimentary system of law (international law that a state could invoke on behalf of its cause), within which the US and Japan competed. Complementing that outer structure was an ideology and system of values that should further clarify matters. At the level of ideology, we have a mixture of nationalism and imperialism, with the former claiming that one rightly belongs to a nation—a group of people who have had common experiences of ideals, disappointments, struggles, pain, defeat, and triumphs, grounded in a combination of common

---

[121] Bemis, op. cit., p. 689.

[122] It became part of a scandal when the Bolshevik government in Moscow published a list of secret treaties concluded by the tsar, including some with Britain.

territory, language, ethnicity, religion, or ideology, among other things, and aspire to have a common future together. That belonging requires one (a citizen or national) to support and promote the interests of the nation, especially its self-government or sovereignty, which makes it the equal of other nations and, concomitantly, makes each citizen or national the equal of citizens or nationals of other nations. Because the nation's self-government or sovereignty enables it to protect its nationals or citizens—including their family, property, experiences, identity, and opportunities for equal exchanges with other nations, each of which could become a threat or an enemy—each national or citizen owes her or his nation her or his highest loyalty.

If the nation-state's self-governing or self-determining status is respected, it follows that its territorial integrity and political independence should likewise be. A rival ideology, imperialism, contradicts this logic, however. While present throughout most of recorded human history, imperialism, as an ideology, gained special standing during the nineteenth and twentieth centuries. It is rooted in notions of glory, majesty, superiority, and domination and espouses the view (and policy) that a nation-state should extend its rule over other countries, employing military, economic, and cultural instruments (often all three) to gain control of them, if doing so were deemed beneficial to the ruling or the ruled country—always a judgment of the former.[123] This control may assume the form of an empire, which is usually a territorially extensive political unit made up of many national, ethnic, religious, and/ or linguistic communities that answer to a dominant center. The Persian Empire (against which Athens and Sparta fought), the succeeding Athenian Empire, the Roman Empire, the Chinese Empire, and the Byzantine Empire are all examples. In the nineteenth century (and the first half of the twentieth century), "great power status" was defined by the presence of an empire—the more extensive it was, the more prestigious and influential it was, assuming demonstrated effective control, material returns, or broad strategic advantages. States, which

---

[123] See Erich S. Gruen, *Imperialism in the Roman Republic* (Berkeley: University of California, 1970). This is an interesting, though selective, study of Roman imperialism and its exploitative features. Edward W. Said, *Culture and Imperialism* (New York: Alfred A. Knopf, 1993).

were not empires, strove to become them, always insisting that the sought or exercised control of other countries was for the benefit of the peoples or countries controlled.

The British, Russian, Ottoman, German, Austro-Hungarian, French, and Italian empires all competed among themselves to strengthen and expand their respective empires, using characterizations such as "spheres of interest," "protectorate," or "colony" to define the status of peoples under their respective controls.[124] The US, which has always avoided any self-identification as an imperial power, had in fact begun empire building early with its Monroe Doctrine but had not moved beyond the Americas and the Caribbean until the previously referenced 1898 war with Spain, as well as its annexation of Hawaii that year, to establish additional colonies and protectorates. When Washington, in 1853, coerced Japan into opening itself to trade with the US, it was, as later depicted by TR, the work of peace. One cannot have peace, he argued, where countries fail to trade; one cannot have peace where countries are unstable, disorderly, non-prosperous, or exhibiting an "inability or unwillingness to do justice, at home and abroad [or have] violated the rights of the United States or . . . invited foreign aggression."[125] The quoted portions of the preceding sentence are part of a statement (called the corollary to the Monroe Doctrine) that was made with Latin America and the Caribbean in mind. It was, however, applicable to the world at large because the US was merely repeating the often-stated norms of state motivation within the ideology of imperialism—the norms of peace, stability, and order, sometimes simply referred to as

---

[124] A "sphere of interest" refers to an area (Latin America or Manchuria, for instance) or country that, by reason of its location—its physical proximity or "contiguity" to another country, its resources or markets, or its potential as a defensive buffer—is recognized by other states as subject to the dominant influence (including the right to defend it militarily) of another state. A protectorate is a country that, although acknowledged as nominally independent, is seen as incapable of defending itself and is, therefore, taken under the protection of a dominant state. Lastly, a colony is seen as "owned" by the colonial power.

[125] See Pres. Theodore Roosevelt's Fourth Annual Message to Congress, December 6, 1904.

"law and order." These norms are what were ostensibly being advanced, not the aim of imperial domination.

When Japan could not resist the US, in 1853, it capitulated, but it wanted to know about the international authority (including international law) that the US had used to force it to open its markets so that it too could acquire the means (power) and legitimacy to act as the US and other Western countries had.[126] The Japanese proved to be exceptional students, learning the "law of nations" (as elaborated by the then dominant West) even more quickly than the rapid pace at which it mastered industrialization as well as other features of Western culture, such as certain managerial approaches to improving public administration, education, and military proficiency.

It was this learning, coupled with outstanding achievement in economic and military capabilities and combined with their own cultural refinements, that enabled them, as described earlier in this chapter, to wrestle so successfully with the US, in China, within the context of the multipolar distribution of power. Japan, for example, expertly learned and practiced Western concepts such as "spheres of influence" (sometimes used interchangeably with "special interest"), "protectorate," "contiguity," "propinquity," "territorial integrity," and "political independence" and applied them with utmost dexterity. In the case of the latter concept, for example, Tokyo quickly came to know that under certain procedural observations within the context of war and peace, a weak state had little weight when facing a powerful one—as was its case when it faced the US in 1853. A great power, by virtue of its international standing, could dismantle the territories of other weaker countries during times of war and incorporate those territories into its own or put in place "political elites" who are dependent on the good mercies of their conqueror. All they had to do was to plausibly claim, as did President Roosevelt, that they were pursuing peace. In the case of China, its weakness, despite its enormous potential and unparalleled past, was an invitation to the strong to exact more and more concessions from it.

---

[126] See Hathaway and Shapiro, op. cit., pp. 138–157, which deals with "What Kind of Thing Is the Law of Nations?"

On account of that weakness, many Western countries used their influence to penetrate Chinese society not only economically, as sketched earlier, but politically, legally, and religiously as well. In the latter regard, Christian missionaries and their institutions, for example, became cultural arms of their respective governments. In 1899, a group (called the Boxers) engaged in an uprising against this foreign influence. Responding to that uprising (which was viewed as a "law and order" matter), an international force of some twenty thousand—composed of troops from Austro-Hungary, France, Germany, Italy, Japan, Russia, Britain, and the US—was able to quash the revolt and impose an even more humiliating subjugation of China. The latter country, among other things, not only had to pay some $300,000 million to the occupying foreign governments as well as forego importation of arms for a stipulated period but also had to accept those terms in the face of a rising national fervor among citizens, thus impairing its own legitimacy. The regime (the Qing dynasty) never recovered, was overthrown in 1911 by Sun Yat-sen, and was replaced in 1912 by a republic led by Sun Yat-sen and the KMT (nationalist party) he had founded. It was this government on which Japan imposed the Twenty-One Demands in 1915.

Old and New Norms in Conflict

We now turn, in this narrative, to the post–World War I period to 1941, when the attack on Pearl Harbor took place and during which the rivalry between the US and Japan escalated as each country self-consciously advanced policies in conflict with the other's declared or otherwise known interest. At the heart of the conflict was China, but underlying it was the struggle of two political peers that had come to the "imperial game of great powers" in China relatively late. For the US, China represented an extension of its expanding reach from the Americas and the Caribbean; for Japan, it was the site of its potential to become, if successful, the equal of other great powers or to remain, if unsuccessful, a third-class country subject to those powers' control and exploitation. For the other powers, in China, the latter was an unexampled market.

If one were to take the populations of some of the countries involved in China, for example, one may gain a sense of the enticements that Beijing represented. In 1900, the population of Japan was about forty million, that of the US about seventy-six million (that of Germany was about fifty-six million, and that of Britain, outside the empire, was about thirty-eight million). The population of China, on the other hand, was four hundred million. It was resource rich, although it had become progressively socially poor, largely because of foreign exploitation, but returns from commerce and investment were still promising.[127]

In this part of the narrative of the period under discussion, that of the normative conflict between old and new practices and aspirations, one can gain a fair understanding of US–Japan relations through four subthemes: the legal and diplomatic; the military and political; the socioeconomic and cultural; and, finally, the combination of all three during the latter part of the 1930s.

The legal and diplomatic might be properly grasped through the Covenant of the League of Nations, which sought to overcome the human slaughter of World War I, by changing the way that international relations were conducted before the league came into being on January 10, 1920. Foremost among its terms were those of Article 16, which espoused the idea of "collective" rather than "national" (the individual state's) security. This meant that instead of viewing a military attack by one country against another as a matter for the attacked state to address by finding the means to defend itself, that attack, under defined circumstances, would be regarded as an attack on *all* members of the league. If that attack were against all, then by extension, all members would be expected and obliged to come to the aid of the victim.[128]

[127] See, for example, an eighteenth-century physiocrat's view of China, that of Francois Quesnay, from his "Despotism in China," which he saw as a model for Europe, in Franz Schurmann and Orville Schell, eds., *Imperial China: The Decline of the Last Dynasty and the Origins of Modern China* (New York: Vintage Books, 1967), pp. 115–120.

[128] See Article 16 of the text of the Covenant of the League of Nations through the *Avalon Project: Documents in Law, History and Diplomacy.* avalon.law.yale. edu

Further, Article 10 of the covenant required each member "to respect and preserve as against external aggression the territorial integrity and existing political independence" of all members of the league.[129] The key here is "existing political independence," which left those countries and peoples that were not then independent confined to their existing status, and those imperial countries that controlled them could continue to do so. It also meant that new imperial states that saw military conquest as a means of territorial expansion were at a great disadvantage. A new class of territorial and political subordination also emerged, although it was not generally understood as such, except for those countries that benefited little or not at all from it. This class emerged under what was known as the mandate system of the league, a system by which colonies and other territories of defeated countries were transferred under varying levels of control to non-defeated or victorious countries and their allies. Some, like those areas belonging to the former Ottoman Empire, were transferred to Britain and France with the understanding that they were sufficiently politically mature that they could gain independence within a reasonable time. Others, such as the German colonies in Southwest Africa or certain areas of the Pacific (because of their distance from "centers of civilization" or their "geographical contiguity" to the territory of the state to which they were being transferred), were to be administered as "integrated portions" of the transferred-to country.[130]

Furthering the law and diplomacy efforts at new norms creation, the covenant, under Article 8, and the 1928 Kellogg–Briand Pact (also called the Pact of Paris) created a particularly sharp distinction between the old and the hoped-for new order. In the case of Article 8, it recited that members of the league "recognize that the maintenance of peace requires the reduction of national armaments to the lowest point consistent with national safety and the enforcement of common action of international obligation."[131] This article, while espousing limitations on arms and, as a result, limitations on war, still assumed the indefinite presence of

---

[129] See Article 10 of the covenant.

[130] See Article 22 (6) of the covenant.

[131] See Article 8 of the covenant.

war in human affairs. Many people were disappointed in this feature of the covenant's provisions. The 1928 Pact of Paris, however, gave those disappointed persons something to cheer for in that it brought, with its terms, a qualitative change in attitude toward war, as indicated in Articles 1 and 2 of the pact. The first article says that nation-states "condemn recourse to war for the solution of international controversies and renounce it as an instrument of policy in their relations with one another." The second article, reinforcing and extending the first, states that "the settlement of all disputes and conflicts of whatever nature or whatever origin . . . shall be sought by peaceful means."[132]

As the preceding paragraph is saying, the league itself accepted war as an important feature of international relations, although it sought to reduce its frequency and brutality. The Pact of Paris, however, sought to criminalize war and abolish it. The creation of the Permanent Court of International Justice (PCIJ), as part of the league, along with the court's support for international arbitration to facilitate "pacific means" of dispute settlement, afforded potentially powerful institutional backing toward the criminalization of war. At this stage, we should go into a discussion of the ways in which the legal and diplomatic changes outlined above bore on US–Japanese rivalry. An inclusion of parallel military and political developments, however, should help illuminate that period of rivalry. So we shall, for a few paragraphs, delay that discussion.

Emerging from World War I and consistent with Article 8 of the covenant's call for reductions in armaments, a series of naval conferences were held, led by the US and Britain, beginning with the 1921–1922 Washington Naval Conference (WNC). The latter, convened by the US, was designed to take advantage of public sentiments that, while keeping the US out of the league, was deemed to be favorably disposed to such a conference of its own calling on US soil. Certainly, the conference appealed to a war-weary world, which was anxious to see steps taken to reduce the prospects of war. The conference became associated with, if not defined by, a disarmament formula pushed by the US and, with some

---

[132] See *United States Statutes-at-Large*, Vol. 42, Part 2, p. 2343. The pact is also named after the then US secretary of state Frank B. Kellogg and his French counterpart, Aristide Briand.

sought modifications, supported by or acquiesced in by other naval powers. That formula was for the five great naval powers (Britain, the US, Japan, France, and Italy) to maintain, respectively, the naval balance of capital ships in the ratio of 5:5:3:1.67:1.67.[133]

What is less well known or even seriously considered are some other areas of agreements and disagreements that had consequences for the 1927 Geneva Naval Conference (GNC) and the 1930 London Naval Conference (LNC), both of which had meaning for what culminated in the same disastrous development in the 1935 LNC. For example, Japan was dissatisfied with its ratio and sought unsuccessfully to change it to gain greater parity with the US and Britain. It bowed to the formula only after getting Washington and London to limit fortifications in certain strategic locations to improve Japan's security. For the US, it pledged "not to [add] to existing fortifications on Guam, Tutuila, the Aleutians, and the Philippines."[134] This concession was seen as limiting the US's capacity to enforce its open door policy in China. Likewise, while the UK conceded naval equality with the US, that concession was unsettled, which we will touch on, and Japan learned from it. Japan was also pressured into a dissolution of its alliance with Britain, a strategic military and political arrangement, as the reader will remember, that it had since 1902; worse, from Tokyo's standpoint, in a separate agreement with the US, it had to return Shandong to China.[135] Finally, Article 1 of a 1922 Nine-Power Treaty, ensuring from the WNC, had the contracting parties, except China, agreeing "to refrain from taking advantage of the conditions in China to seek special rights or privileges which [could] abridge the rights of subjects or citizens of friendly states and from countenancing actions inimical to the security of those states."[136]

---

[133] See Merze Tate, *The United States and Armaments* (Cambridge: Harvard University Press, 1948), pp. 124–140. This work is a classic in the field of disarmament for the period under discussion. Bemis, op. cit., p. 701.

[134] Ibid., p. 140.

[135] Bruce A. Elleman, *Wilson and China: A Revised History of the Shandong Question* (London: M. E. Sharpe, 2002). This is a rather thorough revision.

[136] See Bemis, op. cit., p. 702. See also, for the full text, Williams, op. cit., pp. 707–708.

The statement means many things. Among them is that, as had been the case since as early as the 1840s (when the US could do little about it), the interest of the US in China was consistently that of ensuring for itself the broadest possibilities for economic activities in China; a domination of Beijing by any external power was viewed as unfriendly to those possibilities. Second, in exchange for preserving those possibilities, Japan could be assured against actions that might prejudice the rights of subjects or citizens in China. What were the "conditions in China" of which states should not take advantage? The regional and other political divisions that the KMT, despite its efforts, was unable to control; the emergence of the CPC the year before; and the conflict generated by those who opposed the dominating presence of foreigners in China, including Japan.

In the case of the 1927 and 1930 naval conferences, earlier mentioned, the first turned out to be a failure because the US and Britain could not agree on a quantitative and qualitative understanding about what naval equality between them meant. Each was willing to concede equality to the other but never superiority. Japan also came to understand the distressing fact that even its "minor" undersea vessels were likely to be called "capital ships." One thing was certain—Tokyo came to agree with Britain that the character of an "island empire" that got most of its goods from outside its national borders (unlike the US) should be taken into consideration in assessing the security needs of those engaged in matters of arms limitation. The London conference (after the US and the UK had partially ironed out their respective problems) saw the development of a common US–Britain position to which other naval powers were largely expected to accede.[137] Japan again raised the issue of its being allowed an improved ratio in non-capital ships and was turned down, and as London and Washington had calculated, "the united front of the two great naval powers" would be enough to have Japan back down. It did.

We now turn to the third of the four subthemes, the socioeconomic and cultural matters within which old and new norms operated, as a

---

[137] Tate, *The US and Armaments*, op. cit., pp. 182–183. The issues between the US and Britain were not fully solved, as comments in both the US Congress and the British Parliament attest.

preliminary to an integrated analysis of the issues that controlled the 1930 US–Japanese relations. A major aspect of the socioeconomic and cultural was the issue of *racial equality*, a discussion of which took place during the negotiations of the Treaty of Paris (which brought World War I to a close) at the initiative of Japan. Tokyo wanted it to be incorporated as a principle in the treaty, but the US, led by Pres. Woodrow Wilson, vetoed it. Britain, as we will learn later, had a like position. Japan would not be allowed to keep Shandong, as before indicated, despite promises during World War I (understandable given its cultural and economic importance to China but seen as a betrayal by Japan); led by Australia, issues were raised about Japan's gaining control of former German colonies north of the equator, in the Pacific.[138]

In the midst of other "concessions" that Japan was making to the West and the US in particular (the dissolution of the 1902 alliance—accepting, although reluctantly, the ratios in naval power—and the terms of the Nine-Power Treaty), the US Congress passed the immigration law of 1924, which excluded from admission to its territories "aliens not eligible for citizenship." The latter term could, in fact, apply to all Asians, but since others, including the Chinese, had been included in previous legislation, the 1924 law was specifically intended to operate against the Japanese. "To Japan, it was a bitter blow,"[139] bitter indeed because in its efforts to become more and more like the West, it found less and less acceptance and now public international discrimination and humiliation.

It was this discrimination that, in part, influenced the UK (its white colonies or dominions), in collaboration with the US, to advance the dissolution of the 1902 treaty of alliance between Japan and Britain; it was also part of that which influenced adverse reactions (the "Yellow

---

[138] Japan's disappointment, given the values of the day, was understandable. China, however, pleaded its case effectively with support from the West, noting that Shandong held special cultural importance. It is the birthplace of Confucius and Mencius. To separate it from China is to engage in a cultural amputation.

[139] Bemis, op. cit., pp. 708–709.

Peril") to Japan's expectations to assume postwar control over former German island colonies "north of the equator."[140]

Going through the preceding narrative has, as part of its aim, the accomplishment of many things. First, it demonstrates that unlike what Allison implied, the rivalry between the US and Japan preceded 1898, when the US got the Philippines from Spain. Second, the rivalry was not between a ruling power and a rising one; it was between two rising powers (note, for example, how the US had to fight to gain naval equality with Britain in the 1920s), although the US, by virtue of the role of the dollar, carried greater weight and influence in the world after World War I. Third, the rivalry between the US and Japan in China was really part of a multilateral rivalry for influence in the latter country with Russia, Britain, France, and Germany, among others. Indeed, in respect of Russia, division among Japanese decision makers made it a toss-up in 1941 as to whether Japan should move north, against Russia, or south, against the US, with the move south resulting in the attack on Hawaii.[141] Fourth, as mentioned before, despite the US's consistent inclusion of China's political independence and territorial integrity, in its objections to Japanese expansion in China, Washington's overwhelming interests and aims were economic (trade and investment in particular). All one needs to do (if one did not deduce this from the language of US–Japanese agreements on China we have thus far reviewed) is to analyze what the US agreed to at Yalta without even consulting China—to the independence of Mongolia from China and to Russia's sought "interest" in the Manchurian railways (meaning banks, factories, electrical power grids, harbor facilities, warehouses, and other wherewithal to dominate Manchuria), one of the very areas we sought to deny Japan. In addition, the US agreed that Russia should receive, after World War II, Southern Sakhalin from Japan. All these were concessions made to win Russia's participation in the war with Japan.

There are four other aims of this narrative that we must now touch on. One is related to differences that decision makers make, but we will

---

[140] See William Roger Louis, "Australia and the German Colonies in the Pacific, 1914–1919," in *The Journal of Modern History*, Vol. 38, #4 (December 1966), pp. 407–421. The League of Nations did give Japan some of these colonies.

[141] See "Japan's Fatal Decision" in Williams, op. cit., pp. 824–828.

wait until we cover the case study of Germany. The other three are as follows: the use to which new norms introduced in the international system, after World War I, were put; the ongoing operation of the rules of the old order (a form of hypocrisy), as exhibited in the Yalta agreement, to which we just referred; and a return to the issue of equality.

With regard to the new norms, as already touched on, we had the effort of the Covenant of the League of Nations and the Pact of Paris, both of which (along with some other treaties) sought to promote collective security and place limitations on war or its actual criminalization and abolition. The new norms were used by states to condemn, disapprove, or oppose prohibited conduct associated with enemies while justifying or supporting their own and their allies' conduct based on the old norms. A quote from one who served as the leader of Japan's delegation to the talks in Paris (that ended World War I) and who later served as prime minister of that country should be instructive:

> The pre-war European condition might have suited Anglo-American powers best, but it never served justice and humanity. At an early state, Britain and France colonized the "less civilized" regions of the world and monopolized their exploitation.[142]

The author of the quote, Fumimaro Konoe, went on to note that the Anglo-American powers, for example, advocate "a peace at any price" with "nothing to do with justice and humanity" but to maintain the status quo, including the monopoly of exploitation of the less civilized regions of the world. Japan, he saw, was caught in this effort by the Anglo-American powers to preserve the status quo. Were it to join the league (the document from which the quote is taken was written before the negotiations at the peace conference), it should demand as a minimum an end to "economic imperialism and [the] discriminatory treatment of Asian peoples." If "the peace conference fails to suppress this rampant imperialism, the Anglo-American powers" would, he argued, "become the economic masters of the world" and, in the name of the status quo (territorial integrity, for example), dominate the world

---

[142] Quoted in Boyle, op. cit., p. 163. The quote is from Fumimaro Konoe.

"through the League of Nations and arms reduction" and thereby "serve their selfish interests."[143]

We will be returning to this leader, Fumimaro Konoe, because of his importance in the relations between the US and Japan. At this juncture, let it be sufficient to observe that Japan, to prove itself a trustworthy collaborator, did join the league despite its misgivings: how the US and the UK used the WNC to ensure their indefinite naval supremacy; how interwar tariffs were used for their respective advantage; how, in the midst of fighting Japan's acquiring a "sphere of interest" in Manchuria, the US succeeded in having the most pronounced expression of that concept and practice, the Monroe Doctrine, incorporated in and protected by the text of the covenant of the league itself as an instrument of peace[144]; and how, in the face of even stronger opposition to Japan's having a sort of protectorate over China, the US was establishing protectorates over Haiti, Nicaragua, and Panama. The old legal and practiced order supported US actions; the new legal and aspirational order fought and condemned Japan. Racial equality was not recognized.

The equality, the legal or sovereign equality that Hugo Grotius had offered the world and that the Japanese had studied so diligently, was not being applied except in favor of the US and the West in general. Nowhere was this more evident than the Kellogg–Briand Pact, which, despite its focus on abolishing war, supported it in defense (a state that sought to preserve the status quo that is detrimental to another country could always refuse to change anything, hoping that the dissatisfied victim would commit a breach of peace). Added thereto, the fruits of aggression before 1928 could be kept and enjoyed by states; new aggressions should be disapproved, and their fruits should not be kept. As well, the pact outlawed neutrality in the case of aggression. We will see, as we move from the 1930s to 1941, how the concerns of the US and those of Japan became implicated in them and played themselves out. Before we do, let us return to the issue of equality because it will prove to be the proximate cause of the war.

---

[143] Ibid.

[144] See Article 21 of the covenant, which recites that nothing under the terms of the league shall "affect the validity of . . . regional understandings like the Monroe Doctrine for securing the maintenance of peace."

When Japan was compelled, under the threat of force in 1853 and 1854, to open its society to US trade, it was humiliated and seen and felt as inferior, not morally but in military, technological, and economic terms; it also realized that it had to change and committed itself to that change, in large measure emulating much of the international political behavior of the West, especially militarily, economically, and technologically. It succeeded in transforming itself and, as earlier shown, gained "great power" status. It therefore sought to win for itself (be it in colonial possessions, ratios of capital ships to be made, or respect for its sovereignty and its citizens) affirmations of this status. When the US Congress in 1924 enacted the Immigration Act, it came as "a monumental insult" to the Japanese[145] because it alone, among nations sending immigrants to the US, was disallowed even a quota. It was "singled out for total exclusion"[146] and, far from being a moral and political equal, was left to wear the "stamp . . . of an inferior race."[147]

While newspapers such as the *Washington Post* and the *New York Times* may have actually viewed the action of Congress as an "affront" or an "outrage," the position of the *Cincinnati Enquirer* was more accurate in noting that the "crux of the matter [was] that the United States, like Canada and Australia, must be kept a white man's country."[148] It was being threatened by, among other things, the successes of Japanese immigrant farmers, especially in California. Additionally, the world had to remain, as Konoe had claimed, under a like racial control.

The latter sentiment was expressed in a 1921 confidential memorandum from the British Foreign Office—a document whose message became a basis for US–UK collaboration on matters of race, including the broader area of human rights, after World War II.[149] The

---

[145] Boyle, op. cit., p. 151.

[146] Ibid.

[147] Ibid., p. 152. One may fruitfully review some of the stereotypes of Japan and the Japanese people on pages 150–151.

[148] Ibid.

[149] Paul Gordon Lauren, "First Principles of Racial Equality: History and Politics and Diplomacy of Human Rights Provisions of the United Nations Charter," in *Human Rights Quarterly*, Vol. 5, #1 (Winter 1983), pp. 2–13.

memorandum noted how the issue of racial equality was a concern that had "no cure" in the US as well as the British dominions of Australia, Canada, New Zealand, and South Africa. "Only one of the aggrieved colored races," however, "had acquired sufficient material strength to demand a hearing, and that [was] Japan."[150] In other words, while the colored people of the world might, on the basis of racial discrimination, deserve a hearing to remove that discrimination, Japan was the only one that had the power to *demand* such a hearing.

"Japan is the only non-white first-rate Power," the memorandum admitted. "In every respect, except the racial one, Japan stands on par with the great governing nations of the world. But however powerful [she] may eventually become, the white race will never be able to admit her equality."[151] These statements have many meanings. Among them is an unequivocal admission of Japan's de facto great power status; that in all respects, it deserved to be treated as an equal; and that the only reason that equality is not and cannot be publicly conceded and recognized is the incurable issue of racial identity. The memorandum continued to say that if Japan can "enforce" its claim to equality (an admission that Japan has been making that claim), as the reader will recall, "it will become our superior; if it cannot enforce it, she remains our inferior, but equal she cannot be."[152]

The foreign policy of the UK and the US was designed to ensure that Japan would not gain the capacity to "enforce" the claims for equality. Events of the 1930s and early 1940s furnish persuasive evidence for those who seek it.[153] Long before the international norms (as opposed to the US's unilateral policy declarations, such as the "open door" stance), both London and Washington had seen enough of Japanese potential

---

[150] Ibid., p. 3.

[151] Ibid.

[152] Ibid.

[153] The reason for including the UK in this portion of the discussion is that, as the reader will see, London began preparations for a war with Japan after World War I, even before the US did, although the US seems to have begun thinking about that prospect earlier. In any event, they became collaborators after the war. It is instructive to note also that London's plans for a war with Japan began during a period when the two countries were still allies.

as a "great power" to contemplate the meaning of that greatness for themselves and the world. Japan, like Haiti (when the latter won its independence from Napoleon's France in 1804), was a bad example to much of the world. What if the success of Japan were to be treated by other colored peoples as what is actually possible for them, resulting in Tokyo not being the lone case of "aggrieved colored races" having the capacity to *demand* a hearing for equality?[154] What if India, China, Indonesia, Iran, Egypt, Mexico, or other dominated peoples were to follow Japan?

As early as 1906 (one year, as the reader will recall, after President Roosevelt had mediated the conclusion of the Russian–Japanese War), the US began discussing plans for a war with Japan and went beyond discussions to the adoption of a plan in 1911. Known as "War Plan Orange," it was updated over a period of years and, in substance, called for the economic isolation of Japan and then the striking of "a decisive military blow."[155] Britain had also, by 1919, begun the development of plans to fight Japan; these plans, by 1920, had begun to be concretized and entailed three phases, the third of which called for a blockade of the country, informed by and grounded on an inventory of the goods on which Japan depended.[156] The reader will, at this juncture, recall how concerned Japan was about its physical and cultural "island identity" and how much it depended on resources from other countries during the discussions on naval power.

Those resources, which included oil (over half of the then known world's reserve of which the US and the UK had gained control, in part through the mandate system, as it applied to the Middle East),[157] became

---

[154] See the statement in footnote 149.

[155] See Mitch Rogers, "From Freeze to Five: How Economic Sanctions against Japan Led to the War in the Pacific," in *The Thetean: A Student Journal for Scholarly Historical Writing*, Vol. 47, #1 (2018), p. 163.

[156] See Christopher M. Bell, "The Singapore Strategy and the Deterrence of Japan," in *The English Historical Review*, Vol. 116, #467 (June 2001), pp. 608–612.

[157] J. A. De Novo, "The Movement for an Aggressive American Oil Policy Abroad, 1918–1920," in *American Historical Review* Vol. LXI (July 1956), pp. 854–876. See also Anthony Sampson, *The Seven Sisters* (New York: Bantam Books, 1974).

very important in both the US's and the UK's calculations as both countries increasingly coordinated their respective war strategies.[158] The UK also understood that even in a blockade, the trade between Japan and the latter's trading partners, such as Korea and China, may not be as fully disrupted as desired; so tactics such as making insurance unavailable to neutral shipping involved in trade with Japan was included in the planning.[159]

Neither Britain nor the US was able to give any immediate, direct effect to their respective plans. In the case of Britain, it was hobbled, in large measure, because of its postwar economic problems, including repayment of the debt it owed to the US, the 1923–1924 Ruhr Crisis, colonial challenges (especially in India, which began more assertive claims for independence), mercantilist international economic policies (including some from Washington), as well as reparations controversy and the economic depression that began in 1929/1930.[160] With respect to the US, it was engaged in protecting the markets it had gained during the war, claiming an isolationist orientation but, in fact, very much engaged in interventionist initiatives in Nicaragua (1926), in Mexico (1927)—when the government of the latter state moved to begin oil expropriations and, more generally, the expropriation of subsoil properties—and in the 1928 fight at the Sixth International Conference of American States, convened in Havana, Cuba, against a resolution, stating that "no state has the right to intervene in the internal affairs of another,"[161] sponsored by Latin American countries. (The reader might compare this stance of the US with its position toward Japan in the latter's intervention in China.) Of course, one must always think in terms of the impact of the Great Depression, beginning in 1929, on the US.

[158] Andrew Field, *Royal Navy Strategy in the Far East, 1919–1939* (London: Frank Cass & Company, 2004); David W. McIntyre, *The Rise and Fall of the Singapore Naval Base, 1919–1942* (London: MacMillan Press, 1979).

[159] Christopher M. Bell, *The Royal Navy, Seapower and Strategy between the Wars* (Stanford University Press, 2000), pp. 76–85.

[160] See "Reparations and War Debt" in the British Parliament in HC Debates, December 14, 1932, Vol. 273 CC 353–483, to gain a sense of the debt and its relationship to reparations.

[161] Bailey, op. cit., p. 680.

When Tokyo, however, in response to the September 18, 1931, dynamite explosion on the tracks of the Japanese-owned SMR, used the "incident" to take control of Manchuria and incorporated it by early 1933 into the empire of Japan, it aroused strong international reaction. It turns out that the "incident" was a staged one by the Japanese military (not an action by radical Chinese, as alleged) that was increasingly at odds with the civilian government—a government that the military saw as "soft" and insufficiently forceful in dealing with the West, especially the US. The fact that the civilian government accepted the fruits of this staged action, however—perhaps fearful of exhibiting internal divisions—made it an accomplice.

The major challenges for Japan, at this juncture, were the conflicts between the old and new international orders, to which we earlier referred, the reaction of the League of Nations that was part of the new order, the reaction of the US, which had cast itself as the advocate of China's sovereignty, and the reaction of China itself. The new order's international norms called for the nonuse of force in dealing with international problems except in self-defense. The old order allowed for force, and Japan took the position that its behavior was defensive in nature (hardly accurate, if the "incident" were staged) and that in any event, the new norms such as those expressed in the Pact of Paris were but aspirational and, therefore, did not replace the old order, under which the UK, the US, and Russia, among others, acquired territories.[162]

The League of Nations, failing to impose economic sanctions on Japan for the "incident" in China, was pushed by small countries that feared for their independence to support the conclusion of a fact-finding commission that the action of the Japanese was not defensive in character.[163] As such, its use of force in China was illegal. Frustrated by this unexpected development (and both US and British diplomatic influence was present in the effort to have the league support this conclusion), Japan walked out of the league and, later, in February 1933, renounced its membership in that body. In the case of the US, which

---

[162] See Hathaway and Shapiro, op. cit., pp. 153–160.

[163] That fact-finding body is known as the Lytton Commission (1931–32), named after its chair, V. A. G. R. Bulwer-Lytton, specifically tasked by the league to determine the cause of Japanese invasion of Manchuria.

never joined the League of Nations, it provokingly attended the league's debate on Japan's conduct, using the norms of the new order to do so. It, along with Britain, understood the huge economic resources that Japan would command by controlling Manchuria. When Britain, which was willing to support economic sanctions against Japan, sought to canvass Washington's support, however (London thought that the league could not succeed in such sanctions unless Washington committed itself to help enforce them), the US elected to embrace the benefits of the old order. The US wanted to continue the old practice by which neutral states could legally trade with belligerents in war (in this case Japan) rather than accept the norms of the new order, which made it illegal to remain neutral.[164]

On the other hand, the US was acting "outside" the league in the sense that it was not a member, continuing to employ the norms of the new order (as it suited its interest) against Japan. In no instance was this diplomatic tactic more evident than in what has come to be known as the Stimson Doctrine (named after US Secretary of State Henry L. Stimson), enunciated on January 7, 1932, and stating that the US would not recognize any new agreement that interfered with its economic rights under the open door policy in China and, as well, that the US did "not intend to recognize any situation, treaty, or agreement which may be brought about contrary to the covenants and obligations" under the 1928 Pact of Paris.[165] Here, we have the US again claiming the advantage of the old order to assert its economic interest and bringing with it norms of the new order because they allowed, in its interest, for the containment of Japan. As we will see later, the US will further and further embrace the old order, as its interests urged, while invoking the high moral-sounding claims of the new to limit others, to the utter frustration of Japan.

As regards China's reaction, knowing that it could not successfully confront Japan, militarily in Manchuria, Beijing, under the leadership of the KMT, lodged a complaint with the League of Nations under Article XI of that organization's covenant. After debating the issue,

---

[164] Hathaway and Shapiro, op. cit., pp. 164–165.

[165] Ibid., pp. 166–167.

that international body passed a resolution that not only refused to recognize Japan's push to take over Manchuria but also called upon Japan to evacuate the newly occupied Chinese territory in Manchuria by November 16, 1931. Tokyo, of course, refused to discontinue its expanding control of China (it did find an aspect of the earlier mentioned fact-finding commission's report that it could support)[166] and, in addition, began to lay plans for further actions elsewhere against an enfeebled China. It was about this time that Secretary of State Stimson decided to move ahead with his doctrine, fearing that a weakened China, under pressure from Japan, might sign a treaty conceding Japan's sovereignty over Manchuria.

Confrontation: Economic, Military, and Strategic

At this stage, it might be helpful to recall the quote we earlier used in this work from soon-to-be prime minister of Japan (1937–39, 1940–41), Fumimaro Konoe, whom we met previously in another capacity and who came to be a critical bridge between the armed forces and the civilian elites, especially during his second tenure as prime minister. The quote, as presented, said a number of things that, with additional portions and further elaborations, should help shed more light upon certain aspects of Japan's past behavior as well as help explain what is to come.

The quote,[167] taken from an article of his, called for a conditional rejection of what he saw as emerging out of World War I—what he saw as a likely "Anglo-American–Centered Peace," not one that had anything to do with humanity or with justice; an international arrangement that would protect, in their favor, the unequal distribution of natural and industrial resources of the world; a worldwide territorial framework that would have most of the "less civilized" regions of the world under US and European control, leaving little, if any, space available to other nations; and an international monopolization of capital that, among other things, limited or prevented the free development of nations. In addition, there was another major feature of the article that we should

---

[166] See footnote #162.

[167] See footnote #141.

reflect on—that the West (the US and Britain in particular) engaged in "monopolized exploitation" of the rest of the world, discriminated against Asians to an unusual degree, violated the "principle of equal opportunity among men, and threatened the equal rights of existence for all nations."[168]

Without seeking to measure the results of the Paris Peace Conference against the projected outcomes, as seen by Konoe (and one has but to look at the extent of US and UK control of worldwide oil reserves or the additional territories under their influence or control through the mandate system, to touch on a few areas of his predictions), the Japanese (through the eyes of Konoe) were presenting themselves as embodying the norm of equality. While the US may have been pursuing investment and commercial equality in China, including Manchuria, it and the UK (and the West in general) were seeking to maintain a most unequal system internationally. Japan, on the other hand, was using its great power status to pursue equal opportunity for individuals, races, and nations everywhere. Would the US, for example, be willing to allow equal access to the countries of Latin America? Would Britain entertain the same access to its empire?

The Anglo-American "peace at any price" advocacy, therefore, should be taken (Tokyo was contending) as nothing more than an appeal to ideals to preserve their worldwide advantages, including the opening of its own markets to them. Since they are unlikely to make any changes in those advantages except through the use of force by others, they (the US and the UK) would present to the world their use of force as a defensive response to protect peace, law, and order. In the latter context, one can imagine how Tokyo viewed the previously mentioned Nine-Power Treaty of 1922, which it felt pressured to support, one involving imperial states—Belgium, Britain, France, Italy, the Netherlands, Portugal, and the US (with China included because the treaty focused on China)—the expressed purpose of which was "to stabilize conditions in the Far East"; respect "the sovereignty, the independence, and the territorial integrity of China"; and maintain "the principle of equal

---

[168] Ibid.

opportunity for commerce and industry of all nations throughout the territory of China."[169]

When Japan showed that it was not disposed to succumb to the pressures from the US and the League of Nations, Washington amplified its efforts to coerce Tokyo economically, militarily, and strategically, although it took some time for the incoming Franklin D. Roosevelt (FDR) administration to deal with strong opposition in Congress and the country to the seeming drifting into war and the weakening of the US's proclaimed neutrality.[170] Japan, by the time it had left the league in February 1933, had not only created the state called Manchukuo (out of Manchuria) but also "recognized" its independence despite the fact that it was but a vassal of Japan. When, in the same month and year, the league, using some of the same language found in the text of the Stimson Doctrine, said that it was "incumbent on" its members "not to recognize any situation, treaty, or agreement which might be brought about by means contrary to the Covenant of the League or the Pact of Paris," Tokyo fully understood what that meant for its actions in Manchuria but, even more so, that the US, although it was not a member of the league, was (with Britain) exercising a dominant influence in that international body.

Japan faced a major challenge, independent of Britain and the US, however, as it sought to control China. The latter country, although riddled with weaknesses based on internal factions—some independent but mostly those associated with the CPC and the Chinese Nationalist Party, referred to as the KMT, as previously indicated—was able, through the often-disorganized exertions of those very factions, to

---

[169]   See the text of the treaty in Williams, op. cit., p. 707.

[170]   FDR faced a number of problems. He had appointed Sen. Hugo Black to the Supreme Court, who, it turned out, had earlier been a member of the Ku Klux Klan. As well, before the appointment, he (FDR) had lost considerable public support because he was defeated in his proposed judicial procedures reform, often referred to as the "court-packing plan." For some of the expressed fears concerning actions by the government likely to lead to war, the reader could gainfully read a variety of materials in Williams, op. cit. pp. 727–804. Within the body of the pages just indicated are the conclusions of the Special Committee on the Investigation of the Munitions Industry, which released its unflattering report in June 1936, showing how a neutrality stance to gain war profits can lead to war.

frustrate Japan's efforts to control it in its entirety. Neither KMT-led China nor any of the factions, however, was able to mount a serious challenge to Japan, which came to use the hatred of the KMT for the CPC, on several occasions, as a means to "divide and rule" China. Tokyo also feared what it saw as a possible alliance between Soviet Russia and the CPC. So it offered support to the KMT for brutal attacks against (and as a broader attempt to eliminate) the CPC completely. Tokyo's 1931 attack on Manchuria and subsequent developments there as well as elsewhere induced a search for a common effort against Japan. That search resulted in an agreement (Chiang Kai-shek, leader of the KMT, was arrested and forced by troops to enter that agreement) to form a "united front" against Japan.[171] A more united China stymied Japan's push to control that country, and the US (along with Britain) was able to use this united front to its advantage while dealing with what it saw as international challenges that Japan posed.

The first challenge that a depression-tormented FDR and his secretary of state, Cordell Hull (1933–1944), faced was that of ensuring that Japan did not gain the capacity to be an equal, and it was centered on arms limitation. Any further reduction in arms would allow for fewer dollars to the military and more toward ministering to some of the social problems that were incident to the deep economic downturn. As well, further limits would also allow for a curbing of likely Japanese buildup.[172] The hoped-for success in arms limitation was dashed, however, for the planned 1935 London Naval Treaty (a follow-up from its 1930 predecessor) was a failure. On December 24, 1934, persuaded that neither Britain nor the US would concede naval force equality to Japan, Tokyo denounced the 1922 Washington Naval Treaty and thus the 5:5:3 ratio it had put in place among the US, Britain, and Japan.

---

[171]   James C. Hsiung, *China's Bitter Victory: The War with Japan* (New York: M. E. Sharpe Publishing, 1992).

[172]   President Hoover was less of a "hawk" toward Japan but had gradually yielded to his secretary of state, Stimson, including the previously discussed Stimson Doctrine. FDR essentially accepted Stimson's stance on Japan and, as we will later see, brought him back into government to help him wrestle with Japan. For a sense of some important differences between Hoover and Stimson, see Williams, op. cit., pp. 723–726.

The "Rolls-Royce–Rolls-Royce–Ford" treatment of Japan, as voiced by the Japanese ambassador in Washington, Hiroshi Saito, had come to an end.[173]

The denunciation would only take effect two years later, 1936, so efforts were made to see whether, at the convened conference, any compromises could be struck. At the conference, the US used much of the traditional arguments used by Britain to secure certain advantages (its long coastlines and far-flung possessions) to justify refusing Japan's insistence on rough equality. FDR decided that the US could not risk failing to spend what was deemed required to prevent Japan from enforcing its claim to equality and asked Congress (using trumped-up fears of "falling behind" that have been so prevalent since) for funds to support a two-ocean navy, one capable of confronting the combined "fleets of the so-called aggressor nations—Japan, Italy, and Germany."[174] Secret military plans (in collaboration with Britain) to deal with Japan, although surfacing in the 1940s, started decades earlier (as previously discussed) and resumed as early as 1937. Then the US began to seek and establish common understandings with London respecting a war with Japan. Those understandings varied from the use of bases, including that of Singapore, to certain divisions of labor and diplomatic postures to be taken as well as how Washington might be drawn into such a war.[175]

The plans, in part intensified by what has come to be called the Second Sino-Japanese War (1937–1945), could not be immediately implemented, however, because the economic returns from the New Deal were declining, FDR's "Quarantine Speech" in October 1937 provoked considerable adverse reactions because it provoked fear of war, and some admirals objected to blockade plans because of concerns

---

[173]   See quote in Bailey, op. cit. p. 653.

[174]   Ibid., p. 654.

[175]   A fair summary is found in Williams, op. cit., pp. 756–757. It must be mentioned that even "commanding generals of technical services" who would ordinarily be part of these plans were reportedly unaware of them.

that Japan may not react, as hoped, by backing down in its ongoing expansion in China.[176]

FDR was not to be sidetracked. He, unlike almost any other president or prime minister, thought in terms of what he called "national purchasing power," which he saw as having been damaged and revised by the Great Depression, and he was determined to remove that damage and resume the vigorous economic growth and national purchasing power of individuals and society.[177] To do so, he would have to retain old and then expand into new markets. This was part of the reasoning for his move to extend diplomatic recognition to the former Soviet Union after the US had, for about sixteen years, refused to do so (even deferring discussion of "confiscated property" in doing so). Another reason for this policy initiative toward Soviet Russia was the hope that the recognition would help secure the US's strategic interest in containing Japan in the "Far East,"[178] where both Tokyo and Moscow had some rival claims. The further penetration into and effective control of China by Japan was seen as threatening the opportunities that FDR was seeking to expand markets so that he could augment his national purchasing power, and he saw it as a zero-sum game.

Japan—which, as early as 1934, began to make reference to "Greater Eastern Asia" under a broader umbrella of a claim of "Asia for the Asians" to suggest its version of the Japanese Monroe Doctrine—aimed to limit, if not exclude, activities that non-Asian countries sought to exclude non-American nations from the Americas, such as the US's Monroe Doctrine. The US's 1934 promise to continue its colonial control of the Philippines for another ten years and the reaction of the European-dominated League of Nations to the 1935 Italian invasion of Ethiopia (where there was no policy of non-recognition of Italy's actions or the inclusion of oil, the most crucial commodity, in supposed sanctions against Rome) only intensified Tokyo's sense of the hypocritical and

---

[176]   Ibid., pp. 798–799, 805.

[177]   See FDR's 1938 State of the Union Address.

[178]   See the documents and readings in Williams, op. cit., pp. 763–764.

unequal application of international standards or aspirational ideals.[179] It therefore redoubled it efforts to control *all* of China, using as an excuse for its deepening and expanding actions the 1937 "China Incident" or "China Affair"—the fighting that broke out at a picturesque bridge, Lukouchiao, in Beijing or the "Marco Polo Bridge," as Westerners have called it, between Chinese troops and a Japanese detachment that was stationed nearby.[180]

Quickly, Beijing was overrun, and Japan moved to Shanghai, where Chiang Kai-shek is estimated to have lost over 250,000 of his finest troops, followed by the devastation of Nanjing, where atrocities mounted. Over one million of that city's population is said to have fled, including the national government, which moved to Wuhan and, after its fall, to Chongqing. Over twenty million people became part of one of the largest human migrations. While Japan gained control of most of North China, the coastlines of that country (including many of its biggest cities), the lower Yangtze River valley, and the railroads that line the major population centers, the war became "something near a stalemate."[181]

This stalemate was the result of several factors, however, including Japan's having to disperse resources to deal with Soviet Russia in the northeast; the relative effectiveness of the united front (the CPC was very effective in its guerrilla tactics against Tokyo); the possibility of a war with the West, especially the US and Britain; and, as weighty (perhaps the weightiest), US–British collaboration to get monies and other resources, including minerals such as scrap iron, to China. Here, one must bear in mind that with Japan controlling the coastline and railroads, the Chinese government would have collapsed without the Washington–London collaboration, which increased after FDR's Quarantine Speech of October 5, 1937. The speech was designed to achieve a number of ends: to inform and warn the American people (and the world at large about the US's views) that the political situation in the world has gotten

---

[179] Hathaway and Shapiro, op. cit., pp. 172–173. For the Japanese Monroe Doctrine, see George H. Blakeslee, "The Japanese Monroe Doctrine," in *Foreign Affairs*, Vol. XI, #4 (July 1933), pp. 670–681.

[180] Boyle, op. cit., pp. 180–182.

[181] Ibid., p. 191.

"progressively worse" (the Spanish Civil War, the ascendency of Hitler in Germany, the invasion of Ethiopia by Italy, and the "war" between China and Japan); that "worse," as used in the speech, encompassed a "reign of terror and international lawlessness" that was not only undermining ideals such as the Kellogg–Briand Pact and giving "way to a haunting fear of calamity" but also threatening the "landmarks, the traditions which have marked the progress of civilization" itself "toward a condition of law and order and justice"; and that the threat is motivated by "a greed for power and supremacy . . . devoid of all sense of justice and human considerations," as attested by wars without a "declaration" of one, with civilians "ruthlessly murdered [by] bombs from the air" and ships "attacked and sunk by submarines without cause or notice."[182] The US, he warned, after the above-presented horror, should not suppose that it will escape "those things" happening elsewhere in the world or that "mere isolation or neutrality" would provide any immunity or refuge. What must happen instead is for 90 percent of the world's population that were being terrorized by a mere 10 percent to make a common cause in containing the "epidemic of lawlessness" and reversing the violations of international agreements,[183] restoring international order for peace-securing, trade barriers–removing, business-increasing, and wealth-producing activities rather than "producing military planes and bombs."[184]

He was not about (as Japan and other countries suspected) to limit, as earlier indicated concerning secret military preparations, the production of planes and bombs, but on account of the public's opposition to what it accurately perceived as a getting-ready-for-war speech, he moved quickly to the area of moral combat to create what was called "moral sanctions," a kind of quarantine against "an epidemic of lawlessness," as

---

[182] See Roosevelt's "Quarantine Speech," https://millercenter.org/the-presidency/presidential-speeches/october-5-1937-quarantine-speech

[183] He specified the Covenant of the League of Nations, the Kellogg–Briand Pact, and the Nine-Power Treaty.

[184] FDR, in the "Quarantine Speech," also referred to the solidarity and interdependence of the world technically and morally. However, in the midst of his condemnation of war, he was getting Congress to allocate more and more funds for war and secret planning for war.

we are about to see. In addition, in December 1938, FDR authorized the use of funds from the Export–Import Bank, which had been created in 1935, to further the building of the Burma Road, a highway of over seven hundred miles linking Lashio, in Eastern Myanmar (then called Burma) and Kunming, in Yunan Province, China, so that goods could be sent through this British colony to China and help thwart Japanese control of the coastline of China. Support in the form of credit (particularly to purchase goods) was also extended to Beijing.[185]

Japan, as one may expect, was not pleased by this development, in part because, from its perspective, the sending of aid of the kind that the US and Britain were providing had the effect of stiffening China's resistance and extending the stalemate, increasing the cost of the war in material and human terms and reducing opportunities for strategic maneuvering. As well, as early as 1934 (consistent with the idea of the Japanese Monroe Doctrine), Tokyo had taken the position that it opposed China's availing itself of "the influence of any other country" that sought to enable Beijing to "resist Japan" or was bent on supplying China with "war planes . . . the detailing of military instructors and advisors" or contracts" for loans aimed at proving "funds for political uses."[186] To Japan, any or all of the identified opposed-to activities, if engaged in, would be viewed as hostile to the "friendly" relations between China and Japan and subversive to the "peace and order of Eastern Asia."[187] The reader is hopefully seeing the parallels in the views of the US and Japan about each other.

The US was not to be deterred. Instead, it sharpened its "moral sanctions" in two ways: it successfully increased its economic sanctions against Japan, a course of action not as objectionable to the public as military action,[188] and accentuated a refocus on the ideals of international law and international moral values (including the many in the Atlantic

---

185 Bemis, op. cit., p. 829. See Rogers, op. cit., for further elaboration.

186 Bemis, ibid., p. 824.

187 Ibid.

188 Blackwill and Harris, op. cit.

94

Charter), neither of which constrained our action.[189] In the area of economic sanctions, the Department of State in 1938, for example, despite claiming "neutrality," worked with manufacturers to limit the sale of aircrafts to Japan on the grounds that they would be used against China. In 1939, an embargo was imposed on metals—aluminum, magnesium, and molybdenum, among others—but more was to come. In July 1940, Washington, seeking to wreak even greater damage to the Japanese economy, extended the "moral sanctions" to scrap ferrous materials. The latter course of conduct by the US—combined with its July 26, 1939, termination of the 1911 Treaty of Commerce and Navigation (TCN) with Japan (this termination would take effect in 1940 because of the required six-month notice)—left little guesswork about the determination of the US to contain, if not cripple, Japan.

By May 1940, Germany had defeated Allied forces in and gained control of France, Belgium, Denmark, the Netherlands, and Luxemburg and had effectively concluded (until the Normandy operation of 1944) its Western Front mission. This defeat, Japan opportunistically used to move into certain areas of French colonial territories in Asia, especially Northern Indo-China, and (in part as a reaction to the US's termination of the 1911 TNC but more so to improve its international strategic standing) to align itself with the Axis powers, led by Germany, in September 1940. The thinking then, on the part of Japan, appears to have been that Britain too would be defeated and that it should be preparing itself for that eventuality. Meanwhile, the US, secretly preparing itself for war, sought to create the obverse psychology, at home and abroad, in matters pertaining to Allied prospects in general and Britain's in particular.

American political leaders before and after the tenure of Secretary of State Stimson, who was a strong advocate of sanctions against Japan but also understood their political and moral potential to undermine the US's policy toward Latin America—after all, Washington was acting against Japan's Monroe Doctrine—were often sensitive to the invocation of "world [moral] judgement against Japan."[190] Indeed, Tokyo's effort to

---

[189]   Nigel Hamilton, *The American Caesars: Lives of Presidents from Franklin D. Roosevelt to George W. Bush* (New Haven: Yale University Press, 2010), 23–24.

[190]   Williams, op. cit., p. 701.

exercise virtual sovereignty over East Asia was not unlike the claims of the former secretary of state Richard Olney, who proclaimed that the US was "practically sovereign of this [American] continent, and its fiat is law upon the subjects to which it confines its interposition."[191]

FDR took the latter into consideration, as we are going to see. However, he, who (as earlier indicated) had been preparing the US for war militarily and had gotten Congress to increase military spending after the failure of the previously discussed 1935 LNC, also successfully got Congress—after Hitler had, in 1938, taken over Austria and later Czechoslovakia—to approve a two-ocean navy along with commensurate increases in military spending. For the fiscal year 1939, "total arms expenditures increased more than twice what it was in 1935. The navy drew on the treasury for over $670 million in 1939, almost $900 million in 1940, and over $2 trillion in the fiscal year ending in June 1941."[192] With this armed forces buildup, the US was ready to pursue greater national psychological mobilization, offer greater threats to Axis powers, and prevent Japan's use of mounting weaknesses among European Allied powers (especially in their colonies) to gain the equality that it sought with US and other great powers. He pursued these ends in three areas of sanctions, sensitive to the context of the preceding paragraph but with much greater boldness and comprehensiveness against Japan.

Perhaps no single document fully captures FDR's and the broader government's disposition at the time than the text of his December 29, 1940, "fireside chat" speech.[193] In a sense, a follow-up to his Quarantine" Speech of 1937—with developing international issues more favorable to his stances, coupled with a degree of "I told you so" toward his critics—FDR told the radio audience that he wanted to speak with them on "national security" for the purpose of keeping "you now and your children later and your grandchildren much later out of

---

[191] Quoted in Bailey, op. cit., p. 441.

[192] Williams, op. cit., p. 805.

[193] The term actually refers to a series of evening radio addresses that FDR gave, with considerable degree of collegial "intimacy," between 1933 and 1944.

a last-ditch war for the preservation of American independence."[194] In fact, he sought to indicate that he was seeking to avoid going to war and sought to summon from the American people—the "girl behind the counter," the "workman in the mills, the mines, and factories," the "small shopkeeper," the "farmer doing . . . his ploughing," the "widows and old men wondering about their life's saving"—the same "courage and realism" that they had given in 1933 when the country faced the Great Depression.[195]

The problem, according to FDR, was the "presence of a world in crisis" that, never "before since Jamestown and Plymouth Rock," had posed "such a danger as now" to American civilization and independence."[196] He then identified the epicenter of the crisis and danger: the commitment to take joint action on the part of "three powerful nations, two in Europe and one in Asia," against the US if the latter interfered with their "expansion program . . . a program aimed [at] world control."[197] He then moved to particularize by claiming that Germany was seeking to enslave Europe and use the latter's resources to dominate and control the world, noting how Britain had been valiantly engaged in a defense against that threatened domination, as were the Chinese, in the face of a like threat of enslavement from Japan. Then taking on those who had helped frustrate his efforts to move toward an open war footing in 1937 and now calling for a "negotiated peace," he contended that such calls are "nonsense" and argued that one cannot negotiate with "a gang of outlaws."[198] What the US should aim to do instead was to become "the great arsenal of democracy" and supply Britain and others fighting the Axis powers with not soldiers but "the implements of war"—planes, tanks, guns, and freighters—which would enable them to "fight for our security."[199] He was not going to disturb

---

[194] See Franklin Delano Roosevelt Radio Speech, delivered on December 29, 1940.

[195] Ibid.

[196] Ibid.

[197] Ibid.

[198] Ibid.

[199] Ibid.

the society about losing their loved ones to war but promise security and, from the sale of arms, economic prosperity.

The alleged "frauds" that the Axis powers were engaged in, through the occupation of a country for the purpose of "restoring order" and "protecting it," were, of course, in large measure, what had been taking place under the Monroe Doctrine, especially the corollary thereto, the "civilizing mission" of Britain, and that about which Konoe, earlier in this work, had been accusing the West, especially the US and Britain. It is also part of that which informed Washington's conduct in respect of Greenland (taken in 1941 for security purposes). In respect of the Americas, at the time under discussion, FDR acted quickly under a new focus on Pan-Americanism, beginning in 1938, to promote hemispheric security and reinforce what had come to be called his "Good Neighbor" policy.

The emergence of "regional political order"—in Europe, led by Germany, in East Asia, led by Japan, and in the socialist order, led by Soviet Russia—was seen by the US as a threat to its own led order, encompassing the Americas and the Caribbean, with extensions into the Pacific by way of Hawaii, the Philippines, and Guam. Britain alone (France and other European imperial powers had already been defeated by Germany), with her worldwide empire, merited a special place of trust, although it was understood that there would be (and there were) differences between London and Washington. Japan, of course, had suspicions about its Axis partners and was not about to allow Hitler to extend his developing empire into East Asia.

Nowhere was that suspicion more evident than in the actions of Tokyo, which had moved in 1940 to take control of Northern Indochina (today's Vietnam, Laos, and Cambodia) after the area had passed to Vichy France (the German-controlled regime that succeeded the Third Republic) and again in July 1941, when it moved into Southern Indochina following Hitler's June 1941 launching of his planned attack against Soviet Russia. This move south—bringing Japan in much closer physical proximity to all of Southeast Asia, including the Philippines and Singapore—not only allowed Japan to recoup, potentially, some of the mineral and other resources denied it by US sanctions but also brought with it threats to US and British naval facilities as well as plans in Singapore and the Philippines.

The US responded by freezing all of Japan's assets—a potential disaster for Tokyo since three-quarters of its trade depended on the availability of these assets.[200] In November of the previous year, the US had supported a loan of about $60 million to China for the purchase of needed metals, and while the January 1941 Lend–Lease program was organized for and primarily directed toward Allied powers in Europe (the US was ostensibly neutral), especially Britain, an American mission was sent to China in August 1941, through the Burma Road, to offer major support to China.[201] China, in other words, largely became eligible for the same authorized sale, trade, lease, and giveaway of military hardware that the Allied powers were. It was, from the standpoint of Japan, being strengthened by the US (at least prevented from further weakening because of resource depletion), while Tokyo was being progressively weakened by sanctions.

It is one thing to advance ideals through "moral sanctions" when one is seeking to expand trade and, more broadly, economic interests—a central focus of FDR's administration, as statutorily backed and diplomatically practiced. It is another to progressively expand trade restrictions against an important trade partner. In fact, in his January 3, 1940, message to Congress, consistent with his push after he had first taken office in the middle of the Great Depression with a view to expand trade under the terms of the 1934 Reciprocal Trade Agreements Act, he reminded Congress,

> For many years after the World War [WWI], blind
> economic selfishness in most countries, including
> our own, resulted in a destructive minefield of trade
> restrictions which blocked the channels of commerce
> among nations. This policy was one of the contributing

---

[200] Edward S. Miller, *Bankrupting the Enemy: The US Financial Siege of Japan before Pearl Harbor* (Annapolis: Naval Institute Press, 2007). The work shows the virtual irreversibility, given the financial and political dynamics of the time, of the move against Japan.

[201] See *Department of State Bulletin,* Vol. V, No. 114 (August 30, 1941), p. 166.

causes of existing wars. It dammed up the vast wholesale surpluses, helping to bring about unemployment and suffering in the United States and everywhere else.[202]

The president was referring to the US's tariffs immediately after World War I as well as those that came later, specifically the 1930 Smoot–Hawley Tariff, as the US joined many other countries in trying to become economically self-sufficient. Few knowledgeable persons could, for example, forget the impact of those tariff policies on Germany and their contribution to the rise of Hitler, hence FDR's reference in the quoted statement about the "causes of existing wars." He was therefore fully aware of the potential social and political catastrophes that could result from tariffs and other limitations on the free movement of goods and services. What was it that prompted his openly more aggressive economic sanctions against Japan, eighteen months after his speech to Congress?

There were a number of factors, the contributions of three of which were rather impactful. First, there was the return to government service of the former secretary of state under President Hoover, Henry Stimson, this time as secretary of war. He not only played an important role in fighting the "doves" in FDR's cabinet but also was able to assert his views of Japan as part of an inferior people who could be pressured or "bluffed" into behaving as the US sought to have it behave.[203] Second, there was the now fairly famous "Green Light" message of September 12, 1940, from J. C. Grew, the US ambassador to Japan. For nearly ten years of his tenure in Japan, he rightly cautioned against the exertion of too much pressure on Tokyo for fear of furthering the growing ascendency of the military and undermining the support base of civilian moderates. In the just-mentioned communication to the secretary of state, however, he urged economic pressure because he was persuaded that Japan had been "deterred from taking great liberties with American

---

[202] See President Roosevelt's January 3, 1940, Message to the Congress of the United States.

[203] Williams, op. cit., pp. 674–695, 809–811. We still do not have enough evidence for his alleged maneuvering of Japan into the war (pp. 828–832).

interest only out of respect for our potential power."[204] Third, there were concerns in Washington, adroitly used by Chiang Kai-shek but weightily grounded in experience (given the 1938 defection of the pro-peace-with-Japan Wang Ching-wei from the KMT to Japan), that the KMT might seek a peaceful resolution of differences with Japan. There was a conjunctive what-if that also made Washington nervous: what if the CPC were to outmaneuver or otherwise defeat the KMT and become an ally of Soviet Russia?

Of all the factors that seem to have influenced Roosevelt, none carried the force of the persistent "rumors of impending collapse of the Chinese resistance" in November 1940.[205] Were this rumored possible outcome to mature into fruition or a Sino-Japanese rapprochement to come into being, either outcome would make a "nearly invincible power in the East."[206] This is the very end against which efforts had been marshaled since the end of World War I—prevent the development of a Japan that can enforce its claim to equality. The space for expanded US investment and commercial markets would be so reduced that the US and the West would be rendered, at best, the equals of Japan. So there could be no waiting for the results of the war in Europe, especially in the light of communication from Ambassador Grew, indicating that Japan had been deterred by, among other things, Washington's two-navy buildup, its strengthening of naval bases in the Pacific, and the possibility of joint action with Britain.[207]

What has been insufficiently appreciated is the fact that for all the due resentment that Japan's occupation of China and other countries in Asia had provoked among the inhabitants of these occupied areas, there was equal, perhaps more, resentment of the then existing system of international relations that had been constructed on the humiliation

---

[204]   Ibid., p. 852.

[205]   Boyle, op. cit., p. 202.

[206]   Ibid., p. 192.

[207]   For the entire document communicating Grew's views, see Williams, op. cit., pp. 849–852. One of the reasons why so much pressure was brought to bear on Britain to terminate the 1902 treaty with Tokyo was the fear of some that a London–Tokyo naval collaboration against the US could eventuate.

of Asian peoples. They, in the words of the British, were among the "aggrieved colored races"[208] who found their confinement and subjugation made legal under international law, rebellion against which could be legally met with force, including violence. The Chinese, after 1842, understood this; Japan suffered it in 1853–1854. So when Tokyo launched its "co-prosperity sphere" policy (the creation of a form of commonwealth), it was part of its effort in preparing to "demand" a hearing for a redress of this subjugation as well as the creation of a regional socioeconomic and political system that would ensure that Asia operates in favor of the Asians, "Asia for the Asians," seen and accepted as championed and led by Japan.[209] FDR largely understood this; Japan was expressing a sentiment shared by many Asians. So among other things, he sought to control the extent of Japan's psychological benefits from this sentiment by including aspects of it in his launching of the Atlantic Charter, which promised support for the principle of self-determination after the war.

Japan: Modern Melians?

Whatever the triggering mechanism or combination of mechanisms that prompted Washington's new, more open stances in its long, drawn-out competition with Japan, those stances had ceased to focus primarily on a containment of Japan. They were now directed at ensuring that its capacity to enforce its claim to equality be permanently impaired and reversed.[210] New help to China, further joint planning with Britain, and more damaging sanctions were, in part, calculated to ensure this aim.

---

[208] See Lauren, op. cit., p. 3.

[209] Boyle, op. cit., p. 193. US senator Hiram Johnson's view of "America's Economic Expansion in Latin America" (a form of "America for Americans") can be found in Williams, op. cit., pp. 715–717.

[210] The reader might want to note Article 9 of the US-written-and-imposed Japanese constitution states that "the Japanese people forever renounce war as a sovereign right of the nation and the threat or the use of force as a means of settling international disputes." Paragraph 2 of the same article goes on to say that "to accomplish the aim of the preceding paragraph, land, sea, and air forces, as well

To strengthen China, the largest single loan to the KMT ($100 million) was given in November 1940 to facilitate the purchase of metals and thereby stiffen China's resistance as well as keep nearly a million Japanese soldiers tied down in China.[211] By April 1941 (this prepared the way for the already discussed August 1941 mission to Beijing), China was formally made part of the Lend–Lease program so that shipments of much-needed materials—construction equipment, weapons, and munitions—could be sent through the Burma Road to the KMT. Also, to satisfy "the letter of the law" (the reader must remember that the US was still a "neutral country" and so cannot be legally involved in the war), FDR "authorized Army Air Corps and naval pilots to resign their commissions and join" the American Volunteer Group (AVG)—a body of aviators that became known as the "Flying Tigers"—to be sent to Burma and China to train pilots for the then depleted and largely demoralized China air force.[212]

FDR did more. He followed up the secret British–American staff talks of February–March 1941 (these were so secret that Congress did not know about them, and the president, at the same time, assured legislators and the country that the pending Lend–Lease legislation would have no warlike implications) with a secret "summit" off the east coast of Newfoundland with Prime Minister Winston Churchill on August 9–12, 1941. At the latter meeting, many issues were discussed, including war aims and the possible presentation of an ultimatum to Japan. From this meeting also came the Atlantic Charter, which Nigel Hamilton, a respected biographer of FDR, rightly characterized as "predicated on *moral* principles"[213] to continue containing Japan but, as well, intended to be used as a "clearly articulated moral framework for the world that would come thereafter."[214] This is exactly the type of peace ("Anglo-American peace," especially with Churchill's position that Articles

---

as other war potential, will never be maintained. The right of belligerency of the state will not be recognized."

[211] Boyle, op. cit., p. 202.

[212] Ibid., pp. 202–203.

[213] Hamilton, op. cit., p. 24.

[214] Ibid.

1 and 2 of the charter, which deal with the self-determination and rights of peoples to choose their own government, did not apply to the British Empire) to which the Japanese so scornfully referred and took an oppositional stance toward at the end of World War I.[215]

The Japanese, therefore, understood (in part) what the US was doing but wanted to avoid war with the US, if it were possible. In an effort to become less reliant on the US, following the latter's giving notice that it would terminate the 1911 TCN with Japan, Tokyo moved in July 1940 (as earlier mentioned) to make up for export markets lost and materials that it could no longer purchase in the US by formalizing its shift from "Greater East Asia" emphasis, with Japan as a hegemonic power, to the idea of GEACPS. Within the latter, Japan would still be dominant, but it would be leading with a view toward mutual benefit, derived from a collective effort under Tokyo's technical and other tutelage.[216] Dealing with the immediate effects of US economic sanctions, as economically desperate as Japan was becoming, was not the sole objective that Tokyo was pursuing, however. It was also pushing into the rest of Indochina to make East Asia the equivalent of the Pan-American system under Japan's Monroe Doctrine.

If the freezing of Japanese assets was difficult (and it was because of its earlier mentioned, almost irreversible disabling effects on Tokyo), it was made all the more so when, contrary to the rules of neutrality, the US brought in Britain and the Netherlands East Indies (NEI) to expand the scope of the freeze and bring into being what "amounted to a commercial blockade."[217] Indeed, under international law, a blockade presumes the existence of a war with Japan. The US action did not stop here. It is one thing to be moving toward war; it is another thing to have a mobilized society behind that war. Roosevelt knew he needed to have this mobilized support and extended the US "security zone" as far as Iceland in the summer of 1941 and placed an embargo on oil exports to Japan, hoping thereby to challenge "both the Third Reich and the

---

[215] See footnote #141. Indeed, FDR wanted a postwar period of transition that would see the world administered by a joint US–British effort. Sumner Welles led the opposition to this thinking. See Williams, op. cit., pp. 802–804.

[216] Boyle, op. cit., p. 204.

[217] Ibid.

Empire of the Rising Sun to respond the only way they knew how: by force of arms, thus giving the United States a *casus belli* that would turn the isolationist tide at home."[218]

The decision to adopt an embargo on oil and gas exports to Japan on August 1, 1941, was a course of action that the US had thought about before and decided against for fear of impelling Japan to seek control of the NEI. Tokyo, after having occupied the Cam Ranh naval base in July 1941, had few, if any, incentives not to look toward Malaysia, Borneo, and North Borneo and Brunei (the base was about nine hundred miles from Singapore and the Philippines) as well as the NEI to help compensate for the loss sustained from the embargo. Tokyo was dependent on the US for about 80 percent of its petroleum needs.[219]

What followed were two developments: a series of diplomatic exchanges between Japan and the US and a decision, by the Japanese—reminiscent of the Melians facing the Athenians—not to bow to the US's pressure and not to forego the goal it had set for itself to claim a place of equality in the council of great powers. It would take its chances and the results.

The diplomatic exchanges began when, on November 20, 1941, Japanese ambassador to the US Kichisaburo Nomura forwarded a note to Secretary of State Cordell Hull, who responded, on November 26, 1941, with a "Strictly Confidential Outline of a Proposed Basis for Agreement between the United States and Japan." In the Japanese note, Tokyo proposed that both the US and Japan undertake not to make any "armed advancement" into Southeast Asia (a course of conduct feared by Britain and the US) and the Southern Pacific except for the portions of Indochina where Japanese troops were then presently located; that Japan undertake to withdraw troops then stationed in French Indochina after either the restoration of peace with China or the establishment of "an equitable peace in [the] Pacific area"; that both governments "cooperate with a view to securing the acquisition of goods and commodities which the two countries need" in the NEI; that both governments "mutually undertake to restore commercial relations to those prevailing prior to the

---

218   Hamilton, op. cit., p. 24.

219   Boyle, op. cit., p. 210.

freezing of assets"; and that the US supply Japan "a required quantity of oil."[220]

It should be evident from the note that Japan was anxious, even desperate, to have the crippling freezing of assets and oil embargo removed and was willing to commit not only to stop armed forward movement into Southeast Asia but also to withdraw troops then stationed in French Indochina. Clearly intimated in the note also was the idea of a broader, negotiated "equitable" peace in the Pacific area and cooperation with the US in ensuring that both Tokyo and Washington acquire needed "goods and commodities" from the NEI. These were not confrontational proposals; they were not seeking to exclude the US's commercial and investment interest (a degree of "open door" was being conceded), and they were not, in any way, consistent with its standing as a great power, posing any new threat in China but urged that the US refrain from "measures and actions" (the training and arming of China's military force, for example) that did prejudice its interest in China. Indeed, as will be seen shortly, Tokyo was asking the US to serve as a "go-between" in Tokyo's relations with China.

The US's response was not accommodating. It began with five broad principles (the moral sanctions, at the level of ideas), such as "the inviolability of territorial integrity and sovereignty" of nations; "equality, including equality of commercial opportunity and treatment"; "non-discrimination in international commercial relations"; and "the principle of establishment of such institutions and arrangements of international finance as may lend aid to . . . . the development of all countries."[221] Within the context of the recited principles, the US's position went on to suggest what both and each government should undertake. For example, both governments should endeavor to conclude a multilateral nonaggression pact among the British Empire, China, the Netherlands, the Soviet Union, Thailand, the US, and Japan that Japan would "withdraw" all military, naval, air, and police forces from China and Indochina; that neither government would support "militarily, politically, economically" any government or regime in China other

---

[220] Williams, op. cit., p. 853.

[221] Ibid., pp. 854–855.

than the KMT; and that, along with other matters, both would "enter into negotiations" for the conclusion of a trade agreement based on reciprocal most-favored-nation treatment.

It should be obvious that the US's terms would remove Japan from all means of ever challenging the other great powers—of ever enforcing its claim to equality. First, the general principles that would not limit Washington's behavior would be applied to Japan and make that country but a subordinate of the US and the West. The proposed international financial institution, for example, would—as in the case of what President Wilson was proposing for China—simply be an organization dominated by the US and Britain, and it would limit Japan's influence in the development of other countries, something it had begun to do with non-Japanese areas under its control and in partial fulfilment of its co-prosperity sphere policy. Second, requiring that Tokyo enter into a multilateral nonaggression pact with Britain, the Soviet Union, the Netherlands, and the US was the equivalent of having Tokyo reject its alliance with Germany and Italy—something it could not do without making itself even more vulnerable to the US. Also, asking it to forego support for no other government in China but the US-backed KMT (dissolve its ties with its client state's leader, Wang Ching-Wei) as well as withdraw *all* military forces from the latter country was tantamount to having Tokyo turn over China to Washington. This was not the "equitable peace" for which Japan was looking in the Pacific area. Finally, the US exhibited little hurry in addressing those issues that Japan was in such critical need to have dealt with immediately, such as a restoration of commercial relations that preexisted the freeze and the securing of adequate oil purchase.

Instead, the US promised to "enter into negotiations" to conclude a trade agreement—something that could take years, and under certain reciprocal terms—most likely including some of the nontrade concessions or demands mentioned above.[222] There was no reference to oil, the reserves of which Japan had but for two years. This time would be substantially reduced if there were a war with the US. Neither did the US's response include any reference to the NEI, from which Japan thought both it and the US could have some of their resource needs

---

[222]   Ibid., pp. 853–854.

met. The responses, on the part of the US, gave additional, confirming support to the military sympathizers in the Japanese government, who felt that the West could not be trusted, and when "oil-purchasing missions from Tokyo" to the NEI (the government-in-exile of which was located in London) returned home empty-handed, even greater anxiety must have taken hold of Japan.[223] In a broader sense, while Japan's proposals, had they been accepted by the US, would have left the latter in no worse an international position than it had before such a potential acceptance, the US's counterproposal, if accepted by Japan, would have reduced Tokyo to a third-class power, living user rules, including its own future development, created by Washington.

The December 1, 1941, "Memorandum of Conversation" (MOC) between the secretary of state and the Japanese diplomats in Washington also discloses information pertinent to our present discussions. From it, one gets a fuller sense of the political psychology that defined the stances of each side. The two Japanese diplomats (the earlier mentioned ambassador and a special envoy, Saburo Kurusu) took turns in addressing Secretary Hull, with the special envoy indicting the secretary of state, stating that his response to the November 20 proposal by Japan "[seemed] to fail to take into cognizance the actual conditions in the Far East" and repeated that the offer "to withdraw its [Japanese] troops from [Southern] Indochina still stands"; he also indicated that Japan has shown "its extreme desire to promote a peaceful settlement."[224] Secretary Hull indicated that the US had taken into its calculations the bellicose utterances emanating from Tokyo and that peaceful settlements cannot be "based on principles of force."[225] He also indicated that Hitler was using force to control half of the world and that Japan militarists were moving in a similar direction to control the other half. The ambassador "expressed the view that as a matter of fact," there was "not much difference between Japan's idea of a co-prosperity sphere and Pan-Americanism except Japan's methods may

---

[223] Boyle, op. cit. p. 210.

[224] Williams, op. cit., p. 856.

[225] Ibid.

be more primitive."[226] The ambassador went on to deny that Japan's purpose was to use force. When Secretary Hull asked whether Tokyo was not moving on the territories of other countries, "inch by inch by force," the ambassador indicated that the use of force was a practice of the US (perhaps reflecting on the 1853 experience, among others) and asserted that Japan was motivated by self-defense in the use of force, not unlike Britain in Syria. Japan, he said, needed "rice and other materials at a time she was being shut off [from them] by the United States and other countries," leaving Tokyo "no alternative but to endeavor to obtain access to these materials."[227]

Secretary Hull shifted the exchange somewhat by noting that Japan had taken the stance that the US had "no right to interfere with what Japan [was] doing in [Eastern] Asia" but that when Tokyo sends troops into and keeps them in Indochina" (thus "making it necessary for the United States and its friends to keep large numbers of armed forces immobilized in [East] Asia"), it is engaging in conduct, by so doing, that has the "effect" of aiding Hitler and that the US cannot "sit still" while such developments take place. The special envoy, at this juncture, denied that there was any similarity in the purpose of Japan and that of Hitler, and the ambassador followed up with three very important statements: that the Japanese people believe that the US wanted to "keep Japan fighting with China and keep Japan strangled"; that "they are faced with the alternative of surrendering to the United States or fighting"; and that he was nevertheless "still trying to save the situation."[228] Secretary Hull then rejoined that he had "practically exhausted himself" in dealing with matters, that the American people "are going to assume" there was "real danger to this country [US] in the situation," and that there was nothing he could do "to prevent it."[229]

---

[226] Ibid. The reader will remember the observations of Sen. Hiram Johnson in respect of the US's relations with Latin America.

[227] Ibid. It may be that Iraq, not Syria, is the country to which the Japanese intended to have referred.

[228] Ibid., pp. 856–857.

[229] Ibid, p. 857.

Among the inferences that can be reasonably made from the MOC are that the Japanese felt that they had made as good an offer, through the November 20, 1941, note, as they were disposed to (largely their last offer); that the "moral embargo" organized over the years against Tokyo had limited effects on Tokyo since the latter measured its international behavior against that of the US and Britain and found no substantive difference; that in using force, he had acted defensively (despite attempts to equate its conduct with that of Hitler), acting to defend its right to have access to needed resources, especially in the face of the West's, chiefly the US's, efforts to limit or cut off that access, be it in Manchuria or elsewhere; and that the people of Japan had come to see but two alternatives—to surrender to the US or to fight. The US response was to counter Japan's proposals with terms that it could not possibly accept absent that surrender, and while the Japanese ambassador said he was trying to "save the situation," Secretary Hull indicated that there was little he could do to avoid the feeling, on the part of the American people, that Japan and what it represented constituted a real danger to the US. So it was indeed, as Tokyo's response to Hull's November 26, 1941, confidential communication to the Japanese government disclosed. At the very time that the response was being received by the secretary of state, the Japanese air force was on its way to attack Pearl Harbor.

The December 7, 1941, Japanese Note to the US (JNTUS) began with some recapitulation of diplomatic and other exchanges between the two countries (sometimes including Britain) during the then past eight months, focusing on exchanges during the last three weeks. It claimed that Japan had always had as fundamental to its policy the peace of the Pacific area and the world based on the stability of East Asia and the "enabling of all nations to find their proper place in the world" and that China did not understand this, in part because the US and Britain frustrated all attempts by Tokyo to put in place that which would help ensure that understanding. Despite these claimed attempts, the JNTUS contended, Japan made a series of proposals in the November 20 note to the US, including one for withdrawal from Southern Indochina (the entire text of the latter proposals was included in the JNTUS), and

Tokyo went as far as requesting the US to serve "as 'Introducer' of Peace" between Japan and China.[230] What did the US do?

The US, it contended, was not open; it was, as always, "obsessed with its own views and opinions" and "advocating in the name of world peace favorable to it" (Washington) rather than engaging in a discovery of mutual interests on which peace might be constructed. In addition, the US response sought to have Japan depart from its obligation to its allies, Germany and Italy, while Washington, in the name of self-defense, supported the UK against them. This, seeking further to highlight the hypocrisy, touched on three issues: Washington's advancing of the "unconditional application" of the principle of commercial nondiscrimination throughout China; the call for the *extension* [author's emphasis] of the equivalent of a nine-power agreement over French Indochina without including France; and the imposing with Britain of economic pressures on Japan, some of which were "more inhumane than military pressures."[231] Under these conditions, the JNTUS went on to say, it was "impossible not to reach the conclusion that the American government" desired any end but "to maintain and strengthen, in coalition with Great Britain and other Powers, its dominant position . . . not only in China but in other areas of East Asia."[232] Then in an impassioned statement of general grievance by a member of the "aggrieved colored races," the note stated,

> It is a fact of history that the countries of East Asia, for
> the past two hundred years or more, have been compelled
> to observe the status quo under Anglo-American policy
> of imperialistic exploitation and to sacrifice themselves
> to the prosperity of the two nations. The Japanese

[230] The term "Introducer" as used here is the equivalent of the diplomatic term "good offices," which refers to the use of one's position or influence to facilitate the accommodation of differences between or among disputing international parties. In this specific instance, the US would use its influence with the KMT to help China and Japan explore accommodation of their differences.

[231] See "Japanese Note to the United States — December 7, 1941" in *Department of State Bulletin*, Vol. V, #129 (December 13, 1941).

[232] Ibid.

government cannot tolerate the perpetuation of such a situation since it directly runs counter to Japan's fundamental policy to enable all nations to enjoy each its proper place in the world.[233]

As such, Japan, faced with a collusion between the US and Britain to prevent a new order in East Asia, could not accept Secretary Hull's response as a basis for further negotiations. The "proper place" for Japan, as seen from Tokyo, was one of equality; the proposal that Hull offered, if put in operation, would be not only one in which Japan's international position was that of an "inferior" but one in which "its very existence [as an independent state] would be endangered."[234] Faced with these circumstances, Japan elected to play the role of the Melians, in Thucydides' narrative of the Peloponnesian War.

The Melians, despite being so small when compared with the mighty Athenian Empire, wanted to be regarded as a moral and political equal. Athens wanted domination and would not be denied it by law, custom, values of justice, common practices, or prohibitions of the gods. To the Melians, if the Athenians were willing to risk so much in the pursuit of their self-defined interest, then "it were surely great baseness and cowardice in us who are still free not to try everything that can be tried before submitting."[235]

Tokyo knew how risky the course of action it contemplated was; how comparatively lacking it was in natural, capital, and industrial markets and other resources; the narrow space-time within which it would have to navigate to achieve some success (it knew that it could not win a drawn-out war with the US, for example); and the dire consequences that awaited its failure. It was also faced, however, with the threat of having to return to an international standing of inferiority—the place from which Japan came in 1853, within rules of international law that conferred rights on states, including that to take over other countries or portions of them, if one were deemed victorious in war (this was how the

---

[233] Ibid.

[234] Boyle, op. cit., p. 218.

[235] Thucydides, op. cit., p. 333.

European, Russian, and American empires were created, maintained, and defended). It was the whole point in Japan's dedication to the study of international law and the supposed equality that it recognized among great powers.[236] The same rules of international law make distinctions between belligerents and neutrals. A neutral country (the US, in this case) is not legally allowed to impose an embargo on a belligerent (Japan); it was done by the country that was ostensibly fighting to uphold the international legal order. In the area of trade—which was explained to Japan (at the time of its forced opening) as ordered by God, who was said to have made certain that no country was materially self-sufficient, to promote friendship and a ministry to the mutual needs of peoples and thus advance sociality—it seemed that neither God, friendship, nor sociality mattered. Japan, following God's instructions, allowed itself to become too dependent on the US, a country that the Japanese militarists, led by Hideki Tojo, saw as twisting everything to align with its self-defined interest, while the civilian government in Tokyo (including that of Fumimaro Konoe's) remained irresolute. Not only did he move to replace the civilian government, but also, that move, which had also allowed him political leeway to attack Pearl Harbor, gave FDR what he so exactingly courted through the economic sanctions.

He gave FDR the casus belli that generated the domestic support to go to war. Nigel Hamilton grasped this fully. While "decrypts of Japanese secret signals [revealed] how hysterical the Japanese leaders were becoming, FDR ratcheted up his diplomatic pressure" through Secretary Hull, "not only refusing to lift his embargo on the export of oil and other materials to Japan" but also demanding that Japan must withdraw from all the territories that it controlled in China.[237]

The author went through this fairly detailed narrative not only to show that Allison was wrong in his assessments and demonstrate that equality was the center around which the US–Japanese war revolved but also to show, in this specific case, how much was left untouched by his study to indicate that Japan was challenging not just one country (the US) but also others (especially Britain) in a multipolar world that

---

[236] Hathaway and Shapiro, op. cit., "What Kind of Thing Is This Law of Nations?" pp. 138–153.

[237] Hamilton, op. cit., pp. 24–25.

included Russia (later Soviet Russia), France, and the Netherlands, among others—the very system of Western domination. It is also to demonstrate that the struggle was long, intentional, and planned. Japan could not be an equal, be admitted into the aristocracy of the great powers, because of what it would mean to the system of domination and the West's place in that system. He (the author) also went into the details because, as will be seen in the next three chapters, these details are intimately linked to our study of Britain and Germany, the current relations between the US and China, and the meaning of the UN Charter, including the human rights regime that charter has sponsored.

CHAPTER 8
Germany and Britain

In the case of Britain and Germany, Allison begins his task by quoting a memorandum from Winston Churchill, who was to become first lord of the admiralty, that if one wants peace, one must prepare for war—actually a Roman maxim. This obligatory preparation for "peace lovers" was, at the 1911 date of the memorandum just quoted, intended to deal with the perceived peace-endangering Germany. That country was challenging the naval supremacy that London enjoyed and intended to maintain. On the survival of that supremacy (and "supremacy" here meant maintaining a fleet of battleships equal to that which could be deployed by its next two competitors combined) "floated the might, majesty, dominion, and power of the British Empire."[238] (We will refer to this defined supremacy as the two-ocean or two-power standard.)

Allison then sets up the "excruciating dilemma" that Britain faced. "On the one hand, naval supremacy was non-negotiable." Without it, British outposts in India, South Africa, and Canada—not to mention Britain itself—were vulnerable. Moreover, Britain's long-term security demanded that no hegemon seize control of Western Europe—consistent with the sum of four hundred years of foreign policy stances that London should oppose the strongest and most dominating country on the continent.[239]

---

[238] Quoted in Allison, op. cit., pp. 56–57.

[239] Ibid., p. 57.

Allison then went on to claim that the British were "right to think of this dilemma in apocalyptic terms."[240] Why? After World War I (and this was, for him, caused by Germany's threat), the world lay in ruins, and half a millennium during which Europe had been "the political center of the world came to a crashing halt."[241] The war's "development," in his view, "followed the same bleak pattern—and many of the same dynamics—as other Thucydidean conflicts over the centuries."[242] Britain, the ruling power, Allison argues, became "beset by anxieties typical of many ruling powers," while Berlin was "driven by the ambition and indignation characteristic of many up-and-comers."[243]

What did the ruling power and the up-and-comer do to trigger the war? They engaged in the "heat of rivalry," politically and militarily expressed in "entangling alignments," which, poisoned by reckless myopia across Europe, stoked an assassination in Sarajevo, resulting in "a global [conflagration]."[244] At the center of this rivalry, however, was London's fear that "a powerful Germany left unchecked across the Continent would threaten its existence."[245]

Allison uses the rest of the chapter to marshal proof of this claimed threat by Germany and Britain's response. Among the pillars of the offered proof is the 1907 Crowe Memorandum (TCM) (named after its British Foreign Office author, Sir Eyre Crowe), which created an impressively reasoned documentary justification for subsequent policy actions toward Germany. While taking into consideration Germany's denial of any intention to supplant Britain as a world power and actually acknowledging important contributions that it was then seen as making and could, in the future, make to the world, the memorandum claimed that Germany's *intentions* were of no importance; its *capacity* was that which mattered. If Berlin were, for example, to build a powerful navy that could challenge Britain, the *capability* would pose a threat

---

[240] Ibid.

[241] Ibid.

[242] Ibid.

[243] Ibid.

[244] Ibid., pp. 57–58.

[245] Ibid., p. 58

that was incompatible with the very existence of the British Empire. It was therefore incumbent on London to "stand up to perceived German encroachment and out-build Germany's naval expansion."[246]

Instead of moving directly to the issue of naval rivalry, Allison directs the reader's attention to some factors associated with Britain's justification in its seeking to contain Germany's perceived unfriendly expansion. One of the reasons was psychological, the other ideological. Britain, Allison observes, was the birthplace of the Industrial Revolution and had become the "workshop of the world." By 1880, it accounted for "almost a quarter of the world's manufacturing output and trade"; its "investments powered global growth, and its fleets protected global trade . . . Britain thus saw itself, and expected others to see it, as number one."[247] On the ideological side, he again quotes Churchill, who— embodying the unexampled, modern "images of greatness" attached to the 1897 diamond jubilee celebrations for Queen Victoria as well as the jitters of possible decline—urged his fellow Britons to "continue" the laudable pursuit of "that course marked out for us by an all-wise hand and carry out our mission of bearing peace, civilization, and good government to the uttermost ends of the earth."[248]

In other words, the British Empire had a special mission, above and beyond national interest, that had been assigned to it by an "all-wise hand." Churchill added this feature of ideology, this inheritance or assignment, in a manner reminiscent of Pericles, that of showing that the "vigor and vitality of our race is unimpaired," as was the determination "to uphold the Empire that we have inherited from our fathers as Englishmen."[249]

Allison then directs his readers' gaze to the irony of Britain, in 1914, finding itself aligned with former rivals such as Russia and France (and later the US) to prevent Germany's "gaining strategic mastery in Europe."[250] What immediately follows is a summary of his claimed

---

[246] Ibid., pp. 59–60.

[247] Ibid., p. 60.

[248] Ibid., p. 61

[249] Ibid.

[250] Ibid., p. 63.

"testament to the fear by a ruling power when a rising one appears to endanger its security."[251] The testament is a meandering one—moving from the economic, technical, academic, and demographic to the military (in general), the navy, and the international political alignments. In respect of the economic, Germany had, by 1910, surpassed Britain. In 1913, it accounted for 14.8 percent of global manufacturing, while Britain had fallen from 23 to 13.6 percent. Before its unification in 1871, Germany produced half the steel Britain did, but by 1914, it was producing over twice as much. In industrial potential, Germany was far behind Britain in 1900, but by 1913, it surpassed Britain. Also, if one were to examine exports, part of the offspring of that industrial capacity and growth, while Britain's exports to Germany doubled from 1890 to 1913, this impressive gain was but half of the value of its imports, which had tripled.[252]

In what was then seen as some technical areas that were to form the basis for a second industrial revolution (in the electrical, petrochemical, and organic-chemical industries), Germany outdistanced Britain. Indeed, in 1913, "Britain, France, and Italy together produced and consumed only 80 percent of the electricity that Germany did."[253] Germany's science and technology, emerging from institutes and well-regarded universities, bested those of Britain and the world. "Between 1901, when the Nobel Prizes were first awarded, and 1914, Germany won eighteen prizes . . . more than twice as many as the United Kingdom and four times as many as the United States. In physics and chemistry alone, Germany . . . won twice as many as the UK and the US combined."[254]

Demographically, Britain had more urban living people, but Germany was fast catching up, and its population at about sixty-seven million in 1913 was about 25 percent larger than that of Britain. Among other things, this increase in population allowed for increased recruitments into the armed forces. With these national achievements,

---

[251] Ibid.

[252] Ibid., p. 64. See also Paul Kennedy, *The Rise and Fall of Great Powers* (New York: Vintage Books, 1989), pp. 201, 198–202.

[253] Allison, op. cit., p. 65.

[254] Ibid.

"many Germans felt short-changed. The future, they believed, belonged not to European 'Great Powers' but to what had come to be known as 'World Powers': superpowers whose size, population, and resources" would allow for shared domination of the twentieth century.[255] Britain, because of the mission given it by an "all-wise hand," was opposed.

Germany, as reflected in the well-known statement of Germany's foreign minister, Bernhard von Bulow, without seeking to put "anyone in the shadow," would "demand [its] place in the sun."[256] That place included the establishment of colonies worldwide and a navy that would reflect that worldwide standing. Since any such naval expansion, to please Britain, would have to be done *within* the controlling confines of a London-dominant world system, Berlin's efforts—seeking at once to win the respect of London and reset the latter's control—would have to act *outside* that system.

Through a series of naval laws (1898, 1901, 1906, and 1908), Germany either increased the size of its navy or refined its development. The first, which called for a total of nineteen battleships, under the leadership of Admiral Alfred von Tirpitz, was seen by him as a means to help Germany earn the respect that it desired and deserved. By the time of the Second Naval Law, which doubled the size of Germany's navy to thirty-eight battleships, Britain came to know that the future would be defined by a significant rivalry with Germany. For Allison, the June 1904 visit to Germany by King Edward VII "for the Kiel Regatta" allowed Kaiser Wilhelm the "pleasure [of] showing off as much of the German navy as possible . . . Within a month of Wilhelm's rash display at Kiel, Britain had made the first official plans for war with Germany."[257] By 1914, Germany's navy had grown from sixth to second, after Britain's.

Allison then went into some details to show how the Germans became even more committed to their navy building, using two experiences to help in his explanation. The first focused on the work of the American naval strategist Capt. Alfred T. Mahan. In this case, the

---

[255] Ibid., p. 65.

[256] Ibid., p. 66.

[257] Ibid., p. 71.

kaiser had come upon the rather brilliant work of Captain Mahan, *The Influence of Sea Power upon History*, which became a naval bible for not only some leaders in the US, especially TR, but also elsewhere in the world.[258] Allison noted that the kaiser not only tried to "learn it by heart" but also ordered copies for every ship in his fleet. The contention of the book is that naval forces were indispensable to the development of global military and economic dominance and thus served as confirming evidence for Berlin's strongly held preexisting views. The second point of focus is the motivation that has come to be called the "Copenhagen Complex"—a fear in Germany, especially in the kaiser's mind, that supported the building of a strong navy. In 1807, the British engaged in a preemptive attack on Copenhagen, capturing the Danish fleet to deny its capture and use by Napoleon Bonaparte.[259] This fear of a preemptive naval strike against Germany by Britain emboldened the Germans even more to build a formidable fleet.

Political humiliations (by way of a parenthesis) were visited on Germany during the 1906 Moroccan Crisis, which left it isolated, followed by two others—one in 1908, which had Germany settling for much less than it sought and watching France (aided by Britain) gaining control of Morocco, and the other in 1912–1913, during which Berlin's interests in the Balkans were inadequately protected. These incidents, in Allison's view, reinforced in Germany the felt need to find ways to better protect its interests and at least better test the strength of emerging or established political alignments that Britain, France, and Russia had formed while working to strengthen its own alliance system. The latter, which came into being in 1882, was known as the Triple Alliance, composed of Germany, Austro-Hungary, and Italy. The UK, France, and Russia belonged to the Triple Entente, which was formed in 1907. Both alliances, based on an elaborate system of mobilization

---

[258] Japan, the UK, Russia, Italy, and France were among the countries in which the work gained fame.

[259] See Jonathan Steinberg, "The Copenhagen Complex," in *Journal of Contemporary History*, Vol. 1, #3 (1966), pp. 23–46. See also Hans Christian Bjerg, "To Copenhagen a Fleet: The British Pre-emptive Seizure of the Danish-Norwegian Navy," in *International Journal of Naval History*, Vol. 7, #2 (August 2008), pp. 1–13.

schedule and armed with the then most lethal weapons, were, at different times, tested, including in some of the incidents mentioned that caused embarrassment to Germany. Some also occasioned discomfitures for Russia and France.

For Britain—which, until its 1904 Entente Cordiale with France, had tried for generations to remain free to align itself with whatever continental power's policies complemented its interests—the alliance represented a departure, a realignment of diplomatic orientation, but that realignment was deemed necessary to contain Germany. It was a required complement to the supremacy of the British navy, which, according to Chancellor of the Exchequer David Lloyd George (reminiscent of the earlier quote of Churchill) was "not only essential to our national existence but [also essential] to the vital interests of Western civilization."[260]

From 1909 to 1912, Allison notes that Anglo-German discussions, at different times, took place to determine whether there were grounds for mutual accommodation. Britain wanted Germany to accept its naval supremacy in return for London's help to Berlin in the latter's search for additional colonies. Germany wanted Britain to commit to neutrality, in case of a European war, in return for a reduction in the pace of growth in its naval program. There was no agreement. In February 1913, however, Berlin and London came up with a formula. Berlin accepted a 16:10 battleship ratio, in favor of London, and yet the June 28, 1914, assassination of the Austrian crown prince Franz Ferdinand in Sarajevo, Bosnia, precipitated the long-feared war between Britain and Germany.

For Allison, while the entangling alliances proved to be the "last straw" in the move toward war, the real cause is to be found in the "Thucydidean dynamic." The foundation for the war resided in the arms race between London and Berlin. In other words, "while Germany's growing economic challenge to England had [made] strategic rivalry between the two nations inevitable . . . the growth of the German navy posed a unique existential threat."[261] The just-touched-on conceding, by Germany, of naval superiority to Britain, in Allison's view, was but a

---

[260] Quoted in Allison, op. cit., p. 77.

[261] Ibid., pp. 80–81.

tactical response to domestic constraints that would later change. Thus, when, in 1914, Germany invaded France and the Low Countries, "war seemed preferable to the prospect of Germany achieving dominance on the Continent."[262]

He then posited a second implicated example of the Thucydidean dynamic: that Germany decided to go to war to preempt Russia (which, with French loans, had recovered from its shame-filled defeat by Japan in 1905) from outnumbering, by 1917, Germany's army by "three to one." The latter development would mean the death of Berlin's two-front war strategy (created in 1905 and named the Schlieffen Plan), which called for a quick victory over France and the turning east to extend the war against Russia, the slower mobilization of whose army would allow for such a maneuver. Finally, Allison noted that Germany took the step it did, in part to save its vulnerable ally, the Austro-Hungarian empire, which would have collapsed if it were not able to crush its enemies in the Balkans.

[262]   Ibid.

CHAPTER 9
Another Past

As in the case of the US and Japan, there is another narrative that we will proceed to advance more fully after we shall have identified some weaknesses in Allison's presentation to us. Unlike the examples of Athens versus Sparta and Japan versus the US, where specific claims (apart from the main thesis) were left largely uncriticized because we think such criticism would best be included in the summarizing area of the concluding chapter, we think it is advisable to touch on certain shortcomings of his book to highlight better some area of this alternate narrative. We touch on four points of emphasis: naval supremacy, intention and capability, ascribing to Germany-only sentiments widely shared, and the matter of equality.

With respect to the issue of naval supremacy, which Britain enjoyed before and throughout the period under discussion, Allison's position is that this standing enjoyed by London was "non-negotiable"[263] and, as such, should have been accepted by Germany as a point of departure for its interactions with Britain.[264] This stance, among others, shaped the recounting of events in a way that unduly favored London and, correspondingly, created a view of Germany that was, at times, unreasonably harsh. In fact, if one speaks of negotiations among sovereign entities, the major area of differences among them can never

---

[263] Ibid., p. 46.

[264] Ibid.

be defensibly said to be nonnegotiable. In 1925, at the LNC, not only were negotiations concerning Britain's naval supremacy engaged in, but also, after extended discussions and pressure from Washington, London conceded equality with the US.[265]

The issue of intention versus capability was one in which Allison seemingly took or found ready support from one of the most famous memoranda in international diplomacy, one delivered by Sir Eyre Crowe to the British Foreign Office in 1907, advocating and justifying certain stances against Germany.[266] In that document, he urged Britain to focus on Germany's capability, not its intentions, since even the noblest intentions (ostensibly including those of Britain) can be transmuted to ignoble ends once certain capabilities are achieved. In the depictions of the interactions between London and Berlin, Allison frequently emphasized Germany's capabilities and British intentions. So does Crowe's memo, rejecting Berlin's stated intentions as something London could not trust yet expecting Germany to accept Britain's intentions, not its overwhelming naval capabilities.

The third weakness in Allison's historical recounting (and thus his conclusion) is related to the first and second weaknesses. It concerns what he inaccurately portrays as beliefs that they (the Germans) harbored about the future and casts those ascribed beliefs in a manner implying a failing when it was a body of sentiments shared by Europeans then and, indeed, all the major powers of the world, as the last chapter hopefully indicted. In fact, TCM referred to this idea. It is that the future, as then seen from the major European capitals, would belong not to European great powers but to what had come to be known as world power—what people in the second half of the twentieth century referred to as superpowers. These countries—by virtue of their size, population, and resources—would dominate the twentieth century. Germany wanted to be one of these powers, but a prerequisite to enjoy that status, with its associated respect and prestige, was the gaining of colonies and a fleet that could not only protect them but, as well, augment that protection

---

[265] Tate, op. cit., 161–184.

[266] See "Memorandum on the Present State of British Relations with France and Germany" (hereafter cited as "the Crowe Memo" or TCM).

among other world powers. The ideology of imperialism to which this "world power" sentiment and outlook was linked, we will come to later.

A final weakness in the portrait of events leading to World War I is Allison's references to equality, perhaps the most explicit of which he quotes Alfred von Tirpitz as seeking equality with Britain.[267] He did not take such claims on the part of Germany seriously; they suggest intention. So in this very important respect, his analysis of events is wanting. This brings us to the wider counter-narrative, which contends that the dominant issue then at hand between Britain and Germany (as it was with Athens and Sparta as well as the US and Japan) was never the threatened replacement of an existing leading power but the threat of the presence or the gaining of equality with that power. We will seek to prove this.

"The accomplishment of German unity" in 1871 "may well be regarded, especially in retrospect," said historian Rene Albrecht-Carrie, "as the most important event of the whole nineteenth century."[268] Since then, in large measure because of the reaction of other countries to this unity, that country has been the center of European history. This accomplishment, on the part of Germany, took place within the context of a multipolar balance of power system in Europe and throughout the world with Austro-Hungary, Britain, France, Germany, Italy, Russia, and the US (and later Japan), furthering an agenda of forging, for their respective societies, the coveted status of world great power. That agenda, in turn, was embedded in three dominant ideological orientations: nationalism, liberalism, and socialism.[269] The first, as mentioned in the preceding chapter, espoused the right of peoples constituting a nation to unite as sovereign entities and to pursue their own unhampered development without limitation by other nations.

---

[267] Allison, op. cit., p. 70.

[268] Rene Albrecht-Carrie, *Europe Since 1815* (New York: Harper & Brothers Publishers, 1962), p. 212. There are few books on Europe that are as insightful and integrative as this work.

[269] A reasonable summary of these ideologies may be delightfully read, especially because of the foregrounding of economic issues, in Robert Heilbroner, *The Worldly Philosophers* (New York: Simon & Schuster, 1995).

Explicitly or implicitly, nationalism also accepted as part of its tenet aspects a nineteenth-century belief called Social Darwinism, which claimed that nations, as in the case of other groupings—forests, planets, animals, and plants—evolve. In the process of their evolution, there are struggles and conflicts within and between groups, with some (enjoying capabilities to adapt) surviving and others (lacking those capabilities) progressively becoming extinct. These adaptations, surviving while others perish (called "survival of the fittest"), whatever the "adaptive capacities" happen to be, should not only be protected but also be extended for the good of the human species. These capabilities, of course, include not only the inherited human individual and collective characteristics but culture (civilization) as well—a major justification for imperialism.

In the case of liberalism, which encompasses democracy and the free-market economy (capitalism), it held sway, with some competition from mercantilism, which, although embracing capitalism in principle and practice, believed in more active government involvement in the development and allocation of resources on behalf of society. Socialism, especially its Marxist subgrouping represented by social democratic parties throughout Europe, took up the cause of economic equality and was agitated on behalf of the industrial working class, which became less and less concerned with obeying their "betters" than asserting their claims to their "rightful place in society."[270]

Within the context of the multipolar world, in which every great power was viewed as a potential threat to the other, in which complementary and conflicting ideological values—from nationalism to liberalism and socialism, among others—coexisted, and in which certain oppressed groups (in the Balkans, in South and Southeast Asia, in Egypt, and in South Africa, to identify a few areas) sought a greater say in their own respective development, Britain became preoccupied with one cause: the containment of a feared challenge of Germany to its perceived and actual place in the world. We will look at two statements of this threat from two different sources: the earlier cited January 1907 memorandum from Sir Eyre Crowe and one from Sir Edward Grey, foreign secretary,

---

[270] Albrecht-Carrie, op. cit., p. 163.

in August 1914, as the British Cabinet was deliberating whether or not to go to war.

Expressive of a claimed megalomaniacal ambition of the Germans, TCM argued and warned "that Germany distinctly aims at playing on the world's political stage a much larger and much more dominant part than she finds allotted to herself under the present distribution of material power" and that this aim, "backed by force," would seek to "diminish the power of any rivals, to enhance her own [power] by extending her dominion, to hinder co-operation of other states, and ultimately to *break up* and *supplant* [emphasis the author's] the British Empire."[271] Who "allotted" the then present distribution of power, Crowe did not say (it could be the same "all-wise hand" that sought to limit Germany in favor of Britain). There was "conclusive evidence," argued TCM, for a two-step progression toward the goal Germany had set for itself: "the establishment of a German hegemony . . . in Europe and eventually the world."[272]

Between 1907 and 1914, there were many developments, some of which we will be discussing in some of the pages immediately following. Before we do, however, we should examine the just-mentioned statement in relationship to one uttered by Sir Edward Grey as he sought to remind a divided British Cabinet that a "fundamental premise" of "national interest was bound up with the preservation of France" (one of those countries whose power Germany, according to the 1907 memorandum, would seek to diminish to enhance its own).[273] This reasoning, argued Barbara Tuchman, was best captured in an "epic" sentence by Grey: "If Germany dominated the Continent, it would be disagreeable to us as well as others, for we would be isolated."[274] In this "epic" sentence, Tuchman wrote, was "all of British policy, and from it followed the knowledge that if the challenge were flung, England would have to fight

---

[271] See Crowe's memo.

[272] Ibid.

[273] Barbara W. Tuchman, *The Guns of August* (New York: Bantam Books, 1989), p. 112.

[274] Ibid. This is a quote in the book by Tuchman.

to prevent that 'disagreeable' outcome."[275] Let it be observed here, in reflecting on the two statements, that TCM was submitted to the foreign office led by Grey.

Were one to take the claimed megalomaniacal ambitions of Germany advanced as the only or even the primary source of Berlin's conduct—as some, including Allison, have done[276]—one would have not only an inaccurate sense of what alternatives and important political formations or developments Germany and Britain faced and the more nuanced and all-pervasively subtle containment political tactics recommended by TCM but also, far more important, from the standpoint of the thesis of this chapter, some of the real fears of Britain, as represented by certain conservative elites. These fears are to be found in many areas of TCM and in policy, in statements by German officials, and in the psychological dimensions of imperialism and the then embraced sentimental ideal of world power. TCM offered a clear understanding that Britain would have to deal with Germany. To do so successfully, however, London should follow a basic strategy. While taking an unbending stance against the ambitions that it identified with Germany (whether those ambitions were grounded on "conclusive evidence . . . or unpublished intentions," the latter meaning that for which there is no evidence), London should offer some inducements to Berlin that might allow Germany to change its ambitions.

Included in those inducements or incentives were to be recognition that "the mere existence and healthy activity [as defined by London, of course] of a powerful Germany is a social and moral kinship that is an undoubted blessing to the world"; that it represented "in a pre-eminent degree those highest qualities and virtues of good citizenship . . . which constitute the glory and triumph of modern civilization"; and that the "world would be unmeasurably the poorer if everything that is specifically associated with German character, German ideas, and German methods were to cease having power and influence."[277] An

---

[275] Ibid.

[276] Nail Ferguson, *The Pity of War* (New York: Basic Books, 1999). This work offers an excellent review of those influenced by this outlook.

[277] Crowe Memo, op. cit.

additional inducement would be to indicate that, for Britain in particular, "intellectual and moral kinship creates a sympathy and appreciation of what is best in the German mind" and, therefore, "has made her [Britain] naturally disposed to welcome, in the interest of the general progress of mankind, everything tending to strengthen" the just-mentioned power and influence Germany embodied.[278]

This to-be-constructed disposition to welcome such power and influence had one condition: "there must be respect for the individualities of other nations equally valuable . . . in their own way, in the work of human progress, equally entitled to full elbow room in which to contribute, in freedom, to the evolution of a higher human civilization."[279] Worth mentioning also is that TCM elevated France to a model to be emulated, by virtue of its imputed "sound instinct, [which had] always stood for unhampered play and interaction of national forces as most in accord with nature's own process of development.[280] Would it be prudent for Britain to trust that Germany would use its influence and power, its moral kinship with London, to join Britain (a self-described model) in promoting the "general progress" of humankind, especially if Berlin were to gain universal, preponderant power? We know, of course, that Britain was no such model, but we must pose the question because TCM did and responded no on four grounds: (1) past behavior; (2) world policy; (3) available space; and (4) naval ambitions.

In respect of past behavior, the memorandum went into an examination of many crises linked to colonial issue—from Egypt, Heligoland, Uganda, and Transvaal to Samoa, St. Lucia Bay, and the province of Shandong. These represented areas where Britain faced challenges of conspiracy, hostility, or dishonorable behavior from Germany. This type of behavior was unlikely to change, especially so because there were also earlier examples of like behavior following German Chancellor Otto von Bismarck's (1871–1890) launching, in 1884, of his country "into a colonial and maritime enterprise."[281]

---

[278] Ibid.

[279] Ibid.

[280] Ibid.

[281] Ibid.

This "enterprise" was, in fact, based on a decision by Germany not to be confined, as it had formally been (and Britain had hoped), to a continental focus in its pursued development but to become, instead, what we earlier described as a world power. The latter involved in the political culture of the day, as the reader will recall, the acquisition of colonies—as other world powers such as Britain, France, Italy, Russia, and the US (and latecomer Japan) either had or were vigorously pursuing.[282] London should and did interpret (as recommended by TCM) the move by Germany as a danger—a potential challenge to Britain's supremacy and the British Empire. Germany could not be trusted and needed to be opposed. Britain was compelled to oppose.

On the matter of space (available space for colonial expansion), Crowe sought to demonstrate that Germany could not be a trusted partner of Britain's because Berlin would have to fight to gain more of the rapidly disappearing areas for colonial expansion. Germany could follow the cause of Pan-Germanism (the political idea or principle recommending the unification of all Europeans speaking German) "with its outlying bastions in the Netherlands, in Scandinavian countries, in Switzerland, and the German provinces of Austria and on the Adriatic," but such a racial/ethnic foundation would be constructed on the wreck "of the liberties of Europe."[283] Additional special factors that cautioned against reposing trust in Germany are associated with regional "spheres of interest" or "spheres of influence" that other countries had or claimed. The "acquisition of colonies fit for German settlement in South America [could not] be reconciled with the Monroe doctrine"—a "fundamental principle and political faith" of the US,[284] the memorandum contended, and the "creation of a German India" in Asia Minor (roughly the Asian portion of modern Turkey plus portions of Armenia) would stand or fall on Germany's "command" of the sea and control of Constantinople.[285]

---

[282] One has but to look at French control of Tunisia (1881) and Indochina (1885) or British control of Egypt and Burma, for example, or even the US march into Cuba, Puerto Rico, Guam, the Philippines, and Hawaii.

[283] Crowe Memo, op. cit.

[284] Ibid.

[285] Ibid.

Britain could not entertain such command and control, however, since doing so would be tantamount to ceding to Germany control of Britain and the empire, an end that Berlin was believed to be pursuing in its "our future lies on the water" sentiment and policy. In short, there was no peaceful exit for Germany in its determined goal of achieving sought "world power" status that did not undermine some interest of Britain or other great powers. As such, London could not possibly trust Germany in respect of its likely future behavior, even if one were to overlook its past "dishonorable" conduct.

With little or no available unclaimed space left for colonization (Africa was already divided up, so it did not occupy much of the memorandum) and no opportunities for expansion in Europe, without violating the established rights of other countries and wreaking injury more generally, what might Germany do to gain satisfactory standing as a world power? It could, the memorandum suggested, "with malice aforethought," push for general political hegemony and maritime ascendency and thereby "threaten the independence of its neighbors and ultimately the existence of England," or it could, free of the just-indicated "clear-cut ambition," in an evolutionary way, simply use its legitimate standing as one of the leading powers "in the council of nations" to promote foreign commerce, spread the benefits of German culture, and create new (non-territorial) interest throughout the world wherever peaceful opportunities offer themselves, biding its time "to decide whether . . . changes in the world may not someday confer on [it] a larger share . . . over regions not now part of her dominion."[286] In either case, the memorandum continued, Germany would need as powerful a navy as it could afford.

Britain did not have to elect between the two alternatives suggested because according to the memorandum, it was "clear that the second scheme . . . may, at any stage, merge into the first."[287] So Britain should be prepared, whatever Germany does, to oppose it. For Germany, it would not matter what it did or thought; nor would the motives it had matter. Even if it acted in the most commendable manner internationally

---

[286] Ibid.

[287] Ibid.

and were accepted as a thriving, well-adjusted member of the "council of nations," that behavior and acceptance should be seen, by Britain, as nothing more than an ominous waiting, a biding of time, as long as Germany refused to give up the idea of becoming a global power, an equal of Britain, as opposed to a regional great power. A menacing naval capability will always be required, and this capacity, London could indulge.

Let us now examine at least some of the claims of the memorandum, with the reminder that it was submitted to Sir Edward Grey, whom we previously quoted, leader in foreign affairs. He and Crowe, with due recognition of those who question the memorandum's influence,[288] worked closely in the shaping and implementing of British foreign policy. To be borne in mind also, in carrying out this examination, is not only that all the major national actors were at once, in part or in whole, participants in, proponents of, inspired by, or fighters against liberalism, socialism, nationalism, and its offspring, imperialism, as we shall see, but also that each faced parliamentary or parliamentary-like scrutiny of and pressures on policy. There was also the matter of public opinion, overlooked by Allison but which works such as Niall Ferguson's *The Pity of War* admirably incorporates in his scholarly effort to explain World War I.[289]

A major aim of TCM was that of effecting some changes in public opinion, that of professionals and the public at large, an opinion that, until Grey's tenure at the foreign office, had been largely pro-German and anti-French and anti-Russian. The memorandum sought to reverse this; thus, one finds in its texts the following:

> It has often been declared, as to be a diplomatic platitude,
> that between England and Germany . . . there has never
> been any clashing of material interest, so there [are] no

---

[288] See, for example, Richard A. Cosgrove, "The Career of Sir Eyre Crowe: A Reassessment," in *Albion: A Quarterly Journal Concerned with British studies*, Vol. 4, #4 (Winter 1972), pp. 193–202. One has but to follow the course of London's policies toward Germany to refute claims that the memo had limited influence.

[289] Ferguson, op. cit.

unsettled controversies over outstanding questions. Yet for the past twenty years ... German governments have never ceased reproaching British Cabinets with want of friendliness and persistent opposition to German political plans.[290]

Crowe had gone into the archives of the foreign office to excavate past Anglo-German differences, which he and others used to advance his point of alleged unfriendliness and "persistent opposition," using, among other things, the names of countries or areas of the globe we previously mentioned. Let us use three as examples—Heligoland, Egypt, and Shandong—and, in doing so, show, at least partly, how stilted the memorandum was and how it helps explain what developed in Britain's foreign policy after Edward Grey became foreign minister.

In each case, Berlin and London found ways to settle some actual or potential colonial and other territorial claims, to the perceived interest of each, because up until 1903, Britain and Germany were both exploring the possibility of an alliance.[291] Heligoland, a small archipelago in the North Sea, was historically a part of the Schleswig-Holstein German state (an area that, until 1864, was a part of Denmark) and a part of Britain since 1807. Germany coveted it, in large measure because it offered its new navy control over the Kiel Canal and certain areas of the North Sea. The archipelago was ceded to Germany in 1890 through an Anglo-German treaty in return for Berlin's transfer of the island of Zanzibar to Britain as well as a recognition of the latter country's paramount interest in Kenya. Britain also agreed, as part of the overall accommodations, to Germany's acquisition of Tanganyika. Egypt was controversial, as we will touch on later, because London had occupied the country, beginning in 1882, under the guise of organizing its finances but, in fact, had never left. So other imperial powers, including Germany but especially France, were always criticizing London. Also, in the case of Shandong—a province of China that Germany, between 1891 and 1898, had used force to gain control of—there was special nervousness in London because that province contained Kiao-chau Bay,

---

[290] Crowe Memo, op. cit.

[291] Ferguson, op. cit., pp. 43–53.

which could potentially serve as a German naval base. The province was also rich in resources—a settlement to the detriment of China (which, like the Ottoman Empire in Europe, was seen by imperial Europe as "dying") but to the relative satisfaction of competing powers. Germany got to lease for the territory from China for ninety-nine years, something Britain did one year later in respect of Hong Kong; Russia and France, among others, also joined Britain that year, likewise gaining major concessions from a weakened China.

What is important here, for our consideration, are four points. First, Britain had disputes with Germany—many not mentioned, such as those over Transvaal, Morocco, Samoa, and St. Lucia Bay in the Caribbean—as she did with other imperial powers, especially France and Russia but also with the US. There was no good reason to pinpoint Germany as the primary threat to peace unless there was this felt need to alter public opinion radically. Second, the geographical range of the disputes suggests that Germany's interests were, in fact, global, although scattered and less substantial and, accordingly, less weighty in the political and military scales of imperial power—the result of its late entry into the imperial game. Third, in the mentioned Anglo-German differences, there was demonstrated evidence that Britain was prepared to make some concessions to accommodate Germany's interests and that Germany was willing and able to compromise in favor of Britain's interests. Finally, Britain, as the facts should reveal, far from being committed to the development of humankind, as the memorandum claims, was the leader in holding a view of the world that ensured that the interests of non-Europeans (except for the peoples of the Balkans, as we will see) were never consulted. Nationhood and nationalism were concepts to be manipulated in favor of one's imperial interests and against that of others.

What of London's foreign policy after Britain's April 8, 1904, Entente Cordiale with France, with that agreement's implied favorable linkage to Russia? These were two countries with which Britain had colonial and other differences that made those with Germany appear relatively puny. They were also the two countries against which the two-power naval policy was adopted in 1889 (to be later applied against Germany). The foreign office pursued what a courageous historian might defensibly call an "appeasement" policy, conceding to France and Russia claims that London had formerly fiercely opposed, offering some meagre returns to Britain, but really engaged in to further the cause of a stance of almost uncompromising opposition to Germany in Europe and the world at large.

Let us take Russia as an example since we will return to France on the next issue of alleged German militarism. Britain opposed, for many years, Russian expansion into Afghanistan (Central Asia in general), Persia, the Balkans, the Black Sea area in general, and China, including Tibet. With respect to Tibet and Persia, the latter was secretly divided into two spheres, the north going to Russia, the south to Britain; Tibet was understood to be a "buffer state" under British interest, in return for conceding to Moscow greater freedom in Central Asia. The containing of Russia (since 1853) through the Black Sea straits was dropped (Moscow could freely use it), and expansion into Afghanistan was conceded, providing it did not threaten British interests in India. Also, with respect to the Balkans, Grey, favoring Moscow (especially after Austria had annexed Bosnia and Herzegovina in 1908), "sanctioned the Russian sponsorship of Balkan Slav nationalism,"[292] uncomfortable as he was about making peace in the area, dependent on "Serbia restraining itself."[293] The encouragement of "Balkan Slav nationalism" will, of course, became more and more significant.

The final major theme, from the context of this work, that was explicitly raised by TCM to demonstrate Germany's alleged megalomania is an ascribed culture of militarism. It was this claimed culture of militarism, specifically embodied and expressed in Berlin's navy, that constituted, according to Allison, the claimed "existential threat" to Britain. To Crowe, the threat, the focus on military domination, was the means by which Berlin could gain "on the world stage" a more "dominant part" than that "allotted" to it by the then existing international arrangements.[294] That threat, along with the mobilization

---

[292] Ibid., pp. 60–61.

[293] Ibid., p. 61, quoted in Ferguson.

[294] Crowe's memo, op. cit.

schedule that nations had organized, in Allison's view, occasioned the war. The evidence does not support the claim, however.

While it can easily be shown that Berlin sponsored a succession of navy laws, earlier identified in this chapter, it is the case that following Britain's introduction of *Dreadnought* in 1906,[295] it decided to concentrate more on matching that type of battleship through a focus on disrupting merchant vessels rather than an all-out *Dreadnought* rivalry. Second, while Germany's buildup in the North Sea was impressive, that buildup was itself confining and no match for Britain's continued building and upgrading of a worldwide infrastructure of bases and their support—Gibraltar, Malta, Port Said, Aden, Colombo, Rangoon, Singapore, and even Hong Kong (including Weihaiwei), among others.[296] Britain's leaders knew well the limitations of the German navy, especially its regional capability.[297] Third, the Liberal Party, which led Britain between 1905 and 1914, was generally (as distinct from an elite core that colluded with the Conservative Party) indisposed to go to war with Germany or war generally. Grey's gaining of continuing support for the Entente Cordiale was dependent on his receiving support from those conservatives.[298] In fact, the transformation of the entente from a contingent defense arrangement into a military engagement with joint war planning was a development unknown to the cabinet in general and to the country as a whole.[299] This is why, in the midst of the Balkan crisis, during the summer of 1914, Grey knew he could not receive cabinet support to go to war and, in the end, had to resort to Germany's violation of Belgium's neutrality—an issue discussed long before 1914.

---

[295] This was a type of battleship that revolutionized naval power by virtue of its size, speed, stability (especially in heavy seas), and gun caliber.

[296] Margaret MacMillan, *The War that Ended Peace: The Road to 1914* (New York: Random House, 2014), pp. 120–124.

[297] Ibid.

[298] Ferguson, op. cit., pp. 62–63, 56–80.

[299] Ibid., p. 36. Here, one finds Ferguson's reference to the Liberal League, an important faction within the Liberal Party, to which Prime Minister Asquith, War Minister Haldane, and Foreign Minister Grey belonged. For a broader view of the liberals, see H. C. G. Matthew, *The Liberal Imperialists* (Oxford: Oxford University Press, 1973).

With regard to Germany, there was a consistent anti-militarist position in the Reichstag, especially during the time of Edward Grey and particularly after 1912, when the Social Democratic Party of Germany (SDP) gave a two-to-one lashing to the National Liberals (then the most committed party to an aggressive German foreign policy) and became the largest party in parliament. Unlike the Liberal Party in Britain,[300] the SPD was totally opposed to Germany's imperial project and pledged an increased role in social legislation in favor of workers and in opposition to budgetary increases for the navy (it had influence on the budget and so could only indirectly affect foreign policy, which the kaiser controlled). Indeed, German elites had become fearful of going to war because a defeat of Germany was seen as likely, allowing for a radical reorganization of society, most likely under the leadership of the SPD.[301]

Viewing the military planning under the Entente Cordiale, the wholesale reforms between 1904 and 1910 of the British navy by John Fisher, first sea lord (the professional head of the British Royal Navy), the investments on meeting the two-power standard, and the boxing-in of Germany between rising military pressures of Russia and France,[302] one could see Britain as manifesting more "militarism" than that attributed to Germany. It is not necessary to delve into the issue here; what can be noted is that by 1914, both Germany and Britain had arrived at an understanding.[303] The fear of German naval buildup, contrary to its reputation, was never to surpass Britain but rather to make it unacceptably costly for London to engage Germany in a war, as Grand Admiral Alfred von Tirpitz so clearly indicated.[304] Of course, the Reichstag was less disposed to support a navy to supersede Britain than the British Parliament was to ensure London's supremacy,[305] in

---

[300] See Peter Nettl, "The German Social Democratic Party, 1890–1914 as a Political Model," in *Past and Present*, No. 30 (April 1965), pp. 65–95.

[301] Ibid.

[302] Ferguson, *The Pity of War,* op. cit., p. 85.

[303] Ferguson, *Empire* (New York: Basic Books, 2002), p. 248.

[304] MacMillan, op. cit., pp. 104–105.

[305] Ibid., p. 99.

part, one may say, because of the greater pressures in Germany for support of social programs.

By 1914, Britain had achieved a 2:1 ratio advantage in naval power over Germany[306]; its mercantile marines (always built and organized in anticipation of war) were still more than three-fifths of the world's and its shipbuilding industry unexampled.[307] Militarism, far from being "a dominant force in European politics on the eve of the Great War . . . was in political decline."[308]

Let us now look at the role of colonies as a way of integrating naval policy, industrial-military power, available space, culture, and domestic politics (of Britain and Germany) and also as a route to return to our thesis on equality. The matter of colonies was central to imperialism, as before indicated, the imperial vision (including its claimed ideals), and our understanding of military power, especially the naval rivalry that preceded and followed World War I. In the latter regard, there was a "cult of the navy," through which societies lived, and no one better encapsulates the relationship among the navy, colonies, and economic-military power and imperial dominance than Capt. Alfred T. Mahan. He, one of the originators of the cult, saw sea power as the most effective means of warfare and understood that production in an industrial age was not for personal or even national consumption only but for a broader exchange outside the limits of home, cities, and the borders of states. That exchange, in his view, was facilitated and expanded by colonies, and that expansion was a means to economic wealth and power. Naval forces promote, connect, and protect that expansion and exchange as well as the colonies and the mother country.[309]

In short, colonies, in his view, were linked to economic and military power. They, in fact, reinforce each other, especially in the investment

[306] See Kennedy, op. cit., pp. 198–203. See also Ferguson, op. cit., *The Pity of War*, op. cit., pp. 84–85.

[307]

[308] Ferguson, *The Pity of War,* op. cit., p. 28. This work's first chapter, "The Myth of Militarism," is a fine study.

[309] Alfred T. Mahan, *The Influence of Sea Power Upon History, 1660–1783* (Boston: Little, Brown and Co., 1890), p. 28.

field, with portfolio investments (such as in railroads, harbors, canals, ports, and other units of infrastructure) in general as well as the ever-present financing and refinancing of debts, so exactingly captured by David Landes in his classic work on Egypt.[310] Indeed, but for income from existing foreign investment, Britain would have faced insurmountable problems in pursuing new export of capital.[311] It certainly would have hampered the expansion and upkeep of the armed forces, especially the navy, if one takes into view that in the "two decades before the 1914, overall defense spending took up approximately 40 percent of the British government expenditures, a higher proportion than that of any other great power."[312]

Colonies also served as sites to which excess or undeserving (or less deserving) national population groups were encouraged or forced to go, and they were locations from which military and other pressures could be brought to bear on domestic rivals and rival countries.[313] They were likewise territories where shipping companies, bankers, traders, speculators, explorers, scholars, and missionaries, among others, sought to go, hence the effective and popular lobbying of groups such as the German Colonial League and the Company for German Colonization (and their counterparts in Britain and France).[314]

Colonies served other roles too. Among them, they functioned as outposts for future expansion—especially in the area of practiced "territorial compensation," by which one state is conceded claim to an area of the globe, providing other imperial countries are allowed equivalent "compensation" elsewhere. They also serve the larger role of helping confer important status, socially and nationally, the latter having to do with global reach. Lord Salisbury, who served as both foreign secretary and prime minister of Great Britain, expressed this

[310] David S. Landes, *Bankers and Pashas: International Finance and Economic Imperialism in Egypt* (Cambridge: Harvard University Press, 1958).

[311] Ferguson, *The Pity of War,* op. cit., p. 37.

[312] MacMillan, op. cit., p. 118.

[313] Jan Ruger, *The Great Naval Game: Britain and Germany in the Age of Empire* (Cambridge: Cambridge University Press, 2009).

[314] Knapton & Derry, op. cit., p. 318.

function best when he referred to the need for some colonies, the utility of which was not self-evident. He saw them as "pegging our claims for the future"[315]—that is, they serve as strangleholds, as handcuffs against other countries in terms of what the latter might seek to do without negotiating with the imperial power that owned adjoining territories. International custom then embraced the principle that "propinquity" conferred special interest in territorial claims. This was why those countries that had more territories gained more and why Britain, by 1914, had control of about 24 percent of the land area of the world and 23 percent of its population.

With respect to the issue of social and cultural status, we often think of colonies as offering resources such as minerals and food but less so in terms of how they affect culture, lifestyles, status, and prestige. Woodruff Smith, in his *Consumption and the Making of Respectability*, has, in a significant way, helped us understand this area. Colonies supplied rich, "exotic" art, foods, spices, clothing, condiments, important evidence in the areas of social and natural sciences, and a test of orientation toward cosmopolitanism, which was viewed as a sign of some enlightenment. The opportunity to purchase, possess, have knowledge about, write concerning, and shape lifestyles according to those cultures became a basis for coveted status and respectability in Europe and elsewhere. That respectability has spillover effects on subnational institutions (research and historical societies, libraries, museums, universities, churches, among others).[316] The country whose borders encompassed more of these colonies (and the opportunities they afforded) was viewed as occupying a political sphere above and beyond others. It was an imperial class system in which Britain occupied the top position.

A final sphere on behalf of which colonies served was that of helping in the area of national unity for empire-states and a reinforcement of their identity as well as grounds for military intervention against military power on the home front, in the colony, or internationally in general. Colonies—whether in Indochina, South Asia, the Middle East, Africa, the Balkans, or elsewhere—were sites of unrest, resistance,

---

[315] MacMillan, op. cit., p. 90.

[316] See Woodruff Smith, *Consumption and the Making of Respectability, 1600–1800* (New York: Routledge, 2002)

rebellion, and death.[317] These unrest and resistance were often used as justifications for military interventions (whether in Afghanistan, Bosnia, Egypt, Mexico, or Vietnam). These interventions would often become "worldwide events" providing opportunities for patriotic fulminations, "radical" denunciations, budgetary adjustments, identity formation reinforcement, the increased sale of newspapers, and, yes, augmentation of national unity.

All the paybacks from colonies touched on above were part of the rich returns that Germany sought and against which Britain fought. Britain's containment of Germany in the latter's colonization ambitions did not occasion an Anglo-German war. By 1914, confident in having won the naval rivalry and thus Germany's attempt to expand throughout the world, London began discussions with Berlin concerning their mutual interests in the perceived coming disintegration of the Ottoman Empire.

We can now turn to a continuation of the thesis of the alternative narrative, with the understanding that it was not Germany's megalomania, the colonial issues, the naval rivalry, the militarism, or the control of Europe unified under German leadership that was the foundational cause of the war. Rather, we continue to argue that it was the threat of equality.

Not by Fact Alone

The marshaled facts in support of the case of Germany's alleged race to replace Britain have made it challenging to question the case. Human events are not best understood or reliably embodying of truth by what are presented as facts, however. The flavor and larger context of those facts must be *included*—as we have sought to do in our alternative narrative.[318] That inclusion should take into account here what we mean

---

[317] Albert Camus, *Resistance, Rebellion, and Death*, trans. by Justin O'Brien (New York: Modern Library, 1963). Joseph Conrad, *Tales of Unrest* (Penguin Books, 1977), speaks to the same issue.

[318] John Clive, *Not by Fact Alone: Essays on Writing and Reading of History* (Boston: Houghton Mifflin Company, 1989).

by the term "equality" and the domination involved in what is claimed to be "ruling," ascendant, predominant, hegemonic, or dominant power.

Germany, in 1871, had achieved on a national basis what the American philosopher John Rawls called "the most important primary good, self-respect."[319] The latter includes a person's or nation's sense of (her/his) its own value, a "secure conviction" that its conception of its good, its plan of national interest, is worth carrying out.[320] Self-esteem, which nations (like individuals) seek, stems from, in large measure, the recognition by associates (other countries and people) that one's plan of action is worth pursuing, and this recognition strengthens self-respect and self-esteem since it tends to reduce the "likelihood of failure and provide support against self-doubt when mishaps occur."[321] Self-respect also bears with it an implied confidence in one's ability "to fulfill one's intentions"—with "ability" understood to include power.[322] On the other hand, to the extent that one (person or nation) feels that one's plans are not worth pursuing or is plagued with self-doubt about them, one may become lacking in will to strive for them.[323]

In its relations with Britain, Germany sought the recognition of its plan of action, which included gaining the standing of world power, as was enjoyed by the UK, France, and Russia (Berlin also included the US in this grouping). Its primary focus was on Britain, however, because London, in Allison's phrasing, was the *ruling* power. This pursued aim of Germany emerged in many forms, on some of which we now focus.

Between 1899 and 1901, for example, despite what was then taking place elsewhere, London and Berlin were discussing the possibility of a defensive alliance that, were it agreed to, would have resulted in each country pursuing its own interest (its own plan of action) while being solicitous of its alliance partner's interest.[324] (The reach of that

---

[319] John Rawls, *A Theory of Justice* (Cambridge: Cambridge University Press, 1971), p. 440.

[320] Ibid.

[321] Ibid.

[322] Ibid.

[323] Ibid.

[324] Ferguson, *The Pity of War,* op. cit., pp. 49–50.

alliance would extend to China, where, the reader will recall, Britain worried about the motives and actions of the Russians.) The discussions failed because Germany insisted, as any self-respecting nation seeking equality would, on "full reciprocity"[325]—that is, complementarity, roughly equal give-and-take, as distinct from positions originating primarily or exclusively from London.[326] Were one to look at the pursuit of equality from the standpoint of Admiral Alfred von Tirpitz—who, at the same time, was working closely with Kaiser Wilhelm II—one would find that his view was that if Germany wanted to be one of the major world powers, it was advisable to build a big navy so that it could be one with those world powers (he named four: Russia, England, America, and Germany).[327] In short, Germany was thinking of itself as a member of a group of equals, even if this was not mathematically so. More tellingly, even as Tirpitz sought to have the Reichstag double its support for expansion of the German navy, doubling the naval fleet, he was never seeking to exceed the power of the Royal Navy. On the contrary, he was seeking equality in the sense of not having to bow to the dictates of the ruling power, having the relative freedom to pursue its self-defined plans for the perceived national good of Germany (its emerging envisioned empire), and having the capacity to give effect those plans. In his view, Germany, with forty-four capital ships (he knew Britain had many more), would have opportunities or "good chances through geographical position, military system, torpedo boats, tactical training, organizational development, and leadership" to ensure that London "will have lost [any] inclination to attack us and will, as a result, coincide with your Majesty sufficient naval presence . . . for the conduct of a grand policy overseas."[328]

Stated in another way, what Tirpitz was saying is that Germany sought, above all, to avoid pursuing its own contemplated expansion

---

[325]   Ibid., p. 50.

[326]   The reader may note that Britain, the following year (1902), demonstrating that it had alternatives to an alliance with Germany in seeking to contain Russia in the East, concluded a treaty with Japan.

[327]   Kennedy, op. cit., p. 196.

[328]   MacMillan, op. cit., p. 108.

within the restrictions of a British-dominated world system in which it would have had little or no chance for equality[329] but to create, instead, space outside of that system that would enable it to maneuver according to its self-defined plans. The key phrase in Tirpitz's position is that Germany would have "sufficient [naval] presence," not a superseding one, that would make it so costly for London to attack it that it could have latitude to act independently. (This is what we today call deterrence or deterrence capability, something that North Korea, for example, is pursuing in its acquisition of nuclear weapons, making it too costly for the US to attack it.) Britain, of course, sought to thwart all this effort by exaggerating their meaning, questioning their legitimacy (presenting them in such a way that they were not viewed as acceptable), and finding allies to contain Germany. All these oppositional tactics were central to TCM and tersely captured in the notion that Germany was not to be trusted, even if it were "merely using her legitimate position and influence as one of the leading powers in the council of nations."[330]

The evidence for the pursuit of equality by Germany emerges in other areas—those designed to gain the type of respect and esteem seen as due and incident to equality and those reflecting the view from Britain itself—in Crowe's 1907 document, and the evidence was contained in the view of a third party, namely, Japan. In the case of effort to secure the respect that it thought was its due, one finds Germany threatening to withdraw its ambassador to Britain because, it claimed, Prime Minister Salisbury was treating Germany as if he "cared no more for us than for Portugal, Chile, or the Patagonians."[331] One finds an equivalent stance in an 1897 speech by German Foreign Minister Bulow, insisting that in the partition of China, Berlin "must demand" that German missionaries, entrepreneurs, and goods and the German flag are "just as respected" as those of other foreign countries; that Germany was prepared to respect the interests of other powers in Asia so long as its own are, in turn,

---

[329] Michael Howard, *The Continental Commitment* (London: Ashfield Press, 1989), p. 32.

[330] See Crowe's memo.

[331] Quoted in MacMillan, op. cit., p. 61.

respected; and that while Germany does not seek "to put anyone" in "the shade," it would "demand [its] place in the sun."[332]

Another example on the preceding theme and one linked to how Britain saw Germany in 1907 should be helpful here and for later discussion. In 1893, in the context of discussions about Germany's gaining some influence abroad comparable to other great powers, the kaiser had observed that without "being a world figure [having colonies], one was nothing but a poor appearance," and in 1900, he asserted, as Germany launched a new battleship, that in "distant areas [outside of Europe], no important decision should be taken without the German Kaiser."[333]

If one wants to understand Berlin's frowning at the French (with the UK's support) taking over Morocco (1906 and 1911), without discussions with Berlin, one must understand Germany's search for inclusion, an equal say, not a Berlin that was seeking domination, as Allison suggests. The position taken by Crowe in his 1907 document also supports the view of Germany's search for equality, as the following quote (the emphases are this author's) should help demonstrate:

> Sailing across the ocean in German ships, German merchants began for the first time to divine the true position of countries such as England, the United States, France, and even the Netherlands, *whose political influence extends to distant seas and continents.* The colonies and foreign possessions of England more especially were seen to give that country a recognized and enviable status in the world where the name of Germany, if mentioned at all, excited no particular interest . . . Here was a vast province of human activity to which *the mere title and rank of a European Great Power* were not in themselves a sufficient passport. Here in a field of [portentous] magnitude, dwarfing altogether the proportions of European countries, others, who had been perhaps rather looked down

---

[332] Knapton and Derry, op. cit., p. 330.

[333] MacMillan, op. cit., p. 87.

upon as comparatively smaller folk, were at home and commanded, whilst Germany was at best received as an honored guest. Here was a *distinct inequality*, with a heavy bias in favor of the maritime and colonizing Powers.[334]

The quote captures exactly what the kaiser was saying a few paragraphs ago: that Germany's presence, status, and prestige abroad were minimal; that if it were to be a world power, the status as a "great power" in Europe was insufficient; and that the acquisition of colonies was a precondition for it to escape the inequality the European great power status, by itself reinforced. Even the Netherlands, noted TCM, had political influence that outdistanced Germany's, and France, which Berlin had defeated, had recouped its prestige and influence by virtue of its worldwide colonial reach. Colonies, however, needed sea power, naval power. Britain largely succeeded in its effort to confine Germany to Europe.

Japan, experiencing and reviewing what was taking place on the world stage, also provided some evidence of the equality thesis. In a document prepared before the Paris Peace Conference that ended World War I, it observed that Britain, France, and other countries had "colonized the 'less civilized' regions of the world and monopolized their exploitation. As a result, Germany [was] left with no land to acquire and no space to expand," thus violating "the principle of equal opportunity among men" and threatening "the principle of equal right" for "all nations."[335]

The search for equality again raised its head, very clearly, when Britain wanted Germany to concede to it naval supremacy (Germany knew that Britain had been and would continue to remain supreme), but it refused to concede it unless London was prepared to concede to it a neutrality stance in case of a war on the continent involving Berlin. The latter wanted to retain the capacity to keep London uncertain.

Against what was Germany seeking equality—the ability to pursue its self-defined end? It was the Britain whose grandeur (which

---

[334] Crowe's Memo, op. cit.

[335] Quoted in Boyle, op. cit., p. 163.

magnified vastness, immensity), whose ostentation (meaning splendor and magnificence), whose dignity (that is, solemnity and loftiness), and whose distinction (elevation, prominence, and mightiness) were on display in 1897 at the celebration (at which was present Wilhelm) of the diamond jubilee of Queen Victoria, as experienced by an eight-year-old Arnold Toynbee, historian, who later wrote about it in the third person. (It was the same event that inspired Kipling's *Recessional*.)

"He can still remember his excitement," Toynbee wrote, "at the unfamiliar, picturesque uniforms of those magnificent 'colonial' troops, as they were still called in England then."[336] For "an English child, this gave," he noted, "a sense of life astir in the world" and how he felt that what the crowds, gazing at the spectacle, saw was "their sun standing at its zenith and assumed it was there to stay."[337] Then he further opined, as the crowds saw it, "history . . . was over. It had come to an end . . . and they [could] congratulate themselves on the permanent state of felicity which the ending of history had conferred on them."[338]

This "excitement," sense of "stir in the world," the "sun standing at its zenith" and seeming "permanent state of felicity," and the magnificence, all magnified, elevated, and even ennobled—this is part of the need that all human beings have had, the need to experience grandeur. It is something that even psychologists who study imperialism and empire have often overlooked but that has a very profound impact on citizens, including colonized citizen-subjects.[339] It is part of what Germany sought for itself and so well represented by Joseph Conrad in one of his most compelling stories, "An Outpost in Progress," about colonialism. Here, we meet two white men, Kayerts and Carlier, friends whose images of European political, religious, and cultural elites were unflattering.

---

[336] Arnold J. Toynbee, *Civilization on Trial* (Oxford: Oxford University, 1948), p. 17.

[337] Ibid.

[338] Ibid., pp. 17–18.

[339] For two interesting studies, see Ashis Nandy, "The Psychology of Colonialism: Sex, Age, and Ideology in British Colonial India," *Psychiatry*, Vol. 45, #3 (August 1982), pp. 197–219; Richard C. Keller, "Madness and Colonization: Psychiatry in the British and French Empires, 1800–1962," in *Journal of Social History*, Vol. 35, #2 (February 2001), pp. 295–326.

The two "discounted their [the elites] virtues, suspected their motives, decried their successes, were scandalized by their duplicity, or were doubtful about their courage."[340] They were cynical and questioned their own inducements by material things.

Despite their doubts and broadly negative sentiments, when they reflected on "Our Colonial Expansion"—its mission, which spoke "much of the rights and duties of civilization, of the sacredness of civilizing work, and "extolled the merits" of those who were engaged in "bringing light and faith and commerce" to the "dark places" of the world—they wondered and began "to think better of themselves.[341] Then one evening the men began to imagine what the area in the jungle they occupied might be like in a hundred years and thought there might be townships, quays, warehouses, barracks, and billiard rooms—civilization. However, they could imagine even more; people could read that there were two "good fellows" who were the "first civilized men to live" there.[342] Like those citizens at home, as captured by Toynbee, those in the jungle of the earth could find loftiness, exaltation, and significance. They could even gain distinction. They could substitute or exchange cynicism and doubt for moral and imaginative elevation, for personal greatness.

Let us now turn to how Britain was presenting itself, the identity it cultivated, and the political culture it built to have elicited the experiences of citizens at home and abroad, as touched on above. We can then see more fully the clash between Germany's search for equality and Britain's stance and orientation toward it. We are, in part, being led in this portion of the discussion by historian A. P. Norton and politician John Strachey.

Thornton argues that the imperial system, as he saw it, was grounded on a kind of "unreflecting pride" that emanated from political ideas that caught and fired the imagination and that by the last generation of the Victorian era (certainly coincident with Queen Victoria's becoming empress of India in 1876), people thought they had found that faith.

---

[340] See Conrad, *Tales of Unrest*, op. cit., p. 90.

[341] Ibid.

[342] Ibid.

That faith was that "it was the role of the British Empire to *lead the world* in the arts and civilization, to bring light to dark places, and to teach the true political method, to nourish and protect the liberal tradition."[343] Additionally, it was to "act as trustee" for the weak, teach the arrogant humility, and while encouraging adventure and profits as well as advancing commerce and peace, it was to nourish, command, and deserve a *status and prestige shared by no other*[344] (emphasis is this author's).

The ideals advanced above are largely those recited by Churchill and included in Allison's work, those found in Crowe's memorandum,[345] and they are also those that instruct us about why concessions to Germany were viewed as likely to cede the status of the British Empire to Germany. The status that Britain enjoyed, along with its prestige that could not be shared, would have to be shared, at least in part, by an equal. If there is an equal (and of all the countries of Europe, Germany—with its many accomplishments, especially in the sciences and in the arts—was the only likely equal then), where would be the basis of Britain's identity, linked as it was to the zero-sum game of "by no other"? Britain's elites could not imagine sharing. Even the "ordinary" citizens could not. For them, as Strachey observed, the larger patriotism that we call imperialism inculcated, magnified them in a wider, loftier identity, and took them out of a life of relative insignificance that they otherwise lived. To them, the loss of a colony was a psychological amputation.[346]

Unfortunately, the "permanent state of felicity," the "permanent consummation" that Toynbee had experienced as a boy, was sitting atop social unrest, resistance, rebellion, and death, partly referred to earlier, and in the midst of the celebrations and the grandeur we described, the gratification that the top dog enjoyed was connected to the pain suffered by the part of colonial victims, including those in the Balkans, the nationalism of which London had encouraged to contain Austria,

---

[343] A. P. Thornton, *The Imperial Idea and Its Enemies* (New York: St. Martin's Press, 1959), p. ix.

[344] Ibid., pp. ix–x.

[345] Crowe's Memo, op. cit.

[346] John Strachey, *The End of Empire* (New York: Random House, 1960), p. 204.

Germany's ally. It was the clash between that nationalism and Austrian imperialism that resulted in the assassination that became the proximate cause of the war.[347]

Germany did not attack Britain; it went to war to help a relatively weak ally, one that felt that it had to teach Serbia a lesson or face disintegration, at best watch its status as a great power sink to a second- or third-class country.[348] Britain did not have to go to war, and the cabinet would not vote for one until Grey came up with the subtle device of asking potential combatants whether they would respect Belgium's neutrality. The latter was discussed by Britain in its plot of strategies against Germany, as early as 1912; as a result of those discussions, it was decided that London would not allow either Holland or Belgium to remain neutral in case of a war with Germany. In other words, Britain would have violated Belgium's neutrality had Germany not done so first,[349] yet it used that violation as an excuse to go to war, with London portrayed as the upholder of international law. What of Egypt, which Britain illegally annexed from the Ottoman Empire in December 1914?

---

[347] See Sidney B. Fay's *The Origins of the World War*, 2 vols. (New York: Macmillan, 1928). He was the first historian of note to refute the claim that Germany was solely responsible for the war.

[348] John G. Stoessinger, *Why Nations Go to War* (New York: St. Martin's Press, 1978), pp. 1–32. This is an accessible read about the origins of World War I.

[349] Ferguson, *The Pity of War*, op. cit., pp. 66–67.

PART IV

Dynamics of US–China Relations

CHAPTER 10

China and the US Portrayed

We now return to the primary focus of the book—namely, the challenge that China is seen as posing to the US—in the light of the counternarratives we have developed in the case of Athens and Sparta, Japan and the US, and Germany and Britain. Before we enter into the heart of that discussion, however, we should further examine three areas of Allison's elaboration of his thesis. This elaboration—a review, refinement, and further development of the thesis—is incorporated into Part III of his book, entitled "The Gathering Storm" and consisting of Chapters 5, 6, 7, and 8. We will touch on each, in sequence, except for Chapter 8, which will be included as part of the conclusion following our counternarrative on China and the US. Let us now focus on Chapters 5 and 6, wherein, respectively, Allison asks the reader to imagine if China were "just like us" (meaning the US) and then proceed to the next chapter to inquire into "what Xi's China wants."

In constructing the literary organization of the latter two chapters, Allison significantly succeeds in effecting, perhaps unintentionally, a remarkable sleight of hand. First, he achieves the appearance of "being objective" in his implied criticism of the US's behavior over the years from 1823 to about 1913—essentially saying that Washington pursued imperialistic ends. Second, those implicit criticisms give his presentation and aura of fairness on occasions, especially so as he moves to some rather stilted claims about Beijing's alleged motives in "what Xi's

China wants." Third, it avoids any direct current comparisons between Washington's and Beijing's behaviors, and, perhaps most important, it gives the impression that the US's expansionism and imperialism are matters either of the past or of an accepted status quo.

Within the chapter, Allison touched on the annexation of Hawaii (1898), preempting possible Japanese (or, in my view, Britain's) control of the island; the Spanish–American War (1898); the taking of Cuba, Puerto Rico, Guam, and the Philippines, the latter made protectorate in 1902 and continued in that status until 1946; the taking of Panama from Colombia to build the Panama Canal (1903); and, among other things, the proclamation of the corollary to the Monroe Doctrine (1904). All these courses of conduct were engaged in to establish the US status as a *world power*,[350] with all its implications for colonies and the accompanying ideology of "civilizing mission."[351]

As important, from the chapter, is what was but partially said, implied, or fully overlooked—that the US sought and successfully achieved the removal of Spain from the Caribbean and Asia; the virtual political exclusion (with the corollary to the Monroe Doctrine) of Europe from the Americas; and the putting into place the basis for an international maritime transportation infrastructure (the Caribbean, Panama, Hawaii, the Philippines, and Guam) to go with the Aleutian chain. Together, these areas provided Washington with the foundational building blocks for the pursuit, maintenance, and furtherance of world power. There are at least two other features to the chapter's focus: the use to which moral ideals were put and the commitment to naval power.

In the first, as seen in our discussions of the US's and Britain's dealings with Japan, abstract ideals were used to arm the containment of Japan. They were also used to excite and further the mobilization of domestic support for foreign policy ventures. The Monroe Doctrine was

---

[350] Allison, op. cit., p. 94

[351] See Theodore Roosevelt's Message to Congress, December 6, 1904, with its focus on the "world's work." One should also read his January 18, 1909, address at the celebration of the African Diamond Jubilee of the Methodist Episcopal Church, Washington, D.C., hereinafter cited as ADJ Speech. https://spiritualpilgrim. net/07_Special-Documents/Historical-Documents/1909_T-Roosevelt%27s%20 %27Expansion%20of%20the%20White%20Races%27%20speech.html

grounded on the value of liberty for the Americas, and its corollary—under the guise of "efficiency," that of "decency," and the preventing of sloth and a "general loosening of ties of civilized society"—provided Washington with excuses for intervention and control of countries in Latin America and the Caribbean. With respect to the matter of naval power, the virtual addiction to the view that great power status was linked to that capacity was already touched on in this work (in our discussions on Germany versus Britain and Japan versus the US). Not mentioned here, in Allison's Chapter 5, is the influence of Captain Mahan's thinking on TR's grand strategic vision for the US to become a great naval power, encompassing the Atlantic and the Pacific and perfecting the US's standing as a Pacific Power.[352] That thinking, as will be seen later in this work (especially through the eyes of Douglas MacArthur and others), is of utmost importance to understand the US's strategic and military policy toward China. For the moment, let us move to Allison's Chapter 6 and its focus on "what Xi's China wants."

The starting point of this last-mentioned chapter concerns what Allison ends up saying in the conclusion of his Chapter 5. It is this: if China were to behave now as the US behaved throughout the nineteenth and during the beginning of the twentieth centuries, would the US's political leaders find a way, as Britain adroitly did, to adapt to Washington's growing power? He thinks that while a few Americans appear to be preparing to accept London's fate (had to accept the US's rising power), the "differences between Xi and Theodore Roosevelt," to whom he ascribes much of the US's expansionist impulse, are, in his view, "more striking than their similarities."[353] In other words, while a TR-like posture on the part of China might be duly accommodated by the US, there are more differences than similarities between TR's US and Xi's China. So accommodation is, logically, unlikely.

---

[352] Warren Zimmerman, *First Great Triumph: How Five Americans Made Their Country a World Power* (New York: Farrar, Straus & Giroux, 2002). See also Evan W. Thomas, *The War Lovers* (Boston: Little, Brown and Company, 2010; and Mark R. Shulman, "The Influence of Mahan Upon Sea Power," in *Reviews in American History*, Vol. 19, #4 (December 1991), pp. 522–327.

[353] Allison, op. cit., p. 106.

One would think that at this point in Allison's book, one would find indicated similarities and differences between Xi and TR. Such is not the case; it is all Xi except for a passing reference that his vision for China is grounded on an "iron-willed" determination born out of turmoil, not unlike Nelson Mandala, and encompassing his "China's dream" that "combines prosperity and power"—equal parts TR's muscular vision of an American century and FDR's dynamic New Deal. It captures the intense yearning of a billion Chinese "to be rich, to be powerful, and to be respected."[354] For Xi (using claimed support from the late prime minister of Singapore, Lee Kuan Yew), Allison contends, realizing these three yearnings means "sustaining confidence" in Beijing's economic miracle, promoting "patriotic citizenry," and "bowing to no other power in world affairs."[355]

Operationally, this "making China great again" entails, in Allison's view, four major *intermediate* goals: restoring China to the "predominance" that it had enjoyed in Asia before the West intruded in the area; reestablishing control over the territories of "Greater China," including Taiwan; restoring its "sphere of influence" along "its borders and in adjacent seas" that others customarily concede to great powers and that the latter have always demanded; and "commanding the respect" of other great powers in the council of the world.[356] There is, however, according to Allison, a "civilization creed" around which the just-enumerated intermediate goals are being chased. It is the idea of the "Middle Kingdom," the name of China itself (in Mandarin), which conceives of the country as occupying the center of the world, in which not only is Beijing dominant, but also, the domination is defined by other states accepting of their respective statuses and being treated as vassals of a superior China. The advent of the West's imperial intrusion in the affairs of China during a time of technological and military weakness (particularly throughout the nineteenth and the first part of the twentieth centuries) must be reversed and a restoration of its civilizational place assured. This is the overarching mission of Xi.

---

[354] Ibid., pp. 108–109.

[355] Ibid., p. 109.

[356] Ibid.

To support his civilizational argument, Allison brings in statements of scholars and aspects of Confucianism, offering brief comparisons with the US. John K. Fairbanks, an authority on China, is presented as saying that the latter state's foreign policy has consisted of a demand for regional "dominance," persistence in having neighboring states recognize Beijing's "inherent superiority," and a disposition to use this dominance and claim to superiority to "orchestrate 'harmonious co-existence' with its neighbors."[357] Additionally, Allison favorably presents Fairbank as contending that the "civilizational creed" was "profoundly ethnocentric and culturally supremacist," with China seeing itself as "the apex of all meaningful human activity" and the emperor recognized as occupying the "pinnacle of a universal socio-political hierarchy," with other states actually or theoretically operating as vassals.[358] Allison then reinforced his position by noting that this hierarchical thinking fits with the Confucian injunction to know one's place.[359]

Fortifying the above reinforcing statements of his view by the late Professor Fairbanks, Allison brings to the reader some from Henry Kissinger, a scholar on China and a former secretary of state who, in 1972, played a critical role in helping negotiate a less hostile relationship between Washington and Beijing. While affirming much of Fairbank's view and attesting that "lesser states" around the periphery of China paid tribute to Beijing's greatness, a conduct that Beijing viewed as part of the natural order of the universe, Kissinger softened some of the implied expansionist intentions attributed to imperial China by noting that the use of military force was not esteemed and that any such use was as a last resort only. Kissinger is also quoted as contending that while, as in the case of the US, China espoused a kind of universalism, the latter for China was confined to controlling the "barbarians" at its door or countries that were regionally adjacent. The US, on the other hand, sought to spread its values around the world.[360]

---

[357]   Quoted in Allison, ibid., p. 110.

[358]   Ibid., p. 111.

[359]   Ibid.

360

After owning a sense of self that lacked nothing, needed nothing from the rest of the world, China was shattered psychologically and otherwise, by its experienced decline, linked to the intrusion of foreign powers. The latter's exertion of profound influence on the Chinese government during the abovementioned years of the nineteenth and the first half of the twentieth centuries, along with the attendant humiliation of the society, Allison rightly thinks, is part of Xi's makeup. So he moves to enquire, "Who is Xi Jinping?"

In other words, having presented the reader in Chapter 1 with China as the "biggest player" in the history of the world (with its challenge to the US in economic, military, and strategic terms) and then using Chapter 2 (with its example of Athens and Sparta) to theorize and project what is likely to happen in China–US relations, if the challenge of the first chapter continues (and bringing centuries of history he sees as disclosing comparable challenges in Chapter 4), Allison used Chapter 5 to reduce the US's impact on imperial history to the thinking and behavior of TR. In doing so, he tried to have the reader imagine what the US might do if China were to behave as TR did and counseled.

At this juncture, his view is that the US might accommodate itself to a TR-like China, led by Xi Jinping. What he saw, however, is a China that is less like TR or a TR-like US. So he had to enquire into what kind of person this leader of China is to set the stage for his conclusion respecting whether the US can adjust itself to China, particularly so in the light of Beijing's (Xi's) dreams. The reader will recall that Allison, in part, began this analysis earlier when he favorably compared Xi to Mandela, TR, and FDR. He sought to be more specific, however, and gave the reader a sense that Xi is no ordinary leader. He is, in fact, according to Allison, one whose personal experiences replicate that of his country.

Born a "princeling" of China's revolution (his father a former vice premier and colleague of Mao), he became a victim of the Cultural Revolution, repeatedly forced to denounce his father after the latter had been humiliated and imprisoned, to steal books to study after the closing of his school, and to face the suicide of his elder sister after she had undergone deprivations and abuse and being sent to the countryside for "reeducation." He, like China, was broken by these harsh experiences, claims Allison.[361] Instead of being demoralized and alienated, Xi decided, according to Allison, to become "redder than red" and, with extraordinary determination, "clawed his way back to the top."[362] The latter achievement, he realized by graduating from Tsinghua University (often referred to as China's MIT), joining the CPC (after he had been rejected on nine previous occasions), demonstrating his administrative leadership talents as party chief in Zhejiang Province (2002–2007), and being called back to Beijing on the latter date to join Pres. Hu Jintao and other members of the powerful nine-person Politburo Standing Committee, which was then dealing with the uprooting of high-level corruption in the country. In 2013, he outflanked other potential successors to Hu Jintao to become president, with a focus on achieving the ends defined in the earlier-mentioned "China's dream."

First, he began the pursuit of that dream by way of bypassing the practice of the post-Mao consensus that there should be collective rather than a one-person leadership. Second, in Allison's words, he became "Chairman of Everything,"[363] including chairman of the National Security Council and commander-in-chief of the military, and then made himself "core leader." Third, he reduced the size of the standing committee from nine to seven members and removed certain traditional limits, suggesting that he may remain in office beyond 2022. Linked to all these pointed-to changes, Xi associated himself with an ambitious, interrelated, four-pronged agenda to help realize the "dream." They are those of revitalizing the party, reviewing Chinese nationalism, carrying out the third economic revolution, and reorganizing and rebuilding China's armed forces. Any single one of the four items of the agenda, to Allison, would be enough for most heads of state to attempt in a decade. For Xi, with his determination and "Napoleonic self-confidence," all four are, together, being pursued (and in a hurry), thus making China even more of a threat to the US. Giving a summary of Allison's furnished examples under each of the four agenda items showed further our understanding of his "China versus the US" claims.

361 Ibid., p. 113.

362 Ibid., p. 114.

363 Ibid., p. 115.

With respect to the reanimation of the CPC, Allison argues that Xi's central nightmare has been the 1989 disintegration of the Communist Party of the former Soviet Union and the subsequent fall of Gorbachev from power. This fall, from the "careful analysis" of Xi, was the result of three mistakes that Gorbachev made, mistakes that Xi seeks to avoid—having army commanders swear allegiance to the nation rather than the country (the former USSR was a country composed of many nations), relaxing political control of society before reforming the economy, and allowing the Communist Party of the former USSR to continue its corruption. Xi, finding within his own party continuing corruption and attendant questioning of its legitimacy, launched an "anti-corruption campaign of unprecedented scale,"[364] resulting in, among other things, the disciplining of over nine hundred thousand party members, the expelling of over forty thousand (the latter number included high-ranking military officers and former members of the CPC's 150-person central committee and the standing committee), and shaping a digital system to track citizens' financial and certain other social behaviors.[365] As well, unlike his predecessors (beginning with Deng Xiaoping) who progressively sought to separate the party from the government, President Xi is seen as having increasingly strengthened the party's influence over the government and society in general.

As regards the claim of Xi's reviving China's nationalism and patriotism, to make the Chinese people "proud again," according to Allison, the latter argues also that Xi has known that purifying the party from its corruption is not enough to elicit and sustain support and loyalty. Neither is the realized economic growth ensuing from Deng's market reforms. To realize the "dream," there is a need to have a "renewed sense of national identity embraced with pride by a billion Chinese."[366] The construction of this renewed identity has been accomplished, according to Allison, by "reinventing the Party as the twenty-first-century succession of the imperial [Mandarins], the guardians of a proud civilization with a historical mandate to rule,"

---

[364] Ibid., p. 120.

[365] Ibid., pp. 120–121.

[366] Ibid., p. 121.

instead of continuing the Marxist notion (from Western ideology) of a "new socialist man."[367] With this deep cultural tradition, Xi, in Allison's view, has ordered officials nationwide to attend lectures of classical Chinese thought to "encourage national self-confidence."[368]

As important in inspiring Xi's sought national self-renewal is his claimed focus on reminding the people of China that they should "never forget our national humiliation," which the party now invokes, not a Marxism, which is seen as being outside the market, to promote a sense of unity. Allison then quotes Lee Kuan Yew that a revived China is far more important to that country's people than freedom, which the students of the 1989 Tiananmen Square demonstration sought.[369]

The other two areas—the economic revolution and the reorganization of the military—can now be touched on. Allison thinks that Xi must continue the rapid economic growth of China if the party is to survive but that his goal of 6.5 percent growth until 2021 is unsustainable given rising corporate debt, the demands for greater environmental stewardship to which Xi has committed himself, and the ambitious, risky specific promises of the "Two Centenary Goals," of which the first is to build a "moderately wealthy society" (double the per capita income to $10,000) by 2021, when there will be a celebration of the one hundredth anniversary of the CPC. The second is to ensure the development, by 2049, the one hundredth anniversary of the PRC, of a "modernized, fully developed, rich, and powerful" country.[370]

To achieve the ends sought under the economic revolution, Allison includes certain other particulars that have received Xi's focus, such as the structural reforms toward greater domestic consumption, the reorganizing of state-owned enterprises, the strengthening of the country's science and technology standing, and the advancing of greater entrepreneurialism. No area under the economic initiatives excites more concern in Allison than the priority that China has given to infrastructural investments, especially that constituting OBER, the

---

[367] Ibid.

[368] Ibid., p. 122.

[369] Ibid., p. 122.

[370] Ibid., pp. 118, 123.

acronym for the OBOR infrastructural plan, to integrate economic activities (involving the building of railroads, roads, pipelines, hydroelectric dams, naval installations, and freight moving from Beijing to Rotterdam in two days instead of months) across Asia, Africa, and Europe. Allison sees this enterprise as allowing China "to project power across several continents," promoting "the balance of geo-strategic shifts to Asia."[371] It does more. It "echoes claims made a century ago by Halford MacKinder" (a British geopolitical thinker, often viewed as the father of geopolitics) that the country that rules Euro-Asia, roughly covering much of the area embraced by OBOR, will rule the world. In this case, Mackinder's understanding could come to dominate Mahon's thesis (a major source of the US's military thinking) about the centrality of sea power.[372]

The military emphasis of Xi reinforces (in Allison's view) the threat posed by Beijing's economic revolution. This view, in summary form, is that Beijing is saying to Washington that the latter should "butt out" of Asia. Here, Allison looks at Xi's reorganization of the People's Liberation Army (PLA), which encompasses the army, the air force, and the navy, reducing the general autonomy enjoyed by each of its four departments and reconstituting them into some fifteen bodies that report directly to the Central Military Commission, which is chaired by Xi; at Xi's, as previously touched on, uprooting of "rampant graft" within its ranks; and at the shift from a largely defensive bearing of the PLA to an orientation/adaptation that combines defense with offense—a forward-capable armed force that has seen a substantial reduction in army troops as well as increases in the air force and the navy. Embedded in all this is the question of control of the seas abutting China, including those forming an island chain that runs "from Japan, through Taiwan, to the Philippines and the South China Sea," sometimes called the "first

---

[371] Ibid., p. 125

[372] Ibid., pp. 125–126. We will be discussing Mackinder and other geopolitical thinkers in the coming rebuttal to Allison. We should also note that long before Mackinder and others, we had a brilliant India thinker, Kautilya, who is credited with having authored the *Arthasastra*, which deals with geopolitics on a grand scale.

island chain."[373] Beijing wants to exert control over the area, and the US, which has dominated the same site since World War II, is disinclined to cede that control to China.

Allison, although largely persuaded that corruption in the army—the outright buying of ranks, for example—constitutes an "existential threat" to China's military, as viewed by Xi, wonders why he (Xi) would, at the time he is trying to do so many other things, seek to reorganize the PLA. His conclusion is that such steps were necessary to ensure the military's unquestioned loyalty to the party and his own leadership. By extension, of course, it also means a more unified operation to confront the US.

Allison acknowledges the US's implication in the humiliation of China through its decades of operating spy ships in Beijing's adjacent waters; this is so too in the 1999 accidental bombing of China's embassy in Belgrade (during the Kosovo campaign) and the 1996 backing off that China chose to observe when Beijing sought to pressure the then Taiwan government that seemed determined to move toward independence, and the US, in support of Taiwan, responded by sending two aircraft carriers to the area "in the largest deployment of US military power in Asia since the Vietnam War."[374] To be included, among those factors that Allison sees as having motivated Xi to pursue the reorganization of the PLA, are the display of the US's technological wizardry and dominance during its 1991 defeat of Iraq and the "synergy" (today we call this "network-centric warfare") that the US displayed in the operation of its army, navy, and air force.[375]

What, for Allison, is most important as a motivation, however, is that this reorganization of the PLA is designed to prepare China not only to fight but also to win in a war that might involve the US. Thus, toward the end of the chapter, he focuses on the acquisition or development of a sophisticated weapons system by China, the quoting of an apparently

---

[373] Ibid, pp. 130–131.

[374] Ibid., pp. 127–130.

[375] Ibid., p. 129. See also, for an elaboration on this topic, to be dealt with later, Annie Jacobsen, *The Pentagon's Brain: An Uncensored History of DARPA: America's Top secret Military Research Agency* (Boston: Little, Brown and Company, 2015).

authoritative study by RAND indicating approximate dates when China will achieve "advantage" over or "approximate parity" with the US in certain areas of conventional military capability (2017) and predicting that in the next five to fifteen years, Asia will experience the progressive "receding frontier" of US dominance.[376] In other words, barring changes in trajectory, the US will be obliged to fight or "butt out" of Asia. China is leaving the US few, if any, alternatives. To compound the rivalry implicit in what he sees as China's challenge to the US, there are "deep cultural differences" that exacerbate the rivalry. This leads us to the seventh chapter—the one on the "clash of civilizations."

The title itself is taken from one of his former academic colleagues at Harvard University, the late Samuel P. Huntington, who, in 1993, published an article in *Foreign Affairs* entitled "The Clash of Civilizations."[377] In it, Huntington argued that future conflicts will not be primarily, as in the past, between and among princes, nation-states, economic interests, or ideologies but between and among civilizations. The latter, he defined as "the highest cultural grouping of people and the broadest level of cultural identity people have short of that which distinguishes humans from other species."[378] As important, for our summary and understanding of Allison's contention, is Huntington's identification of seven or eight civilizations: Western, Confucian, Japanese, Islamic, Hindu, Slavic-Orthodox, Latin American, and "possibly" African.[379] While admitting that differences do not necessarily mean conflict and that conflict itself does not necessarily mean violence, Huntington takes the position that "over the centuries," differences "among civilizations have generated the most prolonged and the most violent conflicts."[380]

The latter quote, which Allison also uses, fits into his overall thesis concerning the likelihood of a future war between the US and China. Washington, he sees as the leader of Western civilization and Beijing

---

[376] Ibid., p. 132.

[377] Samuel P. Huntington, "The Clash of Civilizations," in *Foreign Affairs*, Vol. 73, #3 (Summer 1993), pp. 22–49.

[378] Ibid., p. 24.

[379] Ibid., p. 25.

[380] Ibid.

as the leader of the Confucian, each of which, historically and in the present, either has not understood or has had problems understanding the other. To support his position, he followed four approaches: he takes the reader back to some of the earliest encounters between China and the West; then he moves to issues of certain values that he insists define the US (Western civilization) and China (Confucianism); he stresses that differences in values find their way into different concepts of world order; and finally, he pleads his case for "strategic culture clash."

In the first approach, we find Allison's impressive portrayal of Lord George Macartney arriving in Beijing from London in 1793 (as a special envoy of King George III), seeking to establish diplomatic relations between Britain and China. As well, he was tasked "to open new ports and markets for British goods [to] negotiate a more flexible system for conducting trade in the coastal province of Canton [and] rent a compound" for the year-round operation of British merchants.[381] The Chinese government had "no conception" of his proposal for diplomatic relations and indicated that while it understood that King George wanted to "partake" in the generosity of China and had come a long way from Europe to pay it due respect, it could not countenance the establishment of a foreign embassy in Beijing. It would, however, as had been traditionally allowed, permit Britain to continue the then current arrangement for the exchange of goods in Canton. Concessions of the kind that sought the requested year-round arrangement were unacceptable.[382]

The riches of China (about 30 percent of the world's GDP), which Britain then wanted to gain greater access to, were being protected,[383] on the one hand. On the other, as seen by Allison, something far more significant happened—something that aptly captures the danger incident to cultural or, in the language of his chapter, civilizational differences

---

[381] Allison, op. cit., pp. 133–134.

[382] Ibid., pp. 134–135.

[383] Henry Kissinger, *On China* (New York: Penguin Books, 2011), p. 12. See also Kissinger's favorable reference to the appraisal of Chinese society by French physiocrat Francois Quesnay in Franz Schurmann and Orville Schell, eds., *Imperial China: Decline of the Last Dynasty and the Origins of Modern China* (New York: Vintage Books, 1967), pp. 113–120.

that create or exacerbate existing conflicts. "It would not be fair," he contends, "to call an encounter that had no chances to succeed an epic failure. Rather than build a bridge, Macartney's diplomatic mission exposed a gulf between China and the West."[384] He goes on to say that although today China engages in trade and diplomatic relations throughout the world, "fundamental differences between these two ancient systems [Western and Confucian] remain."[385] To illustrate his last point, he constructed a model of nine categories (self-perception, core values, view of government, form of governance, exemplar, foreigners, time horizon, change, and foreign policy) to demonstrate a sort of diametrically opposite cultural orientation between the US (Western civilization) and China (Confucianism). For example, in the cases of core value, view of the good, time horizons, change, foreigners, and foreign policy, the US is identified with freedom, necessary evil, "now," inventiveness, inclusiveness, and international order, while China, in contrast, is associated with order, necessary good, eternity, restoration/evolution, exclusiveness, and harmonious hierarchy. Undergirding all of the US's values, without any effort made to reflect on the difference between statements of abstract values and actual patterns of behavior, Allison presents the Declaration of Independence with its "self-evident truths."[386] We will return to these categories in the rebuttal to the section.

Allison, as part of his emphasis on the importance of the perceived or attributed cultural differences and the confrontational inclinations that they are said to excite, used the categories to examine more closely how Americans and the Chinese "differ in their view of the nature and purpose of government."[387] Also, he thinks that we can presume to get insights into that view by asking who we are, what our rightful place in the world is, and what constitutes order, the latter within our society and in our relations with other nations.[388] From the responses to these

---

[384] Allison, op. cit., p. 136.

[385] Ibid.

[386] Ibid., p. 140. See Jill Lepore, *These Truths: A History of the United States* (New York: W. W. Norton & Company, 2018).

[387] Ibid.

[388] Ibid.

questions, we can better appreciate the cultural forces, outside any structural factor that shapes the Thucydides trap, that make it difficult to manage the US–China relations.

For example, he offers, both countries have "extreme superiority complexes"; each, in its own way, thinks of itself as exceptional, "without peers."[389] So can the US accept another, possibly superior superpower, and can China accept that there are two "suns"? An earlier-mentioned leader, the late prime minister of Singapore, Lee Kuan Yew, indicated that for the US to be displaced, not so much in the world but merely from the West Pacific, by an Asian people "long despised and dismissed with contempt . . . is emotionally very difficult to accept. The sense of cultural supremacy of the Americans [makes] this adjustment difficult."[390] The adjustment would be no less difficult for China, which is claimed to see itself as the center of the universe atop a hierarchy in which everyone, internal to its society and externally, knows his/her/its place. China seeks order and harmony based on that hierarchy, while the US seeks liberty, the pursuit of (along with life and happiness) self-evident truths. The latter have universal application and thus are seen by hierarchical systems, as in the case of human rights, as interfering in domestic affairs.

The US also sees itself as a problem solver, Allison contends, especially so in its short-term view of things. It seeks to settle matters and move on. The Chinese, on the other hand, believe that many problems cannot be solved; they can only be managed. So such problems will be differed for many years. Further, in its conception of world order, the US seeks a law-governed world, the American domestic rule of law extended on a global scale. China, preferring hierarchal rule, is suspicious of law, much of which (in international relations) it sees as having been formulated when Beijing was not on the world stage. The Chinese, he sees also as "ruthlessly flexible," as exhibited by their

---

[389] Ibid.

[390] Graham Allison, Robert Blackwell, and Ali Wyne, eds., *Lee Kuan Yew: The Grandmaster's Insights on China, the United States, and the World* (Cambridge: MIT Press, 2013). The reader is urged to read these comments in the broader context of the work. Hereafter, he is cited as Lee, "the Grand Master."

willingness to negotiate with capitalist states (in 1972), even if it meant weakening international communism.

This flexibility and its attitude toward time also mean that China will not risk conflict "on a single all-or-nothing clash: elaborate multi-year maneuvers" are closer to its style. Allison, at this juncture in his book, quotes the legendary, ancient Chinese military strategist Sun Tzu to support his claim. That strategist claimed that the highest kind of victory in war is to defeat the enemy without ever actually engaging in fighting.[391]

Persuaded that he had successfully formed a cultural factor to the Thucydides trap, Allison concludes by looking at what he sees as China's efforts to restore "power and influence in East Asia and its associated action to hasten" the US's retreat from the area. Beijing, he claims, sees Washington's actions in the area as seeking to "contain" it, and President Obama's Trans-Pacific Partnership (TPP) project reinforced that belief. China's view of the US's intentions may be even more complex, seeing Washington's strategy as encompassing "five to's": to isolate, to contain, to diminish, to internally divide, and to sabotage China or its leadership. The US, on the other hand, has seen itself since the time of President Nixon as welcoming China into the mainstream of the international economic and political system.[392] This misperception, partly culturally shaped, makes miscalculation all the more possibly, if not likely.

We now turn to his Chapter 8, "From Here to War," in which Allison touches on two historical examples and four constructed scenarios to sharpen the reader's sense about the possibility of a US–China war. The historical examples are the Korean War and the 1969 border conflict between the former USSR and the PRC. The first entailed the 1950 pushing of North Korean armed forces by American troops toward the Chinese border and a "dumbstruck" US General MacArthur finding the troops that he was leading confronted by Chinese troops, which proceeded to repulse the American forces to the thirty-eighth parallel line that had divided South and North Korea and that, until today,

---

[391] See Sun Tzu, *The Art of War*, with a foreword by John Minford and translated by Lionel Giles (Singapore: Tuttle Publishing, 2008), pp. 6–12. I will be returning to this work.

[392] Allison, *Destined,* op. cit., p. 151.

divides both halves of the Korean Peninsula. To Allison, who would have thought that a PRC leader, who was "barely in control of his own country after a long civil war, [would] dare to attack a superpower that had crushed Japan and ended World War II five years earlier by dropping atomic bombs?"[393] The second example is in 1969, when a former USSR–China disagreement concerning a disputed border along the Wusuli (or Ussuri) River, bordering on Russia and China, resulted in a sudden attack by China and a brutal response from the former USSR. The latter country is reported to have contemplated the use of nuclear weapons.[394] That China should have attacked a nuclear-wise superior former USSR is, to Allison, instructive, and one should have the two examples in mind as one considers a number of "sparks"— sparks that could light fires, background conditions (such as the constant presence of US naval ships and aerial intelligence flights along the ocean borders of China)—"accelerants," and "escalation ladders." Chief among these sparks are an accidental collision at sea, Taiwan moving toward independence, war provoked by a third party, North Korean collapse, and the escalation from an economic conflict to a military war. We will but briefly touch on each to make a generalization.

As an example of collision at sea, Allison offered "routine operations" of an American destroyer passing near one of China's constructed sites on contested islands in the South China Sea. Assume that a China aircraft, naval, or other system were to challenge the destroyer that refuses to back off. Assume further that the destroyer is confronted by a Chinese cruiser and that the US considers backing off a form of surrender and thus decides to sink the Chinese cruiser. In the case of Taiwan, it is an island that has historically been part of China, but there have been growing sentiments toward independence. What if following demonstrations in Hong Kong, grounded on the claim that China is not fulfilling the 1997 "One Country, Two Systems" commitment, Beijing sends in troops to crush the demonstrations? The US, responding to this development, announces respect for Taiwan's president on the

---

[393] Ibid., pp. 154–155.

[394] Ibid., pp. 157–158. It should be observed that Russia and China concluded agreements in 1991, 1994, and 2004 that resolved the dispute, to the satisfaction of both parties.

latter's claims that what is happening in Hong Kong demonstrates that Taiwan can never ensure its citizens' freedom unless it were a sovereign, independent country. This response, Allison admits, would be a US "break" from long-standing Washington policy. He further moves to imagine Beijing using mine-laying drones to disrupt Taiwan's shipping (Taiwan is heavily dependent on the importation of goods, including food), and the US, in sympathy, sends warships from its Pacific fleet to escort commercial shipping in the affected area.

One unit of activity triggers another until a Chinese antimissile sinks an amphibious transport dock ship, killing nearly eight hundred sailors and marines. Beijing claims it was an accident, but fears of isolationist sentiments developing, pressure from the US military, and commitment to Taiwan all conspire to induce a US retaliation. War provoked by a third party (in this hypothetical case, Russia) follows the same trajectory of escalatory actions over the Japanese-claimed Senkaku Islands (also known as the Diaoyu Islands in China). Here, a group of Japanese ultranationalists moves to build structures, on behalf of Japan, on one of the islands, and China responds by arresting them with the intention of taking them to Beijing for trial. Japan seeks to intercept the ship taking the prisoners, and the PLA's navy and the Japanese Defense Force's warships and fighter planes are both determined not to back down. Tokyo reminds the US of its obligation to honor the over-seven-decades-old US–Japanese defense treaty (which is seen as applicable to the Senkaku). A cyberattack by Russia (initially thought to have been the PLA's action) disrupts the Japanese command-and-control system to prod the US and China faster into conflict so that Moscow can deal more effectively with the Ukraine.

The imagined scenarios of a North Korean collapse and a move from economic differences to war, by and large, follow the same script. The North Korean issue revolves around the collapse of the existing regime. The fact that it has (or is believed to have) warhead and missiles programs or is at the final stages of refining some of them at a level of quality and quantity to target South Korea, Japan, and American bases in Guam, Okinawa, and even Hawaii troubles the US, which opposes North Korea's acquiring the type of described capacities, and it is believed to have plans with South Korea, in case of such a collapse, to march north and unite the two countries. For Beijing, the prospect of having South Korea conquering the north and having, thereby, US troops on China's border would be as unacceptable now as it was in 1950. Allied to all this thinking, there would be rather swift action, on the part of China and the US, to gain control of North Korea's nuclear weapons, among other things, pointing to a resulting US–China conflict.

Finally, there is the escalation from economic to military actions, beginning with the US's resentments about its trade deficit with Beijing. The latter is also imagined to be seeking control of certain strategic industries (the semi-conductor industry, for example) and China's alleged involvement in "massive cyber economic theft,"[395] along with Beijing's claimed effort to manipulate the bond market and a rise in interest rates by selling some of the more than $1 trillion it owns in US treasuries. The US is depicted as responding to these developments in a variety of ways, with the US treasury warning of pending danger and the US having to decide on a course of action, after it is discovered that the Chinese have penetrated the US's military computer network.

All the scenarios suggest that a war between the US and China can emerge from a number of sources, none of which may have been intentionally put in place to advance the results with which each government finds itself confronted. Second, each step in the dynamic of conflicts, per the claims of Thucydides, can take turns that no one can predict. Third (and this is explicitly stated by Allison), tension between great powers creates great stress; for him, however, this stress, in the case of US–China relationships, is due to China's challenge to the US. The latter is responsible for little except in going along in its usual pursuits, including being loyal to its allies and friends. In his own words, "as these scenarios illustrate, the underlying stress created by China's disruptive rise creates conditions in which accidental, otherwise inconsequential events could trigger a large-scale conflict."[396] I will go further to say that some of these "scenarios" mask actual plans in high places.

---

[395] Ibid., p. 182. All the scenarios are, in much greater detail, presented on pages 156–184. I have, by way of making the presentation more concise, left out some of those details.

[396] Ibid., p. 184.

CHAPTER 11

Some Rebuttals of Portrayals and an Alternative Narrative

We now move to another different narrative, including a partial rebuttal of Allison's positions in Chapters 5, 6, 7, and 8 (Part III of his book). Some more general disconfirming arguments will be advanced in the concluding chapter of the book. The rebuttals will focus on China as a disrupter and as a communist state using values of imperial China to ground its legitimacy and survival; Xi as a converging embodiment of those values and imperial ambitions; Beijing as encompassing values (including human rights) diametrically opposed to those of the US and the West (the civilizational component of his argument); and China as the aggressor.

Rebuttals of Portrayals

In the matter of China as a disrupter, one has but to reflect on the quoted statement that ends the final paragraph of the last chapter. It seeks to place in context the variety of scenarios that Allison constructed to show the stress that they could cause to the international system and, in so doing, occasion war between Beijing and Washington. Central to his argument is that the rise of China, in every way, is the cause of and results in (even when one is not aware of it) or produces disruptions. The latter terms, with their underlying negative connotation, suggest that the PRC is and likely will continue to be an agent of damage, impairment, defilement (especially when we deal with values), and even ruin. One could, at this juncture, ask, for whom might the rise of China be an impairment or ruin? Certainly not the over six hundred million persons brought out of poverty in China or those throughout the world, especially in the Global South, whose international economic and social circumstances have been materially improved by China's rise. It certainly has not been for those American industries that have profitably invested in China and are trying to ensure more favorable returns from the increased spending power of Chinese citizens as policy makers in Washington have sought to work with their counterparts in Beijing to find mutual adjustment in economic policies to the ostensible benefit of both countries.[397] Neither can it be said to have been the cheaper prices of goods produced in China for American consumers who were not offered many, if any, pay rises or the decision of China to revalue its currency and engage in deficit spending during the 2007/2008 economic crisis to help the US.[398]

What we want to point out here, however, has less to do with specific points or the particular accuracy of claims and more about an unarticulated assumption and the repeatedly highlighted negative connotations accompanying that highlighting. The assumption is that the US has been or is in constant danger of being victimized by China's rise in international relations. The US, therefore, has no alternative but to defend itself.

Nowhere in the US's positions—as presented in the varying scenarios provided in Chapter 8, for example—do we find China as a possible victim. If one were simply to see China as a country that (and most Chinese see their country as one that) has been undergoing the process of socioeconomic development, then the US, in a number of policy areas, might be seen as disruptive also. The US has been involved, as the alternative narrative will show, in disrupting China's development. All one has to do at this point is to reflect briefly on Taiwan, which, in 1949, came under the control of the KMT, the Chinese Nationalist Party,

---

[397] Kissinger, *On China*, op. cit., p. 493–494.

[398] Ibid., p. 501.

against which the CPC fought and won a civil war. The US's support of the nationalist government of China—which, until recently, continued to assert its claim to be the legitimate government of China—is the equivalent of our having the Confederate Government escaping to Long Island, claiming to be the legitimate government of the US and having the support of the then reigning superpower, Britain, supporting the claim and concluding a treaty of friendship with it, a treaty that, for all intents and purposes, had been a defensive alliance. In addition, Britain had been selling weapons to it and had been giving indications of supporting its indications that it would like to become an independent state, in alignment with the US. Imagine further substituting China, if it had the capacity, for Britain. How would the US feel?

The claim that Xi's China is using values of imperial China (Confucianism) to revive and extend the legitimacy of the CPC is, at best, only partly true and, at worst, unilluminating and even misleading. First, Allison is not consistent in his stance respecting the relative influence of communism and Confucianism in China. Second, he does not elaborate on what Confucianism, as used throughout the book, is or is not except for his claim about its hierarchical values and its subordination of women, with the context of a well-ordered patriarchal family. Third, in Allison's presenting contemporary Confucianism in China, his readers would be unaware of the neo-Confucian project (of which Xi is a part), with all its emerging influence, including its skepticism about and rejection of hierarchies and the subjugation of women.[399] They would also be blind to the reemergence of Maoism, something with which we will be dealing shortly. It is as if one were seeking to invite a disapproving view of the US and that for which it ostensibly stands in saying that Washington seeks to deal with rising skepticism about the liberal democracy it espouses by invoking the Founding Fathers, who were slave owners, racists, and upholders of

---

[399] See Beijing Institute of Wang Yangming Philosophy, *Cultural Confidence & National Rejuvenation* (Beijing: Chinese Intercontinental Pres, 2018). It will be cited later as BIW. Tu Wei-Ming, *Neo-Confucian Thought in Action: Wang Yang-ming's Youth (1471–1509)* (Berkeley: University of California Press, 1976); see also Professor Tu's impressive interview with Bill Moyers at "Tu Wei-Ming." https://billmoyers.com/content/lu-ei-ming-confucianism/

patriarchy. Therefore, it is unnecessary to know anything else about them and the society that they helped produce or how their thinking might have evolved and amended over time.

In fact, as Henry Kissinger notes, "once revolutionaries seize power, they are obliged to govern hierarchically if they want to avoid paralysis or chaos. The more sweeping the overthrow [and China's revolution was the most sweeping in human history], the more hierarchy has to substitute for the consensus that holds a functioning society together."[400] Mao Tze-tung, who had deep suspicions about hierarchies, actually embodied one, although he sought at different times, including through the Cultural Revolution, to dismantle portions of it. Before his death, in a poem to his trusted comrade, Chou En-lai, he expressed his fears about their unfinished mission: "[W]ho will be its guardian?" he asked. "[T]he struggle tires us/our hair is grey . . . can we just watch our efforts being washed away?"[401] Readers who cannot go through all of the previously cited work, *Maoism* by Julia Lovell, are urged to try Chapters 12 and 13 of it to gain some grasp of the various ideological groups with which Xi has had to deal—from neo-Confucianists and those who are more inclined to a stronger Western-like market system to remnants of those Maoists from whom Deng Xiaoping wrested power and neo-Maoists of varying colors. It is in the search for balance among these and other groups to create a social order consistent with the promise of communism and Confucianism and having China internationally strong enough to execute the mission associated with that order that one can properly understand Xi's political agenda. Creating or refining a hierarchy (along with plans to reduce it, as we will see) is but one part of a more complex whole.

---

[400] Kissinger, *On China*, op. cit., p. 107. The US revolution involved little social change, but even Washington was opposed to political parties, and the single members district principle that governs our national elections to legislative bodies makes it almost impossible to have more than two national parties. We know of the fact that senators, for a long time, were not popularly elected, and the electoral college is still with us.

[401] Quoted in Richard Nixon, *Leaders* (New York: Simon & Schuster, 1982), p. 247.

It is now worth touching on the values that Xi is seen as espousing and the older system of values that contemporary China is portrayed as embodying and seeking to export to the rest of the world. These values are seen, by Allison and others,[402] as diametrically opposed to those that the US embodies, as the reader will remember. The values revolve around a core value, views of government, forms of government, attitude toward foreigners, time horizon, change, and foreign policy. While Allison, as before mentioned, sees them as authoring a clash of cultures (civilizations), this writer argues here that there are more features that the US and China have in common than those that they have in opposition.

Freedom, which is the US's ascribed core value, is not possible outside order, which is the core value attributed to China. Indeed, at home and abroad, both countries seek order (the US in the Balkans during the 1990s, in Chile, after the democratic election of Salvador Allende, in the early 1970s, on the general support for authoritarians), and within the US, the focus on law and order has always been a political staple, not to mention the issues of discrimination in education and health care that have wreaked havoc on any claim to freedom or liberty. The opportunity to pursue any ends opposed by powerful groups such as the American Medical Association (AMA) and the National Rifle Association (NRA) is limited when and if it exists. The view of government in the US as a "necessary evil" but as a "necessary good" in China is also inaccurate. This is a position that is often abstractly claimed and pushed by the economic sector in the US that prefers to escape regulations by government, but to the "ordinary citizen"—as she looks to the police, the leaders of public schools, parks, fire persons, the military, highways, social security, health care, and regulations against the depredations of business—government is a necessary good. It is true, of course, that the Confucian (as well as socialist) traditions make more explicit than the US (unlike Western Europe and the world, except for the UK, and Australia, to an extent) the strongly encouraged and

---

[402] See, for example, H. R. McMaster, "What China Wants," in the *Atlantic* (May 2020), pp. 68–74. He is a former national security advisor and one of the most respected American military thinkers.

carefully practiced praiseworthy role of government. What of the role of government in dealing with COVID-19?

Neo-Confucianism holds a humanistic view of government, grounded on a rationalism that argues that the universe is understandable through reason and that human beings can use the faculty of reason to create ideal communities within the context of this rational universe. This is exactly what has been claimed by the West, from Plato to Marx and Rawls, although different thinkers have focused on different historical groups—philosopher-kings, mandarins, priests, proletarians, the middle class, or peasants—to lead in the constitution of this community.[403] That ideal community, for neo-Confucians, is linked to moral obligations at every level of society, including government—obligations to others, to the community, to the environment, and to the universe with which one's actions should be in harmony.[404] According to one of Allison's former colleagues, the late John K. Fairbank (one whom he favorably quotes and for whom the Fairbank Center for Chinese Studies at Harvard University is named), the very rights "of rebellion" are embedded in the duty to others. It is "the last resort of the populace against the tyrannical government" when it fails in its moral obligation to the people.[405] These principles predate John Locke and Jefferson by millennia.

Every government represents a hierarchy. To simply say that in the *form* of government, the US is a democratic republic (China calls its own a people's republic), while China is a "responsive authoritarianism," is not helpful. We will not even release to our own public the powers of our president as those powers have grown over the years. What any American president can do, especially in international affairs, exceeds

---

[403] See Glenn Tinder, "What Should Political Theory Be Now?" in John S. Nelson, ed., *What Should Political Theory Be Now?* (Albany: State University of New York Press, 1983), pp. 153–156. One can fruitfully compare the views of Tinder (with whom I shared many discussions on this subject) and that of Tu Wei-Ming, in his interview cited in footnote no. 398 and his book cited in the same footnote.

[404] See Mary Evelyn Tucker et al., *Confucianism and Ecology* (Cambridge, MA: Center for the Study of World Religion, 1998).

[405] See John F. Fairbank, "The Nature of Chinese Society," in SS, *Imperial China,* op. cit., p. 53.

that which any other leader in the world can. No single Chinese leader, unlike in the US, can (for example) decide to launch a nuclear war. The US itself occupies the top of an international hierarchy, which it wants to maintain, and Allison never refers to this fact. It is, of course, true that freedom of the press in the US is much broader and that freedom, in part, operates to keep government in check, but the Confucian and neo-Confucian notion that "heaven decides what the people decide" (something that the West completely missed in its assessment of the source of the Tiananmen Square demonstrations) is also a moral tool that exerts some limits on every Chinese government. It also speaks to where China was in 1979 and where it is today.

The idea that the US is inclusive toward foreigners while China is exclusive also begs for further inquiry. Although Han Chinese constitute about 85 to 90 percent of the PRC's population, China has historically been welcoming to other peoples and ways of being, including the West (China today has about fifty million Christians). Buddhism originated in India, but China became a major home, from where its teaching moved to Korea and Japan. Islam received the same welcome, and the Manchu (Qing dynasty) ruled China from 1644 to 1911. It is true that because external parties have, at different times, sought to use religion as an instrument of social dissention and that communism frowned on religion as a social institution, religious groups have had many challenges in China. The PRC has changed considerably, however, in this area, as we will later discuss, and the idea that China is exclusive is difficult to support factually. A few neo-Confucian principles, as understood by Xi, might provide some helpful insights.

Focusing on the issue of culture, the external display of the heart's and mind's "inner treasures" (*Xin*) and the "realization of one's bigger self after the removal of the little self" (a type of self that transcends the individual ego in which the US prides itself[406]) is something that neo-Confucianism encourages. China's culture is seen, by Xi, as having been characterized by these "inner treasures," a culture that has been disposed to "open mindedness and inclusiveness throughout the five thousand years of [its] civilization." The results of that orientation are that the Chinese nation has not only "preserved and carried forward

---

[406] See BIW, op. cit., p. 11.

but also studied and incorporated the essence of all fine cultures of the world."[407] Indeed, contemporary China has been among the most open countries to the cultures, technical and other, of the world. One has but to examine, as we will do later, its sending of students to study around the world and its welcoming of students from throughout the world. In the view of neo-Confucianism, however, the openness to the culture of others has been and should be part of a type of "self-cultivation, family regulation, state governance, and benefits for all." President Xi, who has been pursuing "the wisdom and experience" as well as the teachings of the sages, has been espousing the pursuit of "the noble cause of building a community of shared future for [hu]mankind" because "all under heaven" are but "one family."[408]

The US, on the other hand, despite its reputation for inclusiveness, has had some problems since its founding as Protestants persecuted and sought to exclude Catholics and white Anglo-Saxons sought to exclude non-whites, including Jews, the Chinese, the Japanese, and darker peoples, including those from Southern Italy, Greece, "Arabia" (Arabs), and India. Even Native Americans were excluded—and especially people from Africa. The idea that a Catholic might be president was contested until the 1960s; one could note that the US Senate has never even brought up for consideration the 1979 International Convention on the Elimination of All Forms of Discrimination Against Women.

Values linked to time, change, and foreign policy can now be touched on. The US is portrayed as valuing *now*, while China values eternity. The US is short term oriented, while China is long term. This too is false. China acts in the context of "now," with a view toward the future and using the experience of the past, just as the US does. Commercial transactions in the market economy, for example, require it; and China appears to have adapted to the market, very much resembling the US, in this respect. Both also operate strategically for long-term considerations, and they both have long memories—one has but to reflect on the hold of the Civil War on the American psyche, symbolically and in

---

[407] Ibid.

[408] Ibid., p. 20. One, at this stage, might want to read *Basic Writings of Mao Tzu, Hsun Tzu and Hah Fei-Tzu*, translated by Burton Watson (New York: Columbia University Press, 1967).

public policy. The Founding Fathers are a source of legitimacy, and the doctrine of "original intent" and the rule of precedent in common law are constitutional and, more broadly, legal categories. What is really the issue here is the comparative antiquity of each of the respective nations' culture, with China having a longer cultural memory and acting in accord with that memory. The idea that a society (the US), a major cultural feature of which (especially since 1945) has been science and technology, is defined by "now" is simply inaccurate. We also claim to be a Christian civilization, and the latter thinks in terms of "eternity." Finally, who constitute the American that is being depicted by Allison? Does it include Jews, Greeks, Iranians, Indians, Syrians, Ethiopians, the Chinese, the Iraqi, Native Americans, and the Japanese? They too have long memories. They are part of the US.

As respects change, the US is presented as characterized by it, by the new, by ideation, originality, creativity, and innovation. China, on the other hand, is, by nature, a country that improves, restores, and expands what has already been created, originated, and in existence. These are but stereotypes that a glimpse of China's history, if consulted, would refute. They do, however (and we will deal with this in the chapter preceding our conclusion), lend weight to the claim that China's advance in the areas of science and technology is the sad offspring of dishonesty and theft of the US's intellectual property (IP). In fact, nations do engage in some "stealing" of technology from others. The US was the China of the nineteenth century as it was charged with "piracy" of said property, especially from Britain, which was, for much of that century, the leading industrial power.[409] Since 2011, the US has been replaced by China as the top country in the number of inventions, trademarks, and designs registered with the World Intellectual Property Organization (WIPO), and in August 2019, the *Washington Post* reported that Chinese scientists may be at the forefront of the emerging quantum revolution.[410]

---

[409] Doron S. Ben-Atar, *Trade Secrets: Intellectual Piracy and the Origins of American Industrial Power* (New Haven: Yale University Press, 2004); see also Richard Wolff, "'Stealing Intellectual Property' Is Fake News," in *Common Dreams* (September 19, 2018).

[410] Jeanne Whalen, "The Quantum Revolution is Coming, and the Chinese are at the Forefront" in *The Washington Post* (August 10, 2019).

A year before, the same newspaper had reported on China's threat.[411] No country that is unassociated with origination, creating, and innovating can, of course, be a challenge to the world's leading industrial power. The latter will always be ahead, without creative challengers.

As for the claim that the US values international order in foreign policy while China seeks a harmonious hierarchy, readers may see how well it seems to fit into the earlier focused-on hierarchical Confucian order. An examination of the actual structure of international relations since the US has gained dominance within it since 1945 reveals the contrary. It is the US that led in the construction of a hierarchy and has sought to maintain it, with Washington at the top. China may very well have a like ambition, but one can only guess at this time. What China has said to the world, as will be discussed later, is that it seeks the contrary in a multipolar world.

Finally, Allison, using the willingness of China to negotiate with the US in the early 1970s as an example, takes the position that as a people, they are "ruthlessly flexible," meaning that they cannot be trusted morally. They are actually lacking in standards and are thus capable of the most brutal and cruel course of action, if they think it is to their advantage, regardless of what that action may mean for others. They were willing to negotiate with the US, forgetting the communist movement throughout the world. Of course, Allison would not recall that the US was going back on its commitments to the Republic of China (ROC), to allies it had, over the years, pressured to join it in isolating China, or those with which Japan was transformed from the unforgivable enemy to an ally or the rapidity with which we colluded with Nazis after World War II because we sought to confront the former USSR.[412] In short, to the extent that Allison takes seriously the attributes ascribed to the US and China, a review of them suggests that both countries are more alike than diametrically different. Let us now deal

---

[411] See Ben Guarino, Emily Rauhala, and William Wan, "China Increasingly Challenge American Domination in Science," *The Washington Post* (June 3, 2018). One should be careful of these reports since in some cases, they are being publicly aired by sponsors who are seeking additional research funds.

[412] See, for example, Scott Anderson, *The Quiet Americans* (New York: Doubleday, 2020).

with an alternative narrative, where the latter claim of China and other matters will be examined.

Alternate Narrative

The sub-theses of this portion of the book are that the PRC has always been perceived by Washington as a threat to the US, directly or indirectly; that the sources of this perceived challenge have undergone changes over the years and that the US has sought to adapt, often unsuccessfully; and that the current challenge, although seemingly different (and presented as such by Allison), is really the same in character except that, for the first time, Beijing has been able to bring all three major sources of its foreign policy conduct—tradition, socialism-Maoism, and nationalism (the latter with mobile military power)—into an emerging, comprehensive combination. Neither the argued threat of the PRC nor the response of the US to the claimed threat has operated in a vacuum. There has been a context to their behavior that must be responsibly indicated and brought to bear on our discussions if we are to have a reasonably accurate sense of the policy developments and their sometimes failures or successes.

Context and Stage

The context just referred to is four general interacting post–World War II movements that defined socioeconomic and political development in the world—movements that have largely continued, even if only in individual and collective memories. They were a moral revolution, decolonization, within a broader human rights cause; an ideological movement (largely social and economic) that pitted liberalism, led by the US, against communism, then led by the former USSR; the expanding reach of the dominant power, the US; and the renewal of efforts (initially embarked on during the interwar years) at a global governance structure, in the form of the UN, to help deal with postwar reconstruction, global poverty, socioeconomic development, and disarmament, among others.

The PRC, itself a product and agent of the first three movements, employed a strong anti-colonial and anti-imperialism stance, a pro–right-to-self-determination stance on the part of colonial peoples, and an anti-capitalism (anti-liberalism) thrust to its socialism-communism cause as well as to the standing of the US as the leading capitalist state; all were used to advance its objectives, at home and abroad. In a major sense, however, the stances that Beijing took were, to a weighty degree, influenced or dictated by the US's policy positions that preceded the victory of the PRC in 1949—a policy of containment, followed by one of isolation, and then a "new" containment.

The US became a supporter of the KMT (the Nationalist Party of China or Chinese Nationalist Party) following its founding in 1912 to help unify China after the overthrow of the Qing dynasty earlier that year, and following the 1925 death of its leader, Sun Yat-sen (who was also leader of the ROC that had succeeded the Qing dynasty), Gen. Chiang Kai-shek consolidated his power within the party and as leader of the ROC. During the period of power consolidation (especially between 1926 and 1928), Chiang came to be seen by Washington as uncompromisingly anti-Japanese and a possibly strong resister to Russian influence in China. As important, the US saw him as fanatically against the CPC, the bloody purging of whose members he had carried out (contrary to the unity government that his predecessor had cultivated) on his way to the power consolidation just mentioned. Between 1937 and 1945, to shape a more formidable opposition to Japan, a united front was formed between the two parties, but it came apart after World War II as each battled to gain control of China. The civil war, which had begun in 1927, resumed after the 1937–1945 pause.

Finding that Mao and his supporters were gaining more and more control and influence over China while the KMT, steep in corruption, was rapidly losing influence (we will use the KMT and ROC interchangeably going forward), the US made its first major effort to contain the CCP (also used interchangeably with the CPC). Washington sent Gen. George Marshall (later to become secretary of state) to China to pursue the formation of a coalition government that would include the CCP but be headed and controlled by the KMT. The US would then give generous support to ensure China's socioeconomic recovery under Chiang's leadership, Mao would progressively have but a diminishing influence as the social and economic conditions improved, and the threatened revolutionary changes in China would be aborted.[413] The mission failed as Marshall found "irreconcilable groups within the KMT, interested in preserving their own feudal control of China," and "mob actions"; as well, the propaganda and "irreconcilable Communists"[414] had overcome his seemingly initially successful efforts in negotiating what appeared to have been a mutually acceptable basis for future collaboration.[415]

With this failure, the US's chance to exercise control over China was collapsing (and there were groups within the Department of State that unsuccessfully urged greater cooperation with Mao Tze-tung given their assessment of Mao and his associates' broad popular support among the Chinese people and their evaluated declining support that Chiang Kai-shek's was commanding, all largely because of his close links to landlords, political elites who no longer had any "mandate from heaven" to lead, discredited military "war lords," and those others associated with business).[416] In fact, while propaganda and coercive violence were part and parcel of Mao's revolutionary tactics (these too were practices of the KMT), his success in China was due more to other factors that came to define Maoism and posed such an important challenge to the US: mass mobilization among the peasantry; continuous party building; a united front of peasants, workers, intellectuals, students, and what is often called the "national bourgeois"; and the translation of abstract concepts into easily understood narratives, including songs to be collectively sung.[417] Further, the landlords, who were among the principal supporters of Chiang, these perceived agents of peasant oppression, had their lands confiscated and distributed to the peasants in areas where Mao gained

---

[413] See President Truman's December 15, 1945, charge to General Marshall and the statement by General Marshall on January 7, 1947, offering a partial explanation of what happened in China, in Williams, op. cit., pp. 1106–1108.

[414] Ibid.

[415] Ibid.

[416] Ibid. See also some comments on the text of the letter from the secretary of state to President Truman in August 1949 in *Readings in American Foreign Policy*, eds. Robert A. Goldwin and Harry M. Clor (New York: Oxford University Press), pp. 209–301. This work will be hereinafter cited as RIAFP.

[417] See Lovell, op. cit., especially the first chapter, for a review of these issues.

control. The peasants were not blind to the difference between the KMT and the CCP.

The US had aimed to have China, under its direction, serve the Asian cornerstone in a global balance of power system controlled by Washington. Access to China's market was of corresponding importance. Chiang was central to this aim, with Sen. Kenneth Wherry of Nebraska hoping that Shanghai, as a result of projected US efforts to "lift" up China, would one day look "just like Kansas City."[418] After intense courtship, diplomatic missions, the furnishing of military advisors, help in the transportation of troops, and the expenditure of some $3 billion in aid to the KMT after the surrender of Japan in August 1945, Washington failed to stop the advance and triumph of Mao and Maoism.[419]

Many developments flowed from this reversal for Washington. Among them was a strong domestic backlash against those who had "lost China." Internationally, a like strong reaction ensued, expressed, in general terms, under the diplomatic policy called "isolation."[420] China would not only be contained as part of Washington's general policy of containment for the Soviet Union and the expansion of communism but be isolated as well. This isolation, among other things, meant that the US would use its power and influence to cut off or limit the international exchanges in which Beijing could engage with other countries, whether those exchanges were of political, economic, military, or diplomatic character. No single step in that policy of isolation was as important as Washington's decision not to recognize the government of the PRC and to use its power to recognize (and urge others to do likewise) the government of the ROC, which had, in defeat, fled the mainland to Taiwan. In other words, the defeated government in the civil war was to be recognized as the legitimate government of China.

The US, it should be noted here, was the only country that, because of its expanded and expanding post-1945 power and influence, could have successfully mounted and sustained this isolation for some twenty

[418] Quoted in Thomas G. Patterson and Garry Clifford, *America Ascendant* (Lexington, MA: D. C. Heath & Company, 1995), p. 81.

[419] Ibid., p. 83.

[420] See text of earlier mentioned text of statements by John Marshall and others in Williams, op. cit., pp. 106–108.

years. In the political realm, Washington had alliances throughout the world, covering Western Europe, the Americas, and the Caribbean, with Australia and New Zealand and soon-to-be developed alliances in the Middle East or West Asia as well as Southeast Asia. Bilateral arrangements with Japan and South Korea would also follow. Militarily, it had the most formidable force, including submarine aircraft carriers and bases throughout the world, including some physically near China. In the area of economics, the US controlled (through its voting power) the decision making of the world's international financial institutions (the World Bank and the IMF, for example) and, through the General Agreement on Tariffs and Trade (the GATT, which was transformed into the World Trade Organization or WTO in 1995), control of global commerce. In terms of the world's principal intergovernmental organization (IGO), the UN, the US, as a permanent member of the Security Council and then the most influential member of the UN's General Assembly, was able to exercise unexampled power.

The two other areas of context and stage (the human rights movement and the ideological conflict) should be further touched on. In the case of the human rights movement, the brutality, the material and social privations, and the human degradation caused by World War II as well as the role of socioeconomic and political exploitation and oppression in bringing it into being invited a shared need for a general moral transformation of international relations, including that of offering support for the principle of self-determination. Japan's use, as we saw earlier, of the promise of political independence as a means to weaken European colonial control of Asia found reinforcement in Roosevelt's decision to champion its cause as a means to marshal support for the war effort. In 1948, a year before "New China" was proclaimed, the UN General Assembly adopted the UDHR, with a focus on two broad categories of rights: civil and political (the rights to freedom of speech, worship, a free press, assemble, equality, associate, vote, a fair trial, and self-determination, for example) and economic, social, and cultural (such as the rights to education, health care, housing, clothing, food, work, and to form or join trade unions).[421] At the core of these rights is "the inherent dignity" of all members of the human family.

The ideological conflict that was part of the context had to do, as already said, with liberalism and communism, with each claiming to embody certain historical truths, not the least of which was the future socio-political direction of humankind. For liberalism, it espoused a future defined by freedom from all forms of political oppression and the presence of democratic control of society; for communism, it has been the freedom from material oppression, including (particularly, one may say) the social class system to whose tyranny and discriminatory practices are due most, if not all, human ills. According to the doctrinal claims of communism, the very laws of history (not some subjective arguments) contain within them the elimination of capitalism, which is grounded on the universal oppression of one class by another.

Using the above contexts and background, we can now proceed with the evolution of US–China relations, breaking them into three distinct periods: the first, defined by isolation and containment, 1950–1972; the second, containment and detente, 1972–2012; and the third, containment and exclusion, 2012 to the present. We take the periods sequentially.

Isolation and Containment, 1950–1972

Although the US, as shown in the brief discussion of General Marshall's mission to China, sought to contain Mao and his future prospects in China, the official isolation feature of Washington's policy toward China came by way of the Korean War, during which "volunteers" from the PRC repulsed the US-led forces that were seemingly on their way to defeat North Korea, which had invaded the south, and perhaps unite the peninsula under South Korean–US leadership. The stunning reversal to the US-led forces caused what is today referred to as a stalemate.

---

[421] The right to self-determination originally came through the UN Charter (Art. 1, sect. 2), which was incorporated by reference into the UDHR, in the preamble of the declaration. This right was later affirmed and adopted by the UN General Assembly and has become part of customary international law.

It was then that the US formally linked China to the containment policy, which had been in force against the former Soviet Union, meaning Beijing, like the former USSR, was to be subject to "the adroit and vigilant application of counter force at a series of constantly shifting geographical and political points" that correspond to shifts in policy emphasis emanating from China.[422] The associated policy of isolation came about at the same time. Beijing, of course, for tactical and other reasons, did associate itself with the former USSR, but it was not about to play second fiddle as implied in having a policy that was created to deal with Moscow simply extend to it. The PRC's memory of Russian imperial aggression against China had always made it cautious in its relations with the former USSR, and Mao and his associates were not about to forget that the KMT had received significant support from Stalin, including important times when that support came at the expense of the CPC.

On the one hand, China was being isolated by the US, meaning that it was being denied access to the world's trading privileges under the GATT, the loans from the World Bank and the IMF, and what have come to be called regional development banks. As well, Beijing would not have access to investments. Diplomatically, the KMT is the government representing China in the UN and all its associated specialized agencies. Politically, the US entered into bilateral alliance with Chinese neighbors such as Japan and South Korea. On the other hand, Mao and his associates did not want to be too dependent on the former USSR, although its Treaty of Friendship, Alliance, and Mutual Assistance with the former USSR resulted in the settlement of some territorial issues in Manchuria and gained it a loan of some $300 million.[423]

[422] See the text of the original formulation of the policy by George F. Kennan, X "Sources of Soviet Conduct," in Goldwin & Clor, op. cit., pp. 337–355, 348.

[423] Victor V. Cha, "Power Play: Origins of the U.S. Alliance System in Asia," in *International Relations of the Asia-Pacific*, Vol. 17, #2 (2017), pp. 329–332. See a much more insightful treatment of the same issue, by the same author, in *Power Play: Origins of American Alliance System in Asia* (Princeton: Princeton University Press, 2016). The discussion of the US bilateral focus in alliances invites reflections.

Beijing decided to look to itself, deciding to employ its own revolutionary experiences, along with the sense of a new identity ("New China") to guide its path. In doing so, it was rejecting not only what the West, led by the US, was offering to the post-1945 world but, as well, the experiences of its socialist friends in the Soviet bloc, led by the former Soviet Union. Within that self was, it thought, the potential to build the confidence of the Chinese people in their own national capacity to rebuild themselves, trusting in the guidance of the CPC to lead the way in doing so. At a time when the very legitimacy of the government was being questioned and denied (especially in the light of who was representing China in the principal international forums to the world), it was particularly important for the people of China to trust in their own judgments about the path being chosen.

Four interrelated initiatives helped China in its efforts: the "speak bitterness" campaign; the people-to-people diplomacy; the memory and symbol of the Korean War; and the US–Japanese rapprochement. In the case of the first, it was part of a spiritual core used by leaders of China during the early 1950s to effect the desired social transformation that they sought to help people gain a more intimate sense of "New China." This transformation was going to have not only political, economic, and administrative importance and application but also deep psychological meaning. It would be a transformation of consciousness that would generate an organic mobilization of people. Individuals, families, neighborhoods, and communities (and cross-communities) were urged to reenact encounters with class struggle through public confessions of their own experiences with their oppressors, especially landlords, and those confessions served to build a shared common experience, shape solidarity, and instill confidence that their own experiences had national significance and worth. It (like they) would also be part of public history. It also freed people to purge themselves of doubt and self-loathing and helped build a less passive and more assertive civil and political society.[424]

The second, an important complement to the first, was an effort by Beijing to get around and limit the international effect of the US's

---

[424] Guo Wu, "Recalling Bitterness: Historiography, Memory, and the Myth in Maoist China," *Twentieth Century China*, Vol. 39, #3 (2014), pp. 245–268.

isolation policy (a kind of "diplomatic embargo"), which reduced and, in some cases, cut off opportunities for China to have normal government-to-government diplomatic and other exchanges. The PRC launched a transnational people-to-people diplomacy, designed to allow China to engage more directly the peoples of other countries with the aim of generating trust among them, even if the governments of the countries so targeted were distrustful.[425] The other two, the Korean War and the warming up of relations with Japan, were equally important for confidence building, for legitimacy reinforcement, and for influence abroad.

The decision of China to enter the Korean War and its success in forcing a reversal of US-led advances brought with them immense prestige and confidence to the Chinese people and an enormous rise in China's international standing, including in the West but even more so the Global South. "For more than a hundred years, Chinese military forces had been objects of contempt, possessing neither skill, means, or the will to fight,"[426] and now its "peasant army" had successfully confronted and wrestled with the most powerful country in the world, one whose army had crushed Nazi Germany and imperial Japan. The "unmistakable message" from this US–China encounter is not so much that "China would never be intimidated, not even by adversaries that could wipe it off the map," as Allison concludes.[427] All countries, like individuals, can be intimidated. It is rather that even the most powerful has weaknesses and that even the seemingly powerless has strengths. This is a lesson Thucydides offered us through the Melians, something Allison overlooked and about which Mao Tze-tung, coming from a completely different perspective, wrote as early as 1938 as China faced

---

[425] Wang Chao, "People-to-people diplomacy key to tell China's story," in *China Daily* (October 31, 2019). This is an interesting contemporary example of a suggestion that the true story of China can best be told through a people-to-people approach rather than the intergovernmental one.

[426] T. R. Fehrenbach, *This Kind of War* (New York: Macmillan Publishers, 1963), p. 192.

[427] Allison, *Destined,* op. cit., pp. 154–155.

Japan militarily and many were counseling the Chinese people about the uselessness of resisting Tokyo.[428]

The war also embodied, in part, some differences about the attributes of power, with the US emphasizing military capabilities (physical coercion) and China focusing more on people, their unity, will, and moral stance—a sense of rightness, fairness, or injustice as well as trans-border solidarity. China felt that unlike the times when they, like India, were largely in isolation, fighting their oppressors during the nineteenth century, they now (in the 1950s) had the benefit of some intellectual and political support.[429] As important, contrary to Allison's claim, China's entry into the Korean War should not have been seen as Beijing recklessly confronting a nuclear-armed, Japan-defeating US. It knew that if it were shown that it did not act to protect its borders, there would be inferences drawn adverse to its interests—that it was fearful of or unwilling to defend itself, for example. It also knew that if the US were to seek to fight a general war with China, despite its nuclear prowess, Washington would have to prepare for and confront a protracted guerrilla war, in which Beijing would at least be an equal.[430]

The warming up of relations with Japan (its erstwhile enemy), Washington felt, was its only strategic option in Asia (given the "loss" of China and the worldwide ideological and political challenge from the former Soviet Union). In September 1951, it signed a ten-year US–Japanese security alliance, generating considerable anxiety in China about the US's integrity (China had fought with the US against Japan) and intentions. It also gave Beijing some favorable talking points about how honorable the US–KMT association could be.

It was with the authority gained from the "speak bitterness" movement, the people-to-people diplomacy, the prestige gained from the Korean War, and the suspicion about the US's motives in its reorientation toward Japan that Beijing confronted Washington in the 1950s on a range of issue areas, varying from Taiwan, Vietnam, and

---

[428] See "Refutation of the Theory of National Subjugation" in Mao Tze-tung's work on protected war in *Selected Military Writings of Mao Tze-tung* (Beijing: Foreign Language Press, 1967), pp. 198–199.

[429] Ibid., pp. 200–201.

[430] Ibid., pp. 187–267.

the Global South's focus on self-determination to its relations with the former Soviet Union and the very moral legitimacy of the US and its Western allies. The latter confrontation was not always expressed so much through the Marxist-Leninist argument that the center on which human social life and the character of public life are determined is a system, over historical times, by which material goods are produced and exchanged. Neither was it that the system of production and exchange within capitalism is geared to enrich owners at the expense of those who are workers. It was the claim that was part of an effort to offer a concrete demonstration of Washington's alleged lack of commitment to and worldwide opposition against the norm of equality. This norm is at the heart of the idea of human dignity and the right to self-determination. We will use the Global South in general, Vietnam in particular, and the UN as instances of sites where isolation and containment were fought and employ a few other examples, as in the case of Indonesia, for elaboration.

In the case of the Global South (and Vietnam specifically), China's revolution—with its peasant-based efforts at social transformation and Mao as a living embodiment of the claim that peasants are, potentially, revolutionary vanguards—offered an attraction and excitement that equaled or exceeded what the French Revolution offered Europe and elsewhere. Intellectuals, students, workers, and peasants, some of the very groups that made the trans-border people-to-people diplomacy so successful, were ready to be part of beckoning experiments. If what was happening (or had happened) in China were true, then there was a good chance that they could happen in other peasant-based societies. Neither the American-led Western model nor that espoused by the former Soviet Union was seen as capturing a framework that fit the Global South. Beijing's reputation and its revolution, however, were more the products of propaganda and theory to less developed countries (LDCs) than what they had actually experienced from dealing with China or its social system except for the 1954 Geneva Conference (April 26–July 20), called to find solutions to outstanding issues extending from the Korean Wat to the First Indochina War (1947–1954).[431]

---

[431] Laura M. Calkins, *China and the First Vietnam War, 1947–54* (New York: Routledge, 2013). Leaders of Burma and India had negotiated with "New China."

At that conference, Chou En-lai, serving as both prime minister and foreign minister, charmed delegates except for those of the US and South Vietnam, and his work, among other things, gained support for North Vietnam. The conference was limited in the range of ideas and the number of states, represented, however, and it took the African-Asian Conference (frequently called the Bandung Conference, named after the site in Indonesia where it was held), which was held between April 18 and 24, 1955, to give China the first broad-based opportunity to subvert both isolation and containment.

There, at Bandung, twenty-nine countries from Africa, Asia, and Europe (one from Europe, Yugoslavia) met. It was the first meeting of its kind, convened as it was by countries that were either former colonies or, as the expression goes, former semi-colonies. Although all, as in the case of China, had societies that were overwhelmingly rural, they had differences in terms of their respective experiences, how they saw the world, and what models of development they sought for their individual societies. Jawaharlal Nehru of India, for example, espoused nonviolence, nationalism, and a socialism that was comparable to the social democracy found in Western Europe or advanced by the British Labor Party; Achmed Sukarno of Indonesia championed an anti-colonialist stance with a considerable degree of party control that later become known as "guided democracy"; and Abdel Nasser of Egypt and Kwame Nkrumah of Ghana joined with Josip Broz Tito of Yugoslavia and Nehru of India to advocate and become leaders of a collective policy and movement called nonalignment. Obviously, China was aligned with the former USSR, so its role in the latter movement had to be carefully pursued.

The countries were all united, however, in their consensus that they, together, represented over half of the world's population; that poverty elimination and *human* development were central to the future they sought; that imperialism had to come to an end; that decolonization should be accelerated; that self-determination and human rights in general must be part of the focus of international relations; and that world peace should become the foreign policy–focused objective of the future. In short, the conference represented the postwar moral and political movement to which we earlier referred.

China's presence at Bandung, in the person of Chou En-lai, continued to exhibit the impression he had given at Geneva the previous year. Far from being aggressive and divisive, as the US had portrayed China and its leadership as being, delegates found him a conciliating and unifying force. Indeed, while US Secretary of State Dulles condemned "nationalism" and "neutralism," China embraced them, in part because Beijing understood those two terms differently from how they were being distortedly presented by Washington. To the latter, revolutionary nationalism threatened global order (the one that sought to have its imperial allies preserve their colonies), and in the face of the evil represented by communism, neutrality was complicity with that evil. To the conferees, revolutionary nationalism was an important instrument against imperialism and colonialism, and what the US called "neutralism" was really nonalignment—a refusal to be tied in advance to either the USSR or the US-led West, preserving, as the policy and movement urged, the right to choose on the basis of the merits of issues as those issues arise. Preserving the right to choose among alternatives— grounded on the ends embodied, the fairness offered or promised, and the equities they distributed or withheld—was to underscore the right to self-determination, assume that the US-led West and the Soviet-guided East were not the only sites of wisdom, and affirm the importance of the moral dimensions in international relations.

That China, an ally of the former Soviet Union, could be as strongly supportive of nonalignment was a revelation. More revealing to the countries gathered was Beijing's championing of the Five Principles of Peaceful Coexistence (FPPCE), which had come out of a 1949 decision by Mao, refined in 1954 agreements with India and Myanmar (then called Burma) and now advanced at Bandung as norm-candidates for the nonalignment movement (NAM). The five principles are mutual respect for sovereignty and territorial integrity, mutual nonaggression, noninterference in one another's internal affairs, equality and mutual benefit, and peaceful coexistence.[432] These principles, as the reader will see, have remained the core of China's foreign policy—hardly the unprincipled flexibility of which Beijing has been accused.

[432] See "Five Principles of Peaceful Co-existence" (retrieved from http://wiki.china.org.cn/wiki/index.php/five).

An examination of the ten-point Declaration on the Promotion of World Peace and Cooperation (the DOPWPC, a document that contains the summary of commitments by the conference attendees) discloses that the five principles were incorporated throughout that document. Further, recognition of the principle of racial equality—a principle that China advanced but that the US rejected at the 1945 discussions in San Francisco that preceded the adoption of the UN Charter—was one of those ten points. The declaration itself (with its focus on nonintervention, the equality of nations large and small, and abstention from the use of force or threat of aggression against the political independence of states as well as their territorial integrity and its emphasis on cooperation, mutual interests, and peaceful means of conflict resolution) created the basis for an ideological collaboration (the NAM) and the beginnings of the identity called the Global South.[433]

Given the US's actions of interventions in Iran (1953), Guatemala (1954), and Vietnam (1954), the DOPWPC represented not only a warning to Washington but a reverse containment of sort from Beijing. The latter, far from being isolated and confined, had expanded contacts, fellowships, and associational society within which an ideological movement, as one will shortly see, would become more assertive in pushing for human rights and economic justice.[434] As important, the reader will see that the norms advanced at Bandung have served as a source of ties between China and the Global South in general, even as those norms have served as a core for Beijing's foreign policy toward the US.

The returns from Bandung included many more features pertinent to our discussions. Among them was a redoubled effort to dismantle the hold of colonialism on the people of the world, the focus on certain areas of economic collaboration, and the elaboration of the right to self-determination. China, which employed its efforts at Bandung to expand state-to-state relations, strengthened its focus on people-to-people

[433] Tukumbi Lumumba-Kasongo, "Rethinking the Bandung in an Era of 'Unipolar Liberal Globalization' and Movements toward a Multipolar Politics," in *Bandung: Journal of the Global South*, Vol. 2, #9 (2015), pp. 1–17.

[434] See Paterson and Clifford, op. cit., pp. 121–122, 127; see also Lovell, op. cit., pp. 185–222.

diplomacy, especially among students, academics, people who generally had objections to imperialism and colonialism, editors of magazines, public intellectuals, those in labor movements, and ethnic and racial communities against which adverse discrimination reigned, to name a few. In the case of the norm candidate of self-determination, the passionate push for the independence of colonial peoples resulted in an increase in the membership of the UN from seventy-six in 1955 to ninety-nine in 1960. That increase (in large measure the offspring of the NAM's efforts), with the support of the former USSR, enabled the UN General Assembly to adopt the landmark Declaration on the Granting of Independence to Colonial Countries and Peoples (DOGICCP) on December 14, 1960.[435]

The 1960 declaration not only incorporated many of the principles coming out of Bandung but also lit a moral fire among peoples of the Global South and further helped China in its efforts to forge greater solidarity (Moscow and Beijing were increasingly at odds) with those who began to push for a "third way"—a path different from what Washington and Moscow were offering. The text of the DOGICCP, in part, reads that "all peoples have an inalienable right to *complete* freedom (emphasis the author's), the exercise of their sovereignty, and the integrity of their territory; that the "subjugation of peoples to alien subjection, domination, and exploitation constitutes a denial of fundamental human rights"; and that "[a]ll peoples have the right to self-determination . . . by virtue [of which] they freely determine their political status and freely pursue their economic, social, and cultural development."[436]

The document went further, reflecting the NAM's response to the affected concerns of European imperial powers and the US about the extent to which colonial groups were ready for independence and some anxieties, by the latter groups, about actions by imperial powers to sow disunity among them. Paragraph 3 of the DOGICCP states that the "inadequacy of political, economic, social, and educational preparedness

---

[435] GA Res. 1514, UNGAOR, 15th Sess., Supp. No. 16, at 66, UN. Doc. A/4684 (1961).

[436] Ibid., paragraph 2.

should never serve as a pretext for delaying independence,"[437] and paragraph 6 asserts that "any attempt aimed at partial or total disruption of the national unity and territorial integrity of a country is incompatible with the purposes and principles of the UN Charter."[438]

Beijing—which faced the possible alienation of parts of its territory, including Taiwan, and the claim of the KMT to be the legitimate government of China—found much comfort in the DOGICCP. It also, as did members of the NAM, felt that readiness for independence was something achieved by revolutionary or militant collective response to oppression, with collaboration among peasants, students, workers, urban intelligentsia, and small merchants, not the determination from the political capitals of the oppressor.[439] By 1971, as a result of the work of the NAM, the worldwide militant agitations supported by Beijing, the UN's membership had grown from 99 in 1960 to 132 in 1971, with new members overwhelmingly from Africa, Asia, Latin America, and the Caribbean. This allowed the Global South to constitute such a majority in the UN General Assembly that the US's influence could no longer successfully contest it without serious political damage to itself. Led by a resolution from Albania, on its twenty-first application to be seated in the UN, the PRC was supported to become the government representing the state of China, and the ROC was expelled.

Almost as important as the expelling of the ROC and the seat of the PRC as the legitimate government of China, from the perspective of this book, was the economic aspects of colonialism against which the NAM had begun to push rather aggressively after the adoption of the DOGICCP. On June 15, 1964, a loose alliance of LDCs (a true Global

---

[437] Ibid.

[438] Ibid.

[439] James Chieh Hsiung, *Ideology and Practice: The Evolution of Chinese Communism* (New York: Praeger, 1970), p. 70. See also Robert Vitalis, *White World Order, Black Power Politics: The Birth of American International Relations* (Ithaca: Cornell University Press, 2015), pp. 133–134; Rudolf von Albertson, *Decolonization: The Administration and Future of the Colonies, 1919–1960* (New York: Doubleday & Company Inc., 1971). The latter work gives the reader a sense of what, by 1960, the imperial powers thought they might be able to preserve of their imperial influence.

South since Latin America and the Caribbean were more intimately involved) formed what has come to be called the Group of 77 (it was 77 when it had been formed but today has over 130 members). Those members concluded that, consistent with the terms of the DOGICCP, if they were to have *complete* freedom and independence, they could not reconcile themselves to their then assigned role of agrarian and raw material producers and appendages of industrial countries, including those from which they had ostensibly won independence.[440] The purpose of the Group of 77, therefore, has been to provide the means by which the nation-states of the Global South can present and promote their collective economic interests, strengthen their negotiating capacity on all matters of major international significance within the UN system, and augment South–South cooperation on issues of development. To help them in achieving that purpose, on December 30, 1964, the group led in helping create, within the UN Secretariat, the United Nations Conference on Trade and Development (UNCTAD).[441]

China has never been a member of the Group of 77, but Beijing has always worked with it. As we will see in the later presentation of this counter-narrative, this support became a major issue in US–China relations, especially during the Reagan administration and later.[442] It should be observed here that neither Bandung nor the Group of 77 appears in Allison's work. We now turn to Vietnam. The other case study in the area of isolation and containment is the Vietnam War and some of its spillover effects. We will conduct our examination by looking briefly at the First (1945–1954) and Second Indochina Wars, the latter known as the Vietnam War (1955–1975). The US's involvement included both.

---

[440] UNCTAD, *UNCTAD at 50: A Short History* (Geneva: UNCTAD/osg/2014), p. 7.

[441] Ibid. This work is an excellent review of fifty-plus years of economic development.

[442] China's international position as a developing country and concurrently as a potential superpower competing with the US has made it complicated for Beijing to join or be directly a part of the Group of 77. This is why, on occasions, one finds communiqués of the Group of 77 *and* China.

The expression "Indochina" is a term used to reflect the joint cultural influence of India and China in a portion of what is, today, all of Southeast Asia. As Europeans colonized this area during the nineteenth century, the French part of the area came to be known as French Indochina, consisting of Cambodia, Laos, and Vietnam. When Germany took control of France during World War II, the latter country gradually lost control of a number of colonies, including those in Indochina, which came under the control of imperial Japan. With the defeat of Japan, Ho Chi Minh, a Vietnamese revolutionary leader, declared the independence of his country under the name of the Democratic Republic of Vietnam (DRVN) on September 2, 1945. France, which was recovering from World War II, sought to regain control of its colonies (including Vietnam, Laos, and Cambodia) and refused to recognize this declared independence until 1954, when it was forced to concede international recognition through the Geneva Conference of that date. The conceding was itself the result of its defeat at the battle of Dien Bien Phu by a Ho Chi Minh–led Viet Minh (to be later called the Viet Cong), a coalition of Vietnamese communists and nationalists.

The US, which had reached the conclusion that Indochina's association with the West was important to the defense of "the free world," had begun to give the French significant support in the form of ammunition, vehicles, aircrafts, naval vessels, small arms, and automatic weapons, along with hospital supplies and technical equipment. By 1954, it was secretly bearing as much as 80 percent of the cost of what France was then incurring to defend its Indochina colonies.[443] At the Geneva Conference, which was convened in July 1954 to negotiate the end of the war, France agreed to withdraw its troops from North Vietnam; Vietnam would be temporarily divided at the seventeenth parallel, and following elections within two years, a president would be chosen, and the country would be reunited.

The US did not sign the Geneva agreements but publicly indicated that it would not oppose them. Washington made it known, however, that it was not bound by the agreements if there were to be any aggression by

---

[443] Ellen J. Hammer, *The Struggle for Indochina* (Stanford: Stanford University Press, 1954), pp. 64–74.

the communists. Indeed, as early as April 7, 1954, before the agreements just mentioned, President Eisenhower, at a press conference on that day, commented on the strategic importance of Indochina to "the free world" in four categories: first, in the category of important minerals (the area housed, he said, tin and tungsten); second, in the category of geopolitics, the "domino effect" (the loss of Indochina would "set off the loss of Burma [Myanmar], of Thailand, of the Malay Peninsula, and Indonesia" with the forfeiture of all the materials and people of the countries identified)[444]; third, in the category of military readiness and operations (the US would be affected adversely by the effect that the loss would have on "island defenses' chain of Japan, Formosa [Taiwan], and the Philippines," and as such, it would "move in to threaten Australia and New Zealand"[445]; and, finally, in the category of markets (the "loss" would "take away the region that Japan must have as a trading area, or it would force Japan to turn toward China and Manchuria" or communist states in general). The consequences of the "loss to the free world [were] just incalculable," the president concluded.[446]

In short, before the Geneva agreements of 1954, the president of the US was indicating that he was unlikely to find a communist control of Indochina acceptable. The then secretary of state, John Foster Dulles, at a press conference about a month later, took the position that the US would "not stand by and see the extension of Communism by any means into Southeast Asia," in response to a question regarding what the US would do if Ho Chi Minh were to win a free election in Vietnam.[447] He further opined that conditions in Vietnam were not conducive to a free election.[448]

Both the president and the secretary of state made references to collective security as an aid to policy in dealing with the area, and on September 8, 1954, they underwrote and helped give birth to the

---

[444] See text of Press Conference of the President in Williams, op. cit., p. 1119.

[445] Ibid.

[446] Ibid. In 1951, the US had concluded a defense treaty (the ANZUS Pact) with Australia and New Zealand.

[447] Williams, op. cit., p. 1120.

[448] Ibid.

Southeast Asia Treaty Organization (SEATO), a regional security body made up of Australia, Britain, France, New Zealand, Pakistan, the Philippines, Thailand, and the US. The imperial powers were being "brought back;" and it was in this context that the US gradually openly opposed the election, as provided in the Geneva accords, gave support to Vietnam south of the seventeenth parallel, and sought to make the temporary line of ceasefire the border between North and South Vietnam, each of which would be a separate state. The DRVN, led by Ho Chi Minh, on the other hand, sought to unify the country under its control by force in the absence of the electoral provisions of the Geneva accords. The Second Indochina War began, with the US viewing its involvement as preventing the North Vietnamese from gaining control of South Vietnam and thereby containing and isolating China, then seen as enjoying weighty influence on North Vietnam and in containing communism in general.

China, in turn (along with the former USSR)—which had been giving material, organizational, ideological, technical, experiential, and moral support to Hanoi since the time of the First Indochina War—increased that support.[449] For Washington, a challenge of a particular character developed. The more it sought to justify the support for Vietnam as a new launching site for a world revolution that would favor communism if the north were to gain control of the south, the more significance the war emerged to hold for China in two significant senses: it was seen as a laboratory for revolutionary success in the rest of Southeast Asia, including Indonesia, and the rest of the Global South, especially Africa, as well as in Latin America and the Caribbean. It was also seen as an upholder and defender of the DOGICCP, which opposed "disruption of national unity" and any and all attempts to limit the exercise of the right to self-determination, which includes the right of countries to "freely pursue their economic, social, and cultural development." China embraced that significance with eagerness and discipline, and

---

[449] Lovell, op. cit., p. 234. It should be noted here that because of Washington's threat to use nuclear weapons against China over differences concerning Taiwan, Beijing was initially not as enthusiastic about a full-blown oppositional war against South Vietnam but came around quickly to offer whatever support Hanoi needed. See Paterson & Clifford, op. cit., p. 121.

although its success outside of Vietnam was mixed, within Vietnam, it was decisive and, in some cases, determinative. A relatively small, poor agrarian country, with support from China, took on the most powerful country in the world (along with some of its allies) and defeated it over a twenty-year struggle.[450]

The reasons for the US's defeat are many, but the principal one was that South Vietnam provided a socioeconomic environment not unlike Chiang Kai-shek's China, where landlords and socioeconomic elites, along with a corrupt military, were unable to make the type of social reform necessary to confront, successfully, what the US called the Viet Cong (the National Liberation Front of South Vietnam), a mass political organization in South Vietnam (it had expanded its mass organization over the years), which, with help from North Vietnam, was able to do so in prosecuting the war using the principles of guerrilla warfare.[451] Very much, as was the case in China, as the communists gained control of certain sites, the land constituting those sites were distributed to the peasants.

The US, over a period of years under the Democratic and Republican administration, would give reassuring reports to their respective political constituencies at home as well as to allies that victory was at hand; that the push of liberty was defeating the aggression of tyranny; and that the security of the global order would never be allowed to suffer by any irresolution on its part. We have already seen how Republican president Dwight Eisenhower informed the American people about the prospect of a chain reaction in the "domino theory," were North Vietnam to win. We know of John F. Kennedy's stance that committed the country, broadly, "to pay any price, bear any burden, meet any hardship, support any friend, oppose any foe, to assure the survival and success of liberty"; Lyndon Johnson's enabling "the will of the world for peace"; and Richard Nixon's stance of providing a war-weary

---

[450] We often think of the war as one between the US and North Vietnam, but the latter had support from China and Russia (among others) and the US from Australia, Canada, New Zealand, the Philippines, and Thailand, among others.

[451] William S. Turley, *The Second Indochina War: A Concise Political and Military History* (Lanham, MD: Rowman & Littlefield, 2005).

nation with a "victory with honor"—all thinking they could bend North Vietnam to America's will.[452]

As the war continued to expand, especially after the Kennedy administration, it became increasingly difficult for Washington to disguise the breadth and scope of its involvement (something we are not willing to do)—an involvement that had spread to Laos, through whose territory North Vietnamese soldiers and materials reached South Vietnam and whose neutrality the Geneva Conference of 1962 had supported. As soon as the agreement of that conference was signed, the US, China, North Vietnam, and others began to undermine it. By November 1961, the Kennedy administration had authorized an increase in the number of "advisors" in South Vietnam (not unlike China's "volunteers" in Korea), and by the end of that year, there were three thousand such advisors. At the time of Kennedy's death in 1963, those advisors—"troops, helicopters units, mine sweepers, and air reconnaissance aircraft"—had grown to 169,000.[453] By 1965, 200,000 American troops were fighting in Vietnam (no longer a US-supported war but a US war, as the country gradually came to learn), and by 1967, at its peak, the number was 540,000.[454]

During all this escalation—symbolized by the characterization, pace, and size of troop deployments, as touched on above—China was using the political environment not only to offer more support for North Vietnam but also to expand material and moral support to the global insurgency against imperialism, the chief conventional representation of which was Washington. Much of the material aid came in the form of grants, no-interest loans to countries in Asia and Africa (later to some in Latin America), technical assistance in terms of medical personnel, agricultural experts, and road-building specialists. Even failing initiatives at home—such as the harmful 1958–1962 Great Leap Forward, a campaign by Mao Tze-tung to transform his country

---

[452]   See Pres. John F. Kennedy's inaugural address, delivered January 20, 1961; Pres. Lyndon Johnson's speech at Syracuse University, August 5, 1964; and Pres. Richard Nixon's *The Real War,* op. cit., pp. 96–125. The development of Nixon's thinking is, of itself, illuminating.

[453]   Paterson & Clifford, op. cit., p. 162.

[454]   Ibid., p. 173.

from an agrarian economy to an industrialized, communist society that
would be self-sufficient—were met with some admiration in many areas
in the West and in the Global South. This admiration largely stemmed
from the willingness of the USSR, which was being seen as less and less
interested in shaping an egalitarian society and militantly confronting
imperialism, to cut off all aid to China, but it also arose from a Global
South that was increasingly in debt to the West and the deeply felt need
to be part of the idea of self-sufficiency, which China was espousing.[455]

China's no-interest loans (and by 1970, China was giving as much as
5–6 percent of its national budget in aid), its insistence that its technical
and other aid personnel live at a standard that corresponded to the
people they served, and its willingness to challenge the major Western
powers and even its socialist ally, the former USSR—which, under the
claim of "socialist commonwealth," sought to limit the right to self-
determination movements in Eastern Europe—won it wide appeal.
Many students, professors, and public intellectuals in the West (and the
US in particular) began to see China as the true champion of the poor
and the oppressed and began to offer it support, even when they were
anxious about policies such as the Great Leap Forward and certain
aspects of the Cultural Revolution. Additionally, Beijing was growing
in military and in other terms of power, and this too evoked respect, if
not outright admiration, in many quarters. It successfully conducted, in
1964, its first nuclear weapon test (unexpected by the world, especially
after the former USSR had withdrawn technical support from China in
the late 1950s), and in record time, it detonated its first thermonuclear
weapon in June 1967. The latter placed China on the road, potentially,
to be among the first rank of military powers. It also meant that China
could even be more forceful in supporting revolutionary movements
around the world, unlike in the early 1950s, when it could be and was,
in fact, threatened by the US with the use of nuclear weapons.[456]

The US, which (during the 1960s) was having its own problems at
home in the form of the civil rights movement, had some achievements

[455] Alfred L. Chan, *Mao's Crusade: Politics and Policy Implementation in China's Great Leap Forward* (Oxford: Oxford University Press, 2001). See also Lovell, op. cit., pp. 188–189, in the matter of technical and economic assistance.

[456] Paterson & Clifford, op. cit., pp. 119–121.

that won it some applause also. Legislation supportive of rights for minorities and for women won congressional support, and some steps were taken to recognize the damage that was being done to the environment. Perhaps the most significant success was the spectacular landing of humans on the moon in July 1969. These achievements were partly undermined, however, by suspicions about Washington's role in the 1965 brutal overthrow of the China-backed Sukarno regime in Indonesia and in the 1960–1961 Congo crisis, its backing of the apartheid regime in South Africa, and its general support for forces of reaction in Latin America and the Caribbean.

It was within this general political environment that the earlier described PRC replacement of the KMT as the representative of China in the UN took place. By 1969, the US faced not only a worldwide rebellion against its actual or suspected policies but also an internal one, especially after the 1968 Tet Offensive—a coordinated and stunning series of North Vietnamese attacks beginning in January of the latter year on over a hundred South Vietnamese cities and townships. The attacks, intended to incite a popular rebellion against the South Vietnamese government, were unsuccessful in their objective, but it exposed the misrepresentations that the US government officials had made, since the early 1960s, to the American people and to allies. The anger it sponsored, especially on college and university campuses, was widespread and bitter, occasioning President Johnson's decision, in March 1968, not to run for reelection to the presidency in November of that year.[457]

Matters got worse. The entire moral fabric of the country, including its constitutional integrity, came into question when, in June 13, 1971, the *New York Times* began the publication of what came to be known as "the Pentagon Papers"—a highly classified study, requested by former secretary of defense McNamara, on the history of involvement in Vietnam from 1945 to 1967. That publication confirmed, for many at home and abroad, the outright deception of the American people and members of Congress, from the secrecy and lies concerning the character and extent of the US's support of France during the First Indochina War

---

[457] See President Johnson's speech to the nation, March 31, 1968.

through the often-denied bombing of Laos and Cambodia to the hidden coastal marine corps attacks on North Vietnam.

Although the war continued until 1975, the US and South Vietnam were defeated at the time of the Tet Offensive. Thereafter, the US began to seek a way to leave Vietnam with "honor," as the late president Nixon promised he would do during his election campaigns in 1968 and 1972.[458] The US, far from succeeding in using the Vietnam War to isolate and contain China, discovered that the latter country had used the same war to help defeat the US militarily, affirming Beijing's belief and theory that a revolutionary war, led by peasants, can successfully resist powerful conventional armies. President Nixon, reflecting on the war, felt that he had to deal with this point, stating that "Vietnam did *not* prove that guerrilla wars are unwinnable or that 'revolutionary' forces are invincible."[459] By 1971, when the PRC had replaced the KMT in the UN, not only had China succeeded in winning broad support among the peoples and governments of the world, but also, a substantial number of the US's closest allies that had joined the isolation bandwagon—Canada, France, Germany, Italy, and the Netherlands—had gradually moved to establish diplomatic relations or had given indications of intending to do so. The US had lost much of its moral clout throughout the world.

---

[458] See Tad Szulc, "Behind the Vietnam Cease-Fire Agreement," in *Foreign Policy*, Vol. 15 (Summer 1974), pp. 21–69. This article offers an unusually extensive and sensitive summary on the background materials governing the negotiations among the US, North Vietnam, and South Vietnam, with the help of China and the former USSR. One may gain some further insights by looking at Richard Nixon's *The Real War*, op. cit., pp. 106–125.

[459] See Nixon, *The Real War*, op. cit., p. 123.

CHAPTER 12

Containment and Détente

The US, like the PRC (despite the latter's recounted success in the last chapter), faced much of the 1970s with some challenges. Chief among them, for China, was the impact of the Cultural Revolution (to which we previously referred), which sought to transform the PRC culturally—in education, in government, in political party alignment, in generational authority (students became teachers), in the physical or social location of the most morally relevant experience, and in the psychological attitude toward authority, be it in local and national public life or within proletarian internationalism. In the case of the latter, the question of alleged actions by certain countries—in collusion with imperialism, in prolonging the Vietnam War, and in lending support to the idea of a socialist commonwealth—were being alluded to.[460] It also had to begin reassessing its policy of "world revolution" in light of the bloody coup in Indonesia, which overthrew its ally, and the genocide in Cambodia, resulting, in part, from its own support of local political groups there and the US bombing of the country. It also needed to review its relations with the former Soviet Union and the US.

For the US, in addition to the domestic and international trauma of Vietnam,[461] it was facing a financial crisis that led to the dismantling

---

[460] See Chieh Hsiung, op. cit., pp. 200–251.

[461] It should not be forgotten that socialism had some significant expression in the US, especially on university campuses, during this time. In Western Europe,

of the gold standard (which had defined the world financial system since 1945), a brutal civil war between Pakistan and East Bengal (now Bangladesh), and conflict in the Middle East, which triggered an oil crisis that adversely affected most of the world, including the West, caused growing debt in the Global South, and increasingly tense relations with the former USSR. In addition, the popular election of socialist Salvador Allende in Chile and the liberation conflicts in South Africa caused great anxiety in Washington. It was under these described conditions, along with others, that the US decided to pursue a policy of containment and détente toward China, the latter term, as used in this work, denoting a gradual relaxation of tensions. This policy continuity (containment) and change (substitution of détente for isolation) was designed to help the US achieve three major objectives: creating greater political stability (accompanied by competition) with the former USSR; improving economic growth and development; and promoting human rights internationally, including the right to self-determination. These three areas paralleled, in large measure, some of China's emerging interests, although with different emphases. For Beijing, the last two had weightier importance, while the first two, including ending the war in Vietnam, had greater urgency for the US. In the case of the second, on which each sought to place a very heavy emphasis, the US was more interested in growth, while China was more concerned about development. We will look at the policy of containment and détente in relationship to the three objectives.

To a shocked world, the late president Nixon announced on July 15, 1971, a planned visit to China. He had campaigned on the issue of ending the Vietnam War and achieving an honorable peace, but few had imagined that this anticommunist leader would be the one to seek an end to the policy of isolation of China, not to mention a relaxation of tensions with the country that had helped bring such trauma and humiliation to the US. He and his national security advisor (and soon-to-be secretary of state), Henry Kissinger, were not the only ones who thought that the policy of isolating China should be discontinued. Others in the foreign policy establishment—such as Hans Morgenthau from the University of Chicago and Robert A. Scalapino from the University of California,

including Germany, it found weighty expression.

Berkeley, two stalwarts of containment—thought as much and testified to Congress accordingly.[462] The latter thought that isolation freed China from responsibilities toward the international system and was, therefore, a mistake that should be corrected; Morgenthau saw the policy as linked to a frustrated expectation, the recognition of the ROC under Chiang Kai-shek, with the strong belief in its likely return to and control of the mainland. In his view, the prospect of that return became so improbable that he could not see the merit of either continuing recognition of the ROC or the isolation of the PRC.[463]

While these views constituted a consensus among some foreign policy experts, the fact that China was seen as the primary supporter of Vietnam did not predispose them or others to the idea of discontinuing the isolation unless there were important returns to the US. President Nixon had other ends in mind, some of which he thought would yield those returns. He sought the new ties with China as a means to put pressure on the USSR to be more flexible in its relations with Washington; to persuade Beijing to use its influence on Hanoi in the latter's negotiations with Washington; and to contain China by way of including it more and more in the international issues confronting the world, thus giving it a stake, as Professor Scalapino argued, in US-advanced international issues. A major problem in all this, of course, involved Taiwan. The US had continued to recognize the ROC as the legitimate government of China despite the UN's expelling it in favor of China.

The results of Nixon's visit to China (February 21–28, 1972) were many, chief among which was the Shanghai Communiqué of February 28, which textually expressed the separate and joint positions of both countries and has since served as a core document in US–China relations. It incorporates twelve points and indicates that while both sides achieved certain objectives pursuant to the relaxation of tensions, China was as

---

[462] See "New China Policy for the United States," a statement by Hans J. Morgenthau before the US Senate Committee on Foreign Relations, *Hearing, U.S. Policy with Respect to Mainland China*, 1966. See also "Goals of Communist China," a statement by Robert A. Scalapino at the same hearing of the US Senate Committee on Foreign Relations, in Goldwin and Clor, op. cit., pp. 316–325 and 302–315, respectively.

[463] Ibid., p. 319.

adept in seeking to assure its friends as well as in its efforts to contain the US as the latter was in giving assurances to its allies and containing Beijing. In the first six of these points, China, for example, offered good will to North Korea, North Vietnam, Cambodia, Laos, and Pakistan by name and more general gestures to militants throughout the world by noting that "wherever there is oppression, there is resistance"; that countries want independence, nations want liberation, and peoples want revolution; that "nations big and small" should be equal; that big nations should not bully the weak; and that China "will never be a superpower and . . . opposes hegemony and power politics of any kind." (We will see how some of these positions find themselves in President Xi's speeches.) The US, likewise, offered reassurances to South Vietnam, South Korea, and Japan and emphasized the need to reduce tensions and promote peace in Asia and the world.

Both sides acknowledged in the text that there are "essential differences between China and the United States in their social systems and foreign policies" and that the "two sides agreed that countries, regardless of their social systems, should conduct relations on the principles of respect for the sovereignty of all states, nonaggression of against other states, noninterference in the internal affairs of other states, equality and mutual benefit, and peaceful coexistence."[464] In other words, the PRC got the US to agree to the FPPCE, which were adopted at Bandung and have been part of a broader Global South's commitment. The statement goes further under point eight. It states that "international disputes should be settled on this basis [five principles] without resorting to the use of or the threat of force" (present in the UN Charter and the 1928 Pact of Paris also) and that the US and PRC "are *prepared to apply these principles in their mutual relations.*"[465]

Point nine then begins by stating that "with these principles of international relations in mind, the two sides" agree that "progress toward normalization of relations between China and the United States is in the interest of all countries"; that "both wish to reduce the danger of

---

[464] See Joint Communiqué of the United States of America and the People's Republic of China at www.taiwandocuments.org/communique o1.htm (retrieved May 21, 2020).

[465] Ibid. Emphasis is the author's.

international military conflict"; and that "neither should seek hegemony in the Asia-Pacific region and each is opposed to efforts by any other country or group of countries to establish such hegemony" (this was directed to the former Soviet Union, as the US sought and China also wanted). Then in point ten, both sides shared the view "that it would be against the interest of the peoples of the world for any major country to collude with another against other countries or for major countries to divide up the world into spheres of interests."[466]

Of utmost importance was the issue of Taiwan, the return of which to China had been in the November 27, 1943, Cairo Declaration but to which the US-supported Chiang Kai-shek fled with his army after his 1949 defeat in the civil war with the Mao Tze-tung–led PRC. The US and China have had, as the reader should recall, a tense relationship on this matter. Point eleven, therefore, should be seen as their respective and joint attempts to find their way to solving it. "The China side [the document said] reaffirmed its position: the Taiwan question is the crucial question obstructing the normalization of relations between China and the United States: the government of the PRC is the sole legal government of China; Taiwan is a province of China . . . the liberation of Taiwan is China's internal affair in which no other country has the right to interfere." The US, for its part, in point twelve, says that the "United States acknowledges that all Chinese on either side of the Taiwan Strait maintain that there is but one China and that Taiwan is part of China. The United States does not challenge that position."[467] (The US did not challenge or oppose the 1954 Geneva accords either, but it later supported a division of Vietnam that led to war). Nevertheless, the US, in this 1972 communiqué, reaffirmed its often stated "interest in a peaceful settlement of the Taiwan question" and asserted its "ultimate objective" to withdraw "all US forces and military installations from Taiwan."[468]

The Shanghai Communiqué opened political and diplomatic elbow room that each of the two countries sought. For instance, it allowed both

---

[466] Ibid.

[467] Ibid.

[468] Ibid.

to be freer in their respective relations with the former USSR. China and the US knew that Moscow had to be cautious about how it sought expansion in the Pacific since it would have to deal with both the US and China. It gave the US greater flexibility in dealing with Moscow in its ongoing efforts in the area of arms limitation; it also allowed the US to invite help from China in dealing with North Vietnam, although Chou informed Kissinger that he would not, consistent with the communiqué, exert pressure on Hanoi to negotiate.[469] Because of the reduced expenditure on the war in Vietnam (Congress, in 1974, voted less than half the requested aid to South Vietnam, $700 million instead of the asked-for $1.5 billion)[470] and a more relaxed environment in the negotiations of the ongoing strategic arms limitations with Moscow, the US could better focus on economic issues such as the escalating price of oil, the threatened rise in inflation, and the much-sought resumption of vibrant growth. China also could begin to reorder its economy with the death of Mao in 1976, the ending of the Cultural Revolution in the same year, and the containment and subsequent defeat of the political faction within the CCP called the Gang of Four.

Emerging as core leader in China was Deng Xiaoping (1979–1987), who would reorder the earlier-mentioned economic growth and development. A victim of the Cultural Revolution who nevertheless remained an ardent Maoist, he not only publicly acknowledged the mistakes of the revolution as well as the Great Leap Forward but also committed himself and the CCP to the reforming of the country's model of economic development. He did so by first allowing for certain experiments with their existing agricultural system that was based on collective farms throughout the society. One experiment aggregately referred to as the household responsibility system (HRS) or the family production system began in 1979 but was not officially established until 1982. It permitted households to construct machinery, land, and other inputs from collective organizations and to assume responsibility for losses and profits (with a portion to the government). A production explosion took place, with the GDP in agriculture increasing by 60

---

[469] See Szulc, op. cit. p. 44.

[470] Paterson & Clifford, op. cit., pp. 220-221.

percent and the average income of farmers increasing by over 150 percent. With this success, the people's communes (1958–1983) were replaced by townships, food security was assured, and the infrastructure to promote food production, organize or allow trading, and augment household and community (as well as national) income were put in place.[471]

The de-collectivization of agriculture (and it began at the grassroots level before officials in Beijing gave it their blessings) also occasioned other developments: it allowed many who no longer needed to produce food to move to the factory, often within cities; it increased revenues for the government to be used for investments in the emerging industrial sector; and it allowed for the needed broadening of the educational system and the specializations to be emphasized for the deeper and more complex development of the society.[472] Not to be overlooked are two more fundamental insights that ensued from the experiment: a market system (initially strange to socialist China) could be allowed, as part of socialism (with Chinese characteristics); and zones of industrial experimentation could be organized in the pattern of agriculture if the appropriate incentives were introduced. The success of agriculture gave Deng the political clout to act boldly in his overall modernization scheme. (By 1983, state subvention to agriculture was no longer necessary.)

Deng's experiment and success in the field of agriculture was part of a four-goal program called the Four Modernizations, which he saw as necessary for the rejuvenation of China. They were agriculture, industry, defense (the military), and science and technology. The latter, as one might surmise from China's achievements in the nuclear field, had been very important to Beijing, and immediately after the 1979 establishment

---

[471] Kathleen Hartford, "Socialist Agriculture Is Dead: Long Live Socialist Agricultural Organizational Transformation in Rural China," in Elizabeth Perry and Christine Wong, eds., *The Political Economy of Reform in Post-Mao China* (Cambridge: Harvard University Press, Council on East Asian Studies, 1985), pp. 1–62. See also Kathleen Hartford and Steven M. Goldstein, eds., *Single Sparks: China's Rural Revolutions* (Armonk: M. E. Sharpe, 1989).

[472] Justin Yifu Lin, "The Household Responsibility System in China's Agricultural Reform: A Theoretical and Empirical Study," in *Economic Development and Cultural Change* (a supplement), Vol. 36, #3 (1988), pp. S199–S224.

of diplomatic relations between the US and China, efforts were launched to find ways of gaining mastery in wider areas of science and technology. To a certainty, the Cultural Revolution had resulted in the loss of at least a generation of scientists and other leaders in technology and to the undermining of a civilizational commitment of the Chinese people to science and technology.[473] So Deng and his prime minister, Zhao Ziyang, accentuated reforms in this area of modernization. One has but to examine the 1979 US–China Agreement on Cooperation in Science and Technology, a cooperation that ranged from agriculture, forestry, and energy and nuclear safety to public health, telecommunications, space technology, and high energy.[474] What is most important for us to know at this juncture is that science and technology underwent reforms between 1979 and 1986 (with certain continuing refinements) that were not unlike what took place in agriculture and was to take place in industry. The results have been no less spectacular, as we will see.

China's research institutes, until the early 1980s (and most research took place through institutes, modeled after the former USSR), were structured to share results in a vertical hierarchy, and aligned with that practice, these institutes dealt with limited supplies by pursuing self-sufficiency, further reducing the exchange of information or of personnel across the confines of administrative frontiers and the encouraging of non-useful rivalries. Premier Zhao and the central committee of the CCP reformed the system by insisting on coordination between and among scientific fields, fluid communication among and across research units, non-duplication of facilities and personnel, and improved allocation of personnel and funding. Equally important, the reforms encouraged the

---

[473] Joseph Needham (ed.), *Science and Civilization in China* (Cambridge: Cambridge University Press, 1954–2007). This is a series by Cambridge University Press and is more of a culturally focused work than anything else—exceptional historical presentation.

[474] Nitin Agarwala and Rana Divyank Chaudhary, "China's Policy in Science and Technology: Implications for the Next Industrial Transition," in *India Quarterly*, Vol. 75, #2 (June 2019), pp. 206–227. See also Jin Xiaoming, "The China–US Relationship in Science and Technology," a paper presented at the Lally School of Management and Technology–hosted meeting, "China's Emerging Technological Trajectory in the 21st Century," Rensselaer Polytechnic Institute, Troy, New York, September 4–6, 2003.

commercialization of technology, the application of science to the needs of industry, and continuity between basic research (much of it led by China's Academy of Sciences) and the applied variety.

As revolutionary were the encouraged practice of having institutes work directly with industry, the establishment in 1986 of the National Science Foundation (with a range of incentives and greater allocations for budgetary support of research), the decentralization of science and technology, the introduction of markets, the focus on competition, incentives in the form of awards and recognitions for new products, models, or processes, and the complementarity between science and technology and the overall economy. The latter too got its opportunity at autonomy with the introduction of private ownership, special investment zones, and strong support of the government by way of subsidies.

Affecting the sought containment of China were two complementary policy emphases: the neoliberal push of the Reagan administration (which had almost the exact temporal correspondence with Deng's tenure as core leader) and a passionate shift in the focus on self-determination, this time with an economic emphasis, in contrast to the previous, greater political focus. In these unfolding two policy accentuations, one sees more clearly the divergence in paths chosen by the US and China, with the former focusing on economic growth and the latter pursuing growth and development. There was, however, a seeming underlying convergence at the heart of the political economy policies emerging from Washington and Beijing—a phenomenon that was very pleasing to Washington. In pursuit of its neoliberal agenda, the Reagan administration was removing more and more state intervention in or regulation of the market; China was moving from a socialist country to one that embraces what we now call a "socialist market" model, meaning, in part, one with fewer government controls, incentives, and private competition. All this fit well with the idea of "convergence," Washington's policy of containing China by facilitating the latter's "progressive integration" into the US-controlled world economic system. For China, however, while it recognized the market as an important instrument of growth, it also saw the government as the means by which distribution, certain investments, and the broad-based unfolding of all social and societal potential can be realized. There was, therefore, a limit to what the market and growth are seen as capable of doing.

There was more. The ending Vietnam War in 1975 merged with a number of associated problems, some of which, like the dollar, had begun in the early 1960s (some would say late 1950s) but were aggravated by the war and threatened its monetary standing as the world's key currency. Others included its worldwide military commitments that the budget found difficulties accommodating, emerging record unemployment, disturbing amounts of corporate debt, inflation caused by rising oil prices after 1973, and a debt-to-equity ratio that was hostile to the integrity of the US-led economic model and its associated world financial system.[475] The path going forward after the Vietnam War, therefore, had to address in some way, even if by neglect of some areas, all these problems as well as domestic burden sharing. The efforts of Pres. Lyndon Johnson through his Great Society programs, which sought to "buy off" some of the then emerging opposition to the war, had to be reviewed.[476] The review, which expressed a concern about a more equitable sharing of the cost of foreign policy (meaning removing some of the economic burden from the non-affluent classes), was "resolved" in favor of those who sought no fundamental change in the economic structure of society and who, as well, argued that "supply-side economics" (a macroeconomic view that contends that economic growth can best be realized by lowering taxes, decreasing government regulation, etc.) would take care of the concern. Forming the heart of the neoliberal outlook that President Reagan followed, it was paired with the then late president Kennedy's aphorism that "a rising tide lifts

---

[475] See an impressive debate and consensus on "Who Pays for Foreign Policy? A Debate on Consensus" in *Foreign Policy* #18 (Spring 1975), pp. 79–122. Leading the debate were Earl C. Ravenel and Charles W. Maynes Jr., with comments by foreign policy stalwarts such as Richard Falk, Hans Morgenthau, Daniel Moynihan, Bruce Russett, and Arthur Schlesinger Jr. (cited as Ravenel and Maynes).

[476] See Charles W. Maynes Jr., "Who Pays for Foreign Policy?" in *Foreign Policy* #15 (Summer, 1974), pp. 152–168. This article played a role in triggering the debate indicated in the preceding footnote. It may be borne in mind that unemployment, for example, was sufficiently severe that Japan sent care packages to the US.

all boats," which essentially argues that a growing economy left to the unregulated market will benefit everyone,[477] with no concern about how equitably the benefits of that growth are distributed to individuals, social groups, and society at large. Reducing taxes, of course, holds within it the cutting of expenditures for government programs. In the case of the Reagan administration, those cuts were mostly the social programs that benefitted the least advantaged, in part because a decision was made to place pressure on the former Soviet Union by increasing military spending and restoring the pride that the military had lost from the loss of the Vietnam War.

Having gone through sketched outlines of the PRC's economic focus under Deng and the US's under Reagan, let us turn to the issue of human rights, with a special focus on the right to self-determination, and then tease out, more clearly, how China did fit into or failed to fit into the sought containment thesis of the US's policy. We begin with the Carter administration, which lasted from 1976 to 1980.

The Carter administration, it should be recalled, is the one under which the PRC and the US established diplomatic relations. It was also the administration under which the US, despite its prior assertions about its commitments to human rights and its frequent criticism of other countries' human rights records, made human rights a central part of its foreign policy. This course of conduct was, in large measure, an effort to help restore the US's moral standing in the world, as indicated by the then secretary of state Cyrus Vance.[478] This course of action was rather fitting because in 1974, the earlier mentioned Group of 77, as an expression of the human right to self-determination, proposed, through the UN General Assembly, the New International Economic Order (NIEO).

A major part of the justification for the NIEO was the claim that although *political* independence had been largely won from international

---

[477] See "John F. Kennedy on Economy and Taxes," https:/www.jfklibrary. org/learn/about-jfk/jfk-in-history/john-f-kennedy-on-the-economy-and-taxes (retrieved August 1, 2020).

[478] See Cyrus Vance's Law Day address at the University of Georgia, April 30, 1977, "Human Rights and Foreign Policy," carried in *Georgia International Law Journal*, Vol. VII (1977), pp. 223–229.

imperial control, a form of neocolonial structure had remained, defined by and grounded on a worldwide economic system organized by the West, under the US's leadership, which continued to exercise control over former colonial countries. Within that organization, counties of the Global South were expected to accept their place in making their natural resources, markets, and labor available to the industrial countries of the West, without the former groups having any control of any of the terms of exchange—interest rates, prices of commodities they sold (with the possible exception of OPEC), investments, prices for IP, or the industrial goods they purchased.

The perceived threat of the NIEO—especially when viewed from its most important document, the Charter of Economic Rights and Duties of States (CERDS)—were its efforts to reverse the relative powerlessness of the Global South in the just-mentioned identified areas outside their control, to promote an international redistribution of wealth and power, and to reassert the sovereign equality of states. In the latter regard, one finds Chapter I of the CERDS, the principles that came out of the Bandung Conference, and in Article 1 of the document, we find that every state "has the sovereign and inalienable right to choose its economic system as well as its political, social, and cultural systems in accordance with the will of its people, without outside interference, coercion, or threat of any form whatsoever."[479] This is, in part, a central aspect of the Shanghai Communiqué and one of a body of principles violated in the overthrow of the socialist government of Chile in 1973. Articles 2, 4, and 13 created even more potential problems for the US.

Together, those articles assert that every state "has and shall freely exercise permanent sovereignty, including possession, use, and disposal, over all its wealth and natural resources"; to "regulate and supervise the activities of transnational corporations"; and to "nationalize, expropriate, or transfer ownership of foreign property," compensation for which, if not agreed on by negotiations, shall be settled "under the domestic law of the nationalizing state"—not, as the West preferred, to have such cases settled in some forums chosen in the West or at

[479]   See the Charter of Economic Rights and Duties of States, adopted by the US General Assembly, December 12, 1974, UNGA Res. 3281 (XXIX), 29 UNGAOR, Supp. (No. 3050), UN. Doc. A/9631 (1975).

a site selected at the behest of transnational corporations (TNCs) or generally biased in favor of the West. As well, the document further contends that every state, as in the case of individuals under Article 27 of the UDHR, "has the right to the benefits from the advances and developments in science and technology for the acceleration of its economic development in science and technology" and that all countries "should promote international scientific and technological cooperation and transfer of technology, with proper regard for all legitimate interests . . . including the rights and duties of holders, suppliers, and recipients of technology."[480] The right to engage in international trade and other forms of international cooperation and exchange regardless of differences in political, economic, and social systems was also part of the push by supporters of the NIEO—a clear contradiction of the US's and Western policy in general toward socialist countries. In other words, while the then existing incentives for creativity may be preserved, the returns from that creativity, whether product or process, should be shared more broadly, beyond creators and shareholders, and economic exchange between and among peoples—trade, for example—should never be confined to operations within ideological borders.

The Carter administration, which made human rights a central part of its international policies, was caught. Its focus on human rights was from the traditional category of CPR—those emphasizing freedom of speech, religion, press, and democratic entitlement—and it had received ample praise for having done so, especially in Latin America and elsewhere in the Global South. The focus of the NIEO, however, was on economic, social and cultural rights (ESCR)—the rights to housing, health care, food, and education and to share in the returns from science and technology. This is an area of human rights very rarely even acknowledged in the US, and the earlier mentioned lack of consensus on greater domestic emphases on socioeconomic fairness affected Carter. Further, the response to the NIEO, in the broader sense by opinion shapers, including those earlier pointed to in this volume, was bitter.[481] Among the more prominent was Daniel P. Moynihan,

---

[480] See Articles 2, 4, and 13.

[481] See some of those who shared the thinking captured in footnote #474.

former ambassador to India, later to be the twelfth US ambassador to the UN, and debate-loving, public intellectual. He formulated the intellectual base for the US's response.[482]

He argued that the proposed NIEO, with all its claims for a redistribution of wealth, was formulated on the mistaken notion that international relations were being conducted in a "single world community" when, in fact, there existed but "the rudiments of a world society," discussions of which had to do with what it might be like. Dismissing the idea of self-determination (the meaning of which he thought was being distorted), he angrily accused the US Mission to the UN of failing to see the emerging ideology that was gradually shaping the UN's social agenda (thus undermining domestic support for the UN) and to understand that "a vast majority of nations of the world [animated by ideology] feel there are claims which can be made on the wealth of individual nations that are both considerable and threatening."[483]

Apart from the threatening, substantive claims, Moynihan saw another especially fearsome feature undergirding the "tyranny of [this] majority" in the UN, and that feature was, in some ways, even more threatening to the liberal international order than communism since the latter had lost its luster and had not, in fact, since the 1950s, gained any further foothold around the globe. That feature was the coherence of the ideology (which had its historical roots and conceptual grounding in British Fabian socialism) and its attitude toward the past. In the case of coherence, it represented a sort of Hegelian synthesis between the US's and the USSR's models of development. Unlike the former USSR, which sought to control all of society, and like the US, the model espoused by the advocates of the NIEO offers some autonomy to the economy and to private property. Unlike the US, however, and more like the former USSR, it has a socialist commitment to "fellowship" and, therefore, has a preference for community, substituting, when it was deemed appropriate, public for private ownership of property as

---

[482] Daniel P. Moynihan, "The United States in Opposition," *Commentary* 59 (March 1975), https://www.commentarymagazine.com/articles/the-united-states-in-opposition/, accessed June 2, 2020.

[483] Ibid.

well as production for use rather than for profits.[484] As respects the past, unlike the American Revolution, which let bygones be bygones to its British colonial ruler, the states that espouse the NIEO harbor resentments (very much like the working class in Britain, out of which the ideology came) as part of their ideology, representing perceived past wrongs, including exploitation, for which they seek reparations. They are also anti-American.

The US, however, he warned, cannot prudently leave the UN or see itself exempt from the merging international system. Neither should it, as was being urged by the foreign policy establishment, seek to appease (plead what he called nolo contendere) the Global South. Indeed, it should go in the opposition and, among other things, focus on three strategic thrusts: accept that it is in the numerical minority and develop a clearer conscious understanding of the ideological coherence of the claims; contest the claims as contained in the NIEO; and highlight the hypocrisy of the Global South's alleged commitment to the equality it seeks by emphasizing CPR. The ideological coherence, we have already touched on. In the case of contesting the claims, Moynihan urged that the US directly attack the idea that the reason for underdevelopment and relative conditions of inequality that define states within the Global South are the exploitations of the colonial past and the existing economic structures of the international system—the so-called rules of the game or "terms of exchange."

The US should first indicate that "inequalities in the world may not be so much a matter of condition as performance"; that the "difference [between the Global South and the industrial West] is in their [the south's] own making and no one else's, and no claim on anyone else arises in consequence"; and that "development is a matter of hard work and discipline." As such, if the south is not developing fast, "it is not because of the rules of the game [that] are stacked against [them] as [those] structural changes are never easy to bring about [and] because [they] are lazy and undisciplined."[485] As urged, Moynihan himself castigated the Global South for its lack of support for equality in the area

---

[484] Ibid.

[485] Ibid.

of CPR and praised the liberal democratic order, which, he contended, sponsored TNCs, which are the most creative vehicles in the twentieth century.

Despite this criticism, President Carter was disposed to negotiate with the Global South, but he was defeated in the 1980 presidential election by Ronald Reagan. The latter embodied the views of Moynihan and, with the late prime minister of Britain Margaret Thatcher, succeeded in undermining the planned negotiations at the 1981 North–South Summit on Cooperation and Development, held in Mexico. He did more; for the duration of his presidency, his administration executed well the plan of opposition urged by Moynihan. What does all this have to do with the PRC aside from the fact that it supported the proposed NIEO, as previously indicated, and came under criticism in the US for having done so? It is important because it is linked ideologically to and illuminates the character of the containment that the US pursued against China and how Beijing resisted; it provides an early glimpse into expressions of neo-Confucianism that complement aspects of the NIEO; and it helps shape a base on which the Deng regime has been used to compare with successor Chinese leaders. As important (and this will not be evident until later in this section), it will show the complementarity between Moynihan's thinking and "Orientalism," to be discussed.

In the case of ideology, although the Reagan administration was strongly anticommunist, it directed most of its public opposition toward the former USSR (as compared to China), so much so that certain veterans of the foreign policy establishment felt we were being too favorably disposed toward China.[486] The latter country, on the other hand, apart from consistent criticism of hegemonism and imperialism, generally concentrated its efforts on rebuilding its society, which had been fractured and unjoined by the Cultural Revolution, largely withdrawing from stoking violent worldwide revolution, a stoking that had kept the US, by and large, on the political and ideological defensive. Internally, Deng set about creating, in his aim of growth and development, not that aim only but a society with the label "socialism with Chinese characteristics." Some of these characteristics, unknown

---

[486] See, for example, Lucien W. Pye, "Erratic State, Frustrated Society," in *Foreign Affairs*, Vol. 69, #4 (Fall 1990), pp. 56–74.

to Moynihan, partake of some of the feared attributes that he saw in the NIEO as well as the neo-Confucian values, which argue for equal regard for members of a community, giving life to the spiritual impulse "to give rather than to take."[487] This "equal regard" is at the heart of the fellowship so prominent in the thinking of Fairbank and feared by Moynihan.

The Reagan administration (and the president had Californians on his staff who were accustomed to dealing with Asians—William Clarke as national security advisor, George Shultz as secretary of state, and Caspar Weinberger as secretary of defense), seeking to give the fullest expression to the neoliberal focus on the market, saw what they perceived as an emerging, mixed-market effort of the PRC as a sought step in the direction of the desired "integration" of China into the Western economic system. In 1983, Beijing was "transferred into the category of US trade partners" that included members of the North Atlantic Alliance (NATO) and Japan to demonstrate Washington's "commitment to China's economic modernization."[488] Later that very year, pushing back against strong opposition from the powerful US textile industry, Washington "renewed an expired textile accord," thus ending a trade dispute that endangered $1 billion in aggregate exports to China. In the investment field, Atlantic Richfield, Exxon, and Occidental Petroleum won drilling rights to China's potentially "huge offshore reserves."[489]

In the security field, not only did the Reagan administration work out a communiqué on the sale of arms to Taiwan (very important to the PRC), but also, it persuaded China to join the International Atomic Energy Agency (IAEA), thus linking China to the nuclear nonproliferation regime. It also shifted from the earlier Carter administration's focus (led by National Security Advisor Zbigniew Brzezinski) on having China as part of a strategic triangle to a status by which Beijing would be (as was, to an extent, envisioned in the 1943 Cairo Declaration) a major leader in a US Pacific basin defense region. This focus would be

---

[487] See Richard L. Gage, *Choose Life: A Dialogue, Arnold Toynbee and Daisaku Ikeda* (Oxford: Oxford University Press, 1989), p. 179.

[488] Robert A. Manning, "China: Regan's Chance Hit," in *Foreign Policy* #54 (Spring 1984), p. 84.

[489] Ibid.

part of the continuing containment of the former USSR, which, in 1979, had invaded Afghanistan and, by so doing, had provoked considerable anxiety in the US. In short, from the standpoint of Washington, it had succeeded in having China move away from a tripartite strategic structure of power and influence (the US, the USSR, and China) to one in which China would ostensibly serve as a major regional (Asian region) leader, in partnership with the US.[490]

Although Beijing was concerned about the former Soviet Union's influence and power projection in the Pacific region, it saw its focus, as before indicated, on societal development as its primary aim. Coupled with its previously touched-on transformation in agriculture with the latter's sponsorship of lower food prices, increase in farmers' income, and growth in savings was the creation of an infrastructure to accommodate two models of trading activities in manufacturing products: the "processing model," which has been defined by duty-free import zones that have been assembling goods produced outside of China to be re-exported after being assembled; and the conventional model, which was dealing with goods produced in China. The former has been part of a regional network of companies in Asia that have taken advantage of cheaper labor and have long exported these goods to the US. They simply transferred the assembling of the goods to China, a major portion of which comes to the US. In general, the US saw the China market both as a site for investments, with the help of cheaper labor (even if it meant the loss of jobs at home), and as a promising market for goods and services.[491]

Linked to the agricultural and manufacturing emphases by China was the focus on education under Deng. He began by emphasizing better quality in the nine-year primary and secondary education sector and introduced in 1986 what has come to be called the 863 Program for excellence in science and technology—one that encompassed post-secondary education, into which the emphasis on quality of primary and secondary education extended. Unlike the US, in which the Reagan

---

[490]   Ibid., pp. 85–87.

[491]   See Martin N. Baily and Barry Bosworth, "US Manufacturing: Understanding Its Past and Its Potential Future," *Journal of Economic Perspectives*, Vol. 28, #1 (Winter 2014), p. 15.

administration sought to offer little or no help to public schools and actually gave assistance to the expansion of private schools, Deng, while opening opportunities to private institutions, boosted assistance to public schools and made certain that the public sector would be equal to or exceed (and it has exceeded) whatever the private sector had to offer.

We now turn to Deng as a frame of reference in the West for purposes of containing China: he ended the Maoist push for a global revolution, aimed principally at the US but the West in general; he had opened the Chinese market with all its potential for US commerce and investment; he allowed for criticism, especially of those who espoused Maoism, and thus permitted a far wider discretionary assessment of what the latter outlook entailed; and he introduced a market system and, therefore, opened the way for a possible integration within the US-controlled liberal democratic order and the unleashing of China's entrepreneurial impulse to sustain that integration. All successive Chinese leaders would be measured against Deng's policies and the possibilities they offered, from the standpoint of Washington.

We will now turn to the two successors to Deng, each of whom served for ten years, before 2012, when President Xi took over the leadership of China. They were Jiang Zemin (1989–2002) and Hu Jintao (2002–2012). Jiang continued the structure built by Deng and, in fact, reinforced the market system. He also reformed state-owned enterprises and succeeded, perhaps in the single most important international achievement, in gaining membership for China in the WTO, making China eligible for what is called "most favored nation status." This status confers on each member of the WTO the right to be treated on terms equal to every other member—that is, no member should be accorded preferential treatment regardless of the political ties it may have or fail to have. Also, since we are here dealing with worldwide membership, every member benefits from scale. Jiang also successfully negotiated the return of Hong Kong to China. One major problem he found (and he was a beneficiary of it since he became the "compromise candidate" for leadership of the CCP thereafter) the CCP could not escape was the Tiananmen Square student demonstrations of April 15 to June 4, 1989, which the army was called on to suppress and which resulted in the death of an unspecified number of students.

The demonstrations were part of a broad abandonment of communism in Eastern Europe through the extensive use of civil resistance campaigns between 1989 and 1990. These campaigns resulted in the largely peaceful dissolution of the communist parties in the area, with the exception of Romania, where the president was killed, and it appeared that China (which believed that the US and some other Western powers were implicated in the demonstrations) would likewise face the same fate as its European counterparts. The crackdown resulted in the US imposing economic sanctions on China (these sanctions varied from the suspension of military sales to that of licenses for crime control and detection instruments).[492]

It was the debate that ensued from this incident that gives one the best sense of the moral and political containment (using human rights norms) that the US imposed on and used against China as well as China's response and resistance, to which we now turn. Here, we will have help from Henry Kissinger, who lived through this debate and was himself a part of it, engaging both Chinese and US leaders in the process.[493] China wanted the sanctions lifted and a return to pre–Tiananmen Square conditions. The US was contingently agreeable to that return: Beijing would have to accept that "democratic values and human rights" form the core of US values and have universal reach and that American citizens (this became particularly important to President Clinton) will not accept returning to normal relations with China unless the latter accepts these values and begins an effort toward their implementation. These values, the position of the US continued, are part of national

---

[492] David Skidmore and William Gates, "After Tiananmen: The Struggle Over U.S. Policy toward China in the Bush Administration," *Presidential Studies Quarterly*, Vol. 27, #3 (Summer 1997), pp. 514–539.

[493] One may validly question whether Kissinger is a reliable source here given his disregard for human rights in Cambodia, Vietnam, Chile, and elsewhere, but he is the only one who tried to capture the Chinese side, as distinct from presenting the US's. It is also my view that in this instance, he proved to be a seemingly reliable reporter.

security that could not be sacrificed.[494] Indeed, the US saw the wave of social and political changes taking place within Russia, Eastern Europe, the Balkans, Central Asia, and elsewhere as a vindication of its belief system and values, and any obstacle to that wave, to open markets and political democracy, should be "swept away."[495] Former secretary of state James Baker envisioned a society of democratic states from Vancouver to Vladivostok.[496]

Before the fall of the former USSR, confronting China in the above-described fashion, seeking to sweep away the regime, would never have been contemplated because Beijing was seen as a strategic check on Moscow. With the former USSR having crumbled, however (by December 25, 1990), the US could concentrate on China. The extent to which military intervention was seriously considered is uncertain (George Bush is said to have viewed intervention in the most populous nation and one with the longest continuous history of self-government as inadvisable).[497] Apart from the economic sanctions, the PRC came under immense pressures, including media barrage designed to question its legitimacy, if not to reverse its growing prestige in the scales of international economic development. China struck back.

While accepting the view that the socialist system needed to undergo changes, it saw the approach of the former USSR followed (and the approach that the US was praising and advancing, namely, the introduction of greater CPR to be followed by market reforms) as a mistake to avoid. The PRC had felt that reforms should first come in the economic realm and that they should be led by the party. It (the PRC) too was changing, using the socialist market economy as its model. In a less-than-tactful move (perhaps reacting to the 1990 visit to the US of then mayor of Shanghai Zhu Rongi, who was repeatedly referred to as

---

[494] Kissinger, *On China*, op. cit., p. 452.

[495] Ibid., p. 459.

[496] Kishore Mahbubani, *The New Asian Hemisphere: The Irresistible Shift of Global Power to the East* (New York: Public Affairs, 2008), p. 42.

[497] Kissinger, *On China*, op. cit., p. 461.

China's Gorbachev), Jiang told Kissinger that there was no Gorbachev in China.[498]

Jiang's China took two other positions, which indicated that it was not about to bow to the US's pressures. While conceding that there can be universal values such as some of those embodied in human rights (after all, Beijing had been supportive or an advocate of the principles of peaceful coexistence that came out of Bandung, was a part of the CERDS, and was a part of the Shanghai Communiqué—self-determination, mutual respect, and noninterference in internal affairs, all of which were intended to be universal), different countries come from different cultural traditions and may give different emphases to the application of the values. China, in fact, had been focusing on the universal values of human rights, as embedded in the UDHR and the International Covenant on Economic, Social, and Cultural Rights, emphasizing, as it has been doing, food, education, health care, housing, work, etc. As important, he also noted that while China had advocated cross-border support, now that the PRC was likely to be the only remaining socialist country, there was no longer the need to continue such advocacy.[499]

The final stance of China is that it could not be bullied and would rather not have "reopened" the *wound* of its "humiliation by foreign powers" and that while Beijing cherished Sino–US friendship, it treasured its "independence, sovereignty, and dignity even more."[500] Furthermore, Beijing pointed out, the US had plenty of human rights "problems of its own that needed attention."[501] Among the human rights advocates in the US (and one should recall here how moral principles were used against Japan as well as the advice of Moynihan concerning the use of CPR) are those who insist that any commitment to peace presupposes the existence of "a community of democratic states."[502] Compromising on human rights, for them (as they see those rights), is

---

498   Ibid., p. 457.

499   Ibid.

500   Ibid., p. 459.

501   Ibid., p. 468.

502   Ibid., p. 452.

a compromise on peace. The late senator McCain, for example, as he ran for the presidency in 2008, held the view that a worldwide league of democracies should be formed if peace is to be achieved.[503] By this standard, peace with a nondemocratic China is not possible.

Resulting from this unsuccessful, attempted containment of China by the pressure of advocated, selective values is a formula by Kissinger that appears to have been reluctantly accepted by the Clinton administration and has been, to a grudging degree, shared by subsequent administrations until the period of the Trump administration, during which it was modified to incorporate a number of other stances, including that recommended by Moynihan, for the Global South as a whole. The Kissinger formula was shaped to accommodate both wings of the foreign policy establishment—the so-called idealists, who seek to avoid any compromise in values (human rights values), and the realists, who think that values are never real and, therefore, should not serve as the basis for action. It asked the realists to accept that values have their own reality but must be built into "operational policy" and the idealists to believe that "principles need to be implemented over time," with occasional adjustments.[504] The key experience or lesson here is that Jiang's China, although fitting into some of the Deng standards and moving into the WTO, needed to have further integration into the international liberal order.

By the time Hu Jintao assumed his position as "core" leader of China, if the US were convinced that it was unlikely that the unipolar world it sought to lead would materialize, that unlikelihood could not be overlooked by the end of his tenure.[505] First, while China was growing economically at a rapid pace (since 1978, it had been growing at an average rate of 9.5 to 10 percent, but in 2007, for example, it grew by 14 percent and had surpassed Germany to become the third largest economy), it quadrupled during his tenure. By 2010, that economy

[503] See John McCain, "An Enduring Peace Built 'on Freedom': Securing America's Future," in *Foreign Affairs*, Vol. 86, #6 (November/December 2007), pp. 19–34.

[504] Kissinger, *On China,* op. cit., p. 454.

[505] Charles Krauthammer, "The Unipolar Moment," *Foreign Affairs*, Vol. 70, #1 (1990/91), pp. 23–33.

surpassed Japan's to become second only to that of the US. Second, Jiang, in resisting Washington's pressure to introduce more CPR as a means to hasten the integration process into the Western liberal order (meaning dismantle the CCP and expand markets), had shown that China's conception of power differed considerably from that of Washington. The latter thought in terms of its overwhelming military advantage, especially in the light of the disintegration of the former USSR. For Jiang and his foreign minister Qian Qichen (true to the Maoist tradition), power resides in people. Far from being impressed, as Allison claimed, by the military sophistication during the Gulf War and the prospect of a unipolar world, they thought demographically and conveyed to the US that the Muslim world had over a billion people, South Asia had over a billion, and China had over a billion. Indeed, China's population, they observed, exceeded that of the US, Russia, Europe, and Japan combined.[506]

Third, while two important factors tarnished his record as leader—increased economic inequality (contrary to socialism and Beijing's idea of development) and a rise in lawlessness—he introduced measures the impacts of which advanced social programs in housing, in health care (particularly after the 2002 SARS virus), in a minimum wage law, especially designed to help "migrant" workers to cities, and in a more balanced development between the coastal regions and the hinterlands. Additionally, he exposed China to the rest of the world in the 2008 hosting of the Beijing Olympics, and in 2003, he presided over China's first manned space probe. Always a consensus builder, perhaps to please some of those who opposed the admission of capitalists to party membership to move further toward the "harmonious socialist society" he sought, he brought back certain sectors of the economy under government control.

Two developments conferred new confidence in China and brought with them questions concerning containment: the 2007/2008 economic recession in the West, undermining the latter's banking system; and the resulting questioning of the compatibility between the liberal democratic order and modern life. If that order were incompatible, why should countries seek or be asked to be integrated into it? In the case

---

[506] Kissinger, *On China*, op. cit., pp. 463–464.

of the recession, the demonstrated wholesale weakness and collapse of the Western banking system exhibited shortcomings and confusion that persuaded Beijing and leaders in many non-Western capitals that London and New York were not the centers of financial wizardry they had been represented as being. Contrary to the expectations and disseminated contentions that the world should be fully connected with or integrated into free markets, questions began to be raised about the US's model or economic development and whether the Chinese model should replace it.[507] The idea that Washington had a solution, democratic or other, regardless of cultural and other circumstances, was shown to be without merit,[508] and the fact of Beijing's supporting intervention in the form of its increasing purchases of US securities and in the purchase of goods stood uneasily with many US leaders. Further, China's economy, by and large, remained unscathed.

It was within the context of this new confidence that Hu addressed the UN in September 2009, outlining what his administration had been doing and indicating the nature of the developmental model that China had been following and intended to continue as well as the relationship that Beijing sought to build.[509] His stature before that world body was made all the more formidable by his earlier, separate one-on-one meeting with President Obama in April of the same year, during the G20 meeting in London, with both presidents (to calm world markets) pledging to "resist [lurking] protectionism" and to work together to "support global trade and investment flows."[510]

He contended that China was disposed to respond to the "call of our times"—one emphasizing "peace, development, and cooperation"

[507] Harold James, "The Making of a Mess: Who Broke Global Finance, and Who Should Pay for It?" *Foreign Affairs*, Vol. 88, #1 (January/February 2009), pp. 162–168; Roger Altman, "Financial Fallout: The Great Crash, 2008," in *Foreign Affairs*, Vol. 88, #1 (January/February 2009), pp. 2–14.

[508] Henry Kissinger, "America at the Apex," in the *National Interest* #64 (Summer 2001), p. 10.

[509] See Pres. Hu Jintao's address to the UN General Assembly, September 23, 2009.

[510] See Wayne M. Morrison, "China and the Global Financial Crisis: Implications for the United States," in *CRS Report* (June 3, 2009), www.crs.gov.RS, 22984.

in the face of worldwide challenges such as the financial crisis, global unemployment and poverty, worsening trade, and financial imbalances along with issues such as climate change, food, energy, and resource insecurity, and public health, coupled with a menacing new mix of challenges in terrorism, the proliferation of weapons of mass destruction, transnational organized crime, and major communicable diseases. These challenges, he audaciously claimed, offered unequaled opportunities for members of the international community to commit "ourselves" to the call and, by so doing, to help "build a harmonious world of enduring peace and common prosperity" for the "development of [hu] mankind."[511] He then proceeded to sketch how China would approach the call and gave examples of China's help to certain areas of the world.

He gave four approaches. The first is to construct a broader perspective of security to safeguard world peace and security, one that understands that the security of *all* (author's emphasis) countries has never been "as closely interconnected" with political, military, and economic factors and linked to the nontraditional areas mentioned above. In doing so, understanding and constructing, mutual trust and coordination can be forged to "advance the common security of [hu] mankind."[512] Hu then went on to note that China has consistently stood for the "complete prohibition and thorough destruction of nuclear weapons and a world without nuclear weapons."[513]

His second proposal called for "a more holistic approach to development and common prosperity." Pursuant to this end, he noted that "deepening economic globalization has linked the development of *all* counties [emphasis the author's] closely"; without the "equal participation of developing countries," there cannot be "common prosperity in the world" or "a more just and equitable international economic order." As such (and this aligns with the Global South's call for a NIEO), the way to ensuring the "holistic approach" to development is to make "common development" a central attribute of global development so that there are "shared benefits" and "win–win progress"—a progress that focuses on

---

[511] See Hu's 2009 speech to the UN.

[512] Ibid.

[513] Ibid.

increased world trade, poverty eradication, and the honoring of official development assistance (ODA). He also called for greater South–South cooperation.

His third approach urged the pursuit of cooperation "with a more open mind and work for mutual benefit and common progress" in the areas of climate change, food, public health, and employment using the UN Framework Convention on Climate Change and the Kyoto Protocol (the latter largely supported by the West) as key instruments, especially when dealing with "common but differentiated responsibilities," the latter a standard that has evolved out of the world environmental movement by which those countries that are technically and otherwise less able have different levels of responsibilities in meeting common obligations. At the center of this third approach is common and mutual learning—learning from one another.

The last of the approaches calls for tolerance toward one another—if all are to live in harmony. Here, he emphasized not just harmony and mutual learning but also that such learning through an understanding of different civilizations constitutes an "inexhaustible source of strength"; allows for the acknowledgement that all countries, "big and small, strong and weak, rich and poor," should be regarded as equal; and—reminiscent of the Bandung Declaration, DOGICCP, NIEO, and Shanghai Communiqué—reinforces the principle that despite differences in cultural traditions, social systems, and values, countries enjoy the "right . . . to independently choose their respective development paths."[514]

In closing, he summarized some of China's actions to promote its own development and to contribute to that of others, here repeated what is now commonplace—that China has chosen the path of "socialism with Chinese characteristics," not one that fits into specific stereotypes; that it is committed to the FPPCE; and that China has decided to dedicate itself, in foreign policy, to common development. Evidence of the latter are Beijing's assistance to the then over 120 LDC and its fulfillment of the UN Millennium Declaration (a 2000 UN General Assembly declaration concerning certain goals to be achieved, such as universal primary education, halving extreme poverty, enabling more

---

[514] Ibid.

233

girls to attend school, etc. by 2015), the cancellation of the debts of forty-nine heavily indebted, poor countries, and the extension of "zero tariff treatment" for commodities from over forty LDCs. Further, China has created a China–ASEAN Investment Fund providing currency; surplus for countries that, for example, do not have dollars to pay for goods or services; and financing support for the IMF and has begun special arrangements with African countries.

President Obama, who spoke on the same day (and the author asks for the reader's patience because what seems like straying is rather central to what is to come), and he too established a main theme and offered four areas of focus. That theme was "a new era of engagement with the world" (in contrast to the unilateralism under the Bush administration as well as the seeming concern on the part of the US with its own security). He noted that the UN itself was "founded on the belief that nations of the world could solve their problems together" instead of separately or unilaterally.[515] Like Hu, he also called for the "cooperative efforts" of the world at large (including small nations) to build a structure of peace. He then presented "four pillars" that could form the basis for his new engagements, for creating the called-for structure of peace and pursuing the common interest of human beings: nonproliferation and disarmament; the promotion of peace and security; the "preservation of our planet"; and a "global economy that advances *opportunities* [emphasis the author's] for all people."[516] In respect of nuclear nonproliferation and disarmament, he identified three interests that must be satisfied—the interests of *all* nations to enjoy "the right to peaceful nuclear energy"; the interests of nations with nuclear weapons to honor their promise and legal responsibility "to move toward disarmament"; and the interests of nonnuclear weapons countries in living up to their commitments to "forsake" those weapons. He contended that America will "keep [its] end of the bargain," and with respect to the broader goal to promote international peace and security, he focused on issues ranging from peacekeeping and the Arab–Israeli War to dealing with Al-Qaeda and Sudan.

---

[515] See text of Obama's speech to the UN General Assembly on September 23, 2009.

[516] Ibid.

On the preservation of the planet, he linked it to the transformation of the "emerging economy" and the worldwide goals set for the emissions cut for 2020 and, eventually, 2050. Like Hu, he referred to differentiated responsibilities and made it clear that all countries must contribute, including those that are "fast-growing, carbon emitters" (and one should read China here). In the case of the final pillar, a global economy that offers opportunities to all people, he thought of fueling demand, creating new "rules of the road to strengthen regulations" to "put an end to greed, excess, and abuse," pursuing "a moral and pragmatic interest in the broader questions of development," and opening further the market of wealthy to extend "a hand to those with less while reforming international institutions to give more nations a greater voice." He closed by referring to the US commitment to human rights (CPR) and the equality of races and the hope that, quoting FDR, the US has "learned" to be "citizens of the world, members of the human community."[517]

We went into this presentation of the two presidents to achieve a number of things, hopefully reinforcing or clarifying certain features of US–China relations that we have previously covered and helping set the stage for what is to come. Specifically, it is intended to show that both countries behaved as "global actors." China was not acting as a "regional power," as the US's containment policy has wanted it to. Second, the topical areas covered often were identical or parallel to each other—on issues of development (for example, human rights), on the environment, on economic collaboration, on nuclear proliferation and disarmament, and on public health, among others. In the area of human rights, President Obama, consistent with the history of the US's foreign policy actions in this area, focused on CPR such as free speech and the "promise" of equality of races. Nowhere was there any reference to ESCR, which have formed such an important feature of China's position over the years. As well, in dealing with nuclear nonproliferation and disarmament, the US noted its minimum responsibility (and improvement over the George W. Bush administration) as well as that of other countries. Neither is there any reference to the overall context of weapons of mass destruction (as China did); neither was there an

---

[517] Ibid.

expressed willingness, as China did, to eliminate all these weapons, including nuclear weapons—certainly not the aggression-loving China about which Allison informed us.

The area of economic collaboration offers perhaps the most impressive contrast, especially in terms of the Moynihan conceptual categories of world *society* and world *community*. In the latter, cooperation is sought, nurtured, and engaged in for the purpose of ensuring the well-being and common welfare of all members, as if they were of a single family. In the case of society, cooperation is pursued to satisfy the interest of separate individual, social, or national societies with the understanding that the return to each will be more than if each acted separately. Hu's idea is that the development of each member of the international community should be embedded in a more general development so that every and all states benefit mutually. Certainly, this is not the China that Allison depicted, seeking, as he claimed, to exploit the countries of Southeast Asia and elsewhere.

Five milestones, each taking place during President Hu's tenure and the first term of the Obama administration, should be touched on here to help us further understand US–China relations since 2012. The first of these developments was the strengthening of the 2005 US–India ten-year defense framework agreement, which had been entered into with a view toward expanding bilateral cooperation between Washington and New Delhi in the area of international security. This agreement—which involves joint training, joint exercises, and the sale of military arms—has been part of the US's policy of containment of China. The second, having the same end, is the TPP agreement, which was drafted in 2015 but had been in development since 2008/2009, among Australia, Brunei, Canada, Chile, Japan, Malaysia, Mexico, New Zealand, Peru, Singapore, Vietnam, and the US.[518] This was a trade bloc to limit China. Third, as indicated in President Hu's earlier discussed speech to the UN, far from having Beijing becoming progressively integrated in the liberal economic order, that order was being increasingly publicly questioned on the basis that it was not, in fact, sufficiently just and equitable, the very criticism from the Global South. Besides, China had to be brought in to offer support to the socioeconomic disorder that had resulted from

---

[518] It was signed on February 4, 2016, but the US failed to win support at home.

the 2007/2008 financial crisis, causing some questions about whether the China model of development was a more effective one to meet the complexities of the contemporary global economy than that led by the US.

Complementing the idea that China was not being properly integrated, as had been hoped, in the international liberal order was the sense (and I use the term advisedly because there is little evidence to support it, as will be seen in our dealing with President Xi's tenure in office) that the spirit of Deng—that sponsoring of market reforms in China as the latter's path to modernization—was being overthrown.[519] To the extent that Washington believes this, however, it is important that we look at the issue. One of the issues advanced for the claim of the alleged reversal was that China limited foreign direct investment (FDI), something it has always done in certain areas of societal life that some Western socialist refer to as the "commanding heights"— transportation, telecommunications, arms, power generation and distribution, and information technology, for example. It was also said that China was offering protection to "national champions," protecting certain companies from foreign control (one has but to note the US's protection of Qualcomm in 2018 or imagine China seeking control of Boeing, Microsoft, or Google). Japan, South and North Korea, and other close allies of the US likewise have their national champions, the size of which is also important for global competition.[520] Another is that new labor laws that aim to enhance workers' rights were being implemented by the All-China Federation of Trade Unions, which, while "periodically assailing foreign firms," tend to overlook comparable violations or abusive behavior by the government. Other issues involving control of the capital account need not be discussed here except that Beijing cannot possible forget the 1998 "Asian financial crisis," when those Asian nations, following Washington's advice, were victimized by foreign speculators while those countries—such as Malaysia, which had controls—preserved their economies and social order.

---

[519] See, for example, Derek Scissors, "Deng Undone," in *Foreign Affairs*, Vol. 88, #3 (May/June, 2009), pp. 24–39.

[520] Ibid., p. 29.

The last of the five developments is the idea of community, which
we earlier elaborated in relationship to certain demands of the Global
South, the 2009 speech of President Hu to the UN, and the contention of
the late Senator Moynihan that the idea sprang from the British Fabians,
who came to control the British Labor Party. As is the case of most
Western writers and scholars, Asians are not endowed (as is the case
of the Global South, generally) with the capacity for original thought,
part of *Orientalism* so insightfully developed and presented in context
by Edward Said[521] and deftly applied by John M. Hobson, whose work
we have already cited.[522] The presumed British origins of the concept of
community,[523] as defined by Moynihan in relationship to the proposed
NIEO (that sought more equitable sharing of returns from what was then
seen as a common economy), actually has other origin—in this case, a
Confucian origin. Hu's focus on "harmonious" common prosperity for
all is part of this Confucian thinking that he brought to the UN and that,
as we will see, will be further developed in a more elaborate fashion
by his immediate his successor, President Xi. To be borne in mind
also is that since the Reagan administration, the idea of national and
international community (as used in the US, in ordinary parlance, this
means "society") has been associated with more, not less, government
involvement in the economy.

[521] Edward W. Said, *Orientalism* (New York: Pantheon Books, 1978).

[522] Hobson, *The Eastern Origins,* op. cit., pp. 1–26.

[523] Moynihan must not have thought of German, Russian, or Japanese scholarship
in this area. He was simply focusing on a prejudice.

CHAPTER 13

Containment, Confrontation, and Open Door

This portion of the counter-narrative in our discussion covers the US–China relationship from 2012 to the present, although Allison's book was published in 2017. Justification for moving beyond the latter date is to be found in the predictive character of Allison's work; that is, its thesis seeks to predict what is likely to happen between the US and China. The burdens of this chapter are to demonstrate that President Xi's tenure thus far has largely followed that of his predecessors (and thus, contrary to Allison's position, has not represented a radical break with the post-1978 period in China); that where he has differed from his predecessors has reflected more of a difference in the level of the country's socioeconomic development, institutional strengthening or rebuilding, and the external social and political unfoldings that have recommended adaptations; and that the perceived, increased threat of China to the US has been the offspring of certain feelings and knowledge on the part of the US (feelings long recognized but deemed too demanding to address) and their convergence with the efforts of President Xi to offer some ideological coherence to the results of forty-plus years of collective efforts and changes in China. These changes include how the latter relate to envisioned future social and political germinations likely to take place throughout the world. One additional feature has been hidden, one that corresponds to earlier cases of "challenge and response" covered in other case studies.

Continuity and Change

While Hu's presidency focused on alleviating and further reducing poverty in China, Xi's has emphasized its elimination as part of the Two Centenary Goals, the first of which is to finish the building of a moderately prosperous society in all respects by 2021, the one hundredth anniversary of the founding of the CPC. In the pursuit of this end, he presided over the doubling of spending and has directed his principal attention, in this area, on the rural regions of China. As well, he has expanded educational opportunities in all areas, with broad emphasis on research institutes and research universities, as well as in the high technology sector.[524] Likewise, he has promoted the cause of renewable energy as a means of dealing with national and international concerns respecting the environmental impact of fossil fuels, has given strong support to the ongoing exploration of outer space, and moved aggressively to ensure that the already-in-progress transition from an export-driven economy to one that is more balanced with internal consumption would take place as smoothly as possible. Linked to that transition also has been the bringing into being of a greater mix of goods and services (not just the overwhelming reliance on manufacturing) as well as the technologies that support them.

There have also been certain areas of reform worth mentioning here with which he has been associated—the ending in 2015 of the one-child policy, which had been in effect since 1979; the rebuilding of local levels of the party structure, which had deteriorated; the expansion of greater or stricter regulation of nongovernmental organizations in China; and the continuation of President Hu's efforts to reassert government control of certain economic activities, coupled with some supply-side structural reforms such as reducing overcapacity in some state-owned enterprises, cutting corporate costs, and pushing to boost innovation. He has also presided over the amending of the party constitution to

---

[524] One may return to Agarwala and Chaudhary, op. cit., to gain a partial sense of China's efforts.

allow for leadership tenure exceeding ten years, and as before noted, he launched a deep and wide anti-corruption campaign and pushed major restructuring of the military, with less of an emphasis on Beijing having a huge army and more of a mobile and less land-based armed forces, with more balance in the areas of the air force and the navy.

Xi's successes in the areas touched on in the preceding two paragraphs can hardly be factually contested. If one were to take the elimination of poverty, in China, for example (and we are focusing on Xi because, as the reader will recall, Allison made "Xi's China" the identity of danger to the US), by 2016, he had reduced the size to about fifty million, which means he had to eliminate poverty by approximately ten million per year to achieve the goal that the policy envisioned.[525] With the trade disputes involving the US (begun in 2017), a "cooling" of the pace of economic growth in 2019 and 2020, the latter because of COVID-19, it is not surprising that achievements in this area invited weighty government attention.[526] One must watch the results of 2021 for the effect of Beijing's exertions. Another goal has been the rooting out of corruption. Xi has received strong support for this venture and on his focus on putting in place "a powerful investigative force that is loyal to an honest, centralized leadership."[527] His thinking appears to be that "over the course of several years, consistent surveillance and regular investigations will change the psychology of bureaucrats from viewing corruption as a routine . . . to viewing it as . . . risky—and finally to not even daring to consider it."[528]

The corruption campaign included the military, junior officers of which, for example, were routinely bribing higher-ranking ones to gain promotion; very much as in the US—where senior government offices can, after retirement, become "consultants" to private sector

---

[525] Institute for Security & Development Policy (ISDP), "China's Anti-Poverty Efforts, Problems and Progress," in *Focus Asia* (March 2019).

[526] See, for example, Chen Jia and Wang Yu, "Stability, GDP get top priority for year ahead," in *China Daily* (December 16, 2019).

[527] James Leung, "Xi's Corruption Crackdown: How Bribery and Graft Threaten Chinese Dream," in *Foreign Affairs*, Vol. 94, #3 (May/June 2015), p. 33.

[528] Ibid.

businesses—some military and other bureaucratic personnel would become consultants. Some did not even have to await retirement. One should bear in mind also that in highly regulated industries such as finance, telecommunications, and pharmaceuticals, relatives of senior government officials often act as "consultants" as well to private businesses and persons, especially those looking for approvals, permits, and licenses to operate.[529] In short, to the extent that private enterprises seek a corruption-free operation, Xi's anti-corruption campaign and his reforms of the military should be seen in a favorable light. The society as a whole, as before indicated, has been appreciative. The "eight rules and six prohibitions"—prohibiting bureaucrats from taking gifts and bribes, frequenting expensive restaurants, or using government funds and vehicles for personal and private purposes, including travel—have endeared him to all but those against whom the prohibitions have been actually or potentially directed.[530]

Contrary to the impression given by Allison that President Xi's anti-corruption policies and his reforms of the military have been in the pursuit of personal power, he engaged in great personal and political risk in pushing for these reforms. Were he to have failed, that failure would likely have been "catastrophic. Corruption would have likely [resulted in] the destabilizing of the economy, reducing investor confidence and seriously eroding Xi's authority, making it difficult for him to lead."[531] In my view, it would have risked the very legitimacy of the CCP, which, it should be remembered here, is no longer a communist-only party, and those capitalists (within and without) who are hungrily awaiting opportunities to discredit the CCP would find the expanding corruption within the party and the army an inviting environment to undermine the party. As well, none of Xi's post-Mao predecessors would have been unhappy with his efforts; neither would they or anyone willing to offer a fair appraisal of Xi's policies find them a radical departure from those of his predecessors. Where he has differed from them, in my view, has been his more assertive position in international relations and his

---

[529]   Ibid., p. 34.

[530]   Ibid., pp. 36–37.

[531]   Ibid., p. 38.

insistence on culture as something that should be the bedding out of which socioeconomic and political actions as well as social and moral visions should take place or evolve. We now turn to this assertiveness and bedding and the extent to which, if any, they are threats to US.

The China of 2012, 2015, and 2020 is not the China of 1978/79 or of 2000. Neither is the international political and security system, especially that led by the US, within which China has had to operate. Given the nature, pace, and scope of changes within and outside of China, including a Washington less willing to be collaborating with Beijing, it is understandable that a more confident China would become more assertive or would be likely to find it necessary to be so. It is also understandable why Beijing would seek to find, if it could, some greater coherence for all the changes it had undergone and likely to continue undergoing. In the case of the international political and security system, we have already touched on the disintegration of the former USSR and the emergence of a far more potentially powerful EU grouping (from its then ongoing integration of former East European states and the addition of other countries such as Sweden, Portugal, Spain, Austria, and Finland, among others, and the reordering of alignments in the Middle East or West Asia). One should also bear in mind the association of BRICS as potential international collaborators in the area of economic diplomacy, the TPP, and the Transatlantic Trade and Investment Partnership (T-TIP). The Balkan War of the 1990s and its effects should not be forgotten.

With respect to US–China relations, all the mentioned events in the preceding paragraph bear some importance, but we will focus on a certain particular development that seemingly made President Xi decide that the relative reticence of his predecessors to be more public in stating the interest of China should come to an end. Among those developments are some geostrategic ones that, although in some cases begun before the Obama administration, gained substance and form then and continued, some in modified form, during Donald Trump's tenure to the Biden presidency. The policy is what has come to be called the "Pivot or Rebalance to Asia," formally announced in 2011.[532] In fact,

---

[532] Oliver Turner, "US Imperial Hegemony in Asia Pacific," doi:10.7765/97815261 35025.00008 (February 28, 2020), accessed June 20, 2020.

this "rebalance" policy has meant that the era of the US's primary focus on Europe (because of the perceived threat to that continent from the former USSR) as well as its then concurrent focus on the Middle East was coming to an end so that the US could give greater strategic weight to the Asia Pacific region, where China has been seen as a challenge to the US's hegemony. At the center of Obama's shift was the previously mentioned TPP, whose four-continent, twelve-member grouping would form a free market to challenge China's economic rise.

Coupled with the TPP were some two-pronged security and economic initiatives—some bilateral, others multilateral. On the bilateral side, one finds the US forging closer strategic ties with Vietnam and the Philippines, a development from which one can gain an understanding of China's emerging concern about being encircled, at least finding the latitude for political and security maneuvers narrowing. In the case of the Philippines, where people were particularly favorably disposed to President Obama (perhaps because he was born in Southeast Asia), it entered in 2014 into what is called an "enhanced defense cooperation."[533] In the case of Vietnam, not only was it slated to be a member of the TPP, but also, in 2011, it entered into a bilateral defense agreement with the US, and that agreement developed into the 2013 US–Vietnam Comprehensive Partnership, an overarching framework for bilateral relations that grew to the 2015 Joint Vision statement expressing their respective intentions to pursue "shared interest and cooperation at both the bilateral and multilateral levels [and] contributing to peace, stability, cooperation, and prosperity in the Asia Pacific region and the world."[534] On March 5, 2018, the US Navy aircraft carrier USS *Carl Vinson* made a port call in Danang; in the same year, Vietnam participated in the Rim of the Pacific (RIMPAC), a maritime military exercise, hosted biennially by the US.[535]

India could be examined on a bilateral basis also, but the evolving relations between Washington and New Delhi have expanded into a

---

[533] Colin Freeman, "Philippines to Sign Security Pact with the US," in the *Telegraph* (April 27, 2014).

[534] See Press Release, The White House Office of Press Secretary, July 7, 2015.

[535] US Department of State, "US Relations with Vietnam: Bilateral Fact Sheet" (January 21, 2020).

rather robust multilateral plan also. Those ties, which foreign policy experts had been urging since the 1950s,[536] have had to do with the containment of China. For a variety of reasons, including India's proud leadership role in the NAM and the role that India envisioned itself playing in the world at large (as a moral leader, including peacemaker, for example), ties between New Delhi and the US were never very close. In 2005, however, the US signed a ten-year defense framework agreement with India, with a view toward expanding bilateral security cooperation between the two countries, and in 2015, that agreement was renewed under the Obama administration to mold increased "defense [and] industrial ties in Asia as a counterweight to China's military growth and assertion of sovereignty in East and South Asia."[537] Just as in the case of the earlier mentioned advice given by Chester Bowles, who had served as ambassador to India from 1951 to 1953, it came to be accepted that bilateral US–India relations alone would not be strong enough to contain China and that "the heart" of the sought "counter-balance must eventually lie in India and Japan."[538] Whether Hillary Clinton or John McCain (instead of Obama) had become president of the US in 2008, the development of ties with India in a multilateral manner would have been pursued because their respective views represented what had already become a consensus among US foreign policy elites on how to succeed in containing China.[539]

"Having steadily, if unevenly, transformed the leadership of the [Pacific] region" from "Alaska to Guam to the Philippines to Japan and beyond" since the middle of the nineteenth century, the US had

---

[536]   See, for example, Chester Bowles, in "Memo on Our Policy in Asia," Williams, op. cit., pp. 1094–1100.

[537]   See report by Lala Qadir, posted on June 11, 2015, about what had taken place in the June 3, 2015, Global Policy Watch.

[538]   See Bowles, op. cit., 1096.

[539]   See Hillary Rodham Clinton, "Security and Opportunity for the Twenty-first Century," in *Foreign Affairs*, Vol. 86, #6 (November/December 2007), pp. 2–18, and John McCain, in the same issue of the magazine, "An Enduring Peace Built on Freedom," pp. 19–34. There was a time when India felt that the US was not taking it seriously. See Baldev Raj Nayar, "Treat India Seriously," in *Foreign Policy* #18 (Spring 1975), pp. 133–154.

maintained its pursued and currently enjoyed "regional imperial hegemony" through a series of "institutionalized and consensual networks" such as ASEAN, SEATO, and ANZUS (the latter an acronym for Australia, New Zealand, and the US).[540] With Australia frequently added to the India, US, and Japan arrangements, it is not surprising that Canberra would be included in what gradually has become an ever-widening arc of the US's conception of its interests in the Pacific region and the reach of that region.

When the CCP won the civil war with the KMT and established the PRC—which, in turn, successfully did "push back" the US-led military forces on the Korean peninsula in 1950—Gen. Douglas MacArthur (who was the leader of those military forces in Korea), having been removed by President Truman as leader of the Korea effort, sought to assure a troubled (some members were angry) Congress that the US enjoyed much strength in the Pacific if it had the will to defend that strength. He then proceeded to give a strategic and physical outline of that strength—one that the US has, over the years, held on to despite international changes.

In a speech to Congress on April 10, 1951, he contended that before World War II, "the Western strategic frontier of the United States lay on the littoral line of the Americas with an exposed island salient extending out through Hawaii, Midway, and Guam to the Philippines."[541] That salient, he asserted, instead of providing security for the US, was a "weakness along which the enemy could and did attack."[542] All "this was changed by our Pacific victory. Our strategic frontier . . . shifted to embrace the *entire* [emphasis the author's] Pacific Ocean, which became a vast moat to protect us." Indeed, he went on, "it acts as a protective shield for all the Americas and all free lands of the Pacific Ocean area. We control it," he further observed, "to the shores of Asia by a chain of islands extending in area from the Aleutians to the Marianas held

---

[540] See Turner, "US Imperial Hegemony," op. cit.

[541] See General MacArthur's farewell address to Congress, April 19, 1951. https:www.americanrhetoric.com/speeches/douglasmacarthurfarewelladress.htm

[542] Ibid.

by us and our allies."[543] To give a north–south complementary linkage to the largely west–east arc, he said, "from this island chain, we can dominate with sea and air power *every* [emphasis author's] Asiatic port from Vladivostok to Singapore and prevent any hostile movement into the Pacific."[544]

Pivot to the Pacific gradually became more than the *entire* Pacific (emphasis author's), which MacArthur described to Congress as the area constituting the US's strategic frontier. With India added to the landscape of that frontier, a trilateral dialogue (the US, India, and Japan) began in 2011; concurrently, a trilateral strategic dialogue was taking place among the US, Australia, and Japan. It was not surprising, therefore, that diplomats and others began to refer to the Indo-Pacific and "the Quad" (the Quadrilateral Security Dialogue) "among like-minded democracies" in the region: the US, Australia, India, and Japan. What is this Indo-Pacific Asia, as it is sometimes referred to? It is said to encompass a biogeographic region of the world's seas, incorporating the tropical waters of the Indian Ocean, the western and central regions of the Pacific Ocean, and the seas connecting the two, covering the general area of Indonesia and Malaysia. In 2019, the US Department of State published a document formalizing the concept of the "Free and Open Indo-Pacific" (FOIP).[545] When President Trump and Prime Minister Modi met in February 2020, the region is said to have been an important subject of discussion.[546]

---

[543] Ibid.

[544] Ibid.

[545] P. Parameswaran, "Assessing the New US Free and Open Indo-Pacific Progress Report," posted in *thediplomat.com* on November 5, 2019. See also the Department of Defense, "Indo-Pacific Strategy Report: Preparedness, Partnerships, and Promoting a Networked Region" (June 1, 2019). The following articles, which are quite informative, should also be helpful—V. Pant, "Rising China in India's Vicinity: A Rivalry Takes Shape in Asia," *Review of International Affairs*, Vol. 29, #2 (2016), pp. 364–381; Rory Medcalf, "In Defense of the Indo-Pacific: Australia's New Strategic Map," *Australian Journal of International Affairs*, Vol. 68, #4 (2014), pp. 470–483.

[546] See Debidata A. Mahapatra, "Trump–Modi Visit a Boon to US–India Relations," in *Orlando Sentinel* (February 29, 2020).

For those of our readers who feel that we have again drifted, it is hoped that they will quickly be disabused of this feeling by the following justification for the apparent detour. Changes in the international system, described above, bear on US–China relations; these changes constituted defensible reasons in respect of why President Xi might have felt that he had to be more assertive (Allison would say aggressive), and Allison failed to offer the contexts (some of which we provide), thus creating a distorting view of US–China relations. To all the just-mentioned explanations for the seeming roundabout way that we have gone must be added the fact that providing contexts always require details, among which are dates, usually provided so that one can have a better sense of sequence (especially when Allison's work, at times, looks at consequences) and therefore seek to find cause to justify or criticize them. In the apparent detour, we went beyond 2017, the publication date of *Destined for War*, because doing so allows one to assess the predictive accuracy of the work. Let us now turn to Xi's more assertiveness, on behalf of China, and use some of the issue areas around which the accusations leveled against him have been hinged: the South China Sea; Taiwan (and Hong Kong); Beijing's economic reach and its nature; and the role of the state in the economic life of China.

The South China Sea, an area claimed by both the PRC and the ROC (Taiwan), is a marginal sea (a division) of the Pacific Ocean. It is constituted by a body of islands, bays, and sunken reefs that extends from the Strait of Taiwan to the Straits of Malacca and Karimata (off Malaysia and Indonesia, respectively) and the main transport route between the Pacific Ocean and the Indian Ocean on the one hand and the principal shipping route between the South China Sea and Japan and the North Pacific ports on the other. This area is part of the area to which General MacArthur referred—an area that [and he could not have then known and most likely never imagined, given his view of the future of its peoples][547] houses considerable natural resources in the form of oil, gas, and fish, among others, and facilitates trillions of dollars annually in trade.[548]

---

[547] Ibid.

[548] Hugigao Qi, "How to Clear Bottlenecks of Joint Development of the South China Sea" (published online on November 12, 2019), https://olio.org/10.1080/24

As China developed economically and became the world's largest trading nation (2013), it was logical that it would seek to acquire greater naval capacity to protect commerce—something for which, as the leader will recall, the US, the UK, and pre-1945 Japan had, at different times, argued as they sought to deal with limitations on naval forces. As well, given the many earlier touched-on "security arrangements" that the US and its allies or partners were putting in place around the border of sea lanes of China, it was not unreasonable for President Xi to seek to make clear to the international community China's position on its claims respecting its territorial integrity. The latter is a principle that has been one of the legal and moral cornerstones of international system, especially since 1945, and even more so of the PRC's foreign policy, as our previous discussions should attest. When the US-begun 2009 repositioning to the Pacific ripened into a 2011 public declaration, it would have been irresponsible of President Xi not to have ensured that China would be fully capable of defending its interests and protecting its society.

What if the circumstances were reversed and China, accepting the argument of MacArthur, claimed the entire Pacific as its strategic frontier (including the waters abutting the US's West Coast) and it were pivoting through areas such as the Panama Canal, Southern Argentina, and South Africa to the Atlantic so that its trade with the Caribbean, Africa, and Latin America and the security of those areas would be protected? What if its aircraft carriers were in the Gulf of Mexico? What if Mexico and Cuba were emerging allies of China, with South Africa serving as a link between the Atlantic and Indo-Pacific regions? The analogy is not exact, but the reader will understand some parallels. How would the US react? The use of the term "Atlantic and Indo-Pacific regions" is really to capture the meaning of the Indo-Pacific area that has developed since 2005—a region extending from the waters of East Africa, including some islands in the Indian Ocean, all the way through Malaysia, Indonesia, and the Philippines into and including the entire Pacific, with Vietnam, bordering on China and formally an enemy of Washington, shifting from being a trade partner to a security partner of the US, expanding military ties with Washington's allies,

761028.2019.1685427

namely, Australia, Japan, and the Philippines.[549] A US-led blockade of China, because of its control over the Indo-Pacific region, would cripple China's international commerce and, therefore, the economy of that country. It should not be lost to the readers that India, Vietnam, and the Philippines have conflicts with Beijing—the latter two covering islands in the South China Sea and involving New Delhi over a disputed border site in the Western Himalayas.

Part of what Xi did as president was to reaffirm more forcefully China's sovereignty over and hence right to ensure the security of certain islands in the South China Sea—islands and other formations including the Paracel Islands, the Spratly Islands, and Woody Island, on the latter of which Beijing has moved to display fighter jets, cruise missiles, and radar systems. In the case of the Paracel (which is also claimed by Vietnam) and Spratly (which is claimed by the Philippines, for example) Islands, China has been constructing ports, outstrips, and military installations. These actions, accompanied by the exhibition of historical maps showing China's ownership of the islands for hundreds of years, have also included efforts by Beijing to negotiate the conflicting claims over the islands (claims that have largely risen out of the imperialism of the nineteenth century).[550] The US's interest in controlling the Indo-Pacific area is not one that lends itself to any encouragement of such negotiations, as opposed to the hardening of positions respecting the conflicting claims. (China's assertiveness, of course, has some of the same impact, but it has been reacting to encircling military alliances.)

China also, in 2013, declared an air defense identification zone (ADIZ) in the East China Sea, a marginal sea in the western part of the Pacific Ocean that is bound by, among other areas, islands to which there are disputed claims with Japan. The declaration of such a zone—usually covering the airspace over land or water within which the identification, location, and control of civil aircraft are pursued in the interest of national security—is something supported by international law, and in some instances, the area covered can extend over national

[549] Jennifer Lind, "Asia's Other Revisionist Power: Why U.S. Grand Strategy Unnerves China," in *Foreign Affairs*, Vol. 96, #2 (March–April 2017), p. 79.

[550] See Qi, op. cit. See also Jeremy Page and Chun Han Wong, "Beijing Offers to Negotiate in South China Sea Dispute," in the *Wall Street Journal* (July 13, 2016).

territory if the state declaring the zone is engaged in demonstrable efforts to give itself more time to respond to possible hostile incoming aircrafts. This action by China is said to have occasioned "dismay" in Tokyo and Washington.[551]

The question at this juncture is not so much why Xi has unapologetically responded to an apparent military "encirclement" but why has the US become so implicated in so many disputes, from India to Japan? A partial answer has to do with MacArthur's conception of the US's physical and strategic frontier (part of which we have already quoted but may bear some repeating in a fuller context). According to him (and the US followed his view):

> [o]ur strategic frontier [after World War II] shifted to embrace the entire Pacific Ocean, which has become a moat to protect us as long as we [hold] it . . . We control it to the shores of Asia by a chain of islands extending from the Aleutians to the Marianas held by us and our free allies . . . No amphibious force can [be] successful without control of the sea lanes and the air over those lanes in its avenue of advance. With naval and air supremacy and modern ground elements to defend bases, any major attack from continental Asia toward us or our friends of the Pacific would be doomed to failure.[552]

The term "allies," as used in the quoted statement, was intended then, as now, to include the Philippines, Taiwan (the ROC), Australia, and Japan, among others. Taiwan and the Philippines as well as Japan were and are part and parcel of the "chain of islands" and are therefore central to the then defined strategic frontier. The political economy as well as the integrated character of the security and peace to be provided by the frontier (the entire Pacific) is not to be made light of; certainly, it should never be forgotten because without them (encapsulating the domino theory), ruin awaits the US. In MacArthur's words,

---

551 See Lind, "Asia Other Revisionist Power," op. cit., p. 76.

552 MacArthur, op. cit.

[u]nder such conditions, the Pacific no longer represents menacing avenues of approach for a prospective invader—it becomes instead the friendly aspect of a peaceful lake. Our line of defense is a natural one and can be maintained with minimum military effort and expense [and] properly maintained would be invincible defense against aggression . . . The holding of this littoral defense line in the Western Pacific is entirely dependent upon holding all segments . . . for any major breach of that line by an unfriendly power would render vulnerable to determined attack every other segment.[553]

With this protected frontier, at a reasonable cost to defend or maintain (unlike Europe), the political danger normally attending international military spending would be missing. Further, its maintenance would induce "minimum" military effort, thus releasing resources, human and material, to other theaters of actual or potential conflict. (One may ask, however, if the entire Pacific is a needed defensive frontier for the US, how much more so is the South China Sea for China?)

The rise of China is said to threaten this frontier in scope, character, and cost of maintenance, and this perceived threat, while primarily linked to the economic impact of Beijing's economic development, is at least secondarily attached to the military changes associated with Xi's reforms, which, it must be noted, actually began in 2009, three years before Xi became core leader of China. The weight of his reforms has been to make the changes more integrative and coherent. In particular, as before indicated, he has been giving much greater emphasis to the navy and air force, the two branches most intimately linked to expanding international trade and investment, and to the South China Sea. China's military spending, which increased by 6.6 percent in 2020, however, is less than a quarter of the US's defense budget (and this does not include the military spending of US allies).[554] Control of the South China Sea (as in the case of the East China Sea) by a country other than the US

<hr>

[553] Ibid.

[554] Steven Lee Myers, "Chinese Saber Rattles Neighbors, but Signal Is for US," in *New York Times* (June 26, 2020), p. A. 14.

potentially breaks the arc to which MacArthur referred. China wants and insists on having control (as part of its sovereign territory) of some of the sea lanes that the US military had assumed it would continue to control indefinitely; maintaining whatever security arrangement is left, if China were to enjoy the control it seeks, will be quite costly, in the material sense, to Washington. Allison says nothing of the "strategic frontier" in the Pacific and merely presents China as an aggressor.

The US, in part to preserve to itself as much flexibility as possible, has been using the principle of freedom of navigation and overflight, as provided by international law, to move through certain areas of the South China Sea. China, in 2019, however, indicated that while it "respects and safeguards all countries' freedom" under the principle, it resolutely opposes the behavior of any country trying to undermine China's sovereignty and security under "the pretext of such freedom."[555] We turn to Taiwan and Hong Kong, events surrounding which are offered as examples of Xi's aggressiveness. As the reader will recall, Taiwan is an island about 110 miles off the coast of Southeast China, to which the KMT and its leader, Chiang Kai-shek, fled after defeat in the civil war with the CCP and its leader, Mao Tze-tung. There, Chiang and other associated leaders sought to continue the government of the ROC and, in fact, to continue having the latter government to carry on as that which ought to represent the nation-state of China. With the support of the US, the ROC won the right to represent China among most governments outside of the former Soviet bloc, including the UN, from which it was expelled in 1972.

In the Shanghai Communiqué of February 1972, consistent with the Cairo Declaration of November 27, 1943, the US and China jointly affirmed that both sides (the ROC and the PRC) agree that there is but *one* China and that Taiwan belongs to it. The US, however, has never, since the Korean War, morally committed itself to the return of Taiwan to China and, under the guise of wanting to ensure a reunification that is settled peacefully, has sought to encourage the independence of Taiwan, especially as the people of the island have increased their technological capabilities and China has become stronger in the naval sense. The

---

[555] See editorial comment, "US Meddling in South China Sea to no Avail," in *China Daily* (November 25, 2019), p. 8.

PRC, however, which has had at least two crises with the US (1958 and 1995), while not pushing for another crisis, has been uncompromising in its stance that the issue of Taiwan's reunification with Mainland China is nonnegotiable, while the US has begun more openly to encourage the increasingly "democratic" ROC to embrace the principle of self-determination toward independence.

More recently, three issues have brought the matter of Taiwan's independence to the fore: the claim on the part of many young people in Hong Kong (along with others) that the "One Country, Two Systems" principle that defines Hong Kong's relationship with Beijing is being threatened by Beijing; the 2020 attempts to have Taiwan gain membership in the World Health Organization (WHO); and quarrels centered on China's access to US technology. In the first stance, the US government and media have accused China of violating its commitment to the "One Country, Two Systems" principle, which promised to Hong Kong a great degree of autonomy in the conduct of the latter's affairs—autonomy that had induced the US to treat Hong Kong, in commercial and investment terms, as far more favorable than China. As Beijing moved to clamp down on and limit the scope of demonstrations and protests—a scope that included the shutting down of the airport, the transportation system, and the disruption of schools and businesses—the US and some of its allies further accused China of violating human rights and going back on its sacred promise. Former secretary of state Michael Pompeo claimed that China's behavior, in relationship to Hong Kong, should be seen as the emergence of a CCP that is perceived as "different . . . today than it was ten years ago" and that it is now one that is "intent upon the destruction of Western ideas, Western democracies, [and] Western values."[556] As such, the special status accorded Hong Kong (seen as an outpost of Western values) should be withdrawn. The status has been withdrawn.

For China, which had earlier poured scorn on the "West's hypocrisy" as it compared the protests in Hong Kong and their closing down of transportation, businesses, schools, and the airport with "Occupy Wall Street" (OWS) in 2011, when over five hundred demonstrators were arrested for failing to use sidewalks rather than the street (where traffic

---

[556] See *Boston Globe*, June 1, 2020, p. 62.

would be adversely affected), the double standard was all too apparent. Autonomy, in Beijing's view, does not mean that Hong Kong is exempt from regulation if that autonomy is being abused,[557] as the disruption of transportation, schools, and the airport, among other forms of behavior, indicated. One of its media organs, the *China Daily*, carried an article the very day of the accusation of hypocrisy on how well the "One Country, Two Systems" was working in Macao.[558] For the US, the main audience for the demonstrations in Hong Kong was Taiwan, the people of which it wanted to have concluded that since the "One Country, Two Systems" did not work in Hong Kong, it could not possibly work for them. Alternative? Independence.

With respect to the WHO, Taiwan's exemplary success in dealing with COVID-19 (550 cases, 502 of whom recovered, and only 7 deaths) was advanced as an example of an open and transparent system that could benefit the world in contrast to China's nontransparent approach.[559] As such, this small "country" should be accorded membership in the WHO. China's strong opposition helped quash the US's push.

The third area has to do with technology, where the US has increasingly been involved in battle with Beijing, which is seen as moving (where Xi is seen as acting aggressively) to threaten the US's supremacy. In particular, the claim involves Huawei, a Chinese multinational telecommunications company that is a major global smartphone brand and perhaps the world's "largest producer of equipment that powers networks."[560] Huawei, however, is dependent on semiconductor foundries, perhaps the world's most advanced of which is the Taiwan Semiconductor Manufacturing Company (TSMC) in Taiwan. Foundries, in turn, rely significantly on the US's software

---

[557] See Michael Tsai, "West's Hypocrisy over Hong Kong Exposed," in *China Daily* (December 4, 2019), p. 9.

[558] Zhang Yi, "Macao Lauded for Its Successful Practices," in *China Daily* (October 4, 2019), p. 1.

[559] Yu-Jie Chen and Jerome A. Cohen, "Why Does the WHO Exclude Taiwan?" *IN BRIEF* (Council on Foreign Relations, April 9, 2020).

[560] Ana Swanson, Paul Mazur, Raymond Zhong, "US Is Using Taiwan as a Pressure Point in Tech Fight with China," in *New York Times* (May 20, 2020), p. B1.

and equipment. In May 2020, the US announced a regulatory change that "bars companies around the world from using American technology to produce or design chips that are sent, either directly or through an intermediary, to Huawei itself."[561] Among other things, this regulatory change not only limits activities in and the development of Chinese companies located in China's territory but also further sets in motion an expanded basis for conflict.

So why is Taiwan—which, as late as January 5, 1950, the US claimed not to have had any *designs* on or special interests in—now being identified as so important? Why is this island that was then regarded as "historically and geographically" and strategically part of China now being supported to think of itself as not a part of China?[562] The answer lies in in two areas, neither of which had any direct bearing on President Xi. One is Washington's sense that China had never thought of itself as a superpower in the Western sense (with extensive maritime interests, for example, contrary to historical evidence), so it was unlikely that it would want to be one in the future. Far more important was the "strategic frontier" provided by General MacArthur in 1951.

As we left off a few pages ago, MacArthur sought to impress upon Congress the importance of preserving intact "all segments" of the strategic frontier, or it would become vulnerable. For this reason, he counseled, "under no circumstances must Formosa [Taiwan] fall under Communist control."[563] Such "an eventuality," he continued (giving voice to Eisenhower's domino theory), "would at once threaten the freedom of the Philippines and the loss of Japan and might well force our Western frontier back to the coasts of California, Oregon, and Washington."[564] The contemporary presence of aircraft carriers and nuclear weapons–laden submarines makes no psychological difference. Might it be that it is the US's conception of itself and its strategic frontier rather than Xi's alleged aggression that is at issue with Taiwan? The

---

[561] Ibid.

[562] See "Memorandum on Formosa," December 5, 1949, in Williams, op. cit., pp. 1108–1111.

[563] See MacArthur, op. cit.

[564] Ibid.

US's unchallenged presence in the Pacific and its pivot to the area helped induce a more economically developed and confident China to strengthen its armed forces, especially its air force and navy. As China has become so strengthened, the US has become less and less interested in seeing Taiwan as part of China.

Let us return to the two remaining areas, where Xi has been seen as aggressively threatening the US, namely, China's economic reach, and the role of the state in the socioeconomic life of the country. China's economic reach can be sketched by looking in three directions—the established economic order created after World War II by the US, the Global South (which has, from time to time, challenged that order), and some new institutional arrangements that China has been pursuing. The US-led, Western international economic system is anchored by the World Bank, the IMF, and the WTO, within each of which China functions as a member. The anchoring institution within which the behavior of China has been most widely and bitterly criticized is the WTO, in which China gained membership in 2001 as part of the project of integrating it more fully into the Western international liberal order. In a sense, China has integrated all too well. Not only has it expanded trade with the world, but also, it has done so at a pace and a range that has, at times, stunned the world, improving the lives of its citizens and those of other countries and regions of the world. It has also done so by reducing its own average weighted tariffs from 15.6 percent in 2001 to 3.83 percent in 2018.[565] As well, China has promised to continue the process of reducing tariffs as the world's largest trading nation (which it became in 2013), reaching almost every country in the world.

Beijing has been seen, primarily in the West, as not having done what it has implicitly or explicitly promised—that is, reduce the role of the state and, correspondingly, increase the role of the private sector in the economy of China. Additionally, the US has accused China of stealing IP and using it to give itself a certain comparative competitive edge against Western entrepreneurs, including those "forced" to transfer

---

[565] See "Tariffs and Imports: Summary and duty ranges," AI, wto.org (retrieved June 6, 2020). These tariffs compare well with Brazil, Mexico, India, and South Korea, which, respectively, had rates of 8.016, 4.35, 6.35, and 8.67 percent. Japan and others had a weighted average of 2.81 percent.

IP to Chinese partners.[566] In July 2018, following months of threatening to impose tariffs, the US unilaterally imposed tariffs on Chinese goods, and China retaliated. A tit-for-tat battle began, with the US imposing increasing tariffs (in the amount of $552 billion) and China retaliating (in the amount of $185 billion, the difference in amount reflecting the fact that the US imported more from China than the latter from the US). Since that time, some agreements have been struck between both countries, but some of the tariffs remain.[567]

As a poor nation, China was, for a time, among those countries eligible for and receiving loans from the "concessional window" of the World Bank, the International Development Association (IDA). As Beijing moved to the status of a middle-income country (like Mexico, for example), it graduated from the IDA in 2001; by 2007, it began to contribute to the IDA so that the latter institution could offer more funds to poorer nations (hardly the perception one receives from any US administration in relationship to China).[568] As earlier pointed out, throughout its history, the PRC has always given support, in the form of aid, to the poorer countries of the world, especially those from the Global South. As well, through trade, investments, and assistance, the PRC, by 2018, had so significantly extended its reach into the areas constituting that geographical region that the *New York Times* began a series on that reach, although with a tone to invite fear within the US. That tone is that China is aggressively displacing the US in areas of the globe where Washington enjoyed unrivaled economic advantage.[569]

---

[566] See "Trade Wars Are Good, and Easy to Win," *Business Week* (November 18, 2019), pp. 32–36.

[567] See a rather detained presentation of the tariffs in Dorcas Wong and Alexander C. Koty, "The US–China Trade War: A Timeline," *China Briefing* (May 13, 2020).

[568] Scott Morris and Gailyn Portelance, "Examining World Bank Lending to China: Graduation or Modulation?" Policy Paper #135 (Center for Global Development, January 2019).

[569] See, for example, Max Fisher and Audrey Carlsen, "How the Rise of China Is Challenging Longtime American Dominance in Asia," *New York Times* (March 16, 2020), p. A1; Ernesto Londono, "China's Long, Quiet Push into Latin America," *New York Times* (July 29, 2020), p. A1.

Africa has been a geographical region of major focus for China's foreign assistance programs begun in the 1950s, as before touched on. While China has repeatedly denied any exploitative intent toward that continent and its peoples,[570] claims concerning Beijing's alleged predatory and "evil" intent with regard to that socially and politically fragile continent are repeated in the West in general and in the US in particular.[571] The criticism initially seemed to have been innocently grounded on the fact that China, for a number of years, had much of its foreign aid funneled through the Ministry of Commerce. Changes in this approach, including the 2018 establishment of the China International Development Cooperation Agency (CIDCA) to streamline Beijing's development aid, have not removed or abated the charges. Answering directly to the state council (the chief administrative authority in the PRC), which is chaired by the prime minister and composed of the heads of all cabinet-level executive departments, CIDCA will now coordinate China's bilateral foreign aid activities. In some respects, the changes have but increased some of the most negative moral judgements launched at China—a "rogue donor," engaged in "debt trap" practices, in the pursuit of creating neocolonial conditions.[572] Meanwhile, China continues its support of Africa, including important collaborations through the Made in Africa Initiative (MIAI), a UN development program that aims to combine the knowledge of experts, the experience and skills of persons who have worked in China and Africa, and the shift of light manufacturing from the PRC to "other emerging economies" to expand and augment the rise of industrialization in Africa. By the end of

---

[570] Yun Sun, "Africa in China's Foreign Policy" (a paper produced at the John L. Thornton China Center and the African Growth Initiative at Brookings, April 2014), p. 5.

[571] Ibid., p. 1.

[572] Cheng Cheng, "The Logic Behind China's Foreign Aid Agency" (a paper prepared at the Carnegie Foundation for International Peace, March 21, 2019). One should note some of its tortured logic, argued in part because China's approach differs from that followed by the Organization for Economic Cooperation and Development (OECD).

2012, PRC aid to Africa through the China–Africa Development Fund alone had brought investment financing to an estimated $3 billion.[573]

In May 2020, the *New York Times* carried an article laden with the letter and spirit of "debt trap" diplomacy, noting that part of the uniqueness of COVID-19's impact on the poor countries of the world is that China's lending of some $350 billion had resulted in a burden on them. "China's aggressive lending" not only had placed it in a bind but also has saddled those poor countries with debts that they cannot repay.[574] From Sri Lanka to Pakistan, Ethiopia, and Ghana, one learns about the dilemma of these poor countries and (almost triumphantly) some developmentally unfriendly actions that China might be forced to take, thus losing influence among them.

One should, at this point in our discussion, move to the new international institutions that China has created or led in sponsoring because they too deal with the reach and nature of China's development efforts as well as its economic policy in general and their perceived threat to the US. So too should be mentioned two regional economic organizations in which China occupies a dominant position. These international institutions include the New Development Bank (NDB), which China, in 1994, helped create and, in so doing, further linked the economics of Brazil, Russia, India, China, and South Africa with $50 billon in development funding. This was followed in June 2015 by the AIIB, with $100 billion planned for investment. The US was not pleased when, despite its contrary urging, many members of the Organization for Economic Cooperation and Development (OECD) and even some of the G7—including the UK, Germany, France, and Italy—rushed to join. Complementarily, two other multilateral institutions were also created—the 2015 South–South Cooperation Fund (with a promise of $20 million annual support) to assist LDCs in implementing their agendas associated with the 2015 UN Sustainable Development Summit and the $40 billion Silk Road Fund, financed from, among other areas,

---

[573] Yun, op. cit., p. 23. According to Yun Sun, some $5 billion was available for investment, but $3 billion was spent by then.

[574] Maria Abi-Habib and Keith Bradsher, "China Lent Billion to Poor Countries, and Now They Can't Pay It Back," *New York Times* (May 19, 2020), p. B. 1. Countries in Central Asia are included in "poor countries."

the China Investment Corporation, the Export–Import Bank of China, and the China Development Bank and seeking to promote development roughly along the "ancient" Silk Road.

In terms of regional and trans-regional trade organization, the reader will recall that former president Obama's TPP was not supported by Congress and that his successor, President Trump, withdrew from it. It had a successor organization, however. Led by Japan and wearing the name of the Comprehensive and Progressive Agreement for Trans-Pacific Partnership (CPTPP), the latter organization, boasting all the original members of the TPP except the US, came into being in January 2018. It still has the aura of an anti-China grouping and could still be reshaped to include and be led by the US, depending on the views of presidential and business leadership in the US. It would, however, face another like group, one in which China is likely to play a leading role. It is the Regional Comprehensive Economic Partnership (RCEP), constituted by the nations of ASEAN[575] plus six others: Australia, India, Japan, New Zealand, and South Korea. It might here be observed that there are some overlapping memberships in some of these organizations. So efforts at realizing exclusive support from each, as either Washington or Beijing might seek, will not, in some instances, be easily realized or be realizable.

What explains the nature, breadth, and volume of China's economic assistance support if not actuated by the ugly, predatory motives attributed to Beijing? An answer to this question might also help us understand the last area focused on by the US and Allison in characterizing Xi's leadership as aggressive: the role of the state in the social life of a nation. The Kiel Institute for the World Economy, a private nonprofit economic research institution in Germany, claims that China's economic aid to poor countries (mostly for infrastructure building, in contrast to the US's, which is mostly military) is actually about $520 billion and, at that amount, makes China a "bigger lender

---

[575] Members of the Association of Southeast Asian Nations (ASEAN) are Brunei, Cambodia, Indonesia, Laos, Malaysia, Myanmar, the Philippines, Singapore, Thailand, and Vietnam. RECEP, without India (which has withdrawn from membership), houses 30 percent of the world's GDP and 30 percent of its population.

than the World Bank or the International Monetary Fund."[576] China certainly has the interests normally attached to any and all nation-states, including the US, in gaining support for its economy, its international political objectives (including those linked to IGOs), and its security (including access to energy sources and minerals) as well as adequate protection of its transportation routes. There are some values regarding sharing and the role of states with which we will deal more thoroughly in the next chapter but that, in brief, merit our critical gaze at this time if we are to going to further address the issue of the state's role in the economic life of nations.

Speaking at the World Economic Forum at Davos in January 2017 (and some of this material can be found elsewhere, but he was particularly emphatic at this largely business forum), President Xi offers us some examples of these values and, in his view, China's role in giving international effect to those values. By extension, they reveal the role of government in the economy. He argued that globalization represents a *natural* stage in human technological, social, economic, and political progress and development and that it is a good to be embraced, not something to be avoided or withdraw from, because doing the latter is not beneficially possible, and in any event, the ills attributed to it are but the products of "excessive chase of profits by financial capital and the grave failure of financial regulation."[577] The returns from the goods and services that globalization makes possible should be equitably distributed or shared, but such sharing and distribution can only be assured by adaptive and proactive management of the globalization process. The distribution itself should not be to individuals and states but inclusively to different subnational groups and social strata (unlike the US, he is not afraid to address social class, for example). He then returned to an old theme of China's foreign policy: the equality of small and big, poor and rich, and weak and strong states, including the equality of their voices.[578] The final value he espoused (for purposes of our discussion) was that of "common development," which was also

---

[576] Quoted in Abi-Habib and Bradsher, op. cit.

[577] See Pres. Xi Jinping's speech delivered at the opening plenary at Davos, 2017.

[578] Ibid.

pushed by his predecessor, Hu Jintao, and which Xi has seen as globally required because of developmental convergence, if for no other reason. (We will later see that there are "other" reasons.)[579]

How are these values of inclusiveness, individual equality, social equality, international democracy, and common development to be realized? Through two other values: that of change and that of a more active role for the government in national and international societies. He thus called for structural changes, especially in international financial systems and steps to correct the results of uneven development that one finds in the globe at large. The role of China's government in the progressive elimination of poverty, formerly thought to be an unavoidable feature of society, was highlighted; so too, he claimed, was the PRC's focus on the role of technology and innovation as key drivers of change, something he shared with the leaders of the G7 in 2016.[580]

China's help to the Global South, to the poor nations toward which it ostensibly harbors "evil" intent, should therefore be seen as part of a focus on common development, as part of China's model in its own development, and as part of the role of government in that development. This advanced role of government, more than any other single reference or position that Xi may have taken, dis-endeared him to the US. Xi's position in the speech is that the West's ideas about governance and development are not the only paths available to development or to effective governance; that socialism with Chinese characteristics has successfully, factually demonstrated an alternative path; and that this path may well be better suited to other countries, including those in the Global South and elsewhere.[581]

Among the characteristics of this "socialism" are an insistence that polity should control economy; that this control should not be merely to regulate but to manage, adapt, and guide, even to initiate, at times; that such management and guidance includes ensuring that certain social ends are realized—ensuring that the inequalities of the market

---

[579] Ibid.

[580] Ibid.

[581] See a fairly instructive essay on this by Cheng Si, "Global benefits of socialism hailed at forum," in *China Daily* (November 19, 2019), p. 4.

are either eliminated or oriented in the direction of social equality; and that development should be a common endeavor on behalf of all.[582] These characteristics, except for equality and equity, are not strangers, as we will see later, to modified mercantilism, a view that exercised considerable influence on US society until 1929.

We will return to this issue almost immediately. Let it be sufficient to observe here that the many accusations against Xi and China during his leadership are, at best, questionable and, at worst, clear misrepresentations. The issue of expansionism, for example, finds little support if one accepts that the US's interest in the Pacific is grounded on the view that the entire Pacific, under Washington's control, is needed to ensure its security. We already observed, in slightly different phrasing, that if this outlook accurately captures, for Washington, the significance of the Pacific, the sovereignty of China over the South China Sea and Taiwan cannot be reasonably claimed to be less. In any event, as even Allison concedes, China began building up islands, constructing missile batteries, and erecting airfields in the South China Sea largely after the 2001 collision of a US signal intelligence (surveillance) aircraft flying near Hainan Island, the southernmost province of the PRC, with a Chinese fighter jet. China, as any state would, has become strongly opposed to the "consistent presence" of the US's naval ships along its borders.[583]

The major issue for the US is that the policy positions of isolating, containing, including, and excluding China, each having as its principal objective the gaining of an "open door" to China's market, have not worked the way Washington expected. We are, in fact, at a point of another transition in US–China relations, one, according to Allison, defined by China's alleged threat to the US. We have tried to show that the claims of this threat are, thus far, not factually supportable and will add to this showing in the chapters to come. It is the case, however, that when the US supported the inclusion of China in the WTO in 2001, it believed that the PRC would, as in the case of other intended-to-be-excluded states such as Germany and Japan, "accept its place in the

[582] See Lovell, op. cit., Chapters 12 and 13, to get sense of Xi's political balancing actions.

[583] Allison, *Destined for War*, op. cit., pp. 159–160.

American-led international rule-based order."[584] This expectation has been varyingly expressed in other coded expressions, such as China becoming a "responsible stakeholder," a "responsible player in world affairs," as phrased by President Obama, a more "fully integrated" country in the "rule-based international system," or, as stated by Robert E. Lighthizer, US trade representative, "a model global citizen."[585] Each of these coded expressions is sometimes used interchangeably with the liberal democratic order or system or the liberal economic order. What this expectation has, in fact, meant is that China, despite acknowledged to be the embodiment of a civilization, should disregard its own economic and social culture and eagerly take up (without any serious changes) the economic system authored by Washington. Beijing, in doing so, would be betraying its stated commitments to its own people, the sacrifices of those who have fought to develop and support its system, and the undertakings it has assumed with friends throughout the world, including those in the Global South with which it has been collaborating over decades, and acknowledge that its own plans and model of development are not worth preserving. This course of desired conduct from Beijing would, were it to be pursued, be taken (by Allison and others who speak of the "ruthlessly flexible" character of China's policies) as confirming that claimed flexibility. Of course, the qualifiers of "rule-based" or "responsible" imply that a state that operates outside of the liberal order is not responsible and, consistent with that irresponsibility, is also non–law-abiding.

To be noted, before we close this chapter, is the observation that—contrary to the view that socialist or communist China has been pursuing naked self-interest in its expanding economic reach, especially with the Global South, and the implication that Xi, in particular, has been a major agent of this expansion—the founder of the KMT, Sun Yat-sen, held views that parallel Xi's. He (Sun Yat-sen) saw "greatness" for China as partly residing in its willingness to use whatever influence and power it

---

[584] Allison, ibid., p. 220.

[585] See Ely Ratner, "Course Correction: How to Stop China's Maritime Advance," in *Foreign Affairs*, Vol. 96, #4 (July/August 2017), p. 67; Robert E. Lighthizer, "How to Make Trade Work for Workers: Charting a Path Between Protectionism and Globalism," in *Foreign Affairs*, Vol. 99, #4 (July/August 2020), p. 80.

gains to help deliver "those nations which suffer in the same way as we do now."[586] This focus on serving as a non-military example to the less fortunate of the world is something that the US has known and feared that China (and the former Soviet Union) might become, especially in tending to the material needs of the least socially favored. For the US to be such an example, it would mean the entire recasting of its society. It would be too costly.

[586] Quoted in Emily Dong's speech on "Sun-Yat-sen" at the Pan-Asian New Dawn of Peace, the Democracy Center, Cambridge, MA, November 2, 2019. See also Williams, op. cit., p. 1050.

CHAPTER 14

Culture and Ideology in the Contest

We have shown certain alignments and seeming compatibilities
between China and the Global South throughout this section of the
book. We have not, however, indicated the actual source or sources of
these apparent compatibilities with China apart from certain common
social and psychological experiences that have helped form some
common memories, perceptively identified by Daniel Moynihan as
manifested in a "coherent ideology." Unlike Moynihan's contention,
which assumes that anything that is rational and coherent had to have
had its origins in the West (in this case Britain), the ideology has had
diverse cultural roots. This ideology has to do with polity and economy,
state and society, the individual and the group, the political construct
of the terms "East" and "West" within which has been embedded the
ethno-cultural category called race, certain attitudes toward race, and
an orientation toward war and peace.

The main thrust of Moynihan's 1975 *Commentary* magazine piece
was that the proposals in the 1974 UN General Assembly–approved call
for the NIEO assumed the existence of a world or global *community*
instead of what he saw as but the beginnings of a world or global
society. The latter, as before touched on, stemming from the growing
interdependence among nation-states, envisions but continuing (perhaps
augmented) cooperation among otherwise independent countries
without any sentiment concerning one state owing anything to another.

WINSTON LANGLEY

Community, on the other hand, invites images of the family, where the ideas of owing, of mutual obligations, and of common and shared outcomes are understood and pervasive. The NIEO, in the type of sharing for which it called (to achieve the just economic world order that its advocates sought), bespeaks a community. To bring such a social and moral system into being would require much more involvement of government in the life of society than the US-led market economies and their respective governments might ever be ready to tolerate, not to mention support or accept. Further, the broad subordination of the economy to polity (politics, as commonly understood), instead of accepting the economy's autonomy and sometimes subordination of economy, was contrary to the US's belief and its proclaimed fear of what it came to call authoritarianism.

Xi, in seeking to espouse China's tradition (in a neo-Confucian form coupled with socialism), begins with the "idea of community." He argues that for over five thousand years, the Chinese nation has not only carried forward a unique culture (which he defines as a country's or a nation's "soul") but also studied as well as incorporated as part of itself the "essence" of the "fine cultures of the world"; that resulting from this incorporation has been a "great unity"; and that "all under heaven as one family" is, for the PRC, a "worldview" around which it is oriented. He proudly noted that the PRC has, since its founding, united some fifty-six ethnic groups and urges that in China, individuals should regard "other people as their own persons" and regard "the country as their own family." In respect of the world? He said that "the mission of the Chinese people is to promote the building of a community of shared future for mankind."[587] He goes further. As if underlining the synthesis that Chinese culture, in his view, has represented (and we should bear in mind that the idea of synthesis is very much part of Chinese socialism), he espouses a concept central to Buddhism and Taoism as an aim that all individuals should have—the "removal of the little self" (the narrow individualist entity associated with the West) and substitution

[587] See CCNR, pp. 10–11, 96–97.

268

and cultivation, in its stead, of "one's bigger self," a community- or family-embracing identity.[588]

That idea that the economy can or should be allowed to coexist as an autonomous body of activities in a society seeking to embody the above definition of community (especially when one thinks of the ideology of neoliberalism that sees government as a necessary evil) is viewed as a socially unacceptable extreme. Neo-Confucianism, like classical Confucianism, urges one to live by "the Doctrine of the Mean," which, in summary, supports an outlook on life that believes in self-regulation, family regulation, and state governance for the benefit of all as values intimately linked to the worldview of great unity and all under heaven as one family.[589] (Consider family as used here to include workplaces, organizations, schools, neighborhoods, and communities,[590] and "all under heaven" is a reference to a normative category that transcends nation-states in binding all.) The idea of community, as Xi presents it, lends itself to associational analogues, even if partial, with other cultures—Ummah in Islam, for instance, Ujamaa and its equivalent, in much of Africa, obligatory reciprocity among many indigenous peoples, Catholic "social teaching" in Latin America and the Philippines (out of which "liberation theology," which has had a preferential social option for the poor, emerged), and the broadly shared view among socialists, almost everywhere, in social sharing. It is part of that which animated the 1961 European Social Charter.[591] As well, one finds aspects of it in Marxism, which envisioned a world without national borders, often referred to as proletarian internationalism. So too will one find some comparable values among historical and contemporary leaders of the Congress Party of India and even the conservative-leaning People's Action Party of Singapore, the Australian Labor Party, and leading parties in Indonesia, Japan, South Korea, and Vietnam. Israel's Labor

---

[588] Ibid., pp. 10–12.

[589] Ibid., p. 11.

[590] Ibid., p. 19.

[591] See 529 UNTS 89. Europ. TS No. 35. (They are, respectively, the United Nations Treaty Series and the European Treaty Series.)

Party, especially as originally constituted, and social democratic parties throughout the world have shared many of Xi's views.

If we were to confine ourselves to the Global South, however, one can understand why the NIEO ideology brought the fear of what Moynihan saw as an emerging "tyranny of the . . . new majority" and the numerical and ideological minority in which the US found itself.[592] The economic policies/power of China, directed toward the world at large but to the Global South in particular, although a form of state capitalism or market socialism, really have no present goal of limiting the role of the state in the economic life of societies. On the contrary, Beijing is seen as reinforcing, by its example and success, an increase in that role. As well (and this is quite important to the US), China's influence has made countries less vulnerable to the economic and other pressures (nectarously labeled "soft power") that Washington has traditionally successfully applied to get its way internationally.[593] Likewise, reduction of the space within which American-style market economics can emerge, thrive, and expand means, at a minimum, a narrowing of the US's commercial and investment opportunities. Not only is the "open door" not available in China—as Washington has, since the nineteenth century, sought—but also, China could be closing the "open door" possibilities elsewhere, especially in the Global South. Force may be employed by the US, an area in which it enjoys almost prohibitive advantage, to ensure this opening, but its use is not always applicable; and some of the more damaging impacts of economic sanctions—the cutting off of Iranian banks from access to the Society for Worldwide Interbank Financial Telecommunications (SWIFT), for instance—do not sometimes have the intended or desired outcome. Not only has Iran failed to fold, but also, Russia, Western Europe, and China

---

[592] Moynihan, op. cit.

[593] Alexander Cooley and Daniel H. Nexon, "How Hegemony Ends: The Unraveling of American Power," in *Foreign Affairs*, Vol. 99, #4 (July/August 2020), pp. 143–156. See also Robert M. Gates, "The Overmilitarization of American Foreign Policy," in the same issue, pp. 121–142.

are thinking about creating an alternative system—one over which the US would have but limited power and influence.[594]

That Xi has emphasized culture as the germinating and sustaining element in realizing China's dream of becoming a "modern socialist country that is prosperous, strong, democratic, culturally advanced, and harmonious" (that is, enjoying civil peace) and participating in the "reform and construction of a global governance system" to "promote the building of a world with lasting peace, common prosperity, as well as a world that is open, tolerant, clean, and beautiful" strongly suggests that the PRC is acting not only in the pursuit of joining IGOs but also in significantly reforming them.[595] While these reforms, given the ascribed and feared character of the "new majority" (people who are committed to building community and willing to use their votes in the UN to do so), in Moynihan's view, exact international obligations, one to another, the US could become less and less able to elicit willing global support on behalf of its way of life. It could, in its place, face the uninviting prospect of having to negotiate on the long escaped-from and feared grounds of sovereign equality.

Finally, given the manner in which the "unregulated market" behaves—producing socioeconomic privations of many sorts, including social inequality—the modern socialist state to which Xi refers, that which China dreams of building (and this comes from Xi's experience in a China that has had some direct experience with capitalism and witnessed some of its extremes, combining the lack of affirmative spiritual and cultural values), must have a larger role for the state. The role includes encouraging and promoting human agency for good rather than leaving people with the impression that "anything goes" and that they can do little about it. One may call this an empowering function, something Mao taught.[596] In addition, government has a role not only in helping business primarily or only but also in nurturing, in part, what

---

[594]   Eswar Prasad, *Gaining Currency: The Rise of the Renminbi* (Oxford; Oxford University Press, 2016); Paola Subacci, *The People's Money: How China Is Building a Global Currency* (New York: Columbia University, 2016).

[595]   See CCNP, op. cit., p. 20, 152.

[596]   Evan Osnos, *Age of Ambition: Chasing Fortune, Truth, and Faith in New China* (New York: Farrar, Straus, and Giroux, 2014). Xi has been seeking to deal

values serve as the basis for legitimacy and, as important, in arresting and reversing, where it can, the spiritual crises that a society may be facing, as it was in the case of the China over which the CPC assumed control in 1949.

Linking Moynihan's and Allison's thinking has been done in this portion of the work to make a larger point beyond the particulars mentioned above. That thinking shares the common characteristic of helping illuminate something that has aided the West to define itself since the latter's encounter with Islam and refined over time to remove certain explicit and often considered impolite categories. That something is a cultural concept that captures this definition of the Western self and its relationship to the "other" that has come to be known as *orientalism*, which Edward Said, in a book by that name, ably captured and, as touched on earlier, so concretely and persuasively elaborated by John M. Hobson in his book *The Eastern Origins of Western Civilization*.[597]

The central idea about *orientalism* is that the West used the non-Western other to construct its own identity (from roughly the time of the rise and expansion of Islam to the present) and, simultaneously, to shape the identity of the non-West. In this constructing and shaping, the West is portrayed as a desired (ideal) and operational norm and the non-West as what the West is not, usually through a body of failings or weaknesses or, more generally, in terms of a condition of lacking certain desirable capacities that Europe, and now the US, possesses. These claimed failings would then be used as the foundation for the general rejection of what the East purportedly has embodied or represented and, conjointly, to provide the ideological (including moral) grounding for the West to lead in removing those failings and, to the extent deemed possible, substitute the desirable attributes of the West. Moynihan's positions, as presented above, were in the grand tradition of orientalism, with its implicit racism.[598] It mirrored the views of TR during his presidency, whom Allison uses in his book as a frame of reference in

---

with some of the excesses dealt with in this book, especially as seen throughout CCNP.

[597] See Said, op. cit., and Hobson, op. cit.

[598] The author uses the term "implicit racism," very much in the way John Hobson does, to distinguish it from the more explicit and "unrefined" claims made

his comparing China and the US, largely outside TR's racial views, and anticipates those of President Trump's administration as well as the prevailing stances of the opinion shapers or molders of the day. Much of the alleged "lacks" or failings bear little relationship to the truth, as we will come to see, but factual accuracy or truth is not as important as the images that they convey, the psychological orientation that they support, or the moral certainty/ambiguities that they confer or solicit in ideological battles.

Moynihan made five points, in the article examined, from the standpoint of orientalism. First, the non-West lacks originality (a point that the reader will recall was made by Allison, in respect of the PRC, when he indicated that the US is invested with the capacity for innovation, while China had but an ability to restore or evolve what is already in existence).[599] For Moynihan, the ideas of the "British Revolution" did not and could not have come from the Group of 77; members of that group merely imbibed that body of ideas from Britain and were using it in their respective political and economic evolution. Second, they did not really understand it since it came from conflicts between the working class of Wales, Scotland, and England on the one hand and the British upper class on the other and was incorrectly made to be parallel or comparable to the anticolonial struggle. Third, its (ideological) coherence makes it dangerous for the West, the US in particular, because it is seen as coming from the Global South but, in fact, is from Europe (he did offer some limited contribution from a few other European countries, including Holland). Fourth, the ideology harbors a deep skepticism about capitalism and sees government as allowing the requisite regulation and control that are coextensive with that skepticism. The latter is made all the more significant by the fact that—unlike the US (and, by extension, Europe), which has the capacity to forget the differences between itself and its former colonial master, Britain—the people who constitute the Group of 77 do not have that

---

in the nineteenth and early twentieth centuries. We no longer, for example, speak climate, genetics, brain size, and certain geographies as indicating abilities.

[599] Allison, *Destined for War,* op. cit., p. 141.

capacity.[600] They harbor some bitterness. The fact that government, for China (according to Allison), is a "necessary good" suggests that it lacks the capacity for individual self-government and therefore exhibits the need to look toward government for that which individuals should be doing—a perfect fit with Moynihan's paradigm.

Two related additional areas of Moynihan's thinking merit mention here: coherence and the basis for the US's moving into the opposition to the proposal to transform the international economic order. The frequency with which he refers to coherence should not be taken to mean that the ideology of the British Revolution (as he calls it) hangs together, is consistent, or enjoys the quality of forming a unified whole only. What was being said, more than anything else, is that this ideology (with which he so strongly disagreed), although coming from a world in which irrationality is a defining attribute, is, in fact, rational because it originated in the West. This conclusion, in a roundabout way, returns to and carries on the traditions of orientalism, which sees the West as rational and the East as lacking in rationality.[601] The reasoning for the US's moving into "the opposition" is related to the seeing of government as a "necessary good" rather than being viewed as a "necessary evil." The former outlook, in Moynihan's view, had been more or less made an operational norm in the Global South, thereby limiting the full expression of (often subverting) that subcategory of human rights we have come to label as CPR. Since the Global South, in contrast to the West, is so lacking in this area, it (the area) should be the target of the US's attack.[602] Tactically, this meant that the US, in opposition, would place members of the Global South on the defensive—always having to explain and apologize for their ascribed identity, for their lack, and reverse the unusual position that the US found itself in after the NIEO proposals were adopted by the UN General Assembly, one of defensiveness. However, defensiveness is but one of the comprehensive psychological and political results of orientalism. The East (and the broader Global South) was made to be always apologetic for not being

---

[600] Moynihan, op. cit.

[601] Ibid.

[602] Ibid.

like the West (something Xi has been refusing to do, and hence, he has been accused of being arrogant). This brings us to what "like the West" has meant.

In Allison is found, under one of his assigned essential attributes of the West, that of exemplar—that is, the West being an exemplar, model, or ideal (the missionary, one defined by the *habit* of seeking to convert others). As observed by Hobson, because there are so many failings on the part of the East (in orientalism), *cultural conversion* became a major strategy used by Western governments under the guise of transforming the non-West, of making the latter more like the West. This pursuit of cultural conversion, sometimes referred to as bringing "civilization to the natives," brought with it, however, a problem. Making the non-West more like the West ("civilized") ran the risk of making the non-West potential future competitors; so implicit in the cultural conversion outlook and practice was the idea of containment—the non-West must be kept down.

TR, in a 1909 speech to the Methodist Episcopal Church, captured the challenge as he sought to celebrate the work of European governments in their missionary tasks and the work of missionaries themselves, specifying certain particular areas of the globe, as he progressed in his speech—Egypt, India, Indonesia, and the Philippines, among others. He opined that

> the best that can happen to any people that has not already a high civilization of its own is to assimilate and profit by American or European ideas the ideas of civilization and Christianity without submitting to alien control, but such control, in spite of its defects, is, in a very large number of cases, the prerequisite condition to the moral and material advance of the peoples who dwell in the darker corners of the earth.[603]

---

[603] See Pres. Theodore Roosevelt's address, "The Expansion of the White Races at the Celebration of the African Diamond Jubilee of the Methodist Episcopal Church," Washington, D.C., January 18, 1919. https://www.stormfront.org/forum/t77702/

To make the point about the virtue of cultural conversion even more compelling and simultaneously deal with the contradiction of that conversion and containment, Roosevelt looked to India. "In India," he contended, "we encounter the most colossal example history affords of the successful administration of men of European blood of a thickly [densely] populated region in another continent. It is the greatest feat of the kind that has been performed since the breakup of the Roman Empire. Indeed, it is a greater feat than was performed by the Roman Empire."[604] While admitting "occasional wrongdoing" on the part of European and American governments and missionaries in their activities in the "darker corners of the earth," he proceeded to hold up India as an example for the Philippines, Algeria, and elsewhere, including the rest of Africa. He further sought to justify rule from London by noting that aside from the comparatively "fair treatment for the humble and the oppressed" that had come to define Britain's rule in India, "England does not draw a penny from India for English purposes; she spends for India the revenues raised in India, and they are spent for the benefit of Indians themselves."[605] (TR, of course, was pretending not to know better than what the last statement claims given the widely shared knowledge of Britain's depredations in India.)

As such, "every well-wisher of mankind, every friend of humanity, should realize that the part England has played in India has been to the immeasurable advantage of India and for the honor and profit of civilization [and] should feel profound satisfaction in the stability and permanence of English rule."[606] Implying that Britain was against tyranny, he observed that "undoubtedly, India is a less pleasant place than formally for the heads of tyrannical states"—princely states formed part of the political subdivisions that constituted British-ruled India. (Apart from noting here the 1857 First War of Independence, when an estimated eight hundred thousand persons died from the conflict and associated famine and disease—a fact that Roosevelt must have known and could hardly be seen as part of an "occasional wrongdoing"—we

---

[604] Ibid.

[605] Ibid.

[606] Ibid.

will come, in due course, to a juncture at which readers can judge the ideal rule that the president highlighted.[607])

Let it suffice to say that from the quoted passages, one can discern several features of orientalism. First, Roosevelt recognized one of its central contradictions and tried to make light of it morally—the contradiction of cultural conversion and containment. How does one assimilate peoples from the "darker corners of the earth" into the "high civilization" of Americans and Europeans without, in his own words, "alien control" of them? How does one raise them up without keeping them down? After all, if they are not kept down, if the non-West (the reader will remember Japan in a preceding section) is not kept down, the West can no longer be superior.[608] Roosevelt argued for alien rule and control in general. That control and rule, he saw as necessary, not in any neutral historical sense but as a "prerequisite condition" to the "moral and material advance" of the peoples to be converted and assimilated, to be "civilized."[609] The obvious implication of falling short, of multiple failings, necessitating the "prerequisite condition," need not be detailed here. The control was necessary despite or regardless of "occasional wrongdoing."

In completing our discussion of the identified attributes of orientalism that Moynihan and Allison employed in their analysis, let us now focus on three more that Allison used in his assessments of and projections about US–China relations. Operating to summarize the values, attitudes, and orientations rising from some deeper analysis to show their inaccuracies and then to indicate how they envelop the political economy of US–China relations, these three are the following: attitude toward foreigners (here, the US is said to be "inclusive," while China is "exclusive"); their respective time horizons, as earlier touched on but which must further expand, with the US seen as responding to "now,"

---

[607] See Jill Bender, *The 1857 Indian Uprising and the British Empire* (Cambridge: Cambridge University Press, 2016); John Marriott, *The Other Empire: Metropolis, India in the Colonial Imagination* (Manchester: Manchester University Press, 2013); Clare Anderson, *Indian Uprising of 1857: Prisons, Prisoners, and Rebellion* (New York: Anthem Press, 2007).

[608] Hobson, op. cit., p. 241. He makes this point rather well.

[609] Roosevelt, "The Expansion of the White Races," op. cit.

while China deals with "eternity"; and lastly, their intentions in foreign policy. Here, the US is described as pursuing "international order" and China seeking "harmonious hierarchy" (Moynihan preferred the term "tyranny," authoritarianism, or the older expression "despotism," which is less frequently used today but was often employed in the eighteenth and nineteenth centuries as part of orientalism).[610]

A final attribute should be added, one not previously highlighted because it is generally hidden although made evident by its being underlined by TR and forcefully presented by Gen. Douglas MacArthur. That attribute is leadership, implicit in the operation of almost every value in the West, including the US, but largely unrepresented in the East and, by extension, China. MacArthur, in his earlier-cited address to Congress, explicitly expressed this. After outlining certain conditions and assigned characteristics of the countries of East Asia (Japan, South Korea, and the ROC, led by the KMT that occupied Taiwan), he came to the Philippines—"our former ward," he called it. "A Christian nation, the Philippines stand as a mighty bulwark of Christianity in the Far East, and its *capacity* for [emphasis mine] high moral leadership in Asia is unlimited."[611] Here, MacArthur is saying that the capacity for moral leadership is not to be found in the other countries of Asia mentioned— they were not of the West. The Philippines, however, by virtue of its Christianity, is of the West and, because of that association, is endowed with the capacity for moral leadership in Asia. That capacity is not only considerable or ample but also unlimited.

TR's position in his 1909 address to the Methodists captures and anticipates this focus on religion and moral leadership, and he uses this Protestant group, as he has used Britain, as an example:

---

[610] See Francois Quesnay, "Despotism in China," in Schurmann and Schell, *Imperial China*, op. cit., pp. 115–120. The reader should know that Quesnay had defined despotism in such a way that it included all monarchies in Europe, and he compared China favorably with Europe, which he saw as inferior to China. The use of "despotism" changed over the years, however, in a way that saw it routinely applied to the East, unlike the West.

[611] See MacArthur's "Farewell Address," op. cit.

In the redemption of Africa, all sections of the Christian Church must be united, but Methodism, because of the vast members it represents and the spirit and methods of its movements, should have a share of special note. The spirit of Methodism is the spirit of expansionism and worldwide conquest in the kingdom of righteousness. John Wesley's [founder of Methodism] motto was "The world is my parish." I hope Methodists of today will make this statement good.[612]

Among the tenets of Methodism (a Protestant branch of the Christian religion) is not only the love that God has for all but also the unity of all Christians in the single body of Christ. Roosevelt envisioned religion as helping in the cultural conversion to Christianity and the West on a worldwide scale. The West was, to him, the secular "kingdom of righteousness" to which all the conquered (converted) will belong. The "redemption of Africa" meant that Methodism would save it from falling short, from its errors, from its many failings, including the evil that defines its people. The spirit of Methodism is the spirit of conquest by the missionary, which, as the reader will recall, Allison depicts the US as modeling. The goal of that spirit in the US is "worldwide conquest" to the kingdom of the civilized, the Christian, and the Westernized world, to a worldwide liberal order.

Let us now scrutinize the properties of orientalism as they have evolved into contemporary thinking, especially in the conduct of the US's foreign policy, including the three Allison-provided contrasting attributes of the US and China. One will see how they are used to keep China on the defensive as well as provide a path to a justification for continuing conflict with Beijing and, later, even war. A rebuttal of those usages will follow, with a view to answering the question "Why the confrontation?"

---

[612] See Roosevelt, "The Expansion of the White Races," op. cit. It should be understood that many missionaries were genuinely of the view that they were saving people who would otherwise be damned, and their belief in their collaborations with governments and governments with them was to the civilizing benefit of "native peoples."

A summary of the properties of orientalism should disclose that they are institutional, ideological (in the sense of a system of beliefs within which a person or group finds social, philosophic, psychological, and other kinds of balance and justification), and moral, that which shapes our sense of right and wrong. At the center of all these properties is the "self," which the US (and the West) has developed. This self is coextensive with the post-1945 multinational, intergovernmental, political, financial, commercial, legal, scientific, and military institutions that the US led in creating and then managing. These have varied from the UN (and its specialized agencies, including the IMF, the World Bank, UNSECO, and the WHO), the WTO, NATO, and US-led regional military and other institutions such as ANZUS and the Organization of American States (OAS). Washington is also owner of the world's key currency, as before said; the Federal Reserve Bank dominates central banks elsewhere, with the exception of Russia and China.

Linked to institutions are practices that are themselves rightly seen as quasi-institutions because, to quote Francis Fukuyama, they represent and encourage stable and valued recurring "patterns of behavior,"[613] such as periodic voting to shape decisions (be they to sponsor successors in leadership, to formulate policy, or to interpret and enforce policy), and even steps taken or procedures to be followed to facilitate or ensure the enforcement of norms. Temporal matters refer to how time is used to augment the self and diminish the other. Allison, as the reader will recall, depicts the US as concerned with "now," while China is focused on or preoccupied with the long term, the eternal. We have already shown that the US is also long term in its concerns, always referring to the Founding Fathers—covering the entire life of the country—to validate or legitimize what it does or seeks to do. China employs the same approach, pointing to its own long history, which extends further back than that of the US,[614] but China also deals with "markets," the operations of which are often "now," for the short term.

---

[613] Francis Fukuyama, "America in Decay," *Foreign Affairs*, Vol. 93, #5 (September/October 2014), p. 8.

[614] Unfortunately, this emphasis on the part of Allison begs the question about those US citizens whose historical memories go back further than 1620 or 1776. Are they Americans?

What is at issue here is something far more important substantively and symbolically. The US (and the West, generally), as part of a cultural leaning, has followed the practice of constructing a self at or from a *laudatory present* and then restructuring the past in a sequence to "demonstrate" an almost inevitable historical move to that present. Modernization, industrialization, and liberal democracy, for example, are the inexorable results of the Renaissance, the Reformation, the Scientific Revolution, and the Enlightenment, and the demonstrations of their claimed inevitability are often done with limited and limiting historical contexts—the excluded role of the non-West, for example, in those "inexorable results." The effect, in part, is the ability to construct a superior self, as we will shortly show,[615] a self that is the agent, the subject of historical change. For the US, it has been the chief agent of that change since 1945.

The ideological is clothed in a system of ideas called liberal democracy (claimed to have evolved from the time of ancient Greece), which is defined by representative government, individual liberty, private property, limited government involvement in economic life (which should enjoy an autonomy captured in the French expression "laissez-faire"—that is, let things take their own course), a body of civil liberties referred to as inalienable rights (the right to free speech, to press, to practice one's religion, and to equality before the law), and an overarching body of basic moral norms called human rights. The latter, Washington selectively employs and often chooses to call those so employed as American values to reinforce certain images of the self. As part of the heart of human rights law and morals but also of the heart and lung of international law is the Latin term "pacta sunt servanda" (agreements, be they private or public, must be kept), indicating the importance of law in governance. So the liberal order is seen as committed to a law-governed world.

When one now speaks of the liberal democratic order, the Western system of political economy, or the world or international liberal order, one is generally referring to the US-led system of political economy, with all the institutional, practical, temporal, ideological, and moral features just mentioned above. The identity of the US as leader of

---

[615] See Hobson, op. cit., Chapter 10.

this largely self-created system has been buttressed by two additional qualities: "public goods" and exceptionalism.[616] The former refers to those international products or services that a country can use (or consume, as the expression goes) without reducing, by that use, its availability to others—for example, the security of transportation on the high seas or the relative absence of anarchy in the international system. The US (through its military forces, as was the case with Britain during the nineteenth century) is seen as providing these public goods. With respect to exceptionalism, it is the view (a type of "civic religion," according to Jeffrey Sachs) that the US has been chosen, has a "divine mission to deliver not only success for itself but global salvation."[617] As mentioned earlier, the late senator John McCain, voicing a bipartisan tradition from George Washington to the present,[618] took the position that "God created us and brought us to our present position of power and strength for some great purpose."[619] As the reader will recall, the sentiments of the late senator replicate that of Churchill, who sought to use it to justify Britain's imperial control throughout the world.

With the exception of Japan (made a honorable member of the West)—because it had "undergone the greatest reformation in recorded modern history," had erected "an edifice dedicated to the primacy of individual liberty," had committed itself to "the advance of political morality [and] freedom of economic enterprise," and had given evidence that it "will not again fail the universal trust" reposed in it[620]—other non-West countries were admitted as "wards" under the guardianship of the West (the US) until they are deemed capable of managing their

---

[616] Joseph B. Nye Jr., "The Rise and Fall of American Hegemony from Wilson to Trump," in *International Affairs*, Vol. 93, #1 (January 2019), pp. 63–80. https://doi.org/10.1093/ia/iiy212

[617] Jeffrey D. Sachs, *A New Foreign Policy: Beyond American Exceptionalism* (New York: Columbia University Press, 2018), p. 23. The entire first chapter is quite insightful.

[618] Conrad Cherry, *God's New Israel: Religions Interpretations of American Destiny* (Chapel Hill: University of North Carolina Press, 1988).

[619] See McCain, op. cit., p. 19.

[620] See MacArthur's speech to Congress, op. cit.

own affairs.[621] The ROC, under the converted Christian leadership of the KMT's Chiang Kai-shek, was to have been the preferred political form of China to play its part as a partner of the US in the post–World War II order of the Far East, as the US envisioned things, and is largely playing the role of Japan today, the latter understanding its place as serving a subordinate role to the US's interest in the region. However, the CPC won the civil war, as we earlier discussed, followed by the Korean War, and visions had to be modified.

The PRC was admitted but only partially into the US-led international order in 1971, when the ROC was removed from the UN, and the PRC began to serve in its stead in that worldwide IGO, followed by the visit of the late president Nixon to China in 1972 and the mutual diplomatic recognition in 1978/79. The latter date marks the time when the US, seeking to have the PRC play the role of a counterweight to the former USSR[622] as well as a candidate for cultural conversion, moved to join Deng Xiaoping's efforts to launch features of the capitalist market system in China. By 2001, the PRC had shown enough promise of convertibility that it was admitted to the WTO.

The promise has not been realized, from the standpoint of the US, because Beijing has refused to see government as a necessary evil (COVID-19 is causing people within the US to question this attribute of US liberal democracy) and has been bent on celebrating government as a necessary good for all people. It has refused to pursue the missionary spirit as a model and has shown that it is more comfortable with honoring the principle of political and cultural right to self-determination, including in its behavior toward the Global South, to which it has extended billions of dollars in foreign aid. As well, while not as inimitable, as characterized by Allison, it prefers to live by example as it builds its own society. As far as the issue of inclusivity is concerned, Xi's position is that China not only boasts a civilization that has learned from and absorbed many of the world's cultures but also continues today in that inclusivity by

---

[621] Here, we are dealing with the use of networks of international institutions, such as the IMF and the World Bank, as well as regional military arrangements, instead of "national" action, which is used less frequently because it raises issues of authority and legitimacy.

[622] 22 Richard Nixon, *Real War*, op. cit., pp. 150–201.

way of the number of students it sends to study abroad (nearly 700,000 in 2019, with 350,000 to the US, and the number of students it accepts from over 190 countries about 500,000; in contrast, the US, during the same period, sent but 21,000 to China).[623]

All the preceding paragraphs illustrate part of China's efforts to create the "socialist society with Chinese characteristics," including the merging of time horizons—now and eternity, not now versus eternity, as might be suggested. The late senator Henry M. Jackson—advisor to Presidents Nixon, Ford, Carter, and Reagan and a known foe of socialism and China—urged as early as 1983 that Washington accept the fact that "overt pressure" will not generally change China, in large measure because its "political system . . . reflected deep tendencies of Chinese culture,"[624] not some recently Xi-constructed, unprincipled self-promoting system of practices. Jackson's concern about having China serve as "balancer" for the former USSR in East Asia, however (and he feared that there might be people in Beijing who preferred Moscow to Washington), led him to support the extension of most-favored-nation trade treatment status to the PRC.[625]

With China refusing to fit into the orientalist paradigm and demonstrating an unwillingness to undergo cultural conversion (while employing parts of the US-led liberal demographic order to further its own advantage and that of other countries that come under the umbrella of orientalism), a decision had to be made, it was felt, to confront China more directly and overtly. That decision was publicly made in 2017 to find ways of halting and possibly reversing the "peaceful rise" of China as the CPC's leaders have been seeming pleased to describe the nature and tenor of that country's development. No longer was the world going to be primarily faced with the coded expressions from the

---

[623] Sources: https://www.statistica.com/statistics/233880/international-students-in-the-us-by-country-of-origin/; Ministry of Education, People's Republic of China, moe.gov.cn (April 17, 2019).

[624] See "The China Policy of Senator Henry M. Jackson," Staff Report to the Committee on Armed Services, United States Senate, December 1983 (Washington: Government Printing Office, 1983).

[625] Ibid. The reader might want to consult the annex to the document for further elaboration.

US's political leaders of both major parties—from former president Obama and Sen. Marco Rubio to chief trade negotiator Robert E. Lighthizer—concerning China's *capacity* (emphasis the author's) to be a "responsible stakeholder," a "responsible player," or a "trusted" and "responsible" member of the global order.[626] China—in addition to the military arrangements that the US has, over the years, built to contain it—will be forced to defend itself not simply as a threat in the South China Sea but as a strategic menace to the entire system of institutions and practices as well as the ideological framework within which they are embedded.

Vice President Pence was assigned the task of publicly delineating the sweep of the decision in a lecture he delivered at the Frederic V. Malek Memorial Lecture at the Conrad Hotel, Washington, D.C. In that lecture, he noted that President Trump had, through his 2017 "National Security Strategy," changed "forever" the substance and narrative of US–China relations and that the decision had come about because the "United States now recognizes China as a strategic and economic rival."[627] He then proceeded to identify a number of areas or activities in which the PRC had failings—areas that, together or separately, constituted a peril to the US. It was engaged in "debt diplomacy and military expansionism," pursuing the "repression of people of faith," and embodying an "arsenal of policies inconsistent with free and fair trade, including tariffs, quotas, forced technology transfer, and industrial subsidies."[628] Throughout the lecture, Pence also focused on the US's values and interests, including democracy and private property. Then Secretary of State Mike Pompeo buttressed and sharpened the area of values in calling for greater emphasis, in relations with China, on private property and religion as human rights.[629]

---

[626] See, for example, Jennifer Lind, op. cit., pp. 74–82, and Lighthizer, op. cit.

[627] See text of "Remarks by Vice President Pence at the Frederic V. Malek Memorial Lecture," October 24, 2019.

[628] Ibid.

[629] See Pranshu Verma, "Pompeo Says Human Rights Must Reflect Religion's Role," in *New York Times* (July 17, 2020), p. A. 19.

Let us review each of the specific allegations within the framework of orientalism. Debt diplomacy and military expansionism, we have touched on already, and we have noted that China's military spending (without considering the expenditures of Washington's allies) is no more than a quarter of the US's and that the latter has allies and friends, many enemies of Beijing's, surrounding China, such as Australia, India, Japan, South Korea, New Zealand, and Vietnam. The differences concerning the South China Sea are not any alleged expansionism by Beijing but rather a combination of two factors: the differences that China has had with disputed claims with some of its neighbors to islands in that sea; and Washington's electing to begin taking sides with those neighbors against China and the US claiming that the entire Pacific Ocean constitutes its own strategic frontier, thereby unwilling to share power with China in that frontier. We will return to this for refinement.

Allison may not have remembered his own essay as he accused China of expansionism, and Vice President Pence may have been unaware of it as he leveled the same accusation. It shows that the expansionism may be a truer portrayal of the US's behavior than China's. In Allison's own words, the "main feature of postwar international politics," as he saw them, "would not be the expansion of the [former] Soviet Union, the resurrection of Japan and Europe, or the multiplication of independent nations [but] the *global expansion of American influence*" (author's emphasis) by social, political, economic, and cultural means.[630] This expansion was not by influence only—if "influence," as used here, refers to the social and psychological effects that ensue from the presence of immense power. It has included control through economic instruments (banking—private and public, such as the IMF and the World Bank), industrial organizations in the form of multinational business corporations, trade networks and organizations, political alignments, intelligence sharing, and a vast telecommunications infrastructure that

---

[630] See Graham Allison, "National Security Strategy for the 1990s," in Edward K. Hamilton, ed., *American Global Interests: A New Agenda* (New York: W. W. Norton & Company, 1989), p. 200. Hereafter, this essay will be cited as "National Security Strategy." This author thinks that the most important post-1945 development was a moral one, the adoption by the UN General Assembly of Universal Declaration of Human Rights.

included the dissemination of information to countries and regions through the acquisition of additional territories (including bases for the navy, the air force, and the army) throughout the world. After the end of the Cold War, the influence extended into Eastern Europe, to an extent Russia (since then reversed by Putin but still courted by Washington), and the Balkans, where Henry Kissinger observed that the US began doing the same things that the Austro-Hungarian and Ottoman empires had done to preserve peace through the establishment of protectorates in the area.[631]

The economic, for instance, has always been part of what, in the US's diplomatic history, has been called "dollar diplomacy"—the using of money to control outcomes in Latin America, the Caribbean, Asia, and elsewhere. One has but to look at how Florida was acquired, how the Panama Canal came to be, the establishment of protectorates over Nicaragua and Haiti, and the post-1945 returns from the destroyers-for-bases deal of 1940 which allowed Britain, in its war crisis, to get American destroyers in exchange for bases in Antigua, Newfoundland, the Bahamas, Bermuda, Guyana, Jamaica, St. Lucia, and Trinidad and Tobago, thus making the Caribbean an American lake.[632] We find some of the same things developing in the Indian Ocean (not unlike the move by the US to take over London's "responsibilities" in the Mediterranean through the Truman Doctrine, thus accepting the baton from Britain in controlling bases in the eastern areas of that sea) in Washington's acquisition of the base on Diego Garcia—so too, if one were discerning, in Washington's "persuading" London to make the pound sterling convertible into dollar in return for a loan of $3.75 billion to a debt-ridden Britain, thus accelerating the decline of the latter's international influence after World War II, or in the manipulation of the dollar and the "oil debt" during the 1970s and early 1980s to retain existing control of the international political economy.[633]

---

[631] Kissinger, "American at the Apex," op. cit., p. 9.

[632] See Bailey, op. cit., pp. 164–173, 546–554, 718–725.

[633] See Ferguson, *Empire*, op. cit. pp. 300–301, and Jan Joost Teunissen, "The International Monetary Crunch: Crisis or Scandal?" *Alternatives*, Vol. XII, #3 (July 1987), pp. 359–395.

The collaboration of the Department of State and members of the business community, including bankers, to work through the American China Development Company or banking consortium to build railroads or partake on broader levels of investments in China is well known; it was certainly well known to TR, who refused to accept the right of the Chinese government to refuse the particularly onerous terms of a proposed deal in 1903.[634] Noteworthy also is the 1932 chagrin of Sen. Hiram Johnson at the profits that bankers (linked to the expansion of the US's influence into Latin America) were taking from the countries of the area compared to what they had invested in those countries. So too was the extent of our investment in the late Boris Yeltsin's survival in Russia during the 1990s,[635] in large measure to help realize James Baker's already-mentioned vision of liberal democracy regimes from Vancouver to Vladivostok.[636]

We went through all this discussion of the preceding few paragraphs in part to say that to the extent that China engages in "debt diplomacy," the US has pursued this as a major part of its own history. Thus, the real reason for criticizing China for doing what the US has done and continues doing cannot be because China's actions are inherently bad, as Washington would have one believe; the reason must reside elsewhere. That elsewhere is to be found in the claim that Beijing has been or has become a "rogue" state and that it has failings (from the standpoint of orientalism) because of its deviations from the Western patterns of dealing with economic aid, grounded on a "winner take all" model and substituting in its stead a non-zero-sum or "win-win" approach, which China seeks to practice.[637] It entails more. It is a claim made to invoke the value of trust, in which the West is trustworthy (despite major questions about the debts sponsored by the West through multilateral

---

[634] See Bailey, op. cit., pp. 529–533. Williams, op. cit., pp. 452–465.

[635] See Senator Johnson's remarks of March 15, 1932, in Williams, op. cit., pp. 715–717. See also Peter Conrad, *Who Lost Russia* (London: One World, 2017).

[636] See quotation in Kishore Mahbubani, *The New Asian Hemisphere* (New York: Public Affairs, 2008), p. 42.

[637] See Anand Giridharadas, *Winner Take All: The Elite Charade of Changing the World* (New York: Alfred A. Knopf, 2018).

institutions[638]) while China is not. In China's case, its history of foreign assistance is not long enough to draw a fact-based conclusion, although all the evidence thus far suggests that Beijing has been largely living up to its "win-win" policy position. The charge also involves the fear, on the part of the US, that aid by Beijing to the Global South (within which there remain the greatest opportunities for investments and trade) is, in effect, aid by government, which "crowds out" available opportunities for private investment—the dominant mode of Western economic transactions. This too is a question of trust—Beijing cannot be trusted to be a responsible carrier of the Western model.

The second body of accusation by then vice president Pence (and this cuts across partisan rhetoric in the American foreign policy establishment) is that Beijing suppresses people for their religious profession. The charge is part of a broader human rights weakness or failing, encompassing freedom of speech, press, conscience, and religion and the right to associate (the latter gaining special attention in relationship to Hong Kong and the broader issue of political democracy). In July 2020, then secretary of state Pompeo brought to the fore the right to private property: "It is important for every American and every American diplomat to recognize how our founders understood unalienable rights" and that "[f]oremost among those rights are property rights and religious liberty."[639]

First, it should be noted that the source of human rights claims above by the secretary of state, the vice president, and earlier by Allison and others is national. In the case of Allison, he is perhaps the most explicit and direct: "Are Chinese citizens less deserving of the human rights America's Declaration of Independence declares to be the God-given endowment of all people? If democracy is the best form of government for all nations, why not for China?"[640] One could, of course, ask why it is the duty of the US to ensure that its own declaration is the source of human rights for all people, as distinct from those of the French,

---

[638] See Cheryl Payer, *The Debt Trap: The International Monetary Fund and the Third World* (New York: Monthly Review Press, 1975).

[639] Pranshu Verma, op. cit., p. A. 19.

[640] Allison, *Destined for War*, op. cit., p. 223.

the British, South Africa, India, or China. One could also ask what democracy we are dealing with in this instance—that which enslaved blacks, discriminated against women, and left non-property owners without the right to vote? What is of central importance here for our discussion is that Allison (as will Pompeo and Pence) substitutes the limited focus of national institutional reference for the globally agreed-on norms of human rights that *deliberately* have sought to avoid being linked to any one cultural tradition, as evidenced by "God-given," which is expressive of the Western tradition. The purpose of doing so, of course, is to demonstrate failings in the relationship to the West, specifically the US, and all the defensiveness that doing so invites. We will first take the issue of democracy and then touch on other issues, including religion, and we will use the UDHR, which is the "common standard of achievement for all peoples and all nations."[641]

Article 21 of the declaration, which deals with the principles of democratic entitlement, reads as follows:

1. Everyone has a right to take part in the government of his [or her] country directly or through freely chosen representatives.
2. Everyone has a right of equal access to the public service in his [or her] country.
3. The will of the people shall be the basis of the authority of government; this will shall be expressed in periodic and genuine elections which shall be by universal and equal suffrage and shall be held by secret vote or by equivalent free voting procedures.

The US (and the West), under the orientalist view, has treated its claim to being democratic as if the latter came by way of an "immaculate birth" at its creation and has since defined its evolution, as before noted, using the present state of things for itself and twisting the past to "confirm" it and then offering its "present self" as an example to others

---

[641] See preamble to the UDHR. It should be noted here that the two covenants—which, together with the UDHR, constitute the international Bill of Human Rights (IBHR)—were given the name "covenants" to remind those who make use of them that the universal principles and values, which they incorporate and to which nations pledge themselves, are not ordinary responsibilities; they are sacred.

to follow. When did the US become democratic in the normative sense referred to in the UDHR or in the practice of the West, including the US? In the case of the practice of the West—which has, by and large, had three features (a national loyal and centralized bureaucracy, which is supposed to operate in an impartial, non-arbitrary manner; the "minimalist state" in partnership with laissez-faire capitalism; and political citizenship, which empowers or entitles all to vote)—we find that the US had no valid claim to being called democratic until 1965, offering on that date, for the first time, the rights of all to vote after 189 years of calling itself a democracy. We will not mention here the end of the Civil War or the abolition of slavery, the continuing division of the country about equal rights (including the ongoing suppression of the right to vote), or the virtual purchasing of votes as a routine in political campaigns. The rational, color-blind, neutral bureaucracy that is supposed to guarantee impartial treatment to all has its problems,[642] from the police and the courts to the Department of Education and to the operation of the Department of State, that organ of government principally tasked with directing the country's relations with other nations. The US record of supporting democracy abroad, including the 2019 "fall" of Evo Morales in Bolivia, is, at best, troublingly inconsistent.[643]

China today is not the China of 1950 or of 2000, and it admits that it has a distance to go to realize *political* democracy, as defined in the UDHR. Its goal is to have that end fully realized by 2049, the one hundredth anniversary of the establishment of the PRC, much earlier than it took the US to achieve the goal, if China were to succeed. Beijing has not been sitting idly; it has been trying to establish another model of democracy, with priority given to *social* democracy—something that liberalism has been afraid of because it requires some fundamental

---

[642] See Richard Rothstein, *The Color of Law: A Forgotten History of How Our Government Segregated America* (New York: W. W. Norton & Company, 2017). One can also review the development of democracy in the US and the West in Chapter 12 of Hobson, op. cit.

[643] See Melvin Gurtov, *The United States Against the Third World: Antinationalism and Intervention* (New York: Praeger, 1974); see also Stephen Kinzer, "In Bolivia, American 'democracy promotion' is a farce," in the *Boston Globe* (February 9, 2020), p. K2.

redistribution of power and wealth—and then moving in a more integrative manner toward democracy in general. This appears to be part and parcel of President Xi's model of development. In this respect, it is not surprising that in the cases of Hong Kong and Macau, China has seemed willing to accept the constitutional principle of "One Country, Two Systems" as well as the allowing of capitalists to be members of the CCCP (we should not forget that Macao operates on the "One Country, Two Systems" principle). One sees in these modes of conduct a far more democratic spirit or impulse than what the US often manifests in finding it so difficult to accept Cuba, with its socialist system, as neighbor or any serious public discussion of socialism or social democracy, an identity that even Bernie Sanders, a democratic socialist, recently tried to avoid by pointing instead to desirable social programs (social security, for instance) that have broad popularity among US citizens. Would the US, emulating China, allow the people of Long Island to have a socialist system coexisting with the rest of the country under the principle of "One Country, Two Systems"? We will deal with the "minimalist" state under our discussion of free trade.

With respect to religion and private property, we must put them in some historical context rather than simply positioning the US as if it were always what it is today to facilitate the orientalist contrast with China. Despite beginning their history on the North American continent as persons fleeing religious persecution, the early settlers and their successors were neither advocates of religious freedom (other than their own) nor advocates against discrimination based on religion, although one would never suppose this to be the case from the US's stance toward China. Contemporary norms of human rights, as enshrined in the UDHR and the 1981 Declaration on the Elimination of All Forms of Intolerance and of Discrimination Based on Religion or Belief (DEAFIDBRB), textually speak of the right that everyone has "to freedom of thought, conscience, and religion" and allows for limits "only . . . as are prescribed by law and are necessary to protect public safety, order, health, or morals or fundamental rights and freedom of others."[644] The US partly holds China to this normative standard using

---

[644] See UN Doc. A/36/51 (1981), reprinted in *ILM*, Vol. 21 (1982), p. 205. This declaration is an elaboration on Article 18 of the 1948 UDHR.

its own attempts at current practice, however, and bypassing its own history as it developed even its own.

An examination of US history will disclose instances from the 1637 trial of Ann Hutchinson, who espoused the idea of salvation through faith and the grace of God instead of one based on law and on works[645]; the persecution of Catholics (the idea of a Catholic president before the time of John F. Kennedy was not thought possible), largely because of the idea of separation of church and state, which the Vatican does not accept; the continued repression of Native Americans; and recent attacks on Muslims. In the case of Native Americans, this has been primarily through the reckless taking of their lands and the destruction of their sacred places (and Native Americans do not make the distinction between church and state either), and discrimination against Muslims has increased under the umbrella of "Islamic terrorism." Allowing for the arbitrary arrests and detention of people, including even Sufi members of Islam, who had nothing to do with terrorism is well known.[646] The US, in part, has often sought to justify its just-mentioned conduct under the public safety exception provisions of the DEAFIBRB. The associated torture during the detentions at many sites, including Guantanamo Bay in Cuba, does not allow for *any* exception.[647]

China's tradition bears close resemblance to that of the Native Americans in the sense that religion was not seen as something separate from society; there was no separation of church and state, in part because of the normative concept of "all under heaven," which has operated above

---

[645] See David Hall, ed., *The Antinomian Controversy, 1636–1638: A Documentary History* (Durham: North Carolina: Duke University Press, 1990), pp. 312–316, 336–337.

[646] See Claudio Saunt, *Unworthy Republic: The Dispossession of Native American and the Road to Indian Territory* (New York: W. W. Norton & Company, 2020). This book had a particularly impressive review in an essay, "This Land Is Not Your Land: The Ethnic Cleansing of Native Americans," by David Treuer, in *Foreign Affairs*, Vol. 99, #4 (July/August 2020), pp. 171–175.

[647] See Article 2 (2) of the Convention Against Torture and Other Cruel, Inhuman, or Degrading Treatment or Punishment, in UN Doc. A/39/51/ (1985). See also Matt Apuzzo, Sheri Fink, and James Risen, "How US Torture Left a Legacy of Damaged Minds," in *New York Times* (October 9, 2016).

and beyond human law, conventions, and practices and has governed all. When Christianity arrived in China, it brought with it the suspicions that the West had about the relations between church and state; its agents were also bearers, especially among the Protestants, of the orientalists' outlook espoused by TR in his advocated "worldwide conquest [to] the kingdom or righteousness"—that is, the "religious other," throughout the world, should be converted to Christianity regardless of its disruption to traditions and practices in non-Christian societies, including China's. Although these disruptions and conflicts were not the main source, they were nevertheless "significantly influential in the cause of events" that led to the Boxer Rebellion (1899–1901) in China, with Christians from the US playing a very important role.[648]

Given this background plus communism's very negative attitude toward religion, it was not surprising that the PRC would be suspicious of this sociocultural institution. The ugly and unacceptable excesses in respect of religion during the Cultural Revolution have been acknowledged by the post-1979 leaders of China, who have moved to accommodate many religions in China—including Taoism, Buddhism, Christianity, and Islam, among others—with a view to realizing a return to having religion enjoy a broad societal identity rather than one that lends itself to being Judaic, Christian, Hindu, Muslim, Buddhist, and so forth.[649] The pursuit of social harmony (a kind of civil order by which public safety, health, order, and morals are assured) as a central policy objective as well as core social value by China—and this, as we before said, is a civilizational tradition in that country—is seen by Beijing as being threatened by certain internal groups aided and abetted by external actors.[650] The work of born-again Christians in influencing the

---

[648] See Mary Katherine Duncan, "Fumbling the White Man's Burden: US Missionaries, Cultural Imperialism, and US Intervention in the Boxer Rebellion" (thesis submitted to Department of History, University of North Carolina Wilmington, 2012); see also Ian Johnson, "China's Great Awakening: How the People's Republic Got Religion," in *Foreign Affairs*, Vol. 96, #2 (March/April 2017), pp. 82–95.

[649] Johnson, ibid., pp. 85–86.

[650] My last two visits to China exposed me to this point of view, and the US is seen as the main external abettor.

US's foreign policy and the presence of international networks (such as the US-founded World Congress of Families, which has been working with Euro-Asian groups[651]) as well as the long-standing British–China rivalry in Central Asia, primarily over the control of Tibet, are all factors affecting the PRC.[652] The claimed presence of radical Muslims in the Xinjiang region of China, prompting Beijing to place significant numbers of Muslim Uighur and Kazak minorities in detention centers, must be considered in the broad context of this search for a harmonious civic order and society, the memory of conflicts in Central Asia (including concerns about Tibet), the colluding role of religion in the weakening of China during the nineteenth century, and the worldwide branding, led by the US, of certain Muslim groups as terrorists.

Both China and the US agree that detention exists. There are disagreements, however, respecting the number detainees, the purpose of the detention, and its nature and intended duration.[653] China takes the position that detention is a relatively accommodating way of dealing with "extremism," using vocational school programs as a means to confer skills that offer the detainees a deeper stake in society and, as well, enabling them to contribute to overall development while it monitors them. It also maintains that some of these detainees are allowed opportunities to visit their families[654] and that the detentions themselves fall within the earlier mentioned exception of the DEAFIBRB, especially

---

[651] See Craig Unger, *American Armageddon: How the Delusions of the Neoconservatives and the Christian Right Triggered the Descent of America and Still Imperil Our Future* (New York: Scribner, 2007); see also Alexander Cooley and Daniel H. Nexon, "How Hegemony Ends," in *Foreign Affairs*, Vol. 99, #4 (July/August 2020), p. 152.

[652] Alastair Lamb, *Britain and Chinese Central Asia: The Road to Lhasa, 1767–1905* (London: Routledge and Kegan Paul, 1960). See also Lamb's book, *The China–India Border* (London: Oxford University Press, 1964).

[653] Nick Comming-Bruce, "22 Countries Issue Plea to Beijing to Stop Its Persecution of Uighurs," in *New York Times* (July 11, 2019), p. A9; Pranshu Verma and Edward Wong, "US Imposes Sanctions on Chinese Officials Over Rights Abuses," in *New York Times* (July 9, 2020), p. A13; Yang Jianli and Lianchao Han, "US Takes Steps to Stop China's Abuse of Uyghurs—as Should Other Countries," in the *Hill* (June 17, 2020).

[654] Verma and Wong, ibid.

in the area of "threats to public safety"—what China more broadly called "security."[655] The US, using its own conception of religion in society, with no reference to the accepted international standard, sees China's actions as a patent abuse of CPR, and some US officials, including a former national security advisor, have used terms such as "internment" or "concentration" camps (with all their morally repulsive historical images and meaning) to characterize the detention centers.[656]

What is really at stake here is not the particular areas of alleged or actual human rights abuse (after all, China began what it has called "reeducation" at the centers years before 2019, and the US then seemingly had no objections, especially as Washington had been actually pursuing a variety of actions, including torture, against "Islamic terrorists"). It is rather Washington's efforts, following the spirit of behavior recommended and followed by Moynihan (and refined by Allison), to drive a strong contrast between the West and the Global South. China is the current focus, if not part of the Global South then as one of the countries under the umbrella of orientalism. The US is what China is not; the latter is a flagrant, ongoing violator of our universal moral norms, while the US is the universal upholder and embodiment of those norms. Had Pope Francis not rejected the Department of State's effort to have the Vatican repudiate understandings concerning certain religious practices it had struck with Beijing, China would have been portrayed even worse than it has recently been.[657] Is the US, in fact, an upholder of and practitioner of human rights, as claimed and portrayed? The body of human rights is divided into two general categories, as we before indicated—the category of CPR and that of ESCR. The US has but selectively focused on rights in the first category and has ignored and abused those in the economic, social, and cultural division. What should be observed also is that the US media, the academy, and most of the nongovernmental organizations have followed the pattern of the government in that selective focus. Let us focus on a few examples.

---

[655] Ibid.

[656] See, for example, John Bolton in his book *The Room Where It Happened: A White House Memoir* (New York: Simon & Schuster, 2020), p. 312.

[657] See Jason Harowitz, "Vatican Defies U.S. in Bishop Deal with China," in *New York Times* (October 23, 2020), p. A11.

The US views itself as the foremost promoter of democracy, but it has helped focus that political value primarily on elections. Other areas such as the right to vote or the availability of the ballot are rarely touched on—even at home, where gerrymandered voting districts exclude and guarantee the elections of political parties. In elections, it has participated in the overthrow of popularly elected governments and tolerated, at home, the intimidation of voters. In the area of "equal access to the public service of [one's] country," as required by the UDHR, there has been little by way of democracy. According to a recent article by former US diplomat Chris Richardson entitled "Closed Doors at the State Department," one learns how lacking in equality and inclusion are the operations of this area of government. The exclusion and discrimination extends elsewhere. What we have in the Department of State, he observed, is a "pervasive and entrenched system of white supremacy."[658] In my view, social class, gender, and religious as well as other cultural factors are also present.

With respect to private property, the US has been a very strong advocate; this form of property ownership has, of course, been the foundation of the economic system we call capitalism. The UDHR, however, offers no preference for this form of ownership and specifically states that "everyone has the right to own property alone as well as in association with others."[659] Countries that have deemphasized private property have been criticized by the US (said to have authored, by this de-emphasis, many social ills) and otherwise made to feel "less than," but seemingly unknown to the Department of State is what we should remember—one has a right to own property "alone" or "in association" with others. China has a mix of ownership but overwhelmingly emphasizes ownership "in association with others," with "others" including future generations.

In the area of torture (and we touch on this merely because of the suggestion, without any evidence at all, that this form of conduct has been taking place in Xinjiang, thus the need to show that the US has not had a good record on this matter either), the US cannot, with integrity,

---

[658] See *New York Times* (June 6, 2020), p. A27.

[659] See Article 17 of the UDHR.

set itself up as an upholder of human rights while China has not been. From the Philippines, in its 1899–1902 war with the US, to Guantanamo, Cuba (2002–2003), and Abu Ghraib in Iraq (2003–2006), the US has been implicated. The Philippines presented the world with what was then called the "water cure,"[660] what we today refer to as "waterboarding," the act of pouring water into the nose and mouth of a victim who lies strapped on her or his back, with feet above her or his head, knowing that the victim will experience the physical and psychological sensation of drowning. This practice by the US, during the above war with the Philippines, became an important feature of Washington's human rights abuse at Guantanamo, Cuba.[661] Abu Ghraib was more of a "traditional" torture, accompanied by rape and murder.[662]

In the sources cited in the preceding paragraph, the reader will find a wide-ranging body of views, not including those of TR and Hillary Clinton. The latter—in outlining in 2007 her vision for the country, the presidency of which she would seek in 2008—simply passed off Guantanamo and Abu Ghraib as something "we [the US] will have to talk about."[663] In the case of TR, the "water cure" was part of the "occasional wrongdoing" that was naturally incident to rule by the West. In general, the US has treated its own complicity in torture— despite its rather prominent role in prosecuting, judging, and punishing Nazi leaders for torture committed during World War II and the long unequivocal tradition in customary international law that forbids the

[660] See New York Times (March 6, 1902), p. 9; (April 17, 1902), p. 3. See also Richard E. Welch Jr., "American Atrocities in the Philippines: The Indictment and Response," in Pacific Historical Review, Vol. 43, #2, pp. 233–253, https://online.ncpress.edu/phr/article-pdf/4312/233/322006/3637551.pdf (accessed July 15, 2020).

[661] See free online access to relevant documents, which have been reviewed by Robert Jarvis in "The Torture Blame Game" in Foreign Affairs, Vol. 94, #3 (May/June 2015), pp. 120–127.

[662] See Mark Danner and Hugh Eakin, "The CIA: The Devastating Indictment," in New York Review of Books, LXII, #2 (February 5, 2015), pp. 31–32. Julian Borger, "Chilling Role of 'the Preacher' Confirmed on CIA Waterboarding Hearing in Guantanamo," in the Guardian (January 25, 2020).

[663] See Clinton, op. cit., p. 15.

practice—as if it were a course of conduct that should be condemned and punished according to certain conditions. Discussions, including debate by members of Congress, often treat torture as something allowable depending on the character of threat that a nation believes it faces from an actual or perceived enemy.[664] This view would, of course, leave the US, in political discourse, to hold itself up as not committing torture because of its perception of threat to the US while saying China or other countries, in their circumstances, committed torture. The international convention on torture leaves no doubt. Article 2, Section 2 of that treaty states, "No exceptional circumstances *whatever* [emphasis the author's], whether in a state of war or a threat of war, internal political instability or any other public emergency, may be invoked as a justification for torture."[665] Further, it goes on to say, an "order from a superior officer or public authority may not be invoked as justification for torture."[666] In other words, one cannot argue that a president, prime minister, king, or queen commanded him or her to commit torture. The argument will hold no validity.

With respect to ESCR—the right to housing, health care, education, clothing, and food—they are part of the sought human "security in the event of unemployment, sickness, disability . . . or lack of livelihood in circumstances beyond [one's] control," among other objectives.[667] The US has never sought to support these rights. On the other hand, they are among the rights to which China has given priority in its effort to advance national economic, social, and cultural development. They are also among the body of rights that Xi has been championing in his efforts to rid China of every expression of material poverty. The US, in deemphasizing and actually overlooking the ESCR, has been able to achieve four ends: it has been able, internationally, to use its economic power ("soft power") to impose the harshest of sanctions against countries with which it has had differences, some in the area of CPR, without being held accountable for human rights abuse. Washington,

---

[664] See Jarvis, op. cit.

[665] See Convention on Torture, op. cit.

[666] Ibid., Article 2 (3).

[667] See Article 25 of the UDHR.

for example, under the claim that a country has violated the right to religious freedom, can impose sanctions that affect people's rights to food or health care.

Indeed, usually, such sanctions weaken a targeted country generally by impairing its ability to trade and its capacity to maintain desirable levels of employment, to avoid shortages of food, medical supplies, and sometimes even water, and to support education, the paying of rents, and the sustaining of transportation and social security. Iran furnishes a good recent example in this respect, weakened as it had been by COVID-19.[668] No one in the US's media establishment will accuse Washington of human rights violation; neither will human rights organizations such as Human Rights Watch or other like NGOs ostensibly committed to human rights, as opposed to using the term to support the official stance of governments. The fact that these sanctions sometimes result in the "fall" of governments, thus defeating the expressed will of voters, has often been treated as irrelevant, an event that can set back a country many decades on its road to development.

Third, the US, by this practice, contributes to its objective to make ESCR of tertiary importance when, in fact, they are of first importance. All one needs to reflect on is the fact that COVID-19 has taught the world that health care is fundamental to economic growth, development, and even economic life and that food, rent, and education have much to do with security and even the right to life. One author, making some comparisons between some of the social conditions brought on by COVID-19 and the Great Depression, observed how people, weeks earlier, thought they were "doing well," only to find that two weeks later, they were broke—without food, rent payment, and health care—and in debt, with house parents hiding their allotments of supplies into empty baby carriages because they were ashamed,[669] feeling "less than" because they have had no sense that their condition is hinged to rights

---

[668] See Stephen Kinzer, "Sanctions-Mad America Turns On Its Friends," in the *Boston Globe* (July 12, 2020), p. K7. As admirable as his analysis is, he, as is the case with most opinion shapers or journalists in the US, did not relate all the criticisms of sanctions to ESCR.

[669] See Andrew Coe, "Free Food, with a Side of Shaming," in *New York Times* (June 25, 2020), p. A27.

denied them; those leaders of traditions that boast of commitment to the democratic norm of equality as well as representatives of the "best economy" in the world have, in fact, been colluders in their humiliation and on assaults on their dignity.

Fourth, it allows the US to attack China on the latter's weakness in the area of CPR (with a US-led successful worldwide dissemination that they are the only areas of human rights worth fighting for and reflecting on) while remaining virtually immune from criticism because Washington is seen not as a perpetual violator of ESCR but as the upholder of human rights in general. China, of course, despite its focus on ESCR, is placed on the defensive, and the US maintains the aura of moral superiority, which the West, in orientalism, enjoys over the Orient and thereby works to *keep* China on the defensive, always trying to explain itself. The current speaker of the House of Representatives, Nancy Pelosi, went so far as to accuse Beijing of "barbarous actions" in its alleged actions in Xinjiang,[670] a characterization she would hardly perhaps never use for a Western country, just as Alexander of Macedon has been called Alexander the Great despite his having "subjugated, pillaged, raped, and destroyed," as did Attila the Hun and Genghis Khan. The latter two were "invading savages" from Asia; Alexander was from the West and became great for behaving savagely.[671] Is it more or less "barbarous" to deny people of their ESCR?

It should here be mentioned that part of the reason for the social crisis (especially in health care but also education) is the idea of "minimalist government," which left the overwhelming percentages of research labs to the private sector and the having of entire counties (not just a city or town, as socially and morally troubling as doing so is) without a single intensive care unit (ICU).[672] The private sector has the answer, it is claimed, to all of society's problems and challenges; government has but a minimal role to play.

---

[670] See Yang and Han, op. cit.

[671] *Smithsonian* (July/August 2020), p. 3.

[672] See Fred Schulte et al., "Counties with No ICU Beds as Pandemic Intensifies," in *Kaiser Health News*, khn.org (March 20, 2020).

There are three remaining areas that the Trump administration had focused on in relationship to its complaints against China, areas on which there is broad agreement with the Democratic Party. They are that China is building a surveillance state; is pursuing unfair, nontrade practices; and has been engaging in forced transfer or theft of technology as well as industrial subsidies. Let us look at the change of "surveillance state."

The former vice president Pence accused "China's Communist Party [of] building a surveillance state unlike anything the world has ever seen."[673] "Unlike *anything* [author's emphasis] the world has ever seen" sounds ominous and should rightly invite anxiety in every human being who understands what the building of such a state could mean. Pence proceeded to describe what he claims is being built—"[h]undreds of millions of surveillance cameras staring down from every vantage point," and ethnic minorities (who constitute about 8.5 percent of China's population) "must navigate arbitrary checkpoints where police demand blood samples, fingerprints, voice recordings, and multiple angle head shots and even iris scans."[674]

As just indicated, minorities constitute a relatively small percentage of China's population; from my own research in China (including in the northwestern province of Shaanxi), the description of what is taking place in China toward minorities is not accurate. It might be that in Xinjiang, the claimed activities are taking place, but I have found no reliable source of any evidence to that effect. Of course, we have had examples of surveillance of minority and women's groups seeking the recognition of their CPR. With respect to the "hundreds of millions" of surveillance cameras, this is part of what we have in the US today, although citizens are seeming largely unaware of them, and more so in the UK (defended on the grounds of fighting terrorism). Far more important, we have expressed little concern about the far more potentially controlling surveillance by private companies, as aptly captured by the work *The Age of Surveillance Capitalism*, authored

---

[673] See Pence, MML, op. cit.

[674] Ibid.

by Shoshana Zuboff.[675] The contention of the volume is that private companies are using and will further use the entirety of the human constitution and experiences as "raw material to be tracked, parsed, mined, modified, and used" in the pursuit of knowledge, wealth, and power.[676] We are dealing with and should be concerned about individual freedom and dignity, and if we truly are, the source of threats, public or private, to them does not matter. The US government itself, however, is also implicated further in what it has been accusing China of doing.

In Stephen Kinzer's *Poisoner in Chief*, we have a distressing narrative of the CIA's search for mind control[677]; in Edward Snowden's *Permanent Record*, we have the anxious awakening of how our government has been secretly pursuing the collection and control of every phone call, text message, email, travel, etc. of citizens.[678] Unlike the surveillance cameras indicated above that may or may not be tracking criminal activities only, the surveillance disclosed by Snowden has little to do with suspicion of criminal conduct. It targets all citizens.[679] It is difficult to accept that the government that presents itself as the embodiment and defender of liberty and freedom and China as the opposite is so largely implicated in doing what it contends that China should not be doing. As regards the pursuit of an "arsenal of policies" inconsistent with reciprocal trade (again, while this claim was shaped by the Trump administration, representing the Republicans, it is generally shared by business leaders throughout the country and Democrats as well), one may best approach the issue through a body of denials in which the US has engaged and a furthering of images (a denial as well but also a

---

[675] Shoshana Zuboff, *The Age of Surveillance Capitalism: The Fight for a Human Future at the New Frontiers of Power* (New York: Public Affairs, 2019).

[676] Winston Langley, *While the U.S. Sleeps* (Bloomington, IN, NC: Xlibris, 2021), Chapter 6.

[677] Stephen Kinzer, *Poisoner in Chief: Sidney Gottlieb and the CIA Search for Mind* Control (New York: Henry Holt & Company, 2019).

[678] Edward Snowden, *Permanent Record* (New York: Metropolitan Books, 2019).

[679] The reader may want to read a 2014 interview of Edward Snowden by Anthony Romero, executive director of the American Civil Liberties Union (ACLU). See *American Civil Liberties Union* (Summer 2014), pp. 15–19.

claim that has fed a myth) of orientalism. Let us begin with the first of the denials.

The first concerns the US's trade deficit with China, which one must admit had been increasing over a period of years. Like Britain (during the high days of its worldwide imperial rule), which had a balance of trade deficit every year between 1796 and 1931,[680] the US has had a balance of trade deficit, except for a single year, since 1981.[681] This type of deficit that the US has been able to maintain has been because it holds the world's key currency, the dollar. A proper response to the deficit is to address the cause, not its symptoms, including blaming others for it. In this case, the cause is the lack of sufficient domestic savings. In short, the US has been consuming (spending) more than it has been saving and has been depending, as a result, on the investments of other countries to bail it out. Reducing our "current account deficit" would require foreigners to purchase fewer US assets. That, in turn, would require increasing domestic savings or, to put it in less popular terms, "reducing consumption."[682] Reducing consumption, however, is difficult; it causes pain to many people, especially those who rely on certain services. It is also always fraught with risks for political leaders and political parties, such as electoral and other losses. So when modest proposals such as a consumption tax are suggested, there are not, generally, many takers. It is easier to blame others.

One should also reflect on the fact that trade deficits are often associated with increases in employment. One has but to look at the fact that the US's Great Recession of 2007/2008, which resulted in the loss of nearly nine million jobs and an increase in unemployment to 10 percent of the labor force, was followed by both a steady decrease in unemployment and an increase in the trade deficit (including that with China).[683] It is likely that our COVID-19–induced deficit spending will likewise result in another steady decrease in unemployment and

---

[680] See Hobson, op. cit., p. 253.

[681] Douglas A. Irwin, "The Truth About Trade: What Critics Get Wrong About the Global Economy," in *Foreign Affairs*, Vol. 95, #4 (July/August 2016), p. 86.

[682] Ibid.

[683] Ibid., pp. 87–88.

an increase in current account balance (this is really the relationship between the cost of goods and services that a country imports or buys and what it exports or sells). By the end of the Obama presidency, unemployment had declined from 10 percent to under 5 percent; by the time President Trump decided to confront China in overt economic terms (2018), unemployment had decreased to about 3 percent. So deficits with China could not have been the *cause* of our deficit. The US never accepted the view that its trade surpluses with the world, from the time of the middle of World War I to the 1960s, or its current favorable balance with many countries were the product of unfairness or lack of reciprocity on its part. It has always treated such advantageous outcomes as the natural or proper returns from a praiseworthy system of trade practices.

Another denial of the US is that related to strong involvement of China's government (contrary to the US's conception of democracy with its laissez-faire or minimal government relationship with the economy) in trade and investment in the Chinese economy. This, we partly touched on earlier in Chapters 10 and 11 by pointing to the mercantilist policies that Alexander Hamilton set as the grounding of the US's economic development—the very policies that the PRC has been following, arguing now, as Hamilton did during his time, that China (as the US, then in relationship to Europe) cannot exchange with the US "on equal terms" (in this sense through private enterprises and levels of technology) unless it were concomitantly willing to confine itself to the production of goods and services that, at best, served as support for the US's industries. That type of production (in the case of the US in relationship to Europe, it was agricultural goods instead of manufacturing), far from promoting China's development and competitive capabilities, would make it dependent on the US and the West that Washington leads.[684] As with China today, the US government assumed a major role in society's development, in fact resisting the economic interests of the day that wanted to make agriculture their primary focus and emphasized manufacturing with protective tariffs (tariffs to protect emerging

---

[684] See "Report of Alexander Hamilton" in George T. Crane and Abla Amawi, eds., *The Theoretical Evolution of International Political Economy: A Reader* (New York: Oxford University Press, 1991), pp. 3–41.

industries),[685] subsidies to help in competition with foreign producers of like goods, bonuses, special recognitions, and the invitation of talent from abroad through immigration policies, among other actions.

It is also the case, which the US is denying (but which Moynihan acknowledged and inveighed against), that increasingly more and more states throughout the world, including some of its closest allies—Japan, Germany, and France, for example—have embraced a wide variety of government involvement in the economy. To the names just mentioned, one can add India, South Korea, Singapore, Norway, and Saudi Arabia. In short, the free market in its ideal "Anglo-Saxon" form that the US espouses (at least as an abstract standard by which to inform others that they have fallen short and level criticism) has, over the years, been facing rejection, even in Washington, D.C., where that rejection—in the forms of long-term planning, subsidies, protective tariffs, insurance against risk (the latter in the case of the Export–Import Bank), and currency manipulation—have been hushed up.[686] As I write, the Federal Reserve Bank, to help businesses confront COVID-19, assumed responsibility in 2020 for a variety of debts and supporting loans and promised low interest rates for years to come, with praise-filled responses from Congress to Wall Street. As well, on October 26, 2020, the WTO authorized the European to impose tariffs in the amount of about $4 billion worth of the US's exports annually as a retaliation of sorts for the US's illegal subsidies to Boeing.[687] Sovereign wealth funds (investment funds owned by states that invest in real and financial assets such as stocks, bonds, real estate, precious metals, hedge funds, or private equities around the world) now operate routinely. From the preceding few paragraphs, one can see that the accusation about China's use of non-tariff barriers can easily be lodged against the US.

Among all the denials (and these are denials because Washington is unable to admit them as part of its history or current conduct if it is to successfully criticize or otherwise confront China) are two

---

[685] Ibid., pp. 37–47.

[686] See Ian Bremmer, "State Capitalism Comes of Age: The End of the Free Market," in *Foreign Affairs* (May/June 2009), pp. 40–55.

[687] Bryce Baschuk, "WTO authorizes the EU to impose tariffs on US," in the *Boston Globe* (October 27, 2020), p. D2.

others that we will deal with here: the contributions of China's rise to the global economy and the most important objective that is being courted. In the case of China's contribution to the world's economy—a contribution that, in turn, redounds to the US's economic interest, including countries with which Washington enjoys favorable balance of trade—it has been impressive, offering a contrasting image of the PRC to the selfish and self-serving one that the US has been trying to project. Between 2000 and 2013, China made the largest contribution (23 percent) to global economic growth, with the US, contributing 12 percent, occupying second place.[688] That level of Beijing's contribution was projected to increase to about 25 percent by 2020,[689] but the emergence of the COVID-19 pandemic as well as the trade conflict between the US and China most likely will prove to have been reducing of that projection. The point to be made here is that China's contribution to the world's economy not only is unacknowledged by Washington but also contradicts the propaganda-induced image of the former's economy being a closed and self-serving one.

The final area—the most comprehensive, future-oriented, and promise-filled ideological feature—is that which feeds the myth concerning the Anglo-Saxon (the US's and the UK's) model of free-market economy that is deployed to offer the broadest levels of contrast to the weaknesses of orientalism, one seeking to place China in the most inclusive of defensive positions, and to prod or induce its opening its economy to the historical march of laissez-faire capitalism. This ideological assertion is centered on the claim that the US–UK free-market economy (the US refining what the UK had done in the latter's industrialization while continuing its spirit) is the greatest creative, wealth-creating, technology-calling, social-transforming, freedom-producing-and-protecting, and morally responsive force in human history. The American and British pattern of governance has been that which has ensured that the government's role in the development of society has largely been confined to providing the conditions within which the creative energies of markets and individuals have flowered

---

[688] Hu Angang, "Embracing China's 'New Normal': Why the Economy Is Still On Track," *Foreign Affairs*, Vol. 94, #3 (May/June 2015), pp. 10–11.

[689] Ibid., p. 11.

and expanded. We will deal with the issues of technology and creativity, among the attributes that are featured by the ideology, because they are so important to our understanding of the conflict between the US and China. Preliminary to doing so, we will look at the idea of the US and the UK providing the conditions within which free-market capitalism has unfolded. We will use information from the economic development of both countries to rebut the claim.

The UK's embrace of the free-market idea (despite the 1776 publication of Adam Smith's *The Wealth of Nations*) came at the *end* (author's emphasis) of its industrialization, when it enjoyed immense comparative advantage over other countries, not at the beginning.[690] At the beginning, in the seventeenth century, one finds the UK a staunch mercantilist country in outlook, with large percentages of government spending used to support state and society and the capital markets functioning primarily to fulfill the demands of military activities. There were even forced savings, and tariffs, far from being low, were among the highest in Europe. The UK pursued the model of the "Asian Tigers" before there were Asian tigers.[691] True, there was the abolition of the "Corn Laws" in 1846—a series of statutes that, in 1815, imposed tariffs and other trade restrictions on imported food and grains—but it was not fully implemented until the 1860s with Europe, and even after that date, when the US and Germany began to overtake Britain in the area of industrialization, tariffs in Britain remained high.[692] If one were to look at Britain's relationship to India, which had a flourishing textile industry that outcompeted the UK's in quality until about the time of the repeal of the Corn Laws, to avoid competition with New Delhi, London imposed tariffs against Indian textiles but insisted on India opening its markets (allowing free trade) for goods from Britain. The effect was to destroy India's textile and its emerging steel industry.[693] We know of the "open

---

[690] Peter N. Stearns, *Interpreting the Industrial Revolution* (Washington, D.C.: American Historical Association, 1991)—a typical view.

[691] Hobson, op. cit., pp. 256–257.

[692] As late as 1839, the average tariff for Britain was 38 percent. See Hobson, op. cit., p. 250.

[693] Ibid., pp. 255–256.

door" policy that Britain began in the 1840s, seeking the limitation of Chinese duties at treaty ports that it controlled or sought to control.

As regards the US, consistent with its mercantilist focus from 1789 to the 1930s, it provided subventions to industry; built canals, ports, and railroads; established a public university system; and imposed some of the highest tariffs found anywhere, including some in the 1920s, favoring its own industries and contributing to the international economic instability of the latter period and that instability's culmination in the Great Depression. Even in the case of the press, to improve US institutions' competition among international news organizations—Reuters (from the UK), Wolff (from Germany), and Havas (from France)—and garner less adverse portrayal in the news, subsidies were given.[694] Not to be overlooked is the acquisition of territories from Native Americans on behalf of land and gold speculators to Hawaii on behalf of the sugar interests[695] or the collection of debts through the establishment of collector-generals of customs from Haiti to Nicaragua, for example.[696] Like Britain at the height of its imperial standing, the US, in the late 1950s, began to think of "freer" (not "free") trade, culminating in the Kennedy Round of world tariff negotiations that took place between 1964 and 1967, followed by other rounds. This development launched a series of like rounds, all in the direction of "freer" trade, culminating in the latest round, the Doha Round, which began in 2001 but has yet to be concluded because of issues of subsidies that both the West and other groups of countries want to retain, although each group has different sets of goods for which it seeks subsidy.

In going through this focus on the UK and the US, it is hoped that the reader gains an understanding that neither of these two countries (leaders in the ideology of free trade) was a free trader until late in

[694]   Kent Cooper, *Barriers Down: The Story of the New Agency Epoch* (New York: Farrar & Rhinehart Inc., 1942).

[695]   See *United State v. Sioux Nation of Indians*, 448 U.S. 371 (1980), and the 2020 decision by the Supreme Court in favor of the Creek Nation in Jack Healey, "For the Tribe in Oklahoma, Ruling Sparks Emotion Over 'a Promise Kept,'" in *New York Times* (July 13, 2020), p. A16. Merze Tate, *Hawaii: Reciprocity or Annexation* (East Lansing, MI: Michigan State University, 1968).

[696]   Bailey, op. cit., pp. 531–562.

its respective economic development (at the time when each thought certain industries were mature enough to enter into competition with trade partners); that each arrived at "free trade" at about the apogee of its economic domination, when it perceived that it enjoyed certain advantages and that its self-judged capacity to compete was unquestioned; and that China (which is generally just ahead of Mexico in its level of overall industrial development) is offering its relatively infant industries the same protection that London and Washington offered theirs at a comparable stage of development and as Japan, South Korea, and India have done or are doing. Indeed, China has not only indicated that it will be opening its markets further to competition ("freer" trade and investment)[697] but also agreed to allow AXA—a French multinational insurance company, headquartered in Paris—to be the first foreign corporation to own 100 percent equity in China. Equally important, it demonstrates that China—far from being the imitator of the West, including the US—sees itself as capable of conceiving its own good and devising appropriate means to realize it. In truth, the experiment through which that country is going (building a society from a combination of socialist, Confucian, and market economic values) has never been done. From the standpoint of orientalism (which assumes an emulation of the West, if success is to be realized), it is supposed to be impossible, especially when the peasant-based origins of contemporary China are reflected on. This above-indicated, most inclusive ideological accusation of China is and has been to place Beijing on the general defensive in the eyes of the world, including the people of China and the US, to have them think of China as "lacking" when compared with the US, which has been depicted as always being a free trade nation. The factual inaccuracy of the claim is unimportant to those who espouse it.

The final area of expressed concern is that of China's claimed theft of IP and the forced transfer of technology. As the reader will recall, we previously stated that nation-states have, historically, routinely copied or borrowed from one another, including in the areas of science and technology. (When agriculture was the driving force in economic development, copying or "stealing" plant types from other countries

---

[697] See Keith Bradsher, "China Endorses Free Trade, But Finds Deals Are Elusive," *New York Times* (November 6, 2019), p. B4.

was also routine; one has but to reflect on the goods that the US today produces and ask how it got some of these plants.) As with private industry, in their competition with one another in the US and elsewhere, they sometimes copy, borrow, and even duplicate and reproduce what others create. We also pointed out that in its own borrowing (or "stealing," as Pence and others argue), the US in the nineteenth century was regarded, especially by Britain, even less charitably than we today regard China.[698] What we are faced with in respect of the emerging US–China rivalry in technology, however, is the cultural presupposition expressed so troublingly—a prejudiced-filled civilizational bent we have been calling orientalism. Not only are we unable to concede China's developmental contributions to the US and the world, but also, we can but point to the alleged continuing lack of capabilities and values in its culture, political policies, and practices as well as the people of China themselves. Beijing was accused by then secretary of state Pompeo of ingratitude—seeking to "usurp the global order" and to be engaging in a "biting" of "the international hand that fed it."[699] In other words, China is seeking to take power illegally or by force, and it is seeking to do so against the country that had previously helped it.

The current president of MIT, L. Rafael Reif (himself a child of the Global South), understands the central implications of the charge against China respecting the alleged theft of IP, as seen in his article in the *New York Times,* indicating that "China is not an innovation also-ran that prospers mainly by copying other people's ideas and producing them quickly at low cost. The country is advancing aggressively to assert

---

[698] See Ben-Atar, *Trade Secrets*, op. cit. It might be noted that the leader of Facebook, Mark Zuckerberg, admitted to Congress that the private sector copies from one another. In his own words, each gained "inspiration" from another. See his testimony before the US House Judiciary Subcommittee on Antitrust, Commercial, and Administrative Law, July 29, 2020. The author viewed the testimony through the MSNBC television network.

[699] See report on Secretary of State Pompeo's speech at the Nixon Library, July 23, 2020, in Matthew Lee, "At Nixon Library, Pompeo declares China engagement a failure."
https://www.boston25news.com/news/political/nixon-library/akkn31 zpcwerzdosn5AAPmcyga/

technological supremacy in critical fields of science and technology."[700] A *Boston Globe* report, to an extent reinforcing Reif's view concerning Beijing's accelerating bid to assure this supremacy,[701] has little bearing on the wider sense in the West (especially in the US, as expressed by Allison and others who characterize China's inventive abilities as largely confined to that which can restore or evolve what is already in existence). Such views are also the spirit that prompted the December 2019 JASON Report, a National Science Foundation–commissioned study of how the nation may set up a comprehensive system to deny China access to America's science and technology.[702] Even if China is specifically seen as excelling in some particular areas of science and technology, the latter two categories are understood as really from the West, the offspring of the Scientific and Industrial Revolutions. They are part of the hands, through its leadership in them, that have fed and can feed, but is this so?

President Xi—fully aware of the views of the West, especially in the US, that it has been a source of modern science and technology— indicated in his previously cited 2017 speech at Davos that the globalization we have been experiencing is the "natural" outcome of "scientific and technological progress" (note that he did not label it a "revolution") that is not something created by "any individuals or . . . countries."[703] This view, as mentioned above, is largely rejected by the West and by the US in particular. A brief review of some history could at least make one less assertive about it.

Britain, from which the US learned much (far from being the originator of) was a relatively late comer to the Industrial Revolution if one looks at what it copied from China, diffused through a variety of intermediaries, including the Muslims, Spaniards, Venetians, and

---

[700] See L. Rafael Reif, "China's Challenge Is America's Opportunity," in *New York Times* (August 8, 2018).

[701] See "China's New Plan to Overtake the US in Tech," *Boston Globe* (May 22, 2020), p. C2.

[702] See report on "Fundamental Research Security" at https://www.nsf. gov/news/special reports/jasonsecurity/jsr-19-21 Fundamental Research Security.12062019Final.pdf.

[703] See Xi, Speech at Davos, op. cit.

Mongols, among others. The copied innovations included "the seed-drill and horse-drawn hoe, the curved iron mouldboard plough, the rotary winnowing machine, crop rotation methods, coal and blast furnaces, iron and steel production, pound-locks, the idea of the steam engine, and much more."[704] Were one to look at areas seen to be concerned more with theoretical or manifesting more of a mixture of the theoretical and the applied (some of these are from Asia generally, especially the Middle East and India, but mostly from China), one will find algebra, geometry, our numerical system, astronomy, the experimental method (which Bacon popularized in the UK and the West, more generally), inventions promoting maritime navigation (such as the magnetic compass), and paper and the printing press for general literacy. Not to be forgotten are gunpowder and the gun, cannon, sword, lance, crossbow, etc., which advanced the "military revolution."[705]

I have briefly indicated how the UK was indebted to China for the former's industrial and technological development (with the West, at large, benefitting) to say that China, far from being beholden to the West for current scientific and technological developments, is really but sharing in some of the fruits of a diffusion and development of knowledge (in fact and in method or approach) much of which, in what we call modern times, begin with it. Further, China did not seek to accuse Britain of spying or stealing. Neither did it seek to "pull the ladder up" (as the JASON Report is urging), and the US government has begun to do this as part of a broader strategic confrontation with Beijing.

Despite evidence to the contrary (that we have thus far presented and will add to in the conclusion of this work), Washington has overtly decided that China and its behavior are a threat to the US and has begun to escalate in economic and technological terms what it has been less openly doing for over a decade or more in the political and military realm. These escalatory moves may be summed up in three interrelated strategic moves captured in what French diplomat

---

[704] Hobson, op. cit., p. 303.

[705] Ibid., pp. 302–303.

Jean-David Levitte rightly labels "a triple strategy."[706] The first is a military one that entails the evolution with Australia, India, and Japan of the Indo-Pacific Alignment (IPA) to contain China in the South China Sea, Southeast Asia, and the broader Indo-Pacific area. The second is a technological one—the marshaling of departments and agencies of the federal government (and with the sought support of allies in a manner consistent with the JASON Report but with broad international application) to undertake "every effort to curb China's access to primacy in the fields of artificial intelligence and robotics, which will be decisive elements of the future."[707]

In my view, more fields are involved other than artificial intelligence and robotics, unless both are seen to encompass advanced manufacturing (which implicates both fields), data in general since the latter is the oil of the future (and hence the forbidding of the merger of Broadcom and Qualcomm in 2018 because of fears that the latter, which designs chips or semiconductors for mobile phones, and the former, which derives most of its revenues from China, might become subject to Beijing's influence). Both companies are headquartered in the US, but Washington wanted to avoid offering support to China's fifth-generation (5G) technological ascendency,[708] an ascendency defined by the movement of data, which, in turn, is centered on the semiconductor industry. As long as the US controls this industry, it can "curb" China's future access to it and, hence, China's future.

The third area of the "triple strategy," which Levitte sees as "the most ambitious and most dangerous element for the future," is that of Washington's efforts to arrest the "economic rise" of Beijing by breaking, wherever possible, "value chains" that allow for "the assembly of a wide range of products . . . in this workshop of the world that is

---

[706] See "With the End of Four Centuries of Western Dominance, What Will the World Order Be in the 21st Century?" (a speech delivered before the Academy of Moral and Political Science in France, January 7, 2019).

[707] Ibid.

[708] See Adam Satariano, Stephen Castle, and David E. Sanger, "Defying China, Britain Rejects Telecom Giant," in *New York Times* (July 15, 2020) p. 1.

China."[709] "Breaking the chains" may be ambitious indeed, but it does not mean this course of action cannot succeed—most likely with great damage to the significantly integrated regional networks of production by companies in Asia that had formerly exported directly to the US and other countries but that are now part of a manufacturing–processing structure that places those products in China to be assembled and re-exported to the world, including the US.[710] It would, were "breaking the chains" to succeed, disrupt the existing patterns of trade and economic activities throughout the world, with increasing material and other costs to participants but with considerable industrial injury to China since there are complementarities between the activities of the "export zones" in which the "networks of production" complete the assembling of their goods for exports and China's overall manufacturing. Already, the US has begun to try to induce some of its own companies to shift the manufacture of goods from China to the US or elsewhere.[711]

Technology has a central role to play in the "value chain" manufacturing enterprise. One has but to look at the issues associated with Huawei, which was reported in 2019 to have become the world's largest smartphone seller, overtaking Samsung of South Korea.[712] This powerful telecommunications company out of China, as influential as it has become, is currently dependent on the US's semiconductor industry for the parts necessary for its manufacturing of smartphones. In short, it is part of a technology chain linked to semiconductors that are among the most impressive technical achievements of human beings. They control almost everything we call "modern," certainly almost everything we consider to be important—from cars, refrigerators, washing machines, and digital cameras to computers, the internet, software companies, and space exploration. As before said, the US presently enjoys supremacy in

[709] Levitte, op. cit.

[710] See Baily and Bosworth, op. cit., p. 14.

[711] The degree of disruption bears on the status that China is seen to have achieved—the "workshop" or the "processing center" of the world. See Yuning Gao, *China as the Workshop of the World* (New York: Routledge, 2011).

[712] See "Huawei Said to Overtake Samsung in Phone Sales," in *New York Times* (July 31, 2020), p. B2.

this industry and has been employing its technological muscle to induce allies and others not to use Huawei's high-speed wireless network (5G) on the alleged grounds that it constitutes a security danger. The UK, which had initially rejected the US's claims concerning security risks and agreed to use Huawei's network, under pressure from the US, reversed its commitment to Beijing.[713]

"Value chain" also extends to capital formation, which often begins with "seed capital" to get a project off the ground and continue into a step called initial public offering or IPO (the process by which shares of a private corporation are offered for sale to the public). The US, which has the most dynamic stock market in the world, is a preferred site for many IPOs from other countries, including China. The US began, in 2020, to use the threat of "stricter scrutiny" of foreign IPOs and those companies from China listed on the US's stock exchanges. Washington has even moved to demand American ownership of WeChat, a Chinese multipurpose messaging, social media, and mobile payment app that was developed by Tencent (China's Facebook), the very type of action we have been condemning in China.

All this focus on science and technology in a chapter on ideology is to deal, in part, with the issue of progress and the claim by the US that the laissez-faire economy has been the most creative, technology-summoning, wealth-creating, socially advanced, and freedom-promoting system that history has produced. Since successes in science and technology have been seen as the principal expressions of this system, China cannot be allowed to supersede the West. Complementing all this, however, is the view of orientalism on the creation of the new.

---

[713]   See Satariano, Castle, and Sanger, op. cit.

CHAPTER 15

The Real Challenge

The contention of this chapter is that—as in the cases of Athens versus Sparta, the US versus Japan, and Britain versus Germany—the challenge that China poses to the US is not one of threatened *replacement* but one of intimidating *equality*. It argues further that the policy of the US, since 1949, has been to contain China as part of an East Asian extension of the US's worldwide primacy (first through the KMT, even after 1949, when it tried to isolate the PRC and champion the cause of the ROC, and then as part of the Western liberal order and policies into which China's identity would be progressively integrated, thus reducing some of the socioeconomic and cultural traditions that Beijing embodies). Finally, it posits that the issues of China's threatened military and economic domination of the US are but screens that hide the unwillingness to accept or concede equality.

Proof of this claim is amply found in a number of areas, including formal statements by China, policy stances and orientations, and actual practice, from 1950 to the present. No one today can more fully speak to this proof than the current president of the PRC, Xi Jinping, to whom Allison, policy analysts, and like thinkers and commentators have attributed unchallenged power. In his (first) September 28, 2015, speech to the UN General Assembly, Xi stated to the world that in China's development, no "matter how the international landscape may evolve and how strong it [the PRC] may become, China will never pursue hegemony, expansionism, or [what has been realism's practice] sphere of influence."[714] The reader will note that the president is not merely indicating that China does not seek domination (and if it sought replacement of the US, it would be seeking domination) but, as well, territorial expansion (although it will defend what it considers to be its territory). It also seeks to forego the traditional balance of power politics, which is so laden with "spheres of influence" or "spheres of interest" rivalries and maneuvers that have been at the heart of political realist thinkers.

One should not focus on a single statement at any given period, however significant it might be, to use as a reference for the foreign policy of a country. One should preferably seek to establish whether there are patterns that the statement represents, and here, we have more evidence. Were one, for example, to turn to the 1972 Shanghai Communiqué (a document we previously discussed in some detail), one would find China stating to the world that it will "never be a superpower" and that it "opposes hegemony and power politics of any kind."[715] This statement is, in turn, reinforced by an even earlier policy statement of commitments, found in the earlier-discussed 1955 ten-point DOPWPC that came out of the Bandung Conference of that date, a statement that not only was influenced and jointly shaped by China but also won it many friends that it has held since then. A central principle of that declaration is the "equality of nations large and small," a principle found throughout the foreign policy positions and commitments of China.[716] In the above-quoted 2015 UN speech by President Xi, we find him reaffirming and expanding the sixty-year commitments of Bandung in his own words:

> The future of the world must be shaped by all countries.
> All countries are equals. The big, strong, and rich
> should not bully the small, weak, and poor . . . [A]ll
> countries' right to independently chose social systems

---

[714] See full text of Xi Jinping's First UN Address, September 28, 2015.

[715] See JCM, op. cit.

[716] See Lumumba-Kasongo, op. cit.

318

and development paths should be upheld, and . . . all countries' endeavors to promote economic and social development and improve people's lives should be respected.[717]

A country that is seeking to replace another dominant power does not usually speak in terms of having the future of the world "shaped by all countries" instead of one or a few; neither does it speak of equality of the strong and the weak, the rich and the poor. We found no such example in Athens, Britain, Germany, or Japan. We do not find it in the US, although Latin American nations, at different times, have tried to have the US adopt elements of it in Washington's foreign policy. Let us turn to other statements or policy positions that, although bearing on different issues, operate to corroborate the claim or support an inference of China's push for equality rather than dominance.

The last portion of the indented, direct quote from President Xi deals with the principle of self-determination, which the UN, in 1960, adopted as a legal and moral instrument. In Article 1 (2) of the relevant document, one reads, "All peoples have the right to self-determination; by virtue of that right, they freely determine their political status and freely pursue their economic, social, and cultural development."[718] There are some textual differences between the two statements. One refers to "all peoples," while the other refers to "all countries"; one urges that the principle be "upheld and respected," while the other refers to it being "respected." The two differences primarily bespeak the passage of time, which has seen the overwhelming number of colonial peoples becoming states or countries, and "upheld" implies a confirmation and endorsement of something that is viewed as having pre-existing legitimacy. The latter conclusion finds support in the frequency with which the principle is referenced, including the previously mentioned 1974 CERDS,[719] which states that every state "has the sovereign and inalienable right to choose its economic system as well as its political, social, and cultural systems

---

[717] See text of 2015 UN speech.

[718] See DOGICCP, op. cit.

[719] See Article 1 (1) of CERDS, op. cit.

in accordance with the will of its people, without outside interference, coercion, or threat in any form whatsoever."[720]

Except for the phrase "without outside interference, coercion, or threat of any form whatsoever" (which is actually implied in "freely determine"), the principle has found itself in a variety of international legal instruments, including the two covenants that, together with the UDHR, make up the International Bill of Human Rights.[721] It should be obvious that China's championing of the principle of self-determination exhibits some self-interest, its having chosen a social and economic system that differs from that which the dominant country, the US, has adopted and fiercely espouses. Germany, Denmark, Japan, India, Singapore, and Tanzania have also chosen socioeconomic systems that differ from the US's also, but none have varied from the US's as widely as China's. These others are already firmly integrated, although sometimes challenging Washington, in the international liberal order. That China should seek to promote principles of equality so generally while seeking to have a future in which it replaces the US or pursues hegemony (to use Beijing's own term) would be the equivalent of building the basis for its own political, economic, and moral illegitimacy.

What about some material, institutional, and other evidence of behavior, on the part of China, that would further boost the idea of Beijing seeking equality with, not replacement of, the US? One may look at some broad foreign policy areas, beginning with the military and economic institutions it has been creating, its attitude toward IGOs (including part of the liberal order), and the world it seems to be bent on helping build. Let us begin in the sequence in which the suggested areas are mentioned.

With respect to the military, "China's defense policy," according to President Xi, "is defensive in nature. And its military strategy features active defense. Let me reiterate here that no matter how developed it becomes, China will never seek hegemony."[722] We have already, in

---

[720] Ibid.

[721] Two covenants refer to the International Covenant on Economic, Social, and Cultural Rights and the International Covenant on Civil and Political Rights.

[722] See full text of Pres. Xi Jinping's speech, September 22, 2015, in Seattle to a group of political and business leaders. https://www.geekwire.com/2015/

Chapter 13, dealt with Beijing's reform in the area of the armed forces to make it more mobile (what Xi is here describing as "active defense") and defense spending, which is but a fifth of the US's. Let us therefore focus on nuclear weapons since those weapons are the most widely recognized expressions of unique military capabilities and the military basis for dominance.

While China has but 300 deployed strategic nuclear warheads, the US and Russia have 1,550 each.[723] In addition, the US, since the time of the Obama administration, has been involved in a "nuclear modernization" program. That program, as initially estimated, would cost $100 billion, but it has now moved to $1.7 trillion and is well on its way to $2 trillion.[724] The US has argued that it is engaged in this modernization—entailing "new cyber and space weapons" as well as the application of AI and a range of new weapons capable of carrying either conventional or nuclear warheads—because Russia and China are said to be increasing their nuclear capabilities.[725] This claim that Washington is but responding to international nuclear challenge as the basis for increases in nuclear capabilities is a well-known and frequently used tactic by the US government and the arms industry to generate public support, as shown by former US secretary of defense, William Perry.[726] A more recent work looking at some of the same issues covered by Perry but examining weapons systems more broadly is even more persuasive.[727]

---

full-text-china-president-xi-gives-policy-speech-in-seattle-pledges-to-fight-cybercrimes-with-us/

[723] See Jessica T. Matthews, "The New Nuclear Threat," in the *New York Review* (April 20, 2020), p. 21. We will forego discussions of nuclear submarines and aircraft carriers that are part of the overall calculation about nuclear capabilities in general because the US is known to be far ahead in these areas.

[724] Ibid.

[725] Ibid., p. 19.

[726] William J. Perry, *My Journey to the Nuclear Brink* (Stanford: Stanford Security Studies, 2016).

[727] Fred Kaplan, *The Bomb: Presidents, Generals, and the Secret History of Nuclear War* (New York: Simon & Schuster, 2020). Every citizen should read this work.

Reinforcing the position of the PRC, as expressed by President Xi, that China's defense policy is a defensive one—not one aimed to replace the US but one designed to deter attacks on China—is the notion of the actual use of nuclear weapons. China has been the only permanent member of the UN Security Council (a group that one may define as the major nuclear weapons power) to have declared and maintained "an unqualified policy of no first use."[728] In other words, China has given a commitment to the world that it will never be the first to use nuclear weapons in any conflict. This is hardly evidence of a state seeking hegemonic influence and power.

In the matter of institutions created, when the NDB was established in 2014 among the BRICS members, Beijing was the leader in its creation. This multilateral development bank has as its objective the offering of loans to public and private entities that are deemed to be contributing to the development of member and other countries. Although Beijing is its dominant member, it is not a dominating one, as seen by the agreed-on voting power of its founding members. Each has an equal percentage of votes, unlike the World Bank or the IMF, in which a single country, the US, has veto power. The AIIB—which China led in creating in 2015, with the objective of providing loans to Asian countries to develop their infrastructure—bears resemblance to the World Bank and the voting power that the latter observes. China has (and is likely to continuing having) a veto power.[729] In general, its terms have been attractive enough, however, that major US allies, including all G7 members (except Japan), became members. What is particularly impressive about China's push for equality is its focus on opening up, through strengthening reforms, the governing structures of international economic life—the IMF, the World Bank, and the WTO—not to replace them.[730] The creation of the AIIB is, in part, to bring pressure in favor of those reforms. That creation also, because of its focus on infrastructure,

---

[728] Sidney Drell, "Reducing Nuclear Danger," in *Foreign Affairs*, Vol. 72, #2 (Spring 1993), p. 145.

[729] Edna Curran, "The AIIB: China's World Bank," in *Quick Take* (August 6, 2018). This article gives a fair summary of how the AIIB is seen in the US.

[730] See Xi's 2017 speech at Davos, op. cit.

increases the prospects of increasing material equality among countries and peoples.

Even more explicit in the pursuit of equality are four proposed areas of international reform by Beijing: the establishment of partnerships among states based on sovereign equality; the creation of a new security architecture; the promotion of open, innovative, and inclusive development; and an increase in inter-civilizational exchange. In the first, the central idea is that states, as equals, would form partnerships *with* rather than alliances *against* one another—a major shift in thinking that does not imply the absence of war but begins with the assumption that peace among countries can exist, with wars experienced as an aberration, rather than the reverse, which assumes war and its culture as permanent, with peace as but a passing interlude. Under the partnership focus, states would reject unilateralism (not the stance of hegemons or would-be hegemons) and the Cold War mindset that one's gain must be another's loss and place in their stead multilateralism and multi-polarity (many instead of one) centers of power through which states benefit from cooperation and dialogue rather than continuous confrontation. Complementing the principle of partnership is the proposed new architecture featuring fairness and shared benefit.

"No country," President Xi contends, "can maintain absolute security with its own efforts, and no country can achieve stability out of other countries' instability. The "law of the jungle" leaves the weak at the mercy of the strong. It is not the way for countries to conduct their relations."[731] Rather than have the law of the jungle, which the Cold War mentality offers, *"a new vision of common, comprehensive cooperation and sustainable security* (emphasis the author's) *should be pioneered."*[732] Expressive of this vision is the giving of "full play to the central role of the UN and its Security Council in ending conflicts and keeping the peace and adopting the dual approach in seeking peaceful solutions to disputes and taking mandatory actions so as to turn hostility into amity."[733] In other words, emphasizing a new security architecture

---

[731]   See President Xi's 2015 US speech, op. cit.

[732]   Ibid.

[733]   Ibid.

of "fairness and shared benefits" must go with the idea of partnership instead of alliances, getting rid of the law of the jungle, and giving "full play" to the UN (not any one state or region of the world) but under the terms of its charter, which, in Chapter VI, emphasizes a range of peaceful modes of dispute settlement and, under Chapter VII, only as a last, sad resort to invoke coercion that is *common*, meaning involving the collective defense of the world community and pursuing "cooperation in both economic and social fields" (which Xi sees as serving to "prevent conflicts from breaking out in the first place"[734]).

Since the UN Security Council structure would largely, as seen by Xi, remain the same but with a culture of comprehensive play of that body's charter, the US would retain all the authority that it currently enjoys but with reduced power because it would have to deal with a world more attached to the principle of sovereign equality holding sway within the context of shared authority. As such, China really makes four distinctions in the use of the term "sovereignty"—sovereignty as authority, the right enjoyed by every state to make the rules (national and international) by which it is governed; sovereignty as autonomy, the capacity to implement decisions independently, without external interference; sovereignty as power or influence, the ability of a state to advance its values and interests in relationship to other states; and sovereignty as legal, moral, and political rhetoric, the deliberate use of the term to limit, foreclose, or advance debate on certain issues.[735] The US, in fact, would remain under Xi's reforms, for some time to come, the most influential state in the sense of its capacity to have its interests met and values advanced, but would it be able, however—in the words of A. Lawrence Lowell, former president of Harvard, who thought that US membership in the League of Nations was desirable because such membership would temper or contain "imperialistic" impulse toward its neighbors—accept such a containment? Far more important, continuing Lowell's thinking, would that influence alone induce the US to abandon the presumption that "the Americas are game preserves in which no

---

[734] Ibid.

[735] See Stewart Patrick, *The Sovereignty Wars: Reconciling America with the World* (Washington, D.C.: Brookings Institution Press, 2018), pp. 7–9. Patrick focuses on the first three.

poachers are allowed but in which [the US] may shoot all he pleases"?[736] One could substitute for the "Americas" the Indo-Pacific region or the even the world at large (under the Truman Doctrine).

The remaining two areas of proposed reform are the matters of open and innovative and *inclusive* development and inter-civilizational exchange. Within China, Xi has sought to advance the idea and practice of inclusive development, meaning the returns from development should involve and benefit all, which is a conveniently forgotten area of human rights—the right of everyone "to share in scientific achievement and its benefits"—particularly important because science and its offspring, technology, have been seen as central to social and economic development everywhere.[737] Among the reasons for President Xi's carefulness about the role of the market is the latter's capacity to act contrary to what an inclusive society requires. He points to the 2008 financial crisis in the West (one could more recently point to COVID-19), which he claims has taught us that allowing capital to blindly pursue its profits can only create crises and that sustained global prosperity cannot be built on the shaky foundation of a market "without moral constraints."[738] He thus points to what has been happening nationally and globally:

> The growing gap between rich and poor is both unsustainable and unfair. It is important for us to use both the invisible hand and the visible hand to form synergy between market forces and government function and strive to achieve both efficiency and fairness . . . Development is meaningful only when it is inclusive and sustainable.[739]

China, through Xi, is saying that sustainable development requires that fairness not be sacrificed at the altar of efficiency (which the market claims as among its most important strengths), of preference for the

---

[736] Quoted in Patrick, ibid., p. 5.

[737] See UDHR, Article 27 (1).

[738] See President Xi's 2015 speech to the UN, op. cit.

[739] Ibid.

invisible over the visible hand, of the behest of the rich at the expense of the poor, or of convenient moral constructs at the bidding of the market. Having entire counties without a single ICU is an example of efficiency, measured by profits. Is there either fairness or equality in the county without an ICU, which has many lives taken by COVID-19, and the country with multiple ICUs within which many lives are saved? The visible hand, the role of government, must be a respected, central part of development; in this regard, equal respect should undergird the path that states follow in their chosen model of development. In his 2017 speech at Davos, he said,

> China has, in the past years, succeeded in embarking on a development path that suits itself by drawing on both the wisdom of its civilization and the practices of other countries in both [the] East and [the] West. In exploring this path, China refuses to stay insensitive to the changing times or to blindly follow in others' footsteps. All roads lead to Rome. No country should view its development path as the only viable one. Still less should it impose its own development path on others.[740]

The economic system in which the role of the state is more (China, for example) and those in which that role is less should be equally respected. China seeks equality.

This brings us to the matter of civilization. To some, including Allison and others, Western civilization, represented by the US, should be emulated, should be the model to be followed. Thus, Allison found it difficult to understand why the US's Declaration of Independence should not be the claim of Chinese citizens. President Xi, far from espousing notions of any clashes of civilization or the superiority of one over another, invites increased "civilization exchanges" to advance inclusiveness and respect for differences. In his view, the "world is simply more colorful as a result of cultural diversity. Diversity breeds exchanges, exchanges create integration, and integration makes progress

---

[740] See text of President Xi's 2017 speech at Davos.

possible."[741] Xi wants more than diversity and respect, however, as important as those ends are. He also wants mutual learning and inspiration as well as cultural equality in the building of what he sees as an emerging "human civilization":

> In their interactions, civilizations must accept their differences. Only through mutual respect, mutual learning, and harmonious coexistence can the world maintain diversity and truly thrive. Each civilization represents the unique vision and contribution of its people, and no civilization is superior to others. Different civilizations should have dialogue and exchanges instead of trying to exclude or replace each other . . . We should draw inspiration from each other and boost the creative development of human civilization.[742]

Nowhere, in all the discussions in this chapter, has there been revealed a scintilla of evidence that China is seeking to replace the US; on the contrary, its focus has been on equality, in all important respects. One, on reading the Shanghai Communiqué, should be persuaded, but if one were not, we have shown that whether one looks at patterns of behavior—including the creation of international institutions that China has led in creating and those that the US has led in creating, including the UN—China has sought equality. One finds the same stance in the area of culture or civilization, including the emerging human civilization. China, contrary to Secretary of State Pompeo, is not seeking to destroy the US. In concluding this chapter, we will look at evidence from one who has had rather long and intimate diplomatic interactions with China: Henry Kissinger.

In his discussions, China's foreign minister, Qian Qichen (1988–1998), for example, candidly told Dr. Kissinger that China would not accept the unipolar world that the US was busily trying to build and lead after the disintegration of the former Soviet Union. He further stated that China represented part of a broader worldwide body of developing

---

[741]   Ibid.

[742]   Ibid.

forces, including a demographic one, that would make it impossible for such a world as the US sought to bring into being.[743] Indeed, the very creation of the NDB among the BRICS grouping might have been induced by attempts at a counterweight to the efforts directed at unipolarity. Recent trade agreements with Asian countries and the EU are in the same spirit. What is being said here is this: China seeks equality, and it opposes domination.

---

[743] Kissinger, *On China,* op. cit., p. 463–464.

CHAPTER 16
US Response to China's Challenge

The US has understood the true challenge of China—the challenge of equality.[744] This equality, were it to develop between Washington and Beijing, however, would remove the US from the identity it has constructed for itself and, even more important, limit its freedom of action internationally (and nationally). It would do more. It would require the US to accept as legitimate China's economic model of development and accord to it equal standing with the free-market model, a course of action that would entail, if the US is to compete successfully, wholesale changes in its social and economic life—a focus on economic, social, and cultural life.

Thus far, the US has rejected this alternative and has, instead, been redoubling its efforts to retain its sought standing as a preeminent state, as the only truly global power in the world, as the only superpower. Doing so successfully requires three strategic actions: reinforcement of the just-touched-on identity; portraying China as a threat to that identity; and mobilizing people as well as scientific and technological resources, domestically and internationally, to confront the threat. A fourth, which will be woven into the discussions of the first three, is rhetorical attacks

---

[744] See Robert D. Blackwell and Ashley J. Tellis, *Revising U.S. Grand Strategy Toward China* (New York: Council on Foreign Relations, 2015). The call for revision is based on an effort to acknowledge that China is not going to be assimilated and thus contained according to the post-1972 formula.

on China, accusing or ascribing to it a variety of attributes, actions, or omissions (regardless of factual accuracy) to support an overall narrative that China is dangerous and cannot be trusted with *world power*. (The term "world power," of course, has meaning beyond challenge to the US; it has implications for all countries that the US wants to bring to the attention of every nation-state. They are being asked to weigh for themselves what is preferable—a world in which the US is dominant or one in which China wields that dominance.)

The identity that Washington claims for itself is centered on the concept of exceptionalism, a concept or belief that the US—as a society, a mix of ideas and institutions, an author of social movements, and the epoch it represents—is different, is exceptional, and therefore is endowed "with the inherent right to make and break the international rules of the game."[745] The making and breaking of law, as characteristic as such a form of behavior has become for the US, has always been linked to another attribute of exceptionalism, as we saw in the case of Britain and Germany before World War I: the presence of an ideal that appears to transcend the ordinary day-to-day interactions of states, linked to a purpose that has evolved to enjoy the status of the sacred, the near-sacred, or something hallowed. For the British Empire, as seen in our discussions concerning London and Berlin, it was to *lead* the world "in the arts of civilization," to bring "light to dark places," to teach the "true political method," and to "civilize" the world, the latter verb including serving as a sort of trustee for the weak and a disciplinarian to the arrogant.[746] The US does not now often use the term "civilize" in this respect, but it has an equivalent purpose, which was indicated earlier on an attempt by the later senator John McCain, quoting Pres. Harry Truman, that "God had created . . . and brought the US [to its] present position of power and strength for some great purpose."[747] This is not something that was discovered by President Truman; "since the dawn of

---

[745] Sachs, op. cit., p. x.

[746] Thornton, op. cit., pp. ix–x.

[747] McCain, op. cit., p. 19.

the Republic, Americans have believed that our nation," McCain noted, "was created for a purpose."[748]

What might that purpose be? It is a mandate, vested in each US president, to build an enduring peace grounded on the supreme value of freedom. This value, which is the natural yearning of all people, is universal, and as such, the US's role is universal—to ensure its enjoyment by all people throughout the world. From freedom comes democracy, equality, security, opportunity, and prosperity—what political economists in the West today ideologically call the liberal democratic order, which the US led in building after World War II. Earlier in the US's history, under the Monroe Doctrine, the US asserted and exercised certain exclusive claims to the Americas and, likewise, employed the Manifest Destiny doctrine to justify expansion across the territories of Native Americans. In 1947, in the defense of a pursuit of a Monroe Doctrine–like claim toward the world (otherwise known as the Truman Doctrine), President Truman stated, among other things, that "it must be the policy of the United States to support free peoples who are resisting attempted subjugation by armed minorities or by outside pressures" because the "peoples of the world look to us for support in maintaining their freedoms."[749]

In 1997, fifty years after the Truman Doctrine was enunciated, former secretary of state Madeleine Albright outlined a plan to organize the post–Soviet Union world in a commencement address at Harvard University, the very site at which her predecessor, George Marshall, enunciated the Marshall Plan, an extension of the Truman Doctrine. In that outline, she depicted the US as a "pathfinder" and, later, as an "indispensable nation" that—as "pathfinder," as the nation able to "show

---

[748] Ibid. One has but to read President Washington's farewell address to Congress to see some of these sentiments. Blackwell and Tellis offer some help in one's understanding of the development of the idea. Many Christians, including early Puritans and today's born-again Christians, have strong views about this purported purpose.

[749] See text of the doctrine in "President Harry S. Truman Address before a Joint Session of Congress, March 12, 1947" in avalon.law.yale.edu (The Avalon Project Documents in Law, History, and Diplomacy). Succeeding presidents, by and large, extended and refined this doctrine.

the way when others cannot"—has "a responsibility . . . to shape history, a responsibility to build with others a global network of purpose and law."[750] Whether one speaks of an "indispensable nation," a "pathfinder" nation, the "exceptional nation," the "greatest nation on earth," or the "chosen nation," one is dealing with the idea of "exceptionalism," making the US unique, as separate, set apart, and singular—as part of what Jeffrey Sachs sought to capture in his reference to Washington's assumed right to "make and break the international rules of the game."[751] As such, the idea of being the "sole superpower" is understandable. Like Britain but even more so, the US's position in the world can be "shared by no other."[752]

China's efforts to be an equal, to help in the development of an international community of equals, run counter to the US's status as a country that is exceptional or the lone superpower. To have equals is to be alike, and to be like or alike is to be the same, is to lose the attribute of being exceptional, of being unaccompanied. It is to forego or lose the status of being exclusive and substitute in its stead a status of being similar, with the limits and confinements that the latter implies and brings. In sum, it is to share with others what it previously shared "with no other."

Equality is seen by the US, therefore, as a threat to its identity (this is what Athens feared more than anything else—law and custom making others its equal), and it has sought not only to reject it but also to treat the claim to it as a moral *attack* or potential attack, where any change attributable to China's development might be seen to touch on the reach of the US's identity, whether that identity be geographic, technological, economic, political, military, ideological, or other. The progressive national and international mobilization or opposition to China developed, especially since 2012, with Washington's policy of containing Beijing through the sought "integration" of the PRC into the liberal international order within which it would play a *regional* (as

---

[750] See Madeleine Albright, "Harvard University Address, Cambridge, Massachusetts, June 5, 1997." https://secretary.state.gov/www/statements/970605.html

[751] Sachs, op. cit., p. x.

[752] Thornton, op. cit., pp. IX–X.

opposed to global) role that would be unthreatening to Washington and defensive of the liberal order. Geographically—from any change in the South China Sea, in Central Asia (with OBOR/the BRI), to the Arctic, or outer space exploration—the actions of China must be placed in most negative light, invite suspicions, and, as plausible, condemned.[753] Likewise, as we have already seen, Beijing's aid to the Global South is being characterized as a "debt trap," while supporting or pushing for reforms of the Bretton Woods system (IMF and the World Bank in particular) is viewed as an assault on the liberal order. It is the case that as China extends ties with the Global South, there is likely to be less investment space within which the US can expand.

The technological space offers no relief. We have already touched on the JASON Report, which, under the guise of protecting the US from governments "that violate the principles of scientific ethics and research integrity" (giving the appearance of taking a stand against those who are without integrity and fail to abide by "scientific ethics"), seeks to keep China from gaining access to scientific and technological knowledge.[754] We also referred to the "triple strategy," as categorized by French diplomat Jean-David Levitte, as he sought to show the degree of national and international coordination that exists or is being or will be attempted.[755] The UK's initial rejection of Washington's appeal to allies and others to refuse telecommunications services offered by Huawei,

---

[753] See Kenneth Chang, "China Launches Mission to Far (but Not Always Dark) Side of the Moon," in *New York Times* (December 8, 2018), p. A5; Zhao Lei, "China Initial Research on Rocket Ends Successfully," in *China Daily* (October 15, 2019), p. 4; Michael Boston and Steven Lee Myers, "China, in Familiar Earth Scene on Earth, Heads to Mars," in *New York Times* (February 24, 2020), p. A12. It should be remembered here that Washington is also attuned to the political geography represented by the "geographical pivot"—the area covering the interior of the Asian continent and Eastern Europe—the control of which is seen as leading to the control of the world, as argued by Halford Mackinder, op. cit. The US is also aware of the "rimland theory" that contradicts Mackinder in shifting focus from the heartland of Asia to the rimlands, the areas surrounding much of Asia and Eastern Europe. See Nicholas J. Spykman, *America's Strategy in World Politics* (New York: Harcourt, Brace & Company, 1942).

[754] See the *Jason Report,* op. cit.

[755] Levitte, op. cit.

for example, was followed by support for that appeal. That reversal will continue to have repercussions.[756]

The political and military—like the geographic, economic, technological, ideological, and psychological—identity of the US is as global in reach and, in some respects, even more so. For example, the US, according to *POLITICO Magazine*, has about eight hundred bases abroad located in over seventy countries. Britain, France, and Russia combined have about thirty.[757] As of 2019, China had but one established military base abroad, in Djibouti.[758] This one base, however, is seen by the US as a threat. Also, in the realm of the political, all one needs to do is to understand it in the context of the fundamental meaning of the West and the US's place in that meaning. That place—consistent with the Truman Doctrine, the US's assumed purpose, and aptly captured by the scholar G. John Ikenberry—is "not just a geographical region with fixed borders," as is generally thought about (with a network of military alliances, a dominant economic system, a worldwide currency that Washington leads), but "an idea—a universal organizational form that could expand outward" (much like the Big Bang theory, which explains the expansion of the universe from a point of origin) "by the spread of democratic government and principles of conduct."[759] Pres. George W. Bush, in his January 20, 2001, inaugural address, gave voice to the US's place in the idea of the West, including the "principles of conduct," just mentioned (otherwise called American ideals and purpose). For him, it is "a place . . . in a long story . . . the story of a new world that became a friend and liberator of the old, a story of a slave-holding society that became the servant of freedom, the story of a power that went into the world to protect but not to possess, to defend, not to conquer."[760]

---

[756] See Satariaon, Castle, and Singer, op. cit.

[757] See David Vine, *Base Nation* (New York: Metropolitan Books, Henry Holt Company, 2015), for elaboration.

[758] The term "established" is used because Beijing is said to be exploring possibilities of a base in Myanmar.

[759] Quoted in Lind, op. cit., p. 78.

[760] See Pres. George W. Bush's inaugural address, January 20, 2001. https://www.whitehouse.gov/news/print/inaugural-address.html

The longer story is seen in the West as beginning in Athens, Greece, followed by more general ideals along the way, like the right to private property, and unfolding into a "timeless promise" that everyone belongs and that "no insignificant person was ever born."[761] This call to equality (political equality) is one that "Americans are called to enact; a cause that "we must follow"; and a "trust we bear" to be passed along.[762] In other words, democracy and its associated values are the entitlements of everyone, everywhere, however seemingly insignificant, and the US is the trustee of these values, which may have begun in a germinating form in Greece but gained their "Big Bang" in the new world and has, through the agency of Washington, been expanding since. What Washington does in politics and law are but the *natural* enactments of what it embodies. Therefore, despite it having developed a network of military alliances in the Indo-Pacific area to "rebalance" development in East Asia, in general, Washington has begun to characterize its actions as pursuing the development of a FOIP, an expression of democracy and its ideals, part of a continuously unfolding America, the America that is exceptional.

To much of the world, the US, which is the self-proclaimed bearer of the value of equality (which Washington has found unacceptable at home and abroad), appears to be a consensus-leading country by way of its created networks of military and economic alignments. Its dominating conduct is also veiled through its co-optation of other major regional powers through the offering to them of what is generally called "public goods"—military security, shared intelligence, and help in gaining access to markets for these powers' products throughout the world (note President Eisenhower's wanting more markets for Japan in Southeast Asia, for instance). These services often go unnoticed, but they are part of which former president Trump was beginning to question and which caused some problems with the US's allies.[763] The history of dominant and dominating powers, however—Persia, Rome, the Tang dynasty, the Mongols, the Dutch Republic, the Ottoman Empire, the British—has

---

[761] Ibid.

[762] Ibid.

[763] See Nye, op. cit.

been a history of co-optation.[764] In the case of the US, it determines what "place" the co-opted or the intended for co-optation will occupy in its system of networks. What countries, for example, may be part of the OECD, and when should they advance to membership? The same is the case of the G7, which began as the G4. Punishment can also be imposed on members, as was done to Russia when the G7 became the G8, and Moscow was disinvited.[765] India, most likely, will become a candidate for co-optation if differences with China escalate.

A central point to be made at this juncture is that what is called "soft" power, co-optation, of shared interest in benefits from "public goods" enables or ensures certain joint international positions. The US and its networks of friends make joint efforts to help Washington extend its claim to be trustee of freedom throughout the world.

When China was allowed to step into the Western system, after 1979, that permission and subsequent additional steps (membership in the WTO, for example) were never intended to help Beijing develop to challenge the US's dominance. On the contrary, the West was certain that it would be integrating within its liberal economic order a soon-to-be-failed communist model because of the dominant view that government-controlled economies subvert growth and that, as shown in the case of the former Soviet Union since the 1980s, socialist or authoritarian regimes cut off or stifle innovation. Other areas that would singly or together generate the failure were the internet and the emerging middle class. The former ostensibly could not be controllable or manageable, and the latter would demand more freedom.[766] That projected failure

---

[764] Amy Chua, *Day of Empire: How Hyperpowers Rise to Global Dominance—and Why They Fall* (New York: Double Day, 2007).

[765] Reference is here being made to the IGO made up of the world's seven largest developed economies (China does not have a "developed" economy). As the US sought to co-opt Russia, it was invited to be part of an expanded body, the G8 (but more of a G7 + 1) to monitor Moscow's behavior over time. It has been disinvited, as of this writing, for actions that it took in relationship to the Ukraine. The US has also, at different times, punished its allies with sanctions.

[766] See a *New York Times* series entitled "China Rules" (November 18 and 25, 2018). See also Megan Specia, "Five Takeaways From Our New Chinese Project," at

would result in the destruction of the PRC's legitimacy and the co-optation of China into the Western system.

Not only did the PRC refuse to fail, as we now know, but also, it achieved a degree of growth and development that caused many in the West to begin questioning whether Beijing's "political and economic system [were not] better equipped and even more sustainable than the American model" that had reigned since 1945.[767] China has had and represents a different model of economic development, as we have seen and repeatedly stated, and it has, from evidence available thus far, exhibited no intention to substitute the American model for its self-chosen model. This insistence on the part of Beijing, on the preservation of its own model—with its Confucian and socialist bias toward community over the individual (the exact opposite of the US's), with commitments to ESCR (social welfare) over private profits, and with equitable sharing over individual accumulation (we have but to observe the claims of business and the community in respect of COVID-19 in China)—has some concrete, long-term meanings that are often overlooked or kept away from public discussion because doing so preserves a level of understanding that generally makes the claims of the liberal order relatively attractive.

Under the semblance of fighting authoritarian governments is, for instance, the real concern that socialist governments' investments crowd out opportunities for private investment. In short, if the CPC spends monies to build railroads, then opportunities for investment are either eliminated or reduced for private markets.[768] What one finds in the case of investment is what one also finds in the area of consumption—wanting to have the population at large spend rather

---

https://www.com/2018/11/21/world/asia/china-rules-takeaways.html.

[767] See Ian Bremmer, "How China's Economy Is Poised to Win the Future," in *Time* (November 13, 2017). See also the series in the preceding footnote.

[768] Robert Madsen, "Comparing Crises: Is Current Economic Collapse Like Japan's in the 1990s?" *Foreign Affairs*, Vol. 88, #3 (May/June 2009), p. 163. Here, we find that in the midst of the financial collapse requiring government bailout of business, the focus of concern was that government spending could crowd out the private sector, so the spending had to be limited.

than save, unlike the practice in China.[769] (Saving is always critical, especially at the earlier stages of development.) As well, to promote social welfare, China limits the amount of interest that can be charged on loans and owns most of the major banks, which control trillions of dollars. Complementing the matter of interest rates are the prices for key services. The government sets and resets prices for utilities, health care, education, and transportation. The reader has but to imagine the trillions of dollars that would be made available to the private industry were the Chinese socialist market economy to be replaced by the American model and how much less of those monies would be left available for the development of society. So the focus is on issues of freedom of the press, religion, speech (matters about which we seem to have little concern in Egypt, Saudi Arabia, or Indonesia and the condition of which has improved immensely since 1972, when we began, in full praise, to establish a more open and interactive relationship with Beijing). The criticisms associated with those issues, however seemingly justified, especially if one bears Moynihan's recommendations in mind, mask other matters.

Having just indicated that there is no evidence that China is disposed to substitute the US model for its own does not mean that China has been deaf to any efforts to find points of convergence and reconciliation between the two systems. It has consistently signaled its willingness to negotiate and, according to two sources that the US considers reliable, is even willing to go further. Henry M. Paulson Jr., US's secretary of the treasury from 2006 to 2009, came to know China well through the US–China Strategic Economic Dialogue (SED), an intergovernmental institution launched in 2006 by Pres. George W. Bush and Pres. Hu Jintao to deal with economic tensions between both countries. Through this institution, the US and China achieved a number of important outcomes, varying from bilateral air services to the Ten-Year Energy and Environment Cooperation Framework. Among the things Paulson observed about China was that it can be a negotiating partner if the party negotiating with it is specific, avoids trying to "manage" China

---

[769] See Frank Trentmann, *Empire of Things: How We Became a World of Consumers, from the Fifteenth Century to the Twenty-first* (New York: Harper, 2016).

(rather engaging it), recognizes that the PRC decides matters rather deliberately (it has lobbyists also) to handle its consensus-style decision making, and is committed to mutual interests and treating "one another as equals" and endeavoring to link the specific issues to "strategic level" concerns, the latter meaning that Beijing is always seeking to merge concrete actions to broader interstate objectives.[770] Paulson, of course, as has been the case with Henry Kissinger and other US officials and businesspersons who have interacted with Chinese decision makers, has had the same overall objective in having China move toward an "increasing integration into global trade, investment, and financial markets."[771] Kissinger, whom the US also trusts, in his discussions with the PRC, specifically with former president Jiang Zemin, had the latter urging that both the US and China should look at themselves and seek to reassess and think through possible modifications in their respective traditional attitudes. "He urged," according to Kissinger, "each side to reexamine its own internal doctrines and be open to reinterpreting them—including socialism."[772]

One will rarely have any reference to Paulson's shared experience with China; even less so would one have an airing of Kissinger's written testimony of President Jiang's suggestion. Having such references would fly in the face of what China must be portrayed as being and becoming. When President Xi, in his 2015 speech to the UN (and reinforced two years later to businesspersons in Davos), indicated that what China sought was to have "the invisible hand and the visible hand" (the market and regulations, respectively) "form synergy between market forces and government,"[773] this too was overlooked, including scholars who are caught up in the felt need to marshal and mobilize national and international sentiments against China, including the previously

---

[770] See Henry M. Paulson Jr., "A Strategic Economic Engagement: Strengthening U.S. China Ties," in *Foreign Affairs*, Vol. 87, #5 (September/October 2008), pp. 59–62.

[771] Ibid., p. 60.

[772] Kissinger, *On China*, op. cit., p. 485.

[773] See President Xi's 2015 speech to the UN, op. cit.

mentioned former secretary of state Pompeo's targeting the country as an enemy of private property.

Participating in the mobilizing are not academics only but scholars in general (as was the case in the seventeenth, eighteenth, and nineteenth centuries, when orientalism had much of its most powerful influence through intellectuals—from Bodin, Montesquieu, Voltaire, and Mill to Marx, Weber, and TR).[774] So as well are the media, significant numbers of businesspersons, charitable organizations, including religious denominations, and governments. Evidence to the contrary of what they espouse (as I write, China is, for example, discussing possible legislation pertaining to its possibly taking anti-monopoly actions against some of its companies to promote the interests of smaller and newly emerging companies, but despite paralleling what the US and Europe are doing, the first reactions are pointedly against China for "punishing" the private sector) will not begin to have persuasive hold in people's minds, in part because the information used and the way it is being constructed will continue to suitably and congruously fit within the arch of images created and reinforced over the years by orientalism. The issue of trustworthiness seeps through most of what is said about China.

Allison's work, for all its other contributions, as before indicated, is part of that orientalist focus—the US is what China is not, and China has the undesirable characteristics of being aggressive, calculating, secretive, manipulative, hierarchical, and dishonest (stealing IP). In addition, it has already surpassed the US in economic power (the implication is that this theft has something to do with it), using, as he did, what has been called PPP instead of the traditional measurement of GDP to support the false claim that China had the largest economy and has surpassed the US. He knows that PPP is but an account yardstick to measure social welfare, *not* a measure of relative power, as his own colleague Joseph Nye rightly pointed out,[775] and yet he repeatedly used the concept because it reinforces his position about the China threat.

---

[774] Hobson, op. cit., p. 224.

[775] See Nye, op. cit.

With respect to the media, we will use two examples in the area of print, each regarded as taking stances considered progressive in US politics. The first is the *Boston Globe*, in a short news item entitled "China's New Plan to Overtake U.S. in Tech," which quickly focused the reader's attention on the development of new technologies (using Huawei and its 5G technology as an example) "at the expense of U.S. companies" and using the latter claim to justify Washington's move to "block the rise of China."[776] There is, of course, no reference to Huawei being ahead of its US counterparts in the relevant (5G) technology or at least exhibiting some pause toward the accusation of IP theft, on the part of the PRC, in the context. It could also invite some uncomfortable questions about why the US fell behind in this important technology.[777] What is important here is that the *Boston Globe*'s focus and tone feed on and reinforces an existing narrative—China is a danger to the US. The *New York Times*, our newspaper of record, fares no better.

In addition to its earlier-mentioned series entitled "China Leads," which conveys images of China as the coming displacement of the US, a major editorial, "Empty Talk on the South China Sea," shows that this highly respected institution not only sought to urge more aggressive action against China over this maritime area but also placed that urging within the rhetorical context of some of the most negative and morally compromising images of China. In this single editorial, the reader is presented with China as destabilizer, predator, bully, harasser, thief, rejectionist, coercer, interventionist, and law breaker.[778] Nowhere in the editorial, if one were to use law breaker as an example, is there an effort at balance—the illegal US–UK occupation of Diego Garcia in the Indian Ocean,[779] for example, in the 2019 ruling of the International

---

[776] *Boston Globe* (May 22, 2020), p. 12.

[777] My own reading of Chinese sources indicates that Beijing might already be working on 6G. See He Ming and Sun Yunchuan, "If 5G is here, can 6G be far behind?" *China Daily* (December 16, 2019), p. 9. See also Sue Halpern, "The Terrifying Potential of the 5G Network," in *New York Times* (April 26, 2020)

[778] See *New York Times* (July 28, 2020), p. A24.

[779] See United Nations, "General assembly Welcomes International Court of Justice Opinion on Chagos Archipelago, Adopts Text calling for Mauritius Decolonization," GA/12146 (May 22, 2019).

Court of Justice (ICJ) since the latter is so importantly related to the 2016 decision of the Permanent Court of Arbitration's (PCA) decision in favor of the Philippines in the latter's territorial dispute with China and to which the editorial refers. Nor would readers, from this editorial, know anything about the relationship between Diego Garcia and its secret base operations, its relationship to the Indo-Pacific corridor and the strategic passageway that is virtually encircling China, and the fact that the disputed territories in the South China Sea have had open and known claims by China (including the ROC) since the 1930s and even centuries before.[780] The reader would not have the remotest idea concerning the suspicions about who really orchestrated the move to have the claim of Manila submitted to the PCA or the fact that China did not participate (and this is an international panel of arbitration) or that one of the arbitrators, a Japanese, is from a country that has interest in the dispute. Why not one of the other panelists, and why should an arbitral body established to facilitate the settlement of disputes conclude that it is facilitating any such settlement by purporting to judge the issues at stake without one of the two disputants? It seems that such a course of action runs contrary to facilitating.

Many businesses will be and are part of the mobilization, largely because of some issues before touched on in this and other chapters, dealing with government regulation of prices, its investing in strategic enterprises (which private industry thinks should properly be the domain of the private sector), and its providing of services such as health care and education. They will not be inclined to note publicly that China jumped some fifteen places between 2019 and 2020—from forty-sixth to thirty-first, according to the World Bank's Doing Business (DB) report, a document that carries the annual assessment of business friendliness of some 190 countries, as measured by regulations, and what it costs

---

[780] See Teh-Kuang Chang, "China's Claim of Sovereignty Over Spratly and Paracel Islands: A Historical and Legal Perspective," in *Case Western Reserve Journal of International Law*, Vol. 23, #3 (1993), pp. 399–420. See also Keyuan Zou and Xinchang Liu, "The Legal Status of the U-Shaped Line in the South China Sea and Its Legal Implication for Sovereignty, Sovereign Rights and Maritime Jurisdiction," in *Chinese Journal of International Law*, Vol. 14, #1 (March 2015), pp. 57–77.

businesses to conduct their affairs.[781] It would be awkward, perhaps even embarrassing (certainly contradicting), to admit this development (New Zealand was number one, Singapore number two, Japan twenty-ninth, and France thirty-second), especially under President Xi, who has been unfairly accused of making it more difficult to do business in China. He, on the other hand, was making sure that people in China understand the type of business environment he has been trying to create.[782]

NGOs, especially religious and human rights ones (as in the case of the other groups whose actual and projected behavior we have tried to capture), will be no less focused on helping mobilize the public, overlooking or denying facts in the process. The religious organizations—some of which, according to Elizabeth Bruenig, have become more of a political bloc with a religious past[783]—will, in the spirit of TR, be seeking to expand the reach of their respective faith and, as integral, conceptual parts of the US's liberal order. Like the US, Christianity is seen exceptional and should oppose conditions that limit the operation of Christ's Great Commission—to make "disciples of all nations."[784] The human rights organizations that, in the US, have consistently sought to influence foreign policy—as previously touched on and somewhat elaborated though the experiences of Henry Kissinger—have insisted that the values that undergird these rights are universal, although they largely use the US's experience as grounds for their claim. Since these values are universal and moral, China is bound by them, and there should be no compromising with Beijing on their worldwide implementation.[785]

The feeling that the US embodies in its constitutional, political, and moral experiences the entire "family of human rights," as former

---

[781] See World Bank, *Doing Business 2020* (Washington, D. C.: 2019).

[782] See the text of President Xi's keynote speech at the opening of the Second China International Expo, November 5, 2019.

[783] See Elizabeth Bruenig, "How Evangelicals Have Changed," in *New York Times* (November 7, 2020), p. A19. This is an insightful article that should be read generally but especially by those interested in religion and politics in the US.

[784] Ibid.

[785] Kissinger, *On China*, op. cit., pp. 452–455.

vice president Pence has so comprehensively phrased it,[786] makes mobilization against China in this area even more potentially powerful and because, according to one scholar, "China is clearly an outsider in the realm of human rights."[787] The US is what China is not. So human rights groups and their supporters in the US, following the orientalist framework of the preceding sentence, are not going to respond to the evidence that China has been implementing one half of the family of rights—the economic, social, and cultural half, such as education and health care. Indeed, it has been implementing that half more fully than the US has its chosen half (the removing from poverty of over 800,000 million people is but one example), as we have seen and will touch on further in the paragraph to come. Nor will they, in their following the US government in promoting CPR, point out that in the most far-reaching post-1945 policy position of the US (the Truman Doctrine), the CPR of all were not considered but of "free peoples" only so that European colonial powers could continue their domination of most of the human family, to which human rights apply; we continue, until today (one has but to reference Saudi Arabia), to be a rather selective supporter of this half of the family of rights.

Under the right to democratic governance, for example, where the US sees itself as a peerless champion, we have chosen to focus on *electoral* democracy, with well-known practices subversive of fair elections, varying from gerrymandering and financial domination of political campaigning to ballot suppression. The non-electoral portion of one's democratic entitlement, such as the right "of equal access to public service" (in delivering those services and in being beneficiaries of them), has historically been disregarded. "The pervasive and entrenched system of white supremacy at the State Department," as observed by a former diplomat, for example, is not something that human rights groups will find a moderating force in their righteous marshaling of attacks against China.[788] The absence of equality—a democratic ideal—in access to

---

[786] See text of Pence's speech as the Hudson Institute, op. cit.

[787] Lind, op. cit., p. 80.

[788] See Chris Richardson, "Closed Door at the Department of state," in *New York Times* (June 26, 2020), p. A27.

public service is also matched by the right to equal representation by citizens. Neither the people of the District of Columbia, the people of Puerto Rico, or those of the Native American communities (because of limits, in the latter case, in economic social and cultural rights) enjoy that ideal. Many of the same issues pertain to some members of minority communities and to the poor in general.

Finally, the marshaling of opposition to China will revolve around some other issues, such as Taiwan, the island off Mainland China to which, as before said, the KMT fled in 1949 after its defeat in the civil war. So too—although less so, except as it relates to Taiwan—might be mentioned the former British colony Hong Kong. The US, as part of its effort to contain the PRC, has had an interest to include both as part of its declared FOIP region (as said before, including India, Japan, and South Korea, among others) as an area of democracy, logically, to be protected by the US. The developments in Hong Kong, following the 2019–2020 unrest there over matters of the island's autonomy, will pose a major challenge to the US's hoped-for extension of its "democratic" reach. Most likely, Hong Kong will remain, as will Macao, part of China's "One County, Two Systems" construct but with broader alignments, including as many as nine cities in nearby Guangdong Province and Macao itself to become part of what China has been calling the Greater Bay Area initiative.[789] With the skills of the people of Hong Kong linked to those other cities, a regional economic and financial powerhouse could emerge that goes beyond anything that Hong Kong may have envisioned for itself.

The notion that Hong Kong would remain "just Hong Kong," without significant political influence from Beijing—a stance that the US and the UK adopted—lent support to the protest movement over the question of the island's autonomy, but that stand flew in the face of historical experiences elsewhere.[790] Would the UK, which controlled the city for over 150 years, have tolerated the protest, which lasted for over

---

[789] See Michael Schuman, "As China Casts Its Shadow, Seeing Upside in Hong Kong," in *New York Times* (November 8, 2020), p. B6.

[790] Hannah Beech, "In the Fight to Be 'Just Hong Kong,' a Daunting New Salvo," in *New York Times* (May 24, 2020), p. A16. See also "US incites violence by passing HK laws," editorial comments authored by Zhu Feng, dean of the Institute of International Relations, Nanjing University, in *China Daily* (December 1, 2019), p. 4.

a year and interrupted business, educational, and commercial activities, the latter including the functions of the international airport—a major hub for global commerce? Would the US—which, in the OWS protests of 2001, allowed for the arrest of over seven hundred individuals as they crossed the Brooklyn Bridge on account of their having walked in the street rather than the sidewalk (thereby blocking traffic)—have been as patient as China were a protest of like kind taking place on Wall Street? The OWS protesters, it should be observed, were not dealing so much with concerns of CPR but with economic and social rights—income and economic inequality—with some reference and opposition to what they saw as a hierarchical and authoritarian structure of society.[791]

The human rights groups had no willingness to reflect on any such comparisons in their united criticism of China, which behaved almost exemplarily. It has been my view that Washington had hoped that China would have acted rashly. The reaction of these groups to Hong Kong will be even less discriminating as the international community will be asked to assess Beijing's future conduct toward Taiwan.

Drawing a close parallel is attempted here because I am about to ask the reader to substitute the US for China in looking at Taiwan as I conclude this chapter. Taiwan, officially (from the standpoint of the PRC) a province of China, had been taken from the latter country by Japan in 1895 and returned to China after World War II by way of a number of international instruments, including the interwar agreements textually contained in the Cairo Declaration of 1943, the 1945 Potsdam Declaration, and the 1951 and 1952 Treaties of Peace.[792] As the reader will recall, however, after the PRC had defeated the ROC, which fled from the mainland to Taiwan, the US backed the ROC and effectively prevented Beijing from taking over and incorporating the island into Mainland China's control. In 1972, the Shanghai Communiqué, earlier

---

[791] Michael Levitan, "The Triumph of Occupy Wall Street," in the *Atlantic* (June 10, 2015). See also Gu Mengyan and Dai Kaiyi, "Damaged Poly U Campus in HK unscaled," *China Daily* (November 30, 2019), p. 4.

[792] The 1951 Treaty of Peace was with Japan to reestablish peaceful relations between Japan and allied powers, often referred to as the San Francisco Treaty (named after the city where the treaty was concluded). The 1952 Treaty of Peace was between Japan and the Republic of China.

mentioned, acknowledged that Taiwan constituted a long-standing dispute between the US and China, defined what they saw as its status, and suggested how a resolution of the dispute might take place.

While China asserted that one China and only one China exists and that Taiwan is a province thereof, the US took a more nuanced stance (in part to fit its position with that of the ROK—which had been contending that there is one China but that it, the ROK, is its legitimate government—and to appease the passionate domestic supporters of the ROK who wanted to get rid of the CCP), stating that "all Chinese on either side of the Taiwan Strait maintain that there is one China and that Taiwan is a part of China."[793] The vagueness of the stance, called the "One China" policy, allowed the Nixon government to avoid any claim of "selling out" a friend, especially in view of the fact that a year earlier, the UN had replaced the ROC with the PRC as the legitimate government of the Chinese state. As important, however, since the US then had hopes of successfully integrating the PRC into the US-led Western liberal international order, it was possible that the ROC could play a role in that integration. It also accorded with MacArthur's counsel that the US should never give up Taiwan if Washington wanted to continue its post–World War II supremacy in the Pacific. Within the US, it also satisfied those who were strong lobbyists, including Christians, for the independence of Taiwan.

This is, in part, linked to a claim concerning the treaties (which I will not focus on here because, in my view, it is the height of bad faith) and the language of the Shanghai Communiqué. If one reads that language carefully, that portion in which the US seems to accept the idea of "one China," one will note that the text says that "all Chinese on either side of the Taiwan Strait maintain that there is but one China." Then the text immediately goes on to say, "The United States Government does not challenge that position." This, among other things, means that if one of the Chinese grouping on either side of the Taiwan Strait were to claim that there is no longer one China, if one side ceases to "maintain" that there is but one China, there would no longer be a position against which the US owes a commitment or with which the US needs to disagree.

---

[793] See Shanghai Communiqué, op. cit.

This, in my view, is the path that the US is pursuing. The independence of Taiwan that was more or less being quietly advanced in 1972 has become, today, more and more an end that is being search for by the US, although within the context of certain contingencies (as so clearly sketched by Allison in his "Taiwan Moves Toward Independence"[794] scenario) and some in Taiwan, especially some from the ruling Democratic Progressive Party (DPP), as opposed to the Chinese Nationalist Party, which prefers closer ties with Beijing.[795] Those thinking and planning in this search have sought to proceed indirectly to avoid, if possible, the likely angry reaction of Beijing, which has made this clear to the US and the world through its insistence on preserving the territorial integrity of China in general and its unflagging opposition to an independent Taiwan. In the latter regard, Beijing has been rejecting the idea that Taiwan's status "remains to be determined" given the explicit positions taken over the years, including the Shanghai Communiqué.

Indirection takes many forms, one or two of which I will touch on before concluding the chapter because they offer a sense of further means that will be employed to mobilize opposition to China and ensure more support for the US. The use of the term "autonomy" in respect of Hong Kong—seeking support for Taiwan's membership in international intergovernmental bodies, increasing "cultural exchanges" with Taipei, increasing departments of the US's government other than the Department of State, interactions with the ROC, and ensuring that the latter has resources to defend itself—is consistent with US "traditional" public support for a peaceful resolution of Taiwan's future.

The use of the term "autonomy" or "greater autonomy" for Hong Kong was given connotations of virtual or approximate independence in the West, and it promoted as such, while the US concurrently gave support to the drawn-out battle that ensued—with ever-escalating demands on the part of the protestors inviting or seeking to invite a brutal crackdown by Beijing. The latter development would lead Taipei, it was hoped, to conclude that the constitutional principle of "One Country, Two Systems" (under which a reunited Mainland China and Taiwan would coexist) is an

[794] Allison, *Destined for War*, op. cit., pp. 173–175.

[795] Edward Wong, "US Tries to Bolster Taiwan Status, Short of Recognizing Sovereignty," in *New York Times* (August 18, 2020), p. A10.

unworkable formula for its future and to generate greater popular support for independence. China frustrated this thinking and planning, by its patience (for over a year) and its relatively careful and benign response, as it sent troops into Hong Kong (after warning that it would) and placed the island under a new national security legislation.

In matters of membership in IGOs and non–Department of State interactions with Taiwan, the US has been busy, beginning with the WHO, and, most recently (May 2020), launched an effort to ensure to Taiwan what is called an "observer status" in that body.[796] Part of the argument used by the US in its unsuccessful effort, over China's objection, was that Taipei had been very successful in its dealing with COVID-19, as before indicated, and thus could be an important contributor to the deliberations of the WHO on confronting the pandemic and public health issues in general. In the matter of non–Department of State departments of the US government dealing with Taiwan (the Department of State interacts with other states or international governmental organizations such as the UN, the EU, or the OAS), the US secretary of health and human services visited Taipei and met with Tsai Ing-wen, the president of Taiwan, in August 2020.[797]

Domestic and international supporters of independence for Taiwan are always dissatisfied with the indirect actions just described. They seek more direct action, such as the increased sale of arms to Taiwan, which the US allowed in October 2020 in the amount of about $4 billion. A statement by one domestic and international supporter can help us in this part of our discussion:

> Taiwan's status as an independent island officially unrecognized by most of the world, including the United

---

[796] See Wong, ibid. The term "observer status" is one sometimes granted by IGOs—the World Health Organization or the UN General Assembly, for instance—to non-members on the grounds that such would-be observers have a recognized interest in the activities of the IGO. Observer status does not allow the entity that has been granted it to vote or propose resolutions in the body in which it is an observer, but the status can be used as a springboard to increased international status.

[797] Ibid.

States, is a geopolitical absurdity . . . the United States' implicit security guarantee of Taiwan has kept China restrained for decades.[798]

The statement has many meanings around which several seminars could be conducted. Let it suffice to observe the terms "independent island" and "officially unrecognized by *most* of the world" [emphasis the author's]. The writers are scholars; they know that the term "an independent island" is factually untrue, yet they use it to persuade the unaware. So too is the term unofficially "unrecognized by most of the world." The word "most" is used to imply that some countries recognize it as independent. These countries (about five of which remain) are a remnant of very small countries that had, before 1971, recognized the ROC as the official government of China. That number has undergone a progressive decline as their fear of the US's sanctions (often through Beijing's support) has been removed. One ought not to confuse recognition of government with recognition of state, however. China's existence as a state has long preceded 1949; the issue was and has been but which of the two competing governments, after the civil war, should be recognized as the legitimate government of China. Thus, it has nothing to do with Taiwan being an independent island; it remains part of the state of China.[799]

There has even been a recently floated idea of increasing cultural exchanges with Taiwan, substituting a language program with the island for that which had been flourishing with Mainland China, through a number of Confucius Institutes (CIs), established by the PRC in the US and achieving a record of exemplary success in Chinese culture and language programs, many serving social and ethnic groups what would never otherwise have had a chance to study Chinese culture and language.[800]

---

[798] Charles Dunst and Shahn Savino, "Stand up for Taiwan," in *Boston Globe* (November 8, 2020), p. K5.

[799] See Bolton, op. cit., pp. 313–314. He generally tries to gloss over Taiwan's true status.

[800] See Baifeng Sun's reports at the University of Massachusetts Boston, where she led a CI, the language programs of which served New England and many

This extended focus on Taiwan is done because the island is closely linked, psychologically and politically, to the emotionally charged idea that the US had "lost China," meaning that the long and extended moral and material investment in that country, until 1949, had gone astray and had been misdirected, allowing the communist, in the organized expression of the CCP and the PRC, to gain control of the country. The ROC's presence in Taiwan, coupled with the isolation of the PRC, represented for many the hope that the CCP would fail and that the KMT would return, opening space for a "free and democratic" China, even when there was little that was democratic about the KMT. Now the sentiments for a "free China" are linked, as the rise of China exhibits little but the tiniest portions of hope merged with large pockets of anger and even hate, to the newly proclaimed FOIP region, which the US is to defend. The mobilization, therefore, that is likely to center on Taiwan will probably incorporate all the other mentioned areas in relation to such mobilization. This will also involve what the late president Dwight D. Eisenhower warned us about—the military industrial complex, an informal alliance between the nation's military and the defense industries that supply it, with an extension of that complex to include the emerging vested interests in the field of artificial intelligence.

We now move to the hypothetical I previously indicated that I would pose to the reader so that one can better see through some of the biased attitudes that will interact with the activation of organized and rallying sentiments against China. Suppose the US fought a civil war in which a side favored by China, the dominant country in the world,

---

states throughout the US. For instance, the Annual Chinese Bridge US High School Speech Contest, which started at UMass Boston's (UMB) campus in 2007, attracted (each year) more than a thousand students from about a hundred schools throughout the US. Over a twelve-year period, it selected 288 students to visit the campus for a final onsite competition. Since 2008, each year, more than ten winning students have participated in the Chinese Bridge Summer Camp, a two-week China tour program. Over 110 participants were a part of it. Since 2011, the UMB CI has hosted a program of the Chinese Bridge Speech Contest for university students in New England. Each year, over thirty or more applied and winners had sponsorships for the two-week Chinese Bridge China tour program. These were potential future professors, diplomats, business leaders, and journalists, among other professional life chances.

lost and escaped to Long Island, where it not only contended, for nearly a quarter of a century, that it was the legitimate government of the US but also actually, with the backing of China, actively exercised that authority in the world's most important international organization, the UN. Suppose further that over seventy years later—after the US and China had, despite remaining differences, reorganized their relations—China began to support the independence of Long Island from the US with the regime that had lost the civil war and its successors to be the new leaders of the would-be independent Long Island. Assume also that the newly independent state would be an independent state allied to China, its waters open to the presence of China's warships, among other military forces. In the meantime, China has been organizing a free and open socialist Atlantic (defined by the rights to food, housing, education, and health care) from the Gulf of Mexico to Nova Scotia, backed by military alliances. China is, in addition, accusing the US of violating the rights of Native Americans and a number of other minorities and the poor in general of their human rights to health care, education, and food, among other areas. How would the US react?

The last few pages (and the chapter, in part), I wrote to culminate what I have been seeking to say—that as in the other case studies, war between the US and China may well come to be, but it will not be on account of any force outside of human control called the "Thucydides trap," the idea of China's challenge to replace the US, as Allison and others may argue, resulting in war between them. If war ensues between these two countries, it will be because the US has elected to fight a war, if necessary, to prevent the value of equality from becoming an operating principle domestically or internationally. At home, this is because China's challenge in the area of ESCR will expose many of the weaknesses of the liberal international order (previously presented as largely flawless), and internationally, this is because the international hierarchical structure (something that Allison left untouched in accusing China of being hierarchically organized), at the top of which the US finds its place, will have to be reorganized to come face-to-face with the principles of sovereign equality earlier discussed.

CHAPTER 17

Conclusion: What Is to Be Done?

It is not because it is difficult that we are afraid to act;
it is because we are afraid to act that it is difficult.

— Seneca

Our conclusion is a five-part one, beginning with a brief summary of what the alternative histories we have covered have revealed and proceeding with the other four areas. Each of these areas is implicit in the idea of China replacing the US in the latter's standing in the world.

The alternative view of the historical patterns we have considered in this work discloses that the conflicts (between Athens and Sparta, Germany and Britain, and Japan and the US) resulted in debilitating wars not because of the anxieties of replacement but because equality would not be conceded by the dominant state in the paired case studies. Athens saw law, practice, and custom (including that portion informed by religion) and the equality they entailed as limiting its search for "world" domination. The US saw Japan's search for equality in "great power" status through territorial expansion as limiting its superior claim to the status of Pacific power and, with the latter, its sought standing as the emerging dominant world power. Britain used its worldwide "rule [of] the waves"—seen as the foundation on which it continued to enjoy the rank, prestige, and honor *shared by no other*—to frustrate all efforts by Germany to gain equality through the acquisition of more

353

colonies and a worldwide navy to protect and defend them as well as the commerce and the envisioned status in the world those colonies and commerce would confer.

The US, as the self-identified "exceptional" power with a global identity (initially only envisioned but subsequently made geopolitically coherent through the "Grand Area,"[801] encompassing the Western Hemisphere, the Far East, and the former British Empire plus the Middle East and South Asia), became even more conscious of the self that benefitted from this identity, with all the influence and power earlier described, as perhaps the most impressive post-1945 international, socioeconomic, and political development. The US has found it unacceptable that China's emergence as a potential economic, technological, and moral rival espouses or seeks an equality that brings with it limits on Washington's hitherto unhindered expressions of global reach, including what is known as the South China Sea or, in China's own un-reunited province, Taiwan.

Each of the dominant states mentioned in the paired case studies adopted an ideological strategy as a self-augmenting, lofty purpose designed to mask or embroider, morally, its sought domination. Athens was "the school of Hellas." It was the exemplar for all in the Greek world; it was the teacher, the example, and the guide, whether it be in the arts, literature, philosophy, or science. In the case of Britain, it claimed a providential calling to lead the world in the arts of civilization and bring light to dark places and even to discipline the arrogant. For the US, it has been that of serving as the unsought but duly accepted worldwide trustee of freedom, the finder of paths to that value, where other countries are unable to find that path, the nation that has the responsibility "to fill the role of pathfinder," including the role of removing obstacles to the finding of that path.[802]

---

[801] This is an area that appears to have come from a study and later a proposal from the Council of Foreign Relations during World War II and later developed and refined though the George Kennan–led Policy Planning Staff (PPS) of the Department of State. See "Review of Current Trends," Memo PPS 23.

[802] See Madeleine Albright's 1997 speech at Harvard, op. cit. She is but one of the latest public officials to invoke US exceptionalism. The president-elect, Joseph Biden, simply speaks of Washington's inheritance and its careful building of the

This is leagued to the claim of Allison and Thucydides that a state that challenges the existing favorable military power of a dominant country sets off *forces* that usually overwhelm whatever restraining political and moral agency that decision makers possess. The implication here is that human moral agency, in those circumstances, lose the freedom to pursue alternatives to war. This claim is not borne out either by the available evidence that has been hinged to any of the case studies we have examined. With respect to Athens and Sparta, we showed the doubts voiced by the king of Sparta, even in the face of overwhelming pressure from his allies. Much more telling is the example of Pericles, the first citizen (the equivalent of prime minister) of Athens. It was his rhetorical and positional stances that brought the Athenians to a decision to go to war after an extended debate that yielded no decision.[803] It was again Pericles (in the face of bitter criticism that those stances that led to war were now threatening to bring ruin to Athens after that city-state was faced with a socially shattering epidemic in the second year of the war) who got Athens to agree that the war should be continued.[804]

The presented cases of Germany and Britain as well as Japan and the US furnish comparable examples. One has but to recall, for instance, the deadlock that Britain's political leaders faced as Germany declared war in 1914 and how, to gain cabinet support, Foreign Minister Edward Grey (who was bent on going to war) "invented" the violation of Belgium's neutrality (a violation that Britain had planned to pursue) as an excuse to enter the war, claiming that it (Britain) had no alternative given the infringement on Belgium's neutrality. London, therefore, could be seen as the upholder of law and civilization. We also have the example of Washington's calculated cutting off of oil to Japan, the extended exchanges between Tokyo and Washington, the refusal of President Roosevelt to meet directly with Japanese leaders, and the decision of Japan (led by Gen. Hideki Tojo) to move south toward Hawaii (the US)

---

global institutions that it must lead. See Joseph R. Biden, "Why America Must Lead Again," in *Foreign Affairs*, Vol. 99, #2 (March/April 2020), pp. 1–23.

[803] Thucydides, op. cit., pp. 79–83.

[804] Ibid., pp. 115–119.

instead of north toward Soviet Russia, with which Japan was also having major differences.

The second feature of this conclusion is an acknowledgement that change on the part of the US or China in a manner that is removing of the emerging differences between them will not come overnight, although each must if it is to survive and thrive, as the third feature should demonstrate. Too much has been invested, in the case of the US, in the identity of exceptionalism and its worldwide reach and attributed meaning. This reach and meaning find themselves in what then president Eisenhower called the "military-industrial complex," denoting the complex intermeshed links between the armed forces and powerful corporations that make weapons systems in the worldwide network of the US's alliances and military bases, on which local national elites and subnational groups often depend for economic and other forms of support, and the organization of millions of men and women (along with their families) from almost every ethnic, racial, social, and religious group who see military service as among the most noble of professional commitments. Undergirding this war system (what we will later call the "culture of war" or the "war culture") is the broad ideological component that emotionally and otherwise approves the system as well as the cultural institutions—including the media, the academy, and the church—that endorse and reinforce the ideology. Rosa Brooks, in her book *How Everything Became War and the Military Everything*, captures this war culture.[805]

Absent a radical alteration in political orientation on the part of Beijing, China is not going to be changing the basic course of its envisioned development either. The nature and scope of that development (and we have seen how China understands development, in contrast to economic growth, only) are viewed by Washington as a threat—the norm of equality that China espouses (very much as the US trumpets freedom) and insists on. As was the case of Japan during the late nineteenth and the first half of the twentieth centuries, the PRC is the only current non-white country potentially capable of demanding it. Beijing is, therefore,

---

[805] Rosa Brooks, *How Everything Became War and the Military Everything* (New York: Simon & Schuster, 2016). See also Andrew J. Bacevich, *The New American Militarism* (Oxford: Oxford University Press, 2013).

a problem—a bad example, especially for states in the Global South that make the same claim to equality, although they cannot now enforce it. China thus (especially in the context of orientalism) embodies and provides too many potential refutations of and social disruptions to the claims of the liberal international order and to orientalism.

The third and fourth areas of the conclusion speak to the direction of globalization and the readiness of the US and China for that direction. They will next occupy our attention and, with the exception of a few examples, will be drawn from our earlier chapters.

Globalization itself is often defined as a process by which the consciousness of companies and individuals (as well as social movements with which they are respectively associated) is expanded beyond national borders and thereby progressively increase the interconnectedness of economies and cultures that a single market of goods and services (including investments) emerges. This is the type of market into which the US envisioned that China would be integrated under "rules of the road" that included the "ruling" currency established by the US and the US-led West. Within this single market, different countries and areas of the world would somewhat freely concentrate on the production of certain goods and services, and these interdependent countries would deal with their differences through existing mechanisms such as the WTO.

The "America first" and other nationalistic stances of the Trump administration highlighted a number of questions and complaints that people have had about globalization, including cultural pluralism and the fairness of material and other distributions from its ample, in some cases, undreamt-of material returns. For China, a principal question has been the extent to which its general emphasis on globalization and international interdependence has been misplaced, especially in view of the US's recent tariffs and other economic policies toward Beijing. This question has so powerfully grown that President Xi himself has begun to speak in terms of increased self-reliance, more of a focus of Maoists, of reducing China's international vulnerability, especially to the US.[806] If either China or the US were to withdraw from the globalization path,

[806] See Chris Buckley, "China Sees Self-Reliance as Essential to Economy," in *New York Times* (September 8, 2020), p. B1.

on which the world at large has been launched, it would be unfortunate for the world at large and counterproductive for each. Fortunately, there are issues that face humankind that frown at de-globalization and strongly push people toward it. Even more important, the issues that now occupy most of the attentive international publics are not so much the process of globalization (although this process has to be reformed) but more so the ends, including whom and what values that globalization ought to and will serve.

Among the issues compelling a global focus by states and thus inducing the development or reinforcement of values that minister to the very constitution of the world's peoples and nature itself are those of the environment and climate change in particular; the global social agenda (the demand for greater social equity within and among countries) led by public health, education, and the eradication of poverty; the global demographic transformation, along with the trans-border movement of peoples; and the social consequences, for both the US and China, of not dealing with those issues. Success or failure in dealing with the demands of the just-mentioned issues requires not only international collaboration but, as well, some agreement on the purposes of globalization—a major source of rivalry between Beijing and Washington. This brings us back to the debate on the proposed NIEO, which took place in the US, led by the late senator Moynihan, who provided the intellectual framework for the debate in the US and for the policies of Washington that followed.

The reader will recall that Moynihan's main objection to the proposed NIEO was that it sought to create, among countries, a new international socioeconomic system (the purpose of which was grounded in the pursuit of "equity, sovereign equality, interdependence, common interest, and cooperation . . . irrespective of their economic and social systems") that presupposed the existence or the creation of a *community* when, in fact, the world was but ready for a *society*. The latter, for him, stands for an association of states wherein, aside from certain elementary actions such as complying with certain basic normative infrastructures (the rule of law, including the honoring of one's contracts, and the right to speak as well as the protection of diplomatic personnel), member states and the societies they represent owe little to one another. The former, on the other hand, suggests an association of states in which international relationships are defined by bonds of mutual concern for one another's well-being as well as the welfare of the association itself.

Moynihan erred in claiming that the focus on community was a sort of unexpected, odd, or "out of left field" push by the Global South because so many efforts of the post-1945 world sought, through a variety of means, to find institutional mechanisms by which the promise of community could be realized. His position fit well with the neoliberalism of the Reagan administration and its influential aftermath, however, and the world has had to live with its consequences, including the failure to offer support to issues pertaining to the global environment, as promised and expected. The human rights regime as well as the Outer Space Treaty and the Law of the Sea are but a few examples on which we can immediately touch, beginning with the first, just-mentioned regime. Here, one speaks not so much of individual rights—to speak, to food, or to health care—but the fact that those rights are linked to a species, a communal identity, a human identity, not an American or Chinese citizen, or women or men, or a Western, Muslim, Hindu, or Christian identity. As well, states jointly "pledge themselves to achieve, in cooperation with the UN . . . the promotion of universal respect for and observance of" those rights.[807] A joint pledge is a communal one. Of course, the rights apply to American and Chinese citizens but only secondarily—that is, they apply to humans who happen to be US or Chinese citizens.

In 1967, seven years before the proposed NIEO, the US, with the former Soviet Union, led the crafting of the Treaty on Principles Governing the Activities in the Exploration and Use of Outer Space, including the Moon and Other Celestial Bodies (also known as the Outer Space Treaty). [808] On the one hand, the treaty states that outer space "is not subject to national appropriation by claims of sovereignty"— sovereignty in terms of authority to make laws, as earlier discussed in this book, governing any area in outer space.[809] On the other hand, the

---

[807] See paragraph 6 of the preamble to the UDHR. See also Article 56 of the UN Charter.

[808] See 610 U.N. T.S. 205, 18 U.S. T.S. 2410.

[809] Ibid., Principle II.

treaty recognizes the openness of outer space to the exploration and use by "all states," but that exploration and use must be on the basis of equality and be "for the benefit and in the interest of all countries." Further, the treaty states that all of outer space "shall be the province of all mankind."[810] The constitution of the oceans—which is named the UN Convention on the Law of the Sea (UNCLOS) and governs an area constituting over 70 percent of the earth's surface, in the same spirit of the Outer Space Treaty—states,

> The area of the seabed and the ocean floor and the subsoil thereof, beyond national jurisdiction, as well as its resources are the common heritage of mankind, the exploration and exploitation of which shall be carried out for the benefit of mankind as a whole.[811]

There are many oceans and seas in the world. Their character and problems are closely interrelated, and human beings saw that they should be considered as a whole on behalf of all.[812] In short, the idea that states, societies, and peoples owe one another some equal regard, the sharing of returns with others from one's efforts (as if they were kin), and the subordination of national interests to mutual benefit and common interest must have been known to Senator Moynihan and to many of his principal colleagues who rejected the idea of a transnational community. The required transformation of our relationship with nature, with the natural world "outside" ourselves, and the reordering of our relationships with one another, are inseparable. These relationships are also conjoined to the idea of community, hence global efforts such as the 2015 Paris Agreement (within the UN Framework Convention on Climate Change), which deals with greenhouse gas emissions mitigation, adaptation, and finance. Such is also the case of the 1987 report of the World Commission on Environment and Development, *Our Common Future*, which, in turn, was part of the spiritual offspring of the 1982

---

[810] Ibid., Principle I.

[811] See paragraph 6 of UNCLOS, UN Document A/CONF., 62/122/Corr. of November 26, 1982.

[812] Ibid., paragraph 3.

World Charter of Nature, which reaffirmed that humankind "is part of nature and life depends on the uninterrupted functioning of natural systems"; that civilization itself "is rooted in nature, which has shaped human culture and influenced all artistic and scientific achievement"; and that "living in harmony with nature gives [us] the best opportunities for the development of [our] creativity and for rest and recreation."[813]

The urged moral code to guide human beings, in the coming to recognize that "every form of life is unique, warranting respect regardless of its [seeming] worth" to humans,[814] has historically found expression in what has come to be known as the "public trust doctrine" that memorializes an ancient and enduring principle that *public property rights* are of first significance (not just private ones), if certain important resources are to be conserved. In the case at hand, expressive of the idea of community—including its intergenerational component—the principle says that governments, as trustees, far from leaving matters to private interests, should have as one of their central functions the protection of natural inheritance such as forests, rivers, and the air for all human beings.[815]

What is true for the environment—its preservation and sustainable development require the collective commitment of every country—is true for education, for the elimination of poverty, and for public health, among other areas of human anxiety. In relation to COVID-19, for example, the ethic of concern for the other (as evidenced by mask wearing and social distancing, for example) is the most effective pre-vaccination approach to countering the pandemic. So the human rights regime that requires states to implement the entire family of human rights enjoins every nation to be as solicitous about the rights to health care, food, and education as it is to the rights to speak, freedom of the

---

[813] See the World Commission on Environment and Development, *Our Common Future* (Oxford: Oxford University Press, 1987). The commission was chaired by Gro Harlem Brundtland and is sometimes referred to as the "Brundtland Report." See also the World Charter of Nature, adopted by the UN General Assembly in 1982, UNGA Res. 37/7, UN Doc. A/37/L.4 and Add. 1/1982.

[814] See preamble of the charter.

[815] See Mary Christina, *Nature's Trust: Environmental Law for a New Ecological Age* (Cambridge: Cambridge University Press, 2013).

press, and freedom of conscience and religion. Support for the family of human rights would prevent the starvation of children because of war. In short, the direction of globalization is one that has been recommending community, rather than society, for the human future. The question at this stage in our discussion, therefore, is whether the US and China are ready for this direction. If they are or can become ready, there will be no war between them.

Here, we should be particularly careful in how we phrase what we say because it is likely to fly in the face of conventional wisdom. Certainly, it will contradict the often-portrayed contrast (orientalism) between the US and China. In the area of the direction of globalization, one may factually say, China seems (especially if it follows a trajectory to become a political democracy by 2049, as it promises) to be somewhat better prepared than the US because many of the values for which the US has proudly stood are increasingly seen as less attractive for human collective future. A brief review will offer some illumination. The US, for example, in its insistence on maintaining the lone superpower status, is carrying on a tradition of domination (from ancient Greece to the present, as Allison has shown). This domination (and "will to domination") is also centrally informed by nineteenth-century European "great power" politics, with its balance of power and political realism bias, as well as moral skepticism orientation, as evidenced in its worldwide system of alliances and military bases.[816] Domination, its war culture, and the tension and mistrust sown by its balance of power system do not generate, not to mention nurture, the type of confidence, integrity, and "caring for" belief system that community demands. (If one were Soviet Russia, with which the US aligned itself to defeat Germany and Japan during World War II, how would one feel when by 1950 Germany and Japan were aligned with the US against Soviet Russia? How did US citizens feel when Russia sought to move into areas of liberated Eastern Europe by 1948?) An unmodified self-regulating market—given its historical record, current practices, and moral commitments—hardly offers a more encouraging prospect for community than military domination.

---

[816] Henry Kissinger, *A World Restored: Castlereagh and Metternich, the Problem of Peace, 1812–1822* (Boston: Houghton Mifflin, 1957)

That market, although admirably potentially supportive of a measurable degree of civic openness and political rights (which every community needs to be self-sustaining), is defined by national and global social and economic inequality (in income and wealth), is supportive of a culture of winners and losers instead of mutual benefits (and mutual suffering),[817] and crowds out the public space it has traditionally helped create with its business way of life and commercial advertisement. It has defeated or sought to defeat every attempt at "social melioration," as shown by the admirable study by Thomas Piketty, and its internal dynamic offers no hope for a less unequal future.[818] Perhaps as important, from the standpoint of community, is the fact that a frequent discussion, at the highest levels of academic discourse, concerns whether one can do well (in material terms) and, concurrently, do good[819] and the insistence on the part of the unregulated market in the US on having economy dominate polity. The business community, in general, seeks to avoid having a "unified government," having one political party gain control of the three political branches of the government. That control could result in polity dominating economy, and the resulting coming-into-being of socially important programs and infrastructure-building initiatives could require higher taxes and, hence, reduced profits for the companies.

China, on the other hand, insists on ensuring that polity controls economy, including the operations of foreign (including US) corporations within its borders, and uses that control to help work toward the fulfillment of ESCR, including the objective of ridding its society of poverty. Gains in the realization of the latter objective, along with the sustained promotion of the other ESCR, contribute to support for the norm of equality that is so much a part of community. President Xi, with

---

[817] See Giridharadas, op. cit. See also Rene Loth, "We Can't Privatize Our Way Out of Poverty," in *Boston Globe* (December 10, 2018), p. A10.

[818] Thomas Piketty, *Capital in the Twenty-First Century* (Cambridge: Harvard University Press, 2014). In a follow-up volume, *Capital and Ideology* (Cambridge: Harvard University, 2019), Piketty exposes the superficial left–right discussions on inequality, something the market encourages to demonstrate openness.

[819] See Michael J. Sandel, *What Money Can't Buy: The Moral Limits of the Market* (New York: Farrar, Straus and Giroux, 2017).

his mix of neo-Confucian and socialist values, espouses the idea of a single family under heaven, as the reader will recall. China's foreign policy, especially in the form of economic and technical assistance, operates to promote ESCR as it does in its domestic policy, thus aligning the country's behavior more closely to the idea of community. Xi's position contrasts sharply with the amoral policy of the deservedly respected father of containment, George Kennan, who, as leader of policy planning in the Department of State, authored the earlier referred-to, declassified memorandum of 1948—one that has been a cornerstone of the US's foreign policy—which cautioned decision makers against becoming "hampered by idealistic slogans" such as "human rights, the raising of living standards, and democratization."[820]

The quote, included in the section of the memorandum dealing with East Asia, became applicable elsewhere, and it is included at this juncture because Kennan argued that the US, while constituting but 6.3 percent of the world's population, had "about 50% of the world's wealth."[821] As such (and the US now has about 24 percent of the world's wealth, with approximately 4.2 percent of its population), improvements in standards of living for the less fortunate would, in the typical zero-sum game reasoning of a political realist, mean a potential loss for the US. Of course, he was not actually dealing with the US as a whole (he was not an advocate for the norm of equality at home); he was referring to a small group of elites who have controlled and disproportionately benefitted from the wealth that the US has been producing. His reasoning explains why it took so long for the US to ratify the International Covenant on Civil and Political Rights (not until 1992) and why it has never ratified the covenant on ESCR. It also explains the resonance of Moynihan's arguments, among national elites, against the idea of an international or global community, its public rejection by the Reagan administration, and its full embracement, by and large, by successive administrations.

China, in the person of President Xi (but fully embraced by his predecessors), far from accepting the culture of great power policies of

---

[820] See Kennan, PPS/23, "Review of Current Trends," op. cit.

[821] Ibid.

nineteenth-century European diplomacy, has indicated that it will never pursue hegemony, is committed to the principle of sovereign equality of all states (however big or small), would like to get rid of "alliances" and substitute in their stead "partnerships" (thus removing some of the major grounds for international fear and suspicion), and will work to bring into being a reformed international system to give expression to a multipolar world community. (This does not mean that, as seen in its relationship with Australia, China does not, at times, follow a realist outlook and behavior. It does, as all states must, because all countries exist within the system structurally and otherwise dominated by realism.)

In broad ideological terms, as we have seen in the counter-narratives, the US is committed to and seeks to extend a single cultural consciousness as containing within itself answers to all human problems—a liberal democratic order within Western civilization. At the core of this ideology's constitution is the idea of the self-making, autonomous individual associated with certain CPR. Those who oppose this ideology are faced with a "clash." China offers in its place the possibility of a plural (this was not the China of the 1950s or 1960s) consciousness in the form of equality of all social systems, the right to national self-determination by which nations "freely determine their political status and freely pursue their economic, social, and cultural development" and, in lieu of a "clash," a "dialogue" among civilizations—a view that finds strong support throughout the world, including Asia, where philosophers and moral leaders, such as Daisaku Ikeda and Tu Weiming, have been its strong advocates.[822] The neo-Confucian outlook that has helped shape President Xi's view of culture and its possibilities bears with it aspects of Buddhism's view of the individual. This view sees the individual not so much as autonomous but as one in a network of relationships expressed through the idea or concept of *dependent origination*. This concept holds that everything in existence (including an as-yet unborn child) exists because other things (including people) are in existence, and therefore, everything is interconnected and interdependent. For this reason, whatever we do,

---

[822] See Tu Weiming and Daisaku Ikeda, *New Horizons in Eastern Humanism* (London: I. B. Tauris, 2011).

whatever we are being and becoming, affects others.[823] This is part of what the earlier quoted World Charter for Nature tells us. One can find few clearer expressions of community and the basis for the ethic of caring for one another; each person or country has responsibilities toward one another and for non-human nature.

We previously, in this chapter, referred to the civic space, the cherished public spaces that the liberal democratic order initially helped create, and how businesses now seek to fill those spaces, thus reducing the quality of people's interactions with one another and their governments. China, in its development, has not allowed for as many such spaces, although in my visits to that country between 2006 and 2015, there were significant improvements. These spaces are important for the sense of communities within community. Within the US, an oligopoly of "business activities," including entertainment, has sought to occupy "humanity's unruly consciousness" and to narrow so thinly the distance between business and culture that "we no longer have a life, a history, a consciousness apart" from or independent of that occupation. Indeed, the latter has sought to put "itself beyond our power of imagining because it has become our imagination, [and] it has become our power to envision and describe and theorize and resist."[824] President Xi has focused and reflected deeply on culture in China and has, in part, been seeking to prevent or contain this occupation. This is understandable, but he has been criticized for it, at home and abroad. The issue for the president is the detailed prescriptions that appear to accompany this reflection on culture. Do they allow enough room for individual and communal development in their plentiful variety and richness? A search for political democracy by 2049 will have to tend to this issue.

The claim above that China is better prepared by history, culture, and policies to deal with the direction of globalization, the reader can

---

[823] For an elaboration of the concept in a richer setting, see Daisaku Ikeda, "Mahayana Buddhism and Twenty-First Century Civilization," in Daisaku Ikeda, *A New Humanism* (London: I. B. Tauris, 2010), pp. 165–175. This was a speech delivered at Harvard University in 1993.

[824] Morris Berman, *The Twilight of American Culture* (New York: W. W. Norton & Company, 2000), p. 4.

agree, has the support of indications just completed. Indeed, this better preparedness does not mean, as indicated, that China does not have weaknesses. We have touched on a few, and we will again. What can be said now is that at this juncture, it is "better prepared" or aligned and is perhaps one of the major challenges that Beijing presents to Washington, especially to the fact that China's economic resources and sociocultural policies hold the possibility of finding greater resonance than the US's in multinational IGOs or conferences within which much of the decisions pertaining to our collective future will be decided. COVID-19 has affected China's growing influence but not in such a manner as would permanently reverse the development of that influence. So the challenge—which, in fact, includes the content and structure of rules that will govern our individual and joint future—is here, although its true character is not being publicly stated. The focus has been on China's alleged military challenge, which former secretary of the treasury Henry M. Paulson rightly dismissed in his speech at the Bloomberg New Economy Forum.[825]

The task before us, therefore, is to find a means to control or influence those "forces" that appear, as political realism contends, to override human moral agency so that the US and China (and the world) can make use of the respective impressive achievements of these two countries—their competitive spirit, their ingenuity, and their other resources—to further and build toward a more mature, self-sustaining, global community, a community in which China can freely learn from the US and, although not often thought about, the US can learn from China. We can do so by soliciting the gradual implementation of claims that both the US and China have made about themselves and the future they seek; link these futures to the broader ends being pursued by groups and institutions within the international system, including the UN; focus on a special commitment within the UDHR to which countries have pledged themselves; progressively reject the lies parading as facts (really propaganda) in international political and social life; and help individuals rediscover their broader selves.

---

[825] See remarks by Henry M. Paulson Jr. at the Bloomberg New Economic Forum, November 16, 2020.

China claims that it is working toward political democracy by 2049, thereby putting in place the entire family of human rights—that is, bringing the civil and political into operational partnership with the economic, social, and cultural. The US, which has championed the civil and the political (although selectively only), could be asked to work on implementing the economic, social, and cultural class of the family of rights by a specified date also, with issues such as voter suppression, campaign financing (should presidential elections cost $6 billion?), and equality in public service employment addressed, the gerrymandering of congressional districts discontinued, and racial equality, not simply nondiscrimination, affirmed.[826] These changes not only would help the US deal with corroding domestic social issues but also could morally help other countries unite the two halves of the family of human rights. As important, the issue of race, which has haunted the country from its origin (masking itself internationally in a variety of guises, including orientalism), could be openly addressed to the benefit of both Washington and Beijing. (David Levitte, diplomat and public intellectual whose position on US–China relations we earlier discussed, was anxious not only that the US might fail in its confrontation with China but also that Europe might not be ready to take the mantle of world leadership from the US. His principal fear was that a non-European state might become the dominant power in the world.[827])

Among the broader ends that political and cultural groups, nations, and IGOs have been trying to achieve is that of the removal of the "war culture," making it fully possible to integrate both of the two categories of human rights that we have been discussing, and open the way for the type of human intellectual and moral solidarity that could make other international achievements possible, including wrestling with the issue of race. This course of action would begin with the Global Zero Action Plan (GZAP), which is an organized effort by

---

[826] The presidential campaign of 2020 alone cost about $6 billion. The campaigns for members of the House of Representatives and for the Senate, combined with the presidential campaign, cost about $14 billion. This is hardly an example for the world. See "2020 election to cost $14 billion, blowing away spending records" by OpenSecrets.org, Center for Responsible Politics, posted October 28, 2020.

[827] See Levitte, op. cit.

governments, NGOs, and individuals, building on the efforts of the US and the former USSR, to dismantle and eliminate nuclear weapons by the one hundredth anniversary of the UN's establishment in 1945.[828] This effort or development could, in the post-2045 period, move to all weapons of mass destruction and help realize the US's goal of saving "succeeding generations from the scourge of war." Indeed, with the emerging network culture, the knowledge of the roles that networks serve in modern culture, new information on the parts that plant and non-human kingdoms play in promoting a sense of community,[829] and the idea of human associations constituting a kind of "social flesh" to be nurtured and protected),[830] the reduction of the war culture would likely offer some space for the emergence of a peace culture.[831]

Since behavior of the kind associated with a nonnuclear weapons future would not only bear with it concrete outcomes in general weapons reduction but, as well, have specific related items of conduct—living up to the international promise to make outer space weapons free, for example—it follows that, like the seabed outside national jurisdiction, humans would insist on ensuring that the exploration and use of outer space be engaged in, as committed to, on behalf of humankind. The spillover effect of all these actions, especially domestically, could be broad investments in education, housing, physical infrastructure

---

[828] See "The Global Action Plan" at https://www.globalzero.org/reaching-zero/.

[829] George C. Williams, through his "Pleiotropy, Natural Selection, and the Evolution of Senescence," in *Evolution*, Vol. 11, #4 (December 1957), pp. 398–411, influenced generations into thinking that we are primarily and even exclusively selfish. So we have had successors such as Richard Dawkins, in his *The Selfish Gene* (Oxford: Oxford University, 1976), among others, following. As a result of seminal research from others, we now know better. See Swami Iyer and Timothy Killingback, "Evolution of Cooperation in Social Dilemmas of Complex Networks," in *PLOS Computational Biology*, Vol. 12, #2: doi:10.1371/journal. pcbi.1004779 (February 2016). See also Ferris Jabr, "The Social Life of Forests," in *New York Times Magazine* (December 6, 2020), pp. 34–41.

[830] See Sharon V. Betcher, *Spirit and Obligation of Social Flesh: A Secular Theology for the Global City* (New York: Fordham University Press, 2014).

[831] See for example, Daisaku Ikeda, *Toward a Culture of Peace: A Cosmic View* (Tokyo: Soka Gakkai International, 1999); Elise Boulding, *Cultures of Peace: The Hidden Side of History* (Syracuse: Syracuse University Press, 2000).

(such as roads, airports, ports, railroads, and dams), and public health, among things. As important, the 2017 Treaty on the Prohibition of Nuclear Weapons (TPNW), with its emerging popular support not only to ban nuclear weapons but also to prohibit their use or threat of use (the countries of Latin America and the Caribbean, the South Pacific, Southeast Asia, Africa, and Central Asia are already committed by treaties to be nuclear-weapons-free zones), should give more political weight to the GZAP.[832]

Coupled with the above moves to remove the culture of war (and the collaboration between the US and China, along with other highly armed countries, would constitute a course of conduct without many parallels in human history) would have to be concurrent and concurring steps taken to deal with the military security needs of the world. This would require using the pressure brought to bear on the elimination of weapons of mass destruction to a reform of the UN in a manner that allows for greater certainty of global *community* action (not any individual country or regional group) against every form of military aggression and strengthen the efforts to outlaw war itself through the work of institutions such as the International Criminal Court (ICC), against which the US has fought and whose chief prosecutor came under sanctions, alienating many allies in doing so.[833] For the first time, indeed, Article 28 of the UDHR could begin its operative application—everyone is "entitled to a social and international order in which the rights and freedoms set forth in the Declaration can be fully realized."[834] (The drafters of the declaration and the two international covenants—which, together, constitute the International Bill of Human Rights—understood that as long as there are wars, the social and international order necessary for the full realization of the rights that the bill embodies could never be realized.)

---

[832] See Tariq Rauf, "Does the TPNW Contradict or Undermine the NPT?" in *Toda Global Outlook,* published by the Toda Peace Institute, Honolulu, November 22, 2020.

[833] See Pranshu Verma, "US sanctions on court alienate allies," in *Boston Globe* (October 19, 2020), p. A2.

[834] See Article 28 0f the UDHR.

Matters of the environment—another area that speaks to the concept of community, as before indicated—could also give offerings to some confidence building as the US and China individually and jointly move to rid their respective societies of the use of oil and gas, from which so much of the fossil fuels that adversely affect the environment come. China is the largest emitter of those fuels in the world, and the US is the largest per capita emitter. Both are also advancing aggressively in the area of electrical vehicles, and they could, in the midst of commercial competition in vehicles, collaborate in accelerating the process of getting these vehicles to the rest of the world. US companies could generate trillions of dollars in so working with China, and other areas of the world could join and cooperate in this effort and in other areas of alternative energy. Likewise, since the armed forces around the world consume much of the fossil fuel we currently use, a reduction in armed forces, especially as more and more of the nonnuclear weapons states are included, would bring with it a reduction in international tensions worldwide, limit the need for networks of national military bases, and open opportunities for the solution of certain problems—the South China Sea, for example, some of the problems associated with which are from a moral and political colonial past that should not be allowed to control our future. One may even see the US join the International Seabed Authority, by way of ratifying the law of the sea convention, to help manage the world's oceans.

The differences between the US and China in the area of economics, especially that which is broadly said to be structural—meaning the US is organized around the concept and practice of private property, while China is built around public property (including an inter-generational public)—will not be resolved soon. Some modifications will take place through the movement of each country toward those dimensions of the family of human rights it has, thus far, least emphasized; others will come through investments and trade. For China, a move to emphasize more CPR will entail a reduction in the role of government in the life of its society; for the US, its shift to focus more on ESCR will require expanded government involvement in the ongoing operations of economic life.

A recent suggestion that *reciprocity* must become a more central feature of US–China relations, if differences are not to exacerbate those relations, should be welcomed because the principle would bring with it some features of community that, properly understood, have been missing from the self-regulating market.[835] It is also a principle that carries with it an aura of fairness, equality, and respect. Defined generally, it is the practice by which, in the exchange of things between or among parties, mutual benefits accrue to each, especially in terms of privileges given or offered by one (a country, for example) to another. Mutual benefits are not always comparable or equal, however. One party to an exchange (A offers to gives up 50 percent of its military vessels in return for B doing the same, with A having five hundred such ships at the time of the offered exchange and B having but ten) could leave the other in a more vulnerable position in relationship to the first party than before. Alexander Hamilton understood this in devising the economic model that the US followed from the 1790s to the 1930s, when, like Britain when the latter was far ahead of other industrial countries, it offered reciprocity.

The reader will recollect that Hamilton's position, very much as Germany's,[836] maintained the stance that "the United States cannot exchange on equal terms with Europe"[837] because equal terms do not mean equal returns. Equal terms between parties who occupy unequal positions guarantee unequal returns; this is why the US sought to protect its less mature industries from 1790 to 1934, when the reciprocal trade act was passed by Congress. This is why China now seeks to protect its less mature industries also and why the US, who has lagged behind China in commercial 5G, has sought to shut China's multinational company, Huawei, out of the US and the markets of its allies, although

---

[835] See "Targeted Reciprocity" by Paulson, op. cit., in his November 16, 2020, speech at the Bloomberg New Economy Forum, hereinafter referred to as "Balanced Relations with China."

[836] See Friedrich List, "Political and Geopolitical Economy," in George T. Crane and Abla Awami, eds., *The Theoretical Evolution of International Political Economy: A Reader* (Oxford: Oxford University Press, 1990), pp. 48–54.

[837] See Alexander Hamilton's "Report on Manufactures" in Crane and Awami, ibid., p. 41.

the reasons that it has publicly offered say nothing about China's current supremacy.[838] A worked-out US–China plan of "targeted reciprocity" that is consistent with the interests of the global community and offers protection to their respective less mature industries would ensure that true reciprocity will have taken place. It is what China claims to be seeking for itself and others, so it could not now possibly reject reciprocity, called for by the former treasury secretary. In the quoted speech, he said nothing about reciprocity, however, for the IP represented by the "best minds from around the world" that he sought to have the US attract and retain; he said nothing about the Global South or of Russia and Eastern Europe. So we are left uncertain about what reciprocity fully entails. One thing is certain—his admission that, as we before said, community means all its members.

Equality cannot be voluntarily conceded by political realists because they view human nature in such a negative light and on account of their further contention that this nature does not and, in fact, cannot change. So the basic selfishness and wickedness as well as its anti-communal character can but be controlled, domestically and internationally. The believers, of course, generally exempt themselves from this selfishness because of how often they portray themselves as acting in the wider national and global interest.

Since there are cultural differences between and among nations, the fixed attribute of selfishness and anti-communal disposition of "foreigners" make them even more dangerous. Power, as in the case of domestic politics, is the only safeguard against disorder and barbarism. Cultural differences, some real and others confected, have therefore been deployed as part of policy (from the ancient Athenians to the present) and are emphasized to instill fear of the other (including the racial other). Power balances abroad, as at home, must be created, manipulated, and maintained as a socialized view of even those, such as former President Obama—viewed as enlightened by some—in his policy toward China.[839] He, for example, in seeking to "put down a set of clear markers on US priorities" in its relationship with China—managing the

---

[838] See Andrew Ross Sorkin, "Huawei Aside, U.S. Lags in the Race for Supremacy in 5G," in *New York Times* (July 2, 2019), pp. B1, B4.

[839] See Barack Obama, *A Promised Land* (New York: Crown, 2020), p. 461.

economic crisis he inherited and the North Korean nuclear program, the need to resolve peacefully the maritime disputes in the South China Sea, the treatment of dissidents in China, and the "push for new sanctions against Iran"—said, in respect of the last item, "I appealed to Chinese self-interest, warning that without meaningful diplomatic action, either we or the Israelis might be forced to strike Iran's nuclear facilities, with far worse consequences for Chinese oil supply."[840]

This blackmail is part of what the apostles of the realist creed often refer to as "soft power," and it had messages, not immediately apparent to others, to China, especially to the South China Sea, around which a blockade by the US could be established to cut off China's oil supply. The reader will also note the number of countries potentially implicated, in addition to many more that depend on Iran's supply of oil and to the world at large. Reflections should also be accorded to Allison's contention about the limited to no moral agency on the part of leaders during crises. Here, we have the realist language—"might be *forced* to strike [emphasis the author's]." Human beings have been morally and socio-politically hijacked by realist thinking, from Thucydides forward, although in a subtle way, the revered historian was seeking to teach his readers about the wages of selfishness.[841] What political realists fear are human connections that they cannot control directly or indirectly, including those, in this volume, that China has been forging with the Global South, whether those connections are across gender, race, religion, nationality, property, social origins, geographies, or other markers. It is why they have a suspicion of *human* rights—because conceptually, those rights call for connections across all the markers. These rights and the community they imply and envision invite the suspicion of political realism because they potentially operate to limit the advantages of power and domination in the form of knowledge (technological and scientific and, more broadly, cultural), property ownership, and what coercive forces confer and nurture. The latter is frequently announcing its subtle presence under the cover of theories

---

[840] Ibid. He was speaking to his Chinese counterpart, Pres. Hu Jintao.

[841] It is my view that Thucydides was teaching us that absent a government structure that is coextensive with the larger universe of states, there was little hope for peace or the containment of the disease of war.

of history, patterns of policies, or, more comprehensively, practices in international relations that include the dispossession of those sources of power in others on various grounds of merit and truth.

The attitude and thinking bequeathed to the world by political realism and political realists gave us World War II, with its horrors of genocide and nuclear weapons, the morally repellant, the wicked instrument that scientists brought into being, the assault that it represented on the house of reason by the very people who were ostensibly our most advanced representatives of that reason, of Western enlightenment, and the thralldom to which it consigned humanity in what we have come to call the Cold War. The UN, representing a partial inspiration against this wickedness and assault, saw the soul of that inspiration tamed and, in some instances, quashed because a focus on domination, broadly approved ideologically, came with heroic standing, with weapons systems pushed by enabling academic and other willing agents, ensured that one side in the Cold War had one step ahead of the other ("the enemy") in armed lethality.

A vicious nationalism (branded as patriotism, as were war departments as defense departments)[842] came to feed the Cold War, and it prevented people, by and large, from seeking the general good that the UN was supposed to have represented; they were, instead, pressured to choose between the "armed lethalities," called the East and the West, and to forget their own moral impulses. A new Cold War is what is being suggested again, in what Paulson rightly characterizes as "pernicious" attacks on China, in the latter's challenge to the US.[843] We ought not to allow a repetition of the Cold War as the earlier idea of community and the efforts to have it define our common future urge.

Another course of action should be pursued in general. We should, as Paulson has done, begin to focus on how these two countries, despite their differences, operate to confer benefits on each other and how their respective traditions have cultural offerings that are admirable and invite emulation. This is part of what we, earlier in the book, indicated

---

[842]   See Stanley, *Einstein's War*, op. cit.

[843]   Paulson, op. cit.

Pres. Jiang Zemin had proposed to former secretary of state Henry Kissinger.

Rather than always pointing to the unilateralism of US conduct in its search to undermine China or vice versa, Beijing, for example, could encourage the portrayal of the US and its market as important for not only the goods and services that China currently produces but also many that it is likely to produce in the future since both countries are increasingly moving to convergences in the type of technological and scientific achievements they boast. The US's position in the all-important climate change area is likely to complement much of that which China has been espousing, and Washington's position on IP, although different from that of China's, is one in which both sides can move to work out a mutually satisfactory, timely solution—one compatible with the interests of the world at large and incorporating some relevant principles contained in the CERDS. Further, China can indicate that it has benefited from some of the knowledge produced by US universities, the organizational emphases of its scientific and business culture, and the products of its agriculture. Collaborations in the energy field have also been mutually helpful. Washington, on the other hand, as Paulson has suggested (and we have touched on previously in the book), could point to China's importance in the purchase of the US's agricultural products and its purchase of debt, thus helping keep interest rates low for everyone and helping the dollar and the US. China's market is and will be important to US multinational companies for the sale of their products, thereby offering employment to the US's workers and other such companies that have invested in China and, thereby, sent cheaper goods to the US, and technologically, while the US has problems with China in the area of IP, far from being a site of IP theft, China has been a seat of a long tradition of scientific and technological excellence.

Representation of the sort above indicated would begin to provide some grounds for an emphasis on good faith "cooperative competition,"[844] as China calls it, and provide for the opening up of the world to the spectacular variety of new discoveries—in methods, processes, and ideas in science, technology, and culture, generally, flowing from

---

[844] Fu Ying, "China and U.S. Can Have Cooperative Competition," in *New York Times* (November 25, 2020), p. A. 23.

Australia, Brazil, Canada, Germany, Ghana, India, Iran, Israel, Japan, Mexico, Russia, South Korea, and Vietnam, among others, in addition to the US and China. The idea of community is not one that the US will ever find easy to accept in the short run, but its own demographic changes, both cultural and generational, will help. With all the efforts to depict it as something inferior to society, something that only the weak in spirit and the less virile aspire to, it would be challenging to make a public case for it today unless one were willing to use the US military as an example of which, institutionally, community thrives and is the basis for success. Businesses, including sports teams, can affirm this experience, if not the concept or principle. A corresponding difficulty will be the idea of leadership, which President Biden sees the US has had as an inheritance.[845] The US sees the future in terms of that leadership, unfortunately confused with domination.

No area of change will have as salutary an effect as that involving the US's self-ascribed concept of itself. That self, which is imbibed by most citizens and directs its society's behavior internally and internationally, has isolated the US from its actual self, from the rest of the world, and from any felt need to reconcile exceptionality (the exceptional self) with actual everyday behavior. If the US were to move toward that reconciliation, it could then justly claim its standing as a great nation but not an exceptional one; that it is heir to the same types of sins it so generously and varyingly claims all other peoples and countries have inherited; that the frequent assertions of "this is not who we are" (denying the unpleasant things it does) are not simply contradictions in terms but unfortunate patterns of practice engaged in to gain approval of untruths; that the ethic that says that what matters, domestically and internationally, is not the character of a given deed but the author or site of the deed (from terrorism to human rights) has to be reversed; and that for it, democracy has, for a long time, been seen as a fine pursuit (domestically and globally) as long as the pursuit does not impair Washington's right to rule.

---

[845] See Biden, op. cit. See also his statement that America is back to claim that inheritance in Jennifer Epstein, "Biden on his team: 'America is back,'" in *Boston Globe* (November 25, 2020), p. A2. See also Peter Beinart, "The U.S. Doesn't Have to 'Lead' the World," in *New York Times* (December 6, 2020), p. SR2.

Needing to be acknowledged too is that "brand management," as many young people are contending, is not the best way to assess conduct; that the free market in every country has never been as free as preached and that every country, including China, has had to face the issue of the proper balance that should exist between economy and polity (as Xi is seeking to do with his private sector and the US and the EU with theirs, including major social media companies); that experiments in this balancing are worldwide and ongoing (from Australia, Brazil, and Japan to Mexico, New Zealand, South Africa, and Spain); that the self-making persons as well as the rational and enlightened society of Jefferson are neither as rational nor as enlightened (one has but to look at our national inability to marshal collective efforts to deal with COVID-19 and the capacity of limited government of preached self-reliance in Texas to deal with an unusual 2021 winter) as has been supposed and posed; and that the US and China are less unlike than is being admitted.

Removing these "hidden inaccuracies" or avoiding having to engage in them is part and parcel of being freed from the lie of exceptionalism. So too would an admission respecting the "clash of civilizations" and the embrace of political realism. In the case of the first, very much like the clamors to "make America great again" (which seeks to ensure continued white domination at home), the clash of civilizations seeks to have Western civilization led by US continue to dominate the world. For over four hundred years, the "clash of civilizations" has been in being, whether one looks at the Founding Fathers' and their successors' conduct toward Native Americans or at Britain's or other European powers' imperial march into Africa, Asia (including China and India), and what are today called Australia and New Zealand, Latin America, and the Caribbean. Allison, Huntington, and other like thinkers took no note of this phenomenon. Only in the beginning of a challenge to Western domination is there, for them, a clash. The permanent presence of political realism in public life is to be seen in like vein.

Alterations in the form of amendments to the US constitution have taken place to reflect cultural and other changes that have taken place since the founding of the republic or, even more tellingly, changes as the world has moved from a pre-Copernican or post-Ptolemian one in science and technology (with the US admirably leading in both).

Washington, however, keeps returning to an unchanged 2,500-year-old mode of thinking that has imparted to humankind an unbroken pattern of historical "killing fields" for the bauble of power and to justify sought and gloried-in international domination. Domestically, the thinking encompasses social-class-dominating and defending states. (China, it should be observed, is also a social-class-dominating and defending state. It, however, gives preference to a social class other than that protected by the US.) Europe, whose reaction toward the Washington–Beijing rivalry could be determining of certain outcomes, before touched on, has been seeking greater leeway in international action, especially as the secondary impact of US sanctions against countries has disrupted the economies of an ever-widening range of countries.[846]

Earlier, in this conclusion, I indicated that at the current juncture on the move toward globalization, as previously defined, it was more in favor of China than the US. Washington enjoyed advantages in the first phases of globalization with its neoliberal outlook and emphasis and the almost unbridled advocacy of selfishness. Now at home (especially among the young) and increasingly abroad, in general, there appears to be (including conservative governments) a converging focus on "the other," although the spotlight on the individual is fighting back. If the social focus continues (and in my view, it should in the face of increased awareness human and human–nature interdependence), it

---

[846] Secondary sanctions refer to the use by the US of its centrality in the effective operation of the global economy to impose economic sanctions against targeted states—Russia or Iran, for example—with reverberating impacts on countries and businesses that are not the targeted state or its companies. The impact of those non-targeted state or companies is referred to as secondary sanctions. At times, the US specifically, using the dollar, stipulates that all companies dealing with the targeted state are subject to the sanction. The European Union, whose economy is deeply integrated with the US's, often finds itself forced to support policies that it finds inconsistent with its own interests. For a sense of how the EU is thinking of its future (greater autonomy in foreign affairs), see Emmanuel Macron, Angela Merkel, and Macky Sall et al., "A Crisis for One Is a Threat to All," in the *Boston Globe* (February 3, 2021), p. A11. One might also look at President Biden's first foreign policy speech on February 5, 2021, in which he indicated that America must lead and "is back" to do so. Transcript from Reuters.

would mean less support for the current US socioeconomic model. Contingent on whether Beijing moves, as promised, toward political democracy (and I would suggest that China change the date from 2049 to 2045 to correspond with the date of other changes mentioned in this chapter), it could become more aligned with the trends in globalization. People are, in addition, unwilling to accept unfairness in everyday life, demanding greater government subsidy (the most remarkable subsidy worldwide is that which the US enjoys by virtue of its owning the world's key currency) to relieve their plight. They will not freely accept the values of an economic system that says that large portions of the human family are disposable. Neither are they inclined to acquiesce in the view that there is no alternative to the socio-political outlook called realism, although a 2021 anonymous memorandum (emulating George Kennan's 1946 long telegram on the former USSR) from a "senior government official" is now urging the forging of the same old balance of power practices, even including an alliance with Russia, to move against China.[847]

At the foundation of all the conflicts narrated above is the threatening norm of equality (and its moral and political twin, self-determination). In political economy in particular but in cultural life in general (including science and technology), it will prove to be the most important single feature of our individual and collective moral life for the rest of this century. Science, which proudly claims to be universal, as seen from the JASON Report, will struggle to sustain that universality and the equality that it implies, and if one were to look at matters geopolitically, the "Grand Area" (and the reader is encouraged to look at the political geography of that area on the third map), especially as seen with the Indo-Pacific area, which effectively gives the US almost unassailable control of the world's oceans, will be the focus of special "protection"

---

[847] See "The Longer Telegram: Toward a New American China Strategy" (Atlantic Council, Scowcroft Center for Strategic Security, 2021). In this longer telegram, which urges a thirty-five-year-long strategic confrontation, we find not only the call for a new Cold War, with all its ugly consequences for the world, but also intimations of the "whispered suggestions" to have China and the Global South become technological colonies (they will have inferior technology), while the Global North will enjoy superior technological sway.

by Washington's policy. That policy will increasingly include, as was the case with Britain during the nineteenth century, Central and South Asia; it will also replicate much of London's efforts to prevent Germany from becoming an equal. As in the case of Japan, which inveighed against the structure of international inequality, China will continue to seek equality. Like Athens, the US will claim that it is a democracy and model for the world, even as its actual behavior rejects equality and knows no legal or moral restraint.

The world could become as Orwell, in his dystopian *Nineteen Eighty-Four* work, warned. States, using realism and a contempt for democracy (as in the case of Athens, which wanted to define and write the rules), will resist broad, collective rule making. It is the hope of this author that this book offers some modest contribution to direct the world away from experiencing the consequences of that warning.[848]

---

[848] Here, we are referring to the emergence of three super states—Oceania, Euro-Asia, and Eastasia—and their reducing human beings to non-human status.

EPILOGUE

Some of developments which are pertinent to the focus of the book have come to be, since its completion. Among them are the March 2021 US-China meeting in Alaska, the Biden administration's reinforcement of its predecessor's charge that China has been engaged in genocide in Xinjiang, the revival of an earlier, alleged Beijing cover-up of the source of Covid-19, the Endless Frontier Act, President Biden's March 25, 2021 news conference, the return of "communist" as pejorative noun or adjective to define China, and discussions concerning certain inter-company collaboration to help deal with Covid-19. We will touch on each, in the reverse order of mention.

The discussion respecting inter-company collaboration refers to the Biden administration's success in getting Merck and Johnson & Johnson (two of the world's largest pharmaceutical companies) to engage in a historic manufacturing cooperation in order to expand the production of the other company's Covid-19 vaccine. This salutary joint effort, in which intellectual property concerns took a backseat to social well-being, contrasts sharply with the difficulties of gaining collective action from the nation's governors. What is not being said or pointed-to is how the selfish operation of private, intellectual property rights have limited rich nation's opportunities to vaccinate the world, and the associated self-justifying attacks on China which, in extending vaccine to countries (especially the Global South) has been depicted as courting political influence. Perhaps the most telling but unacknowledged feature of this discussion is the on-going competition for the future social ordering of the world—an ordering to be weighted in favor of community or in favor of society.

As regards the emerging, intensified focus on China as a "communist state," that focus is the tactical ideological shift that was predicted in other portions of the book—a course of action, by Washington, designed to make more effective questions concerning China's trustworthiness. Evidence of a charge need not be adduced; one has but to associate the charge with the discredited communists who are, naturally, or, needless to say, or it stands to reason, or, inescapably, are untrustworthy. Constructed claims based on events in Hong Kong, Xinjiang, the South China Sea, the WTO, Taiwan, or interference in US' elections can then be lumped together as inarguable evidence of that untrustworthiness.

This sewing of distrust has many adverse effects, nationally, internationally, and globally. It colors the views and feelings of citizens; this coloring limits the range of policy actions governments (in Beijing and Washington, but elsewhere, also) can undertake; it reinforces existing prejudices, everywhere; exposes Asians to all types of human rights violations, including violence; and sabotages the post-World War II commitment, memorialized in UNESCO's constitution, that the stereotyping of others should be brought to an end. It does more: as in the case of some culturally poisoning tactics followed by tobacco and oil companies which, respectively, sought to defeat evidence for the cause of cancer and global warming, Washington is bent on doubt-sewing. The focus of the companies was not to prove that cigarette or fossil fuel was safe, but to sew doubts, distrust, about the evidence that showed tobacco and fossil fuel to be dangerous. Any strength that China represents or embodies that challenges US must be delegitimized, discredited, or doubted, including in matter pertaining to Covid-19.

With respect to President Biden's news conference, apart from reasserting that China has become a strategic challenge to US global leadership and that this challenge will not be allowed to succeed "under [his] watch," the most important statement he made on US-China relations was that the latter country, consistent with Moynihan's advice, will be forced, in an "unrelenting way," to defend its human rights record. Conforming to US' record, Biden was really referring to the civil and political group, within the family of human rights. This group, of course, includes democracy, which is in trouble within the U.S., under the electoral possibilities of the 1964 Civil Rights Act, not to mention under the terms of article 21 section 2 of the UDHR, and of section 3 of the same article, which speaks of universal and equal suffrage, not just ritual elections the results of which are often purchased by money, geographic carvings of electoral districts, or selective exclusions of entire populations such as that of the District of Columbia.

Perhaps most important is that Biden's position ensures the continuation of the use of the civil and political cluster of human rights to mask and confer immunity on US' violations of the economic, social, and cultural cluster of those rights. (Biden's social melioration proposals should not be confused with recognition of the latter body of rights).

This brings us to the Endless Frontier Act (EFA), which was introduced in US Senate in May of 2020 but was given a special legislative push in early 2021 by Senate majority leader, Charles Schumer. The goal of the bill is to ensure US' leadership in "critical technologies" through "fundamental research" in areas such as artificial intelligence, high performance computing, and advanced manufacturing, with centers built throughout the country and with each center conjointly focused on the protection of national security. The reader will note that the "critical" areas covered in this paragraph mirror categories that were previously touched on and, also, have emphasis in China. What is new here, apart from the special push by Senator Schumer, is that unlike the recommendation and operation of the JASON Report (which focuses on the economic weakening of China without an alternative, if that focus fails), the EFA seeks to follow the advice of business, academic, as well as other leaders, who urge a kind of complementary US' emphasis on signal scientific and technological advance that they believe will enable Washington to compete successfully with and outdistance Beijing.

China's alleged coverup of its being the site of biochemical experiments that, by accident, resulted in Covid-19 is something that was "whispered" and occasionally asserted by a few public officials. For some time to come, this country and the world will find themselves at the edge of facing a claim that there is "evidence" of Beijing's concealment of the fact of its being the site of biological experiments that went wrong. Worse, this concealment or absence of transparency, it will be claimed, is what caused the world-wide pandemic. Thus, China owes the world an explanation (US will become a representative of the world, in this respect). The absence of that explanation, or transparency satisfactory to Washington, will be parlayed as the major cause for the breakdown of US-China relations. One, at this juncture, has but to note that the "Spanish Flu" (from which there was an estimated 500 million infections, and 50 million deaths, of which over 650,000 were from US) was first identified in Kansas City; and that the then US' president, Woodrow Wilson's disclosures about the flu (to US and the world) make President Xi's seem garrulous. If the US has evidence that China is concealing, as it alleges, that evidence should be shared with the world—the UN Security Council, for example, and not evidence from some CIA-sponsored agent from China One should also bear in mind that antecedents to (one may even say preparations for) the on-going confrontation with China began before 2010; that presidents and prime ministers, in many countries (including the US), were less than forthcoming to their respective citizens and the people of the world, in their initial encounter with Covid-19. China shared with the world a draft genome of Covid-19 on January 11, 2020.

The issue of alleged genocide in Xinjiang, I initially treated as part of an unfortunate exaggeration, in which the use of terms such as "concentration camps" (given the latter term's historical meaning) was indefensible. When the Biden administration continued to use the term genocide, however, to characterize alleged goings-on in Xinjiang (perhaps as part of the promised "unrelenting" tactic of charging China with human rights abuses), I noticed that the reference would sometimes come with a qualifier--"virtual" genocide, for example. It then occurred to me that US might be referring to article II (b) and (c) of the genocide convention. These two sections, respectively, refer to the intentional "causing of serious bodily or mental harm to members of the group," and the "inflicting on the group conditions of life calculated to bring about its physical destruction in whole or in part" as constituting genocide. The recited, prohibited actions in the identified two sections is part of what is sometimes labeled "indirect" or "hidden" genocide, as distinct from the direct, organized mass killing of members of an ethnic, national, racial, or religious group, with the intent to destroy it, in part or in whole. In short, genocide refers to action deliberately taken, directly or indirectly, to eliminate, partly or wholly, the physical existence of a cultural group.

If, as I suspect, US has been referring to China as embracing an indirect route to genocide, it (US) would have to show how what China has called "reeducation camps"—centers Beijing has used throughout its post-1949 socio-political life to pursue the political indoctrination of people considered subversives, ideological deviants, or political enemies—differ in Xinjiang today from what has always been a PRC's pattern of conduct. Xi himself is a product of such re-education camps which, of course, can vary in the experiences people have in and with them. Second, why would Washington point to China's behavior in Xinjiang and not to that of Saudi Arabia, since 2015, in Yemen, where over 8 million of the latter country's citizens (including over a million children) are at the brink of starvation? Is anyone in doubt that such conditions are causing "serious bodily or mental harm"? Or that such conditions are calculated to bring about the physical destruction, at least, to part, of the group—the Yemeni (or the Houti subgroup)? The US and Britain have been complicit with Saudi Arabia (and complicity in genocide is itself a crime.) And how would such a charge of genocide in Xinjiang, against China, square with the conduct of US-UK in their expulsion of all Chagossians (1967-1973) from their homeland in Diego Garcia (the largest island in the Chagos Archipelago), in the Indian Ocean, to enable the building of a secret military base on that island? No Chagossian lives in Diego Garcia, today; they are scattered, in declining numbers, in the Seychelles, Mauritius, and the UK. How might US respond to a counter charge of continuing indirect genocide in respect of the Native Americans? Genocide, indirect or direct, should never be indulged.

Out of respect for the opinions and moral commitments of the people of the world, for the universal normative force of the legal and moral prohibitions against genocide, and for the intellectual and cultural solidarity supportive of those prohibitions (not in response to the charge of the U.S.) China would be well advised to allow members of the UN's human rights committee, or some other agreed-on independent body) to review its alleged activities in Xinjiang. Such a course of conduct would clarify matters for and to the world.

The final issue area is the US-China meeting in Alaska. In my view, the results of that meeting strengthens what has been argued elsewhere in the book. Like Athens, which preached the realist worldview of self-interest but insisted on defining that interest for others, the US "accepts" that China seeks and is entitled to follow its self-interest, providing it (China) conforms the advancing of that interest to "the rule-based order that maintains global stability," according to the delegation leader, Secretary of State, Anthony Blinken. The rule-based order (including US' model of democracy, which it sees as a model for the world, not that urged by the UDHR), is an expression of Washington's interest defined in the form of rules shaped by Washington; and the United States, as Athens said to ancient Greece, is saying that China's interest must conform to what US' interest, expressed in the rules that make up the order, permit or say it should be. Hence the PRC's angry response to the Secretary of State and his delegation-associates, that US should "stop advancing its own democracy in the rest of the world," including China. The latter country has its own model and will be self-determining.

Not to be overlooked is the psychological atmosphere within which the just mentioned US-China meeting took place. It was one in which China had been accused of a new hacking—the gaining of unauthorized access to US' information systems. The issue here is not so much any complaint about specific hacking actions, but the continuing fact pattern of US portraying itself—and especially its citizens—as victims, as vulnerable victims (which, potentially, every country in fact, including US is).

What is not being said, as in the case of Athens (the UK used it well against Germany), is that the US has become a victim of growing equality, in this case, in cyber warfare. Washington has been engaging in cyber conflict—conflict of a scale grander than anything China can currently boast. But other countries, including China, are catching up. The National Security Agency and the Central Intelligence Agency routinely break into foreign information systems to gain access to and steal secrets. They are highly adept at doing so. The Pentagon even has its own Cyber Command organization, guided by the proactive (not defensive) doctrine of "defend forward," meaning that US, as a matter of policy, seeks to engage in pre-emptive rather than reactive actions in cyber warfare. This doctrine has been amply attested to in the 2007 Stuxnet attack on an Iranian nuclear research facility, sabotaging that country's uranium enrichment centrifuges.

GLOSSARY

AIIB. The Asian Infrastructure Investment Bank, the AIIB, is a multilateral development bank that was created in 2016 by China with a $100 billion capital. Its aim is to help promote the economic and social development of Asia, and it boasts ties with countries in other areas, including the West. It has over one hundred members.

ASEAN. This is the acronym for the ten-member Association of Southeast Asian Nations, which is an intergovernmental, regional organization that promotes economic, political, and security cooperation among its members.

Bandung. Bandung is the capital of Indonesia's West Java province and the site where, in 1955, an Afro-Asian conference took place and has worn its name—the Bandung Conference. That conference is identified with several accomplishments: it was the first time that formerly colonized countries met together as a group; its spirit sponsored the later development of the nonaligned movement (NAM); it elaborated a number of normative categories that have become major shapers of international relations; and the social conditions of its conferees have remained with the world in the group identity we currently call the Global South.

"Burma Road." This expression refers to a highway linking Lashio, in what was Eastern Burma (now Myanmar), with Kunming, in Yunnan Province, China. Completed in 1938, while Burma was still a colony of

Britain, the road allowed for the transport (over seven hundred miles) of materials to China as that country fought the Second Sino-Japanese War and during World War II as the US and Britain sought to help China frustrate the military Japan's push for a military conquest of China.

Cairo Declaration. This declaration was the result of the Cairo Conference of November 23, 1943, to November 26, 1943, attended by Pres. Chiang Kai-shek, Prime Minister Winston Churchill, and Franklin D. Roosevelt. That declaration was made on November 27, 1943, but issued as a communiqué on December 1, 1943. Among other things, it pledged continued support for the war against Japan, that "all the territories Japan had stolen from the Chinese—such as Manchuria, Formosa [Taiwan], and the Pescadores—shall be restored to the Republic of China," and that "in due course, Korea shall become free and independent."

Casus belli. This is the Latin name given to an act, event, or situation that is seen as provoking or justifying war.

Charter of Economics Rights and Duties of States (CERDS). This charter is one of the documents that form the body of the 1974 call for a new international economic order (the NIEO) that was advanced largely by the Group of 77 (many of which are part of the Global South) and adopted by the UN General Assembly.

China-Africa Development Fund. This is a fund (sometimes referred to as the CADF) that was established by China in 2007 as an equity investment fund—that is, it supports Chinese enterprises that invest in Africa.

CIDCA. This acronym stands for the China International Development Cooperation Agency. It is the principal agency of the Chinese government that now deals with foreign aid. It was established in 2018.

Civil and political rights (CPR). The expression refers to a class of human rights that focuses primarily on the protection of an individual's freedom from infringements by government and other individuals—the rights to free speech, to assemble, to receive and impart information, and to participate in the political life of society as well as the freedom of the press, of religion, of conscience and belief, and from torture.

Common heritage of mankind. This (also known as the "common heritage of humanity") is a principle in international law that holds that certain territorial areas ought not to become part of national sovereignty and must be preserved as humanity's common, natural, and cultural heritage and should be held, as such, in trust for the indefinite future.

Communiqué. A communiqué is an official statement, usually made to the media (and thus the world), to announce some important policy. In international diplomacy, such statements are generally associated with the organ of government that deals with foreign affairs or with the position of head of state or head of government.

Containment. This is the name given to a US foreign policy strategy against the former Soviet Union (USSR), aimed at limiting the geographic and political expansion of communism. Containment began in the later 1940s and lasted until the dissolution of the USSR in the early 1990s. Because China was viewed by Washington as part of the "communist bloc," it too was a target of containment.

Cultural Revolution. This phrase refers to the Great Proletarian Cultural Revolution (a violent socio-political effort engaged in by Mao Tze-tung between 1966 and 1976), which aimed to consolidate Mao's own thinking on what communism in China should be and ought to become. Millions died in the process of getting rid of the "four olds"—old custom, old habits, old culture, and old ideas. Every aspect of Chinese society was affected. Abroad, especially among the young and certain left-leaning cultural groups, the Chinese revolution was favorably contrasted with that of the Soviet Union, which was seen as having compromised its ideals. This cultural revolution also fed the view of China, in the West, as a radical, uncompromising, risk-courting, and even dangerous country.

DEAFIDBRB. The Declaration on the Elimination of All Forms of Intolerance and of Discrimination Based on Religion or Belief is a binding instrument adopted by the UN General Assembly in 1981 and has since, along with the International Bill of Human Rights, served as a source of protection against discrimination in the areas of religion or belief.

Debt trap. This is a phrase used in diplomatic and popular circles to describe or characterize a powerful country's or international institution's practice of seeking to gain political or other influence over a borrowing nation by burdening it with huge debt.

Détente. This diplomatic term designates a process of tension relaxation between nation-states that previously had a tense or strained relationship.

DOGICCP. The Declaration on the Granting of Independence to Colonial Countries and Peoples is a 1960 UN General Assembly declaration that is known for supporting several principles in international relations: the right of non–self-governing countries to become sovereign states (self-governing); the right to associate freely, once independence is won, with other sovereign states; and the right to determine, freely, the path they select to follow in their own respective development.

Economic, social, and cultural rights (ESCR). A complement to the civil and political class of rights, economic, social, and cultural rights are a group of rights that focuses on human socioeconomic conditions and prospects. This group or class of rights includes the rights to health care, housing, education, and food and, among others, to partake fully in science and culture.

Entente cordiale. This is a French expression that refers to a friendly or cordial understanding between states that had formerly been opponents. This friendly understanding falls short of an alliance.

Extraterritoriality. This is a term used in international law to denote a condition of being exempted or immune from the legal jurisdiction of a specified territory. Diplomatic representatives or international organizations enjoy this status within the borders of the states in which they are accredited or function. European imperial countries, through negotiations, backed by the threatened use of force, gained that status for their citizens and businesses within the territories of the non-European countries (including China) that they dominated.

FDI. Foreign direct investment specifies a type of investment that is made by individuals or corporations from one country into the business interests that are located in another country. FDI is said to exist when the investor establishes foreign business operations or acquires an existing business operation in another country.

Global South. The phrase broadly refers to those regions of the world—in Africa, Asia, Latin America, and Oceana—generally defined by low incomes, as distinct from the Global North (Europe, the US, and the latter's allies, such as Japan and South Korea in Asia, as well as Australia and New Zealand). It is one of a family of names, including the "Third World" and "the periphery," that are used to identify regions or countries of the world that are, generally, politically and culturally marginalized.

G7. The term refers to the Group of Seven, which is an intergovernmental organization composed of the nation-states with the world's largest developed economies: Canada, France, Germany, Italy, Japan, the UK, and the US. The last country formed and has led the group, which has sought to shape policy for the Western liberal order.

G77. The Group of 77 is a coalition of what is now over 130 developing countries (originally 77 in 1964, when the coalition was formed) that have sought to augment their joint economic and social interests by bargaining collectively.

Hegemony. The term denotes the dominance of one group (a state, for example, in international relations) over another or over others, always supported by practices, ideas, and norms that justify and legitimize the domination.

Hugo Grotius. He was a Dutch diplomat, lawyer, jurist, and playwright who wrote the classic *The Law of War and Peace*. He is considered, by many, to be the father of international law, and his work has had very important impacts on Asia, including China and Japan.

JNTUS. This stands for the "Japanese Note to the U.S." (December 7, 1941).

Kuomintang. It designates the "Chinese Nationalist Party," often referred to in English as the Nationalist Party of China (KMT), which ruled that country from 1912 to 1949, when, defeated in the civil war by Mao Tze-tung and the Chinese Communist Party (CCP), it fled with its leader, Chiang Kai-shek, to Taiwan. The KMT continues to exercise influence in Taiwan.

League of Nations. The first worldwide international organization, the League of Nations, was established in 1920 with the principal aim of providing peaceful resolutions of disputes between and among countries before those disputes erupt into war. It served the world until it was dissolved in 1946, having failed in its aim and mission. It was replaced by the United Nations.

Market socialism. This concept seeks to capture a blend of social or public ownership and the private market economy. Short-term private initiatives are recognized, encouraged, and even supported, in some instances, but those initiatives must be in conformity with the dominant framework provided by the state's long-term planning. China has been developing a market socialist model.

MFN. The "most favored nation" is the term used in international economic relations and politics to designate a status or level of trade treatment extended by one country to another. It is the central feature of the World Trade Organization, under whose terms any concession, privilege, or immunity granted to one nation in any trade agreement must be granted to all members. This is the principle of equality to which many in the US think China should not have been deemed eligible.

MOC. This refers to the Memorandum of Conversation between the US and Japan (December 1, 1941).

NAM. The Non-Aligned Movement was a movement that, although begun in spirit in Bandung in 1955, was formally began in 1961 in Belgrade, Yugoslavia. It is an international association of countries that do not want to be officially aligned against or with any major power or group. The movement has over 120 members.

NDB. The New Development Bank is the name given to the formerly referred to BRICS Development Bank that was established by BRICS states (Brazil, Russia, India, China, and South Africa). Established in 2014, with Beijing's leadership, the bank has as its mission the offering of support to public or private projects through loans, equity participation, guarantees, and other financial instruments.

Neocolonialism. This noun refers to a nation-state's use of economic, political, or cultural compulsion, pressure, or constraints to control or otherwise influence the behavior of other countries, especially former colonies or former non–self-governing peoples. In some countries, the term "soft power" is sometimes used to define this compulsion or pressure.

NIEO. This refers to a set of proposals that called for a different and "new international economic order." They were adopted by the UN General Assembly in 1974. Sponsored by many former colonial countries (especially the Group of 77), which argued that while political independence had been won, such was not the case in respect to economic matters, the proposals sought a major restructuring of the existing international economic system in favor of greater international, socioeconomic equality.

OBOR. One Belt One Road, also known in the West as the Belt Road Initiative (BRI), is a development strategy pursued by China, beginning with the building of a transcontinental physical infrastructure, that involves Chinese investment in about seventy countries. The land passage would link China with East Asia, South Asia, Central Asia,

Russia, and Europe, and the sea route aims to connect China with the East Pacific, West Asia (the Middle East), and Africa.

Open Door Policy. This speaks of a stance or policy (based on a statement of principles enunciated by the US in 1899 and 1900) that the US adopted toward China. Coming relatively late to the imperial game in the latter country—a game in which first-arriving imperial countries carved out preferred territorial and other privileges and rights in China—the US's open door policy self-servingly called for equal privileges and for the protection of China's territorial integrity. China benefitted from the US's insistence on the territorial integrity of China, especially in the latter country's second war with Japan.

Orientalism. This is a phrase that refers to a system or way of thinking that has dominated the West and its perception of (and action toward) the East, including the Islamic and Arab world and China, but later extended to cover much of what, in this book, is identified as the Global South.

Pact of Paris. Also known as the Kellogg–Briand Pact, this is a 1928 treaty that outlaws war as an instrument of policy. Leaders of Nazi Germany, among others, were seen as committing aggression (making war an instrument of policy) and were tried, convicted, and punished under its terms after World War II. During the interwar years, those terms were used to condemn the behavior of certain countries, such as Japan, including Tokyo's military actions in China.

Pacta sunt servanda. This is a Latin term that says that agreements (especially treaties) must be kept. It is a fundamental principle of international law.

Peaceful coexistence. The expression captures a concept that claims that peace between and among nations of widely differing social and political systems is possible and can be successfully pursued under a set of principles, including mutual respect for sovereignty and territorial integrity, noninterference in each other's/one another's internal affairs, and equality and mutual benefit. Peaceful coexistence has been a central stance of China since 1955 and even before.

Rapprochement. This is a diplomatic expression that refers to the process by which there is a warming up of relations between and among states, especially after a period of strained relations.

RCEP. The Regional Comprehensive Economic Partnership is a free trade agreement among fifteen countries in the Asia-Pacific region with about 30 percent of the world's people and 30 percent of the world's GDP, thus constituting the world's largest trading bloc. Although it has a very diverse membership—Australia, Brunei, Cambodia, China, Indonesia, Japan, Laos, Malaysia, Myanmar, New Zealand, the Philippines, Singapore, South Korea, Thailand, and Vietnam—China will likely emerge as the dominant leader and so will significantly influence its rules of engagement.

Shandong. An eastern Chinese province on the Yellow Sea, it and associated territories were part of an area of China that had been colonized by imperial Germany. China entered World War I on the side of the Allies with the understanding that if Germany were defeated, the peninsula would be returned to China. Japan, which had occupied the peninsula during the war, however, used military and other pressures on China (the infamous "Twenty-One Demands") to force the latter country to concede the territory to Tokyo, which, in addition, used Allied need for its naval help in the Mediterranean and elsewhere to elicit support for its gaining the territory in postwar settlements. When the Treaty of Versailles gave the province to Japan, a popular uproar developed in China, and Beijing refused to sign the treaty. The moral embarrassment was removed as part of some agreements in 1922. This province is the birthplace of Confucius.

TCM. As used in the book, it refers to the Crowe memorandum, the famous memorandum from Sir Eyre Crowe of the British Foreign Office, that helped shape British foreign policy toward Germany.

The Quad. This term refers to the Quadrilateral Security Dialogue (sometimes called the QSD), which has been taking place among Australia, India, Japan, and the US concerning what is called a free and open Indo-Pacific region (FOIP).

TPP. The Trans-Pacific Partnership was a proposed trade agreement, pushed by the US, among Australia, Brunei, Canada, Chile, Japan, Malaysia, Mexico, New Zealand, Peru, Singapore, Vietnam, and the US. It was signed in February 2016 but was rejected by the Trump administration. It was intended to serve a curb to the perceived expanding power and influence of China.

TSMC. This stands for the Taiwan Semiconductor Manufacturing Company.

TYP. The phrase "Thirty Years' Peace" refers to the 446 BCE agreement between the ancient Greek city-states of Athens and Sparta that ended the First Peloponnesian War. The violation of its terms contributed to the beginning of the Second Peloponnesian War.

War Plan Orange. This expression deals with plans, on the part of the US, as early as 1907 but partly ripening in 1911, to fight a war with Japan.

BIBLIOGRAPHY

A.

Agarwala, Nitin, and Rana D. Chaudhary, "China Policy in Science and Technology: Implications for the Next Industrial Transition," *India Quarterly*, Vol. 75, #2 (June 2019)

Albrecht-Carrie, Rene, *Europe Since 1815* (New York: Harper & Brothers Publishers, 1962)

Allison, Graham, "National Security Strategy for the 1990s," Edward K. Hamilton, ed., *American Global Interests: A New Agenda* (New York: W. W. Norton & Company, 1989)

Allison, Graham, *Destined for War: Can America and China Escape Thucydides's Trap?* (Boston: Houghton Mifflin Harcourt, 2017)

Altman, Roger, "Financial Fallout: The Great Crash, 2008," *Foreign Affairs*, Vol. 88, #1 (January/February 2009)

Anderson, Clare, *Indian Uprising of 1857: Prisons, Prisoners, and Rebellion* (New York: Anthem Press, 2017)

Anderson, Scott, *The Quiet Americans* (New York: Doubleday, 2020)

Apuzzo, Matt, Sheri Fink, and James Risen, "How the US Torture Left a Legacy of Damaged Minds," *New York Times* (October 9, 2016)

B.

Bacevich, Andrew J., *The New American Militarism* (Oxford: Oxford University Press, 2013)

Bagnall, Nigel, *The Peloponnesian War: Athens, Sparta, and the Struggle for Greece* (New York: St. Martin's Press, 2006)

Bailey, Thomas A., *A Diplomatic History of the American People* (New York: Appleton-Century-Crofts, 1958)

Baily, Martin N., and Barry Bosworth, "US Manufacturing: Understanding Its Past and Its Potential Future," *Journal of Economic Perspectives*, Vol. 28, #1 (2014)

Baschuk, Bryce, "WTO Authorizes the EU to Impose Tariffs on US," *Boston Globe* (October 27, 2020)

Beijing Institute of Wang Yangming Philosophy, *Cultural Confidence & National Rejuvenation* (Beijing: Chinese Intercontinental Press, 2018)

Bell, Christopher M., *The Royal Navy: Seapower and Strategy between the Wars* (Stanford: Stanford University Press, 2000)

———, "The Singapore Strategy and the Deterrence of Japan," *The English Historical Review,* Vol. 116, #467 (June 2001)

Bemis, Samuel F., *A Diplomatic History of the United States* (New York: Holt, Rinehart and Winston Inc., 1965)

Ben-Atar, Doron S., *Trade Secrets: Intellectual Piracy and the Origins of American Industrial Power* (New Haven: Yale University Press, 2004)

Bender, Jill C., *The 1857 Indian Uprising and the British Empire* (Cambridge: Cambridge University Press, 2016)

Berman, Morris, *The Twilight of American Culture* (New York: W. W. Norton & Company, 2000)

Betcher, Sharon V., *Spirit and Obligation of Social Flesh: A Secular Theology for the Global City* (New York: Fordham University Press, 2014)

Biden, Joseph R., "Why America Must Lead Again," *Foreign Affairs*, Vol. 99, #2 (March/April 2020)

Bjerg, Han Christian, "To Copenhagen a Fleet: The British Pre-emptive Seizure of the Danish-Norwegian Navy," *International Journal of Naval History*, Vol. 7, #2 (August 2008)

Blackwill, Robert D., and Ashley J. Tillis, *Revising U.S. Grand Strategy Toward China* (New York: Council on Foreign Relations, 2015)

Blackwill, Robert D., and Jennifer M. Harris, *War by Other Means: Geonomics and Statecraft* (Cambridge: Harvard University Press, 2016)

Blakeslee, George H., "The Japanese Monroe Doctrine," *Foreign Affairs*, Vol. XI, #4 (July 1933)

Bolton, John, *The Room Where It Happened: A White House Memoir* (New York: Simon & Schuster, 2020)

Borger, Julian, "Chilling Role of 'the Preacher' Confirmed on CIA Waterboarding Hearing in Guantanamo," *The Guardian* (January 25, 2020)

Boyle, John Hunter, *Modern Japan: The American Nexus* (New York: Harcourt Brace Jovanovich, 1993)

Bradsher, Keith, "China Endorses Free Trade, But Finds Deals Are Elusive," *New York Times* (November 6, 2019)

Bremmer, Ian, "How China's Economy Is Poised to Win the Future," *Time* (November 13, 2017)

————, "State Capitalism Comes of Age: The End of the Free Market," *Foreign Affairs*, Vol. 88, #3 (May/June 2009)

Boulding, Elise, *Cultures of Peace: The Hidden Side of History* (Syracuse: Syracuse University Press, 2000)

Brooks, Rosa, *How Everything Became War and the Military Everything* (New York: Simon & Schuster, 2016)

Buckley, Chris, "China Sees Self-Reliance as Essential to Economy," *New York Times* (September 8, 2020)

C.

Calkins, Laura M., *China and the First Vietnam War, 1947–1954* (New York: Routledge, 2013)

Camus, Albert, *Resistance, Rebellion, and Death*, trans. by Justin O'Brien (New York: Modern Library, 1963)

Cha, Victor D., *Powerplay: The Origins of American Alliance System in Asia* (Princeton: Princeton University Press, 2016)

————, "Powerplay: The Origins of U.S. Alliance System in Asia," *International Relations of the Asia-Pacific*, Vol. 17, #2 (2017)

Chan, Alfred A., *Mao's Crusade: Politics and Policy Implementation in China's Great Leap Forward* (Oxford: Oxford University Press, 2001)

Chang, Kenneth, "China Launches Mission to Far (but Not Always Dark) Side of the Moon," *New York Times* (December 8, 2018)

Chang, Teh-Kuang, "China's Claim of Sovereignty Over Spratly and Paracel Islands: A Historical and Legal Perspective," *Case Western Reserve Journal of International Law*, Vol. 23 #3 (1991); https://scholarlycommons.law.case.edu/jil/vol23/iss3/1

Chao, Wang, "People-to-People Diplomacy Key to Tell China's Story," *China Daily* (December 31, 2019)

Chen, Yu-Jie, and Jerome Cohen, "Why Does the WHO Exclude Taiwan?" *IN BRIEF* (Council on Foreign Relations, April 9, 2020)

Chen, Si, "Global Benefits of Socialism Hailed at Forum," *China Daily* (November 19, 2019)

Cherry, Conrad, ed., *God's New Israel: Religious Interpretations of American Destiny* (Chapel Hill: University of North Carolina Press, 1988) [There is a 2014 revised e-book edition of this work.]

Chua, Amy, *Day of Empire: How Hyperpowers Rise to Global Dominance* (New York: Doubleday, 2007)

Churchill, Winston, *The Gathering Storm* (Boston: Harcourt Mifflin Company, 1948)

Clinton, Hillary Rodham, "Security and Opportunity for the Twenty-first Century," *Foreign Affairs,* Vol. 86, #6 (November/December 2007)

Clive, John, *Not by Fact Alone: Essays on the Writing and Reading of History* (Boston: Houghton Mifflin Company, 1989)

Coe, Andrew, "Free Produce, with a Side of Shaming," *New York Times* (June 25, 2020)

Coming-Bruce, Nick, "22 Countries Issue Plea to Beijing to Stop Its Persecution of Uighurs," *New York Times* (July 10, 2019)

Conrad, Joseph, *Tales of Unrest* (New York: Penguin Books, 1977)

Cooley, Alexander, and Daniel H. Nixon, "How Hegemony Ends: The Unravelling of American Power," *Foreign Affairs*, Vol. 99, #4 (July/August 2020)

Cooper, Kent, *Barriers Down: The Story of the New Agency Epoch* (New York: Farrar & Rinehart Inc., 1942)

Cosgrove, Richard A., "The Career of Sir Eyre Crowe: A Reassessment," *Albion: A Quarterly Journal Concerned with British Studies*, Vol. 4, #4 (Winter 1972)

Crane, George T., and Abla Amawi, eds., *The Theoretical Evolution of International Political Economy: A Reader* (New York: Oxford University Press, 1991)

D.

Dawkins, Richard, *The Selfish Gene* (Oxford: Oxford University Press, 1976) [A fortieth anniversary edition was published in 2016 by OUP, the reader may wish to know.]

Danner, Mark, and Hugh Eakin, "The CIA: The Devastating Indictment," *New York Review of Books*, Vol. LXII, #2 (February 5, 2015)

De Novo, J. A., "The Movement for an Aggressive Oil Policy Abroad, 1918–1920," *American Historical Review*, Vol. LXI (July 1956)

Drell, Sidney, "Reducing Nuclear Danger," *Foreign Affairs*, Vol. 72, #2 (Spring 1993)

Duncan, Mary Katherine, "Fumbling the White Man's Burden: U.S. Missionaries, Cultural Imperialism, and Intervention in the Boxer Rebellion" (thesis submitted to Department of History, University of North Carolina Wilmington, 2012)

Dunst, Charles, and Shahn Savino, "Stand Up for Taiwan," *Boston Globe* (November 8, 2020)

E.

Elleman, Bruce A., *Wilson and China: A Revised History of the Shandong Question* (London: M. E. Sharpe, 2002)

F.

Fawcett, Peter, "When I Squeeze You with Eisphorai: Taxes and Tax Policy in Classical Athens," *Hesperia*, Vol. 85, #1 (January–March 2016)

Fay, Sidney B., *The Origins of the World War*, 2 vols. (New York: Macmillan, 1928)

Fehrenbach, T. R., *This Kind of War* (New York: Macmillan Publishers, 1963)

Ferguson, Niall, *The Pity of War: Explaining World War I* (New York: Basic Books, 1999)

———, *Empire: The Rise and Demise of the British World Order and the Lessons for Global Power* (London: Penguin Books, 2002)

Field, Andrew, *Royal Navy Strategy in the Far East, 1919–1939: Planning for War Against Japan* (London: Frank Cass & Company, 2004)

Fu, Ying, "China and the U.S. Can Have Cooperative Competition," *New York Times* (November 25, 2020)

Fukuyama, Francis, "America in Decay," *Foreign Affairs*, Vol. 93, #5 (October 2014)

G.

Gao, Yuning, *China as the Workshop of the World* (New York: Routledge, 2011)

Giridharadas, Anand, *Winner Take All: The Elite Charade of Changing the World* (New York: Alfred A. Knopf, 2018)

Goldwin, Robert A., and Harry M. Clor, eds. *Readings in American Foreign Policy* (New York: Oxford University Press, 1971)

Greenberg, Karen J., and Joshua L. Dratel, eds., *The Torture Papers: The Road to Abu Ghraib* (Cambridge: Cambridge University Press, 2005)

Gruen, Erich S., *Imperialism in the Roman Republic* (Berkeley: University of California Press, 1970)

Guarino, Ben, Emily Rauhata, and William Wan, "China Increasingly Challenge American Domination in Science," *The Washington Post* (June 3, 2018)

Gurtov, Melvin, *The United States Against the Third World: Antinationalism and Intervention* (New York: Praeger, 1974)

H.

Hall, David, ed., *The Antinomian Controversy, 1663–1638: A Documentary History* (Durham, North Carolina: Duke University Press, 1990)

Hammer, Ellen J., *The Struggle for Indochina, 1940–1955* (Stanford: Stanford University Press, 1954)

Hamilton, Nigel, *The American Caesars: Lives of the Presidents from Franklin Roosevelt to George W. Bush* (New Haven: Yale University Press, 2010)

Hammond, N. G. L., *A History of Greece to 332 B.C.* (Oxford: Oxford University Press, 1959)

Horowitz, Jason, "Vatican Defies U.S. in Bishop Deal with China," *New York Times* (October 23, 2020)

Hartford, Kathleen, "Socialist Agriculture Is Dead; Long Live Socialist Agriculture! Organizational Transformation in Rural China," Elizabeth J. Perry and Christine Wong, eds., *The Political Economy of Reform in Post-Mao China* (Cambridge: Harvard University Press, Council on East Asian Studies, 1985)

Hartford, Kathleen, and Steven M. Goldstein, eds, *Single Sparks: China's Rural Revolutions* (Armonk: M. E. Sharpe, 1989)

Hathaway, Oona A., and Scott J. Shapiro, *The Internationalists: How a Radical Plan to Outlaw War Remade the World* (New York: Simon & Schuster, 2017)

He, Ming, and Sun Yunchuan, "If 5G Is Here, Can 6G Be Far Behind?" *China Daily* (December 16, 2019)

Heilbroner, Robert, L., *The Worldly Philosophers: The Lives, Times, and Ideas of the Great Economic Thinkers* (New York: Simon & Schuster, 1995)

Hobson, John M., *The Eastern Origins of Western Civilisation* (Cambridge: Cambridge University Press, 2006)

Howard, Michael, *The Continental Commitment: The Dilemma of British Defense Policy in the Era of Two World Wars* (London: Ashfield Press, 1989)

Hsiung, James Chieh, *China's Bitter Victory: The War with Japan* (New York: M. E. Sharpe Publishing, 1992)

————, *Ideology and Practice: The Evolution of Chinese Communism* (New York: Praeger, 1970)

Hu, Angang, "Embracing China's 'New Normal': Why the Economy Is Still On Track," *Foreign Affairs*, Vol. 94, #3 (May/June 2015)

Huntington, Samuel P., "The Clash of Civilizations?" *Foreign Affairs*, Vol. 73, #3 (Summer 1993)

————, *The Clash of Civilizations and the Remaking of World Order* (New York: Simon & Schuster, 1996)

I.

Ikeda, Daisaku, "Mahayana Buddhism and Twenty-First Century Civilization," in Daisaku Ikeda, *A New Humanism: The University Addresses of Daisaku Ikeda* (London: I. B. Taurus, 2010)

————, *Toward a Culture of Peace: A Cosmic View* (1999 Peace Proposal, issued by Soka Gakkai International, Tokyo, Japan)

Institute for Security and Development Policy, "China's Anti-Poverty Efforts, Problems and Progress," *Focus Asia* (March 2019)

Irwin, Douglas A., "The Truth About Trade: What Critics Get Wrong About the Global Economy," *Foreign Affairs*, Vol. 95, #4 (July/August 2016)

J.

Jabr, Ferris, "The Social Life of Forests," *New York Times Magazine* (December 6, 2020)

Jacobsen, Annie, *The Pentagon's Brain: An Uncensored History of DARPA: America's Top Secret Military Research Agency* (Boston: Little, Brown and Company, 2015)

James, Harold, "The Making of a Mess: Who Broke Global Finance, and Who Should Pay for It?" *Foreign Affairs,* Vol. 88, #1 (January/February 2009)

Jarvis, Robert, "The Torture Blame Game: *The Botched Senate Report on the CIA Misdeeds*," *Foreign Affairs,* Vol. 94, #3 (May/June 2015)

K.

Kaplan, Fred, *The Bomb: Presidents, Generals, and the Secret History of Nuclear War* (New York: Simon & Schuster, 2020)

Keller, Richard C., "Madness and Colonization: Psychiatry in the British and French Empires, 1800–1962," *Journal of Social History,* Vol. 35, #2 (February 2001)

Kennan, George F., "X" "Sources of Soviet Conduct" *Foreign Affairs,* (July 1947)

Kennedy, Paul, *The Rise and Fall of Great Powers* (New York: Vintage Books, 1989)

———, *The Rise of Anglo-German Antagonism, 1860–1914* (London: Allen & Goodwin, 1980)

Kinzer, Stephen, "In Bolivia, American 'Democracy Promotion' Is a Farce," *Boston Globe* (February 9, 2020)

————, *Poisoner in Chief: Sidney Gottlieb and the CIA Search for Mind Control* (New York: Henry Holt & Company, 2019)

————, "Sanctions-Mad America Turns On Its Friends," *Boston Globe* (July 12, 2020)

Kissinger, Henry, *A World Restored: Metternich, Castlereagh, and the Problems of Peace, 1812–1822* (Boston: Houghton Mifflin, 1957)

————, "America at the Apex," *The National Interest*, #64 (Summer 2001)

————, *On China* (New York: Penguin, 2011)

Krauthammer, Charles, "The Unipolar Movement," *Foreign Affairs*, Vol. 70, #1 (1990/91)

L.

Lamb, Alastair, *Britain and Chinese Central Asia: The Road to Lhasa, 1767–1905* (London: Routledge and Kegan Paul, 1960)

————, *The China–India Border* (London: Oxford University Press, 1964)

Landes, David S., *Bankers and Pashas: International Finance and Economic Imperialism in Egypt* (Cambridge: Harvard University Press, 1958)

Langley, Winston, *While the U.S. Sleeps: Squandered Opportunities and Looming Threats to Societies* (Bloomington, IN: Xlibris, 2021)

Lauren, Paul Gordon, "First Principles of Racial Equality: History and Politics and Diplomacy of Human Rights Provisions of the United Nations Charter," *Human Rights Quarterly*, Vol. 5, #1 (Winter 1983)

Lee, Kuan Yew, *Lee Kuan Yew: The Grand Master's Insights on China, the United States, and the World,* Interviews and Selections by Graham Allison and Robert Blackwell, with Ali Wyne and Foreword by Henry Kissinger (Cambridge: MIT Press, 2013)

Lepore, Jill, *These Truths: A History of the United States* (New York: W. W. Norton & Company, 2018)

Leung, James, "Xi's Corruption Crackdown: How Bribery and Graft Threaten the Chinese Dream," *Foreign Affairs*, Vol. 94, #3 (May/June 2015)

Levitte, Jean-David, "With the End of Four Centuries of Western Dominance What Will the World Be in the 21st Century?" (speech delivered before the Academy of Moral and Political Science, Paris, France, January 7, 2019)

Lewis, Roger Williams, "Australia and the German Colonies in the Pacific, 1914–1919," *The Journal of Modern History*, Vol. 38, #4 (December 1966)

Lighthizer, Robert E., "How to Make Trade Work for Workers: Charting a Path Between Protectionism and Globalism," *Foreign Affairs*, Vol. 99, #4 (July/August 2020)

Lin, Justin Yifu, "The Household Responsibility System in China's Agricultural Reform: A Theoretical and Empirical Study," *Economic Development and Cultural Change* [a supplement], Vol. 36, #3 (1988)

Lind, Jennifer, "Asia's Other Revisionist Power: Why U.S. Grand Strategy Unnerves China," *Foreign Affairs*, Vol. 96, #2 (March–April 2017)

Lovell, Julia, *Maoism: A Global History* (New York: Alfred A. Knopf, 2019)

Lumumba-Kasongo, Tukumbi, "Rethinking the Bandung in an Era of 'Unipolar Liberal Globalization' and Movements toward a Multipolar Politics," *Bandung: Journal of the Global South*, Vol. 2, #9 (2015)

M.

Mackinder, Halford J., "The Geographical Pivot of History," in *The Geographical Journal*, Vol. XXII (April 1904)

Mahan, Alfred T., *The Influence of Sea Power Upon History, 1660–1783* (Boston: Little, Brown and Company, 1898)

Mahbubani, Kishore, *The New Asian Hemisphere: The Irresistible Shift of Global Power to the East* (New York: Public Affairs, 2008)

MacMillan, Margaret, *The War that Ended Peace: The Road to 1914* (New York: Random House, 2014)

Manning, Robert A., "China: Regan's Chance Hit," *Foreign Policy*, #54 (Spring 1984)

Mao, Tze-tung, *Selected Military Writings of Mao Tze-tung* (Beijing: Foreign Language Press, 1967)

Marriott, John, *The Other Empire: Metropolis, India and Progress in the Colonial Imagination* (Manchester: Manchester University Press, 2013)

Matthew, H. C. G., *The Liberal Imperialists* (Oxford: Oxford University Press, 1973)

Matthews, Jessica T., "The Nuclear Threat," *The New York Review* (April 20, 2020)

Maynes, Charles W. Jr., "Who Pays for Foreign Policy?" *Foreign Policy*, #15 (Summer 1974)

McCain, John, "An Enduring Peace Built 'on Freedom': Securing America's Future," *Foreign Affairs*, Vol. 86 (November/December 2007)

McGregor, Malcolm F., *The Athenians and Their Empire* (Vancouver: University of British Columbia Press, 1995)

McIntyre, David W., *The Rise and Fall of the Singapore Naval Base, 1919–1942* (London: Macmillan Press, 1979)

McMaster, H. R., "How China See the World, and How We Should See China," *The Atlantic* (May 2020)

Medcalf, Rory, "In Defense of the Indo-Pacific: Australia's New Strategic Map," *Australian Journal of International Affairs*, Vol. 68, #4 (2014)

Michael, Franz, "Japan's 'Special Interest' in China," *Pacific Affairs*, Vol. 10, #4 (December 1937)

Miller, Edward S., *Bankrupting the Enemy: The U.S. Financial Siege of Japan Before Pearl Harbor* (Annapolis: Naval Institute Press, 2007)

Mo, Tzu, "Universal Love," in *Basic Writings of Mo Tzu, Hsun Tzu, and Han Fei Tzu*, trans. by Burton Watson (New York: Columbia University Press, 1967)

Morgenthau, Hans, *In Defense of the National Interest* (New York: Alfred A. Knopf Inc., 1952)

——, *Politics Among Nations* (New York: Alfred A. Knopf Inc., 1954)

—————, *Scientific Man versus Power Politics* (Chicago: University of Chicago Press, 1946)

Moynihan, Daniel P., "The United States in Opposition," *Commentary,* #59 (March 1975)

N.

Nandy, Ashis, "The Psychology of Colonialism: Sex, Age, and Ideology in British Colonial India," *Psychiatry,* Vol. 45, #3 (August 1982)

Nardin, Terry, *Law, Morality, and the Relations of States* (Princeton: Princeton University Press, 1983)

Nayer, Raj, "Treat India Seriously," *Foreign Policy*, #18 (Spring 1975)

Needham, Joseph, ed., *Science and Civilization in China* (Cambridge: Cambridge University Press, series, 1954–2007)

Nettl, Peter, "The German Social Democratic Party, 1890–1914 as a Political Model," *Past and Present*, #30 (April 1965)

Niebuhr, Reinhold, *The Irony of American History* (Chicago: University of Chicago Press, 1952)

—————, *Moral Man and Immoral Society* (New York: Charles Scribner's, 1932)

Nixon, Richard, *Leaders* (New York: Simon & Schuster, 1982)

—————, *The Real War* (New York: Simon & Schuster, 1990)

Nye, Joseph S. Jr., "The Rise and Fall of American Hegemony from Wilson to Trump," *International Affairs*, Vol. 95, #1 (January 2019), pp. 63–80; https://academic.oup.com/ia/article/95/1/63/5273551

O.

Obama, Barack, *A Promised Land* (New York: Crown, 2020)

Ober, Josiah, *The Rise and Fall of Classical Greece* (Princeton: Princeton University Press, 2015)

Osnos, Evan, *Age of Ambition: Chasing Fortune, Truth, and Faith in New China* (New York: Farrar, Straus, and Giroux, 2014)

P.

Page, Jeremy, and Chun Han Wong, "Beijing Offers to Negotiate in South China Sea Dispute," *Wall Street Journal* (July 13, 2016)

Paulson, Henry M. Jr., "A Strategic Economic Engagement: Strengthening U.S. China Ties," *Foreign Affairs*, Vol. 87, #5 (September/October 2008)

Pant, Harsh V., "Rising China in India's Vicinity: A Rivalry Takes Shape in Asia," *Review of International Affairs*, Vol. 29, #2 (2016)

Patterson, Thomas G., and J. Garry Clifford, *America Ascendant: U.S. Foreign Relations Since 1939* (Lexington, MA: D. C. Heath & Company, 1995)

Patrick, Stewart, *The Sovereignty Wars: Reconciling America with the World* (Washington, D.C.: Brookings Institution Press, 2018)

Payer, Cheryl, *The Debt Trap: The International Monetary Fund and the Third World* (New York: Monthly Review Press, 1975)

Perry, Elizabeth J., and Christine Wong, eds., *The Political Economy of Reform in Post-Mao China* (Cambridge: Harvard University Press, Council on East Asian Studies, 1985)

417

Perry, William J., *My Journey at the Nuclear Brink* (Stanford: Stanford Security Studies, 2016)

Piketty, Thomas, *Capital and Ideology* (Cambridge: Harvard University Press, 2019)

————, *Capital in the Twenty-First Century* (Cambridge: Harvard University Press, 2014)

Prasad, Eswar, *Gaining Currency: The Rise of the Renminbi* (Oxford: Oxford University Press, 2016)

Pye, Lucian W., "Erratic State, Frustrated Society," *Foreign Affairs*, Vol. 69, #4 (Fall 1990)

Q.

Qi, Huaigao, "Joint Development in the South China Sea: China's Incentives and Policy Choices," in *Journal of Contemporary East Asian Studies,* Vol. 8, #2 (2019) [One can read, for the same author, roughly the same ideas in "Multilateralism in Asia: Rethinking Asian Regionalism in an Uncertain Era," https://doi.org/10./24761028.2019.1685427.]

R.

Ratner, Ely, "Course Correction: How to Stop China's Advance," *Foreign Affairs*, Vol. 96, #4 (July/August 2017)

Rawls, John, *A Theory of Justice* (Cambridge: Harvard University Press, 1971)

Reif, Rafael L., "China's Challenge Is America's Opportunity," *New York Times* (August 8, 2018)

Richardson, Chris, "Closed Door at the Department of State," *New York Times* (June 26, 2020)

Roberts, Jennifer T., *The Plague of War: Athens, Sparta, and the Struggle for Ancient Greece* (Oxford: Oxford University Press, 2017)

Rogers, Mitch, "From Freeze to Fire: How Economic Sanctions against Japan Led to War in the Pacific," *The Thetean: A Student Journal for Scholarly Historical Writing*, Vol. 47, #1 (2018)

Rothstein, Richard, *The Color of Law: A Forgotten History of How Our Government Segregated America* (New York: W. W. Norton Company, 2017)

Ruger, Jan, *The Great Naval Game: Britain and Germany in the Age of Empire* (Cambridge: Cambridge University Press, 2009)

S.

Sachs, Jeffrey D., *A New Foreign Policy: Beyond American Exceptionalism* (New York: Columbia University Press, 2018)

Said, Edward W., *Culture and Imperialism* (New York: Alfred A. Knopf, 1993)

Sampson, Anthony, *The Seven Sisters: The Great Oil Companies and the World They Shaped* (New York: Bantam Books, 1974)

Sandel, Michael J., *What Money Can't Buy: The Moral Limits of Markets* (New York: Farrar, Straus and Giroux, 2017)

———, *The Tyranny of Merit: What Became of the Common Good* (New York: Farrar, Straus and Giroux, 2020)

Saunt, Claudio, *Unworthy Republic: The Dispossession of Native American and the Road to Indian Territory* (New York: W. W. Norton & Company, 2020)

Schurmann, Franz, and Orville Schell, *Imperial China: The Decline of the Last Dynasty and the Origins of Modern China* (New York: Vintage Books, 1967)

Scissors, Derek, "Deng Undone," *Foreign Affairs,* Vol. 88, #3 (May/June 2009)

Shulman, Mark R., "The Influence of Mahan Upon Sea Power," *Reviews in American History*, Vol. 19, #4 (December 1991)

Skidmore, David, and William Gates, "After Tiananmen: The Struggle Over U.S. Policy toward China in the Bush Administration," *Presidential Quarterly*, Vol. 27, #3 (Summer 1997)

Smith, Woodruff D., *Consumption and the Making of Respectability, 1600–1800* (New York: Routledge, 2002)

Snowden, Edward, *Permanent Record* (New York: Metropolitan Books, 2019)

Sorkin, Andrew Ross, "Huawei Aside, U.S. Lags in the Race for Supremacy in 5G," *New York Times* (July 2, 2019)

Stearns, Peter N., *Interpreting the Industrial Revolution* (Washington, D.C.: American Historical Association, 1991)

Spykman, Nicholas, *America's Strategy in World Politics: The United States and the Balance of Power* (New York: Harcourt, Brace & Company, 1942)

Steinberg, Jonathan, "The Copenhagen Complex," *Journal of Contemporary History*, Vol. I, #3 (1966)

Stoessinger, John G., *Why Nations Go to War* (New York: St. Martin's Press, 1988)

Strachey, John, *The End of Empire* (New York: Random House, 1960)

Subacchi, Paola, *The People's Money: How China Is Building a Global Currency* (New York: Columbia University Press, 2016)

Sun, Tzu, *The Art of War*, with a new foreword by John Minford and trans. by Lionel Giles (Tokyo: Tuttle Publishing, 2008)

Swanson, Ana, Paul Mazur, Raymond Zhong, "U.S. Is Using Taiwan as a Pressure Point in Tech Fight with China," *New York Times* (May 20, 2020)

Szulc, Tad, "Behind the Vietnam Cease-Fire Agreement," *Foreign Policy*, Vol. 15 (Summer 1974)

T.

Tate, Merze, *Hawaii: Reciprocity or Annexation* (East Lansing: Michigan State University Press, 1968)

————, *The United States and Armaments* (Cambridge: Harvard University Press, 1948)

Teunissen, Jan Joost, "The International Monetary Crunch: Crisis or Scandal?" *Alternatives*, Vol. XII, #3 (July 1987)

Thomas, Evan W., *The War Lovers: Roosevelt, Lodge, Hearst, and the Rush to Empire, 1898* (Boston: Little, Brown and Company, 2010)

Thornton, A. P., *The Imperial Idea and Its Enemies: A Study of British Power* (New York: St. Martin's Press, 1959)

Thucydides, *The Complete Writings of Thucydides: The Peloponnesian War*, Unabridged Crawley trans. with introduction by John H. Finley Jr., Eliot professor of Greek literature, Harvard University (New York: Modern Library, 1954) [This important work is now part of the public domain and may be copied and downloaded.]

Tinder, Glenn, "What Should Political Theory Be Now?" in John S. Nelson, ed., *What Should Political Theory Be Now* (Albany: State University of New York Press, 1983)

Toynbee, Arnold J., *Civilization on Trial* (Oxford: Oxford University Press, 1948)

Toynbee, Arnold J., and Daisku Ikeda, *Choose Life: A Dialogue, Arnold Toynbee and Daisaku Ikeda,* edited by Richard L. Gage (Oxford: Oxford University Press, 1989)

Trentmann, Frank, *Empire of Things: How We Became a World of Consumers, from the Fifteenth to the Twenty-First* (New York: Harper, 2016)

Treuer, David, "The Land Is Not Your Land: The Ethnic Cleansing of Native Americans," *Foreign Affairs*, Vol. 99, #4 (July/August 2020)

Tsai, Michael, "West's Hypocrisy over Hong Kong Exposed," *China Daily* (December 4, 2019)

Tu, Wei-Ming, *Neo-Confucian Thought in Action* (Berkeley: University of California Press, 1976)

———, "Tu Wei-Ming," https://billmoyers.com/content/tu-ei-ming-confucianism/

Tu, Weiming, and Daisaku Ikeda, *New Horizons in Eastern Humanism* (London: I. B. Taurus, 2011)

Tuchman, Barbara W., *The Guns of August* (New York: Bantam Books, 1989)

Tucker, Mary Evelyn, and John Berthrong, eds., *Confucianism and Ecology: The Interrelation of Heaven, Earth, and Humans* (Cambridge, MA: Center for the Study of World Religions, 1998)

Turley, William S., *The Second Indochina War: A Concise Political and Military History* (Lanham: MD: Rowman & Littlefield, 2005)

Turner, Oliver, "US Imperial Hegemony in Asia Pacific," https//doi.org/10.7765/97815261 35025 00008 (February 28, 2020) [Alternatively, one may read "The United States in the Indo-Pacific" at https://www.manchesteropenhive.com/view/9781526135025/9781526135025.00008.xml.]

U.

UNCTAD (United Nations Conference on Trade and Development), *UNCTAD at 50: A Short History* (Geneva: UNCTAD/OSG/2014)

Unger, Craig, *American Armageddon: How the Delusions of the Neoconservatives and the Christian Right Triggered the Descent of America and Still Imperil Our Future* (New York: Scribner, 2007)

US Department of State, "US Relations with Vietnam: Bilateral Fact Sheet" (January 21, 2020)

V.

Vance, Cyrus, "Human Rights and Foreign Policy," *Georgia International Law Journal*, Vol. VII (1997)

Verma, Pranshu, and Edward Wong, "US Imposes Sanctions on Chinese Officials Over Rights Abuses," *New York Times* (July 9, 2020)

Vitalis, Robert, *White World Order, Black Power Politics: The Birth of American International Relations* (Ithaca: Cornell University Press, 2015)

Von Albertson, Rudolf, *Decolonization: The Administration and Future of Colonies, 1919–1960* (New York: Doubleday & Company Inc., 1971)

W.

Welch, Richard E. Jr., "American Atrocities in the Philippines: The Indictment and Response," *Pacific Historical Review,* Vol. 43, #2 https://online.ncpress.edu/phr/article-pdf/4312/233/322006/3637551. pdf (accessed July 15, 2020) [One may also find access at https://online.ucpress.edu/phr/article-abstract/43/2/233/66676/ American-Atrocities-in-the-Phillippines-The?redirectedFrom=fulltext.]

Whalen, Jeanne, "The Quantum Revolution Is Coming, and the Chinese Scientists Are at the Forefront," *The Washington Post* (August 10, 2019)

Williams Appleman William, ed., *The Shaping of American Diplomacy: Readings and Documents in American Foreign Relations, Vol. II, 1900–1955* (Chicago: Rand McNally & Company, 1967)

Williams, George C., "Pleiotropy, Natural Selection, and the Evolution of Senescence," *Evolution*, Vol. 11, #4 (December 1957)

Wolff, Richard D., "'Stealing Intellectual Property' Is Fake News," *Common Dreams* (September 19, 2018)

Wong, Edward, "U.S. Tries to Bolster Taiwan's Status, Short of Recognizing Sovereignty," *New York Times* (August 18, 2020)

World Commission on Environment and Development, *Our Common Future* (Oxford: Oxford University Press, 1987)

Wood, Mary Christina, *Nature's Trust: Environmental Law for a New Ecological Age* (Cambridge: Cambridge University Press, 2013)

Wu, Guo, "Recalling Bitterness: Historiography, Memory, and Myth in Maoist China," *Twentieth Century China*, Vol. 39, #3 (2014)

Z.

Zhang, Yi, "Macao Lauded for its Successful Practices," *China Daily* (October 4, 2019)

Zhao, Lei, "Initial Research on Rocket Ends Successfully," *China Daily* (October 15, 2019)

Zimmerman, Warren, *The Great Triumph: How Five Americans Made Their Country a World Power* (New York: Farrar, Straus & Giroux, 2002)

Zou, Keyuan, and Xinchang Liu, "The Legal Status of the U-Shaped Line in the South China Sea and Its Legal Implication for Sovereignty, Sovereign Rights and Maritime Jurisdiction," *Chinese Journal of International Law*, Vol. 14, #1 (2015)

Zuboff, Shoshana, *The Age of Surveillance Capitalism: The Flight for a Human Future at the New Frontier of Power* (New York: Public Affairs, 2019)

INDEX

Beijing, xviii, 9–13, 15–16, 62–63, 92, 94, 153–54, 156–59, 162–65, 167–73, 182–83, 188–89, 191–92, 194–98, 208–10, 213, 222–24, 226–28, 230–31, 250, 254–55, 257–59, 288–89, 294–96, 310–14, 320–23, 336–39, 345–46, 348, 356–58

Belgium, 33, 87, 95, 136, 150, 355

Belt Road Initiative (BRI), 38, 333, 397

Berlin, 31, 33, 116, 119–22, 124, 128–31, 133, 135–36, 141–42, 144–46, 330

Bermuda, 287

Biden, Joseph, 243, 354n802, 377, 379, 383–86

Blinken, Anthony, 388

Boeing, 237, 306

Borneo, 105

Bosnia, 121, 135, 141

Boston Athenaeum, xiv

Boston University, xiv

Boxer Rebellion, 294, 406

Brazil, 9, 15, 257, 260, 377–78, 397

Brazil, Russia, India, China, South Africa (BRICS), 243

Britain, xvii–xviii, 4, 10, 30–36, 60–63, 65–66, 70–78, 82–83, 85, 87–90, 94–95, 97–99, 101–2, 104–5, 107, 109–21, 123–46, 148–50, 153–55, 165, 174, 221–22, 273, 276, 282, 287, 308–9, 311–13, 353–55, 392

British Foreign Office, 80, 116, 124, 399

Broadcom, 314

Brunei, 15, 105, 236, 261, 399–400

Bulgaria, 2

Burma Road, 94, 99, 103, 391

C

Cadiz, 30

Cairo Declaration, 211, 223, 253, 346, 392

Cambodia, 15, 98, 199, 206–7, 210, 261, 399

Canada, 9, 30, 36, 80–81, 115, 206, 236, 377, 395, 400

Caribbean, 8, 30, 68, 70, 98, 134, 154–55, 186, 197–98, 201, 205, 249, 287, 370, 378

Carter, Jimmy, 217, 219, 222–23, 284

Central Asia, 135, 227, 260, 295, 333, 370, 397, 412

Charter of Economic Rights and Duties of States (CERDS), 218, 228, 319, 376, 392

Chiang Kai-shek, 89, 92, 101, 183–85, 202, 209, 211, 253, 283, 392, 396

Chile, 144, 176, 208, 218, 236, 400

China, xiii–xx, 8–17, 34–42, 59–66, 74–77, 82–89, 91–95, 105–7, 153–215, 222–37, 239–41, 243–45, 247–68, 270–74, 277–80, 283–86, 288–99, 301–8, 310–22, 324–30, 332–34, 336–54, 356–58, 362–68, 370–81, 391–93, 395–401, 403–5, 407–10, 412–18

China-ASEAN Investment Fund, 234

China Development Bank, 261

China Incident, 92

China International Development Cooperation Agency (CIDCA), 259, 392

China Investment Corporation, 261

Chinese Communist Party (CCP), 183, 185, 212, 214, 225, 230, 242, 246, 253–54, 347, 351, 396

Chou En-lai, 175, 193–94, 212

Churchill, Winston, 30, 35, 103, 115, 117, 121, 149, 282

428

432

National Rifle Association (NRA), 176
National Security Strategy, 285–86, 401
Nehru, Jawaharlal, 193
neo-Confucianism, 177–79, 222, 269
Netherlands, 87, 95, 104, 106–7, 114, 130, 145–46, 206
Netherlands East Indies (NEI), 104–8
New Deal, 90, 156
New Development Bank (NDB), 260, 322, 328, 397
Newfoundland, 103, 287
New International Economic Order (NIEO), 217–23, 232–33, 238, 267–68, 358–59, 392, 397
New Zealand, 8, 30, 81, 186, 200–201, 236, 246, 261, 286, 343, 378, 395, 399–400
Nicaragua, 79, 83, 287, 309
Nine-Power Treaty, 74, 76, 87
Nixon, Richard, 168, 202, 206, 209
Nkrumah, Kwame, 193
nonaligned movements (NAM), 194–95, 197, 245, 391, 397
nonalignment, 193–94
North Atlantic Alliance, 223
North Korea, 8, 41, 144, 168, 170–71, 187, 210, 237
North Sea, 133, 136
North-South Summit on Cooperation and Development, 222

O

Obama, Barack, 168, 231, 234–36, 243–45, 261, 265, 285, 305, 321, 373, 417
Occidental Petroleum, 223
Occupy Wall Street, 254
One Belt One Road (OBOR), 15, 38, 162, 333, 397

open door policy, 14, 28–29, 60, 62–63, 74, 85, 398
Organization for Economic Cooperation and Development (OECD), 259–60, 336
Organization of American States (OAS), 280, 349
orientalism, 222, 238, 272, 274–75, 277–78, 286, 301, 304, 307, 311, 316, 340, 357, 362
Ottoman Empire, 72, 134, 141, 150, 335
Outer Space Treaty, 359–60

P

Pact of Paris. *See* Kellogg-Briand Pact
Pakistan, 30, 201, 208, 210, 260
Panama, 36, 60, 79, 154, 249, 287
Panama Canal, 36, 154, 249, 287
Paracel Islands, 250, 342, 405
Paris Peace Conference, 65, 87, 146
Paulson, Henry M., Jr., 338–39, 367
Pearl Harbor, 27, 65, 70, 110, 113, 415
Pence, Mike, 285, 290, 302, 311
Pentagon Papers, 205
People's Action Party, 269
People's Liberation Army (PLA), 162–63
People's Republic of China (PRC), 11, 161, 168, 173, 178, 182–83, 185, 187, 190, 197, 206–7, 209–11, 217, 222–23, 227–28, 246, 248–49, 253–54, 258–59, 264, 268, 271, 273, 283–85, 291, 294–95, 317, 339, 345–47, 350–51
Pericles, 5, 20–22, 43–45, 52, 117, 355
Permanent Court of Arbitration, 342
Permanent Court of International Justice (PCIJ), 73
Persia, 45–48, 135, 335
Persian Empire, 5–6, 45, 67
Persian Gulf, 30

Treaty of Friendship, Alliance, and
    Mutual Assistance, 188
Treaty of Paris, 76
Treaty of Peace, 346n792
Treaty of Portsmouth, 61
Triple Alliance, 33, 120
Triple Entente, 33, 120
Truman, Harry S., 246, 330–31
Truman Doctrine, 287, 325, 331, 334,
    344
Trump, Donald, 41, 229, 243, 247, 261,
    273, 282, 285, 305, 335, 357, 416
Tsinghua University, 12, 159
Tunisia, 33, 130
Turkey, 2, 9, 130
Tu Weiming, 365
Twenty-One Demands, 62, 70, 399
Two Centenary Goals, 161, 240

U

Uber, 7
Uganda, 129
UN Convention on the Law of the Sea
    (UNCLOS), 360
UN Framework Convention on Climate
    Change, 233, 360
Union   of   Soviet   Socialist
    RepublicsUnion   of   Soviet
    Socialist Republics (USSR), 8,
    38, 66, 160, 168–69, 181–82,
    188, 193–94, 196, 201, 204,
    208–9, 212, 214, 220, 222, 224,
    227, 230, 243–44, 283–84, 369,
    380, 393
United Nations (UN), xix, 42, 80, 182,
    186, 188, 192, 196–98, 205–6,
    209, 218, 220–21, 231–32, 234,
    236, 238, 253, 269, 271, 280,
    283, 319, 323–24, 327, 339, 347,
    349, 352, 369–70, 375

United Nations Conference on Trade
    and Development (UNCTAD),
    198, 423
United States, 4, 11, 15, 68, 80, 100,
    105, 109, 118, 145, 210–11, 231,
    246, 285, 291, 331, 349–50, 372,
    402, 408, 413, 420, 423
Universal Declaration of Human Rights
    (UDHR), xix, 186–87, 219, 228,
    286, 290–92, 297, 299, 320, 367,
    370
University of Massachusetts Boston,
    xiv

V

Vancouver, 8, 227, 288, 415
Viet Cong, 199, 202
Vietnam, 15, 41, 98, 141, 163, 191–93,
    195, 198–203, 205–12, 216–17,
    236, 244, 249–50, 261, 269, 286,
    377, 399–400, 404, 421, 423
Vladivostok, 8, 227, 247, 288

W

Washington, 14–16, 27–29, 61–64, 73–
    75, 88–90, 101–2, 106–8, 111,
    153–55, 172–74, 180–83, 185–
    87, 191–92, 194–96, 208–9, 215,
    223–25, 230–31, 236–37, 264–
    65, 280–82, 284–88, 298–301,
    305–7, 313–14, 319–21, 332–36,
    354–56, 376–77, 379
Washington Naval Conference (WNC),
    73–74, 79
Washington Naval Treaty, 89
WeChat, 316
Weihaiwei, 136
Wilson, Woodrow, 64–65, 76, 107, 386
Woody Island, 250
World Bank, 15, 186, 188, 257–58, 262,
    280, 283, 286, 322, 333, 342